The
Secret Daughter
of the Tsar

The
Secret Daughter
of the Tsar

JENNIFER LAAM

ST. MARTIN'S GRIFFIN
NEW YORK

FOR MY PARENTS

This is a work of fiction. All of the characters, organizations,
and events portrayed in this novel are either products of the
author's imagination or are used fictitiously.

The Library of Congress Cataloging-in-Publication Data is available upon
request.

ISBN 978-1-250-04091-6 (hardcover)
ISBN 978-1-250-02868-6 (trade paperback)
ISBN 978-1-250-02869-3 (e-book)

St. M̶   al, b̶ ̶ess, or
p̶   on bulk purchases, please contact
Mac̶   s Department a̶ 1-800̶ 1-7945,

Prologue

The clanging of the old woman's summoning bell echoed across the kitchen. Annika raised her voice higher with the other girls to drown out the sound. She wanted to hear the latest gossip free from interruption.

The laughter soon gave way to intermittent giggles and then ceased altogether. A moon-faced sous chef regarded her with a sly smile, as though Annika's every move was destined for failure. Annika stuffed another bite of herring in her mouth and let the greasy skin slide across her tongue. The glacial stares sank her spirit like a stone. If Annika proved derelict in her duties, she'd be released without pay. Someone else would inherit the unenviable task of gratifying Marie Romanov's every last whim. She passed a linen napkin over her lips and excused herself.

Upstairs, Annika found Marie perched in her favorite flowered armchair. Despite the frigid autumn chill, the exiled dowager empress had ordered her chair moved from its place in the sun to a less conspicuous corner of the room. Annika suspected Marie didn't want the young visitor to count her wrinkles in the fading light.

The visitor was bent over a tarnished silver samovar now, pressing the wolf's head–shaped spout to refresh Marie's tea. "Nicholas and Alexandra encouraged your granddaughters to pursue sports, did they not?" He spoke impeccable Danish, though his thick German accent struck each consonant like a mallet. "I understand that even at the end, while the royal family was held captive in Siberia . . ." When he spotted Annika at the door, he hesitated mid-pour and forced a tight smile.

"There you are," Marie snapped. "What took so long?" She drew her ratty ermine stole closer around her neck and made a flicking motion with two fingers. "Show Herr Krause to the door. His audience with me has quite come to a close."

Annika lowered herself into one of the quick curtsies that sufficiently pleased Marie without making her calf muscles ache terribly. The German visitor scowled at her and Annika responded with a small shrug. Despite his fine-looking features, she found nothing appealing about this grim young man.

Herr Krause turned the crushing weight of his attention back to Marie. "Dowager Empress, I can't leave yet. You haven't finished telling me of your family's holidays along the Baltic Coast, before the troubles began."

Underneath her thick layer of facial powder, Marie's expression softened. She caressed the gilt edges of the leather album on her lap. Her gaze flashed over a discolored photograph of her four granddaughters standing in a row, shortest to tallest, hands clasped together. The girls wore identical white cotton dresses and giant sunhats with long ribbons. Their heads were tilted coyly to the side, flirting with the camera, untroubled by any hint of the difficulties to come.

"Nicky and Alix are excessively fond of tennis." Marie reached for the delicate porcelain cup perched underneath the samovar. Herr Krause pressed the hot water spout once more. The tea emitted a fragrant aroma of cloves and cinnamon. "They have taught the older girls to play, and lament Grand Duchess Tatiana's weak serve."

"I understand your son Tsar Nicholas was an avid athlete," Herr Krause said. "And even in his final days sought comfort in his daily walks and calisthenics."

Marie snatched her cup back. Boiling water splashed Herr Krause's hand. He yelped and fell back into a chair. Annika found Marie's speed astonishing, given her age. Then again the dowager empress always greeted reality with nasty swipes, like a bear disturbed during winter hibernation. "See him to the door," Marie said crisply.

Herr Krause grabbed a linen napkin from atop Marie's china cabinet and pressed it to his hand. His slender backside melded into the faded upholstery of the guest chair until he appeared intractable. "I don't understand."

"The tsar has not suffered through his last days yet." Marie's husky voice rose in pitch. The thin blue veins in her neck strained against her papery skin. Annika shifted her weight and prepared to stand silently for a quarter of an hour at least, while Marie delved into another bewildering account of how the tsar and his family might have escaped the Bolshevik firing squad to live in hiding in Paris or San Francisco or the Siberian wastelands. Annika had heard a hundred scenarios, each more outlandish than the last.

This evening, however, Marie merely patted the fringed bangs cut high on her forehead. "We will rescue Nicky, Alix, and the children. We will find my missing granddaughter." Her voice cracked and dropped an octave. "Alix will forgive me then."

Herr Krause extended his hand toward Marie. She shot him a withering look and he quickly dropped his hand back into his lap. "Forgive you for what?"

Marie pursed her lips and leaned against the windowsill. She drew the silken curtains back and stared at the gravel beach outside. Marie's sorrowful, searching gaze once again reminded Annika of the precarious nature of the old woman's circumstances. Hvidore belonged to Marie, yet since the Russian Revolution she had lived here only at the pleasure of her nephew, King Christian of Denmark.

"You are fatigued. I have stayed too long." Herr Krause tossed his soiled napkin back on the cabinet, rose to his feet, and started across the room. He stopped abruptly at the door, bony knuckles splayed on the loose knob.

"Don't abandon hope, Dowager Empress. Remain steadfast and true." Herr Krause drew back his right leg and placed his left palm over his heart. A welt blistered beet red on the back of his hand. "We will restore your family's throne. I promise you that." He bowed deeply in Marie's direction, and then followed Annika out to the hall.

Most visitors to Hvidore couldn't keep their gaze from wandering to the domed ceiling, the statuary lining the walls, or the silvery crests of Baltic waves visible from the high windows. This opulence seemed misplaced in the otherwise sensible residence, like the furs and pearls Marie wore with her practical housedress and sturdy black shoes. Yet Herr Krause's gaze remained fixed on each step before him. He removed a handkerchief from his jacket pocket and wrapped it around the welt on his hand. "Does the dowager empress not understand what happened to the tsar's family?"

"The poor creature lost everyone in the Revolution." Annika trailed her fingers along the wrought-iron railing as she led him down the central staircase. "She won't speak of them in the past tense and refuses to indulge those who do so."

Herr Krause winced. "Should I return and apologize?"

"I doubt it will do any good. It looks like she's lost to the world for the evening."

He tilted his head to the side. "Did you understand what she said about a missing granddaughter?"

Annika suppressed a shiver. She didn't care for this topic. On the other hand, once Herr Krause left, she would spend the rest of the night in Marie's room with a needle and colored thread, embroidering flowers on dish towels while the old woman rambled on about the old country and the old ways. "She mentioned a missing granddaughter before. Some of the girls think she's talking about Anna Anderson."

He gave an abrupt laugh. Annika didn't care for the harsh sound of it. "The lunatic who claims she's Grand Duchess Anastasia?"

"No one knows. No one dares remind the dowager what happened. Why should we? The truth is too horrible to bear." Annika imagined the Romanov family on that final night, crowded together in the basement of the house in Siberia where they were kept prisoners. By now, she knew the story too well. She could hear the girls' high-pitched screams, the blast of gunfire, and the sickening sound of flesh ripping underneath the curved tip of a bayonet. Sometimes, she felt as though she'd been in the room herself.

"Besides, the dowager empress dismissed Anna Anderson's petition immediately." Annika quickened her pace. "She called her a silly imposter out for money. Of course, the dowager is eighty years old. She can't distinguish the living from the dead anymore, poor woman." Annika stopped just short of the main doors and opened the hall closet. She stood on her tiptoes to retrieve Herr Krause's overcoat and black fedora from the top hooks. "I wouldn't put much stock in anything she says about a missing granddaughter."

Herr Krause grabbed her arm. Annika tried to wriggle out of his grip. It wasn't painful, but he held her fast. "What does she say? What have you heard?"

His icy blue eyes bored into her, reminding Annika of the Romanian hypnotist who sometimes performed at Tivoli Gardens in the summer. She understood now why Marie had allowed this young man into her chambers when she'd shunned so many visitors before. "Late in the afternoon, when her mind is least clear, I hear her calling out: 'Alix. Forgive me. We'll keep her safe. We'll protect your fifth daughter.'"

"I don't understand." Herr Krause dug his fingers deeper into Annika's flesh. "Tsar Nicholas and Empress Alexandra had only four daughters and a son."

"Yet another figment of the dowager's imagination, I'm sure."

"Of course. Clearly, she is an ill woman." Herr Krause released Annika's arm and allowed her to retrieve his hat and coat. "Perhaps I might speak with Dowager Empress Marie again in the morning, when her thoughts are more lucid."

An entire morning free of the dowager's prattling? Annika

smiled to herself. "I could tell her you were misinformed about the fate of the tsar and his family. She might agree to see you again then."

Herr Krause bent forward to take her hand. He kissed her fingertips with surprisingly soft lips. "I would like that very much."

Annika opened the front door to a freezing coastal gale. Undeterred, Herr Krause placed his hat on his head, tightened his coat around his chest, and took the steps down to the courtyard two at a time. He looked back one last time and tipped his hat in her direction. She found his sudden burst of energy odd, considering he'd spent the better part of his afternoon dealing with Marie's delusions. Then again Marie often commented on the strange quirks of the German race. Perhaps the old woman was more perceptive than Annika realized.

One

"I'm trying to change your life for the better," Jess said. "Just listen for one minute, will you?"

Veronica Herrera rubbed her bare left ring finger, a nervous tic she'd indulged too much lately. For a short while, she felt like a well-adjusted thirty-eight-year-old woman enjoying another glorious Southern California morning. She'd thrown on a dark green sundress, rather than one of the black outfits she usually favored, and walked to the café on Tujunga Boulevard. Nobody walked in L.A., except Veronica Herrera. And Aroma Café lived up to its name. The patio always smelled like cinnamon toast.

But then Jess ruined it all by raising the forbidden topic of Veronica's love life, the one subject guaranteed to reduce Veronica to adolescent gawkiness.

"Eighteen months is enough time to get over anyone or anything," Jess added. "I've made it my personal mission to return you to the land of the living."

"Forget it." Veronica picked at the remains of her muffin and threw the crumbs to a trio of little gray birds gathered at her feet. "No set-ups. It makes me feel pathetic."

"But you'll like this one." Jess gave an authoritative nod.

Veronica imagined her cousin in a tailored business suit, rather than the hippie blouse and Pea in a Pod maternity jeans she wore now. As an assistant district attorney, Jess knew how to grill an uncooperative witness into submission.

"All right," Veronica sighed. "One minute. That's it."

"His name is Michael Karstadt. He's an attorney too and we met at one of those ridiculous social mixers. Since I can't drink and he was the only other halfway-sober person there, we got to talking. He's a huge history buff. So when I found out he's available, I couldn't help myself. I mentioned you. I told him you teach Russian history and you're writing a book about the last Romanov queen. That really piqued his interest."

A gust of Santa Ana wind picked up, scattering the birds. Veronica ran her hand through the shorn layers of hair brushing against her chin, unaccustomed to the breeze on the back of her neck. Let's say she actually agreed to meet this Michael Karstadt. He'd expect a witty, urbane author, not an untenured academic fraud. "Alexandra Romanov wasn't a queen. Her formal title was tsarina, but she preferred empress."

"Excuse me, Professor," Jess said. "I haven't taken any of your classes. Anyway, I showed him your picture. I have tons of pictures of you saved on my phone. He thinks you're gorgeous. Who wouldn't?"

An alarm sounded in Veronica's head. "Which pictures did you show him?"

"The ones from my bachelorette party last summer. Don't you remember?"

Veronica remembered. They'd gone to Cabo San Lucas. It was the first time she'd worn a bikini since college. Big mistake. "You keep those pictures on your phone? And show them to strange men?"

"Look at me." Jess patted her swelling stomach. "I like to keep memories of the glory days readily at hand."

"You do look ready to pop," Veronica said. "You're huge."

Jess laughed. "Still no good at small talk, are you?"

"I didn't mean it like that." Veronica's cheeks flared pink with embarrassment. Now the right adjectives sprang to mind. Jess didn't look huge, but radiant, glowing. Everyone else in her family understood how to behave around Jess. They squealed and cooed, even Veronica's grandmother, and her abuela was hardly the sentimental type when it came to babies. Meanwhile, Veronica hadn't even asked to touch Jess's belly.

"It's okay. I know what you meant," Jess said warmly. "So can I give Michael your number?"

"You met him at some after-hours bar party. You can't say with any confidence he's not a serial killer. That should be a goal in dating: don't get killed by a serial killer."

"Come on, Veronica. You know me. I had him checked out. Not so much as a traffic ticket. Besides, I know it's been a while, but you remember the rules. Meet at a public place. If he creeps you out, leave. Oh! Look what he gave me."

Jess grabbed her purse and pulled out her phone, red lipstick, a case for her sunglasses. "I know it's here somewhere. Ah!" She withdrew a yellow legal pad, detached the first sheet, and flattened it on the table. "Michael wanted me to show this to you. He said he has an entire library and you can borrow anything you want. It was cute that he took the time to write it out on paper. He's an anti-techie—like you."

Veronica set the salt shaker on top of the paper to keep it from flying away in the wind. In elegant handwriting, Michael Karstadt had listed the titles of fifteen books on the Romanov family, some by academic historians and others by survivors of the Russian Revolution. He'd written the list in Cyrillic. Veronica felt a faint tingle along the backs of her ears as she decoded the exotic Russian alphabet.

"I told him you're always complaining about being stuck in your research," Jess said.

Veronica flinched. "Thanks." Not that she could argue. She was stuck. She wasn't in a position to refuse help with her research. She leaned back in her chair, trying to enjoy the feel of the sun on her face, wanting to sound casual. "What does he look like?"

"He's your type." Jess bobbed her head as though this would make it so.

"I have a type?"

"He's everybody's type."

"What's his favorite Joy Division song?"

"Come on, Veronica. Do you expect everyone to pass your impossible tests?"

"Did you ask him?"

"Actually, I did. 'Shadowplay.' He didn't even hesitate. Seriously. It's like I ordered him off of a menu for you."

The Santa Ana wind gusted again, ruffling the edges of Michael Karstadt's list of books and blowing a sugar packet off the table.

Veronica bent to retrieve it, glad for the excuse not to look at Jess. She stuck the white packet at the front of its little caddy and then made sure all of the pink and blue packets were aligned.

"You're organizing," Jess said in a flat voice. "That's never good. What's really the problem here?"

Veronica folded her hands on the table, staring at her cuticles. "You know the problem."

"And you know I'd like to rip that jerk's throat out for what he did to you."

Jess meant this to be reassuring, so Veronica fought the impulse to double over. Thoughts of her ex-fiancé still made her feel as though she'd swallowed spiders—queasy. Couldn't her cousin just play the exultant mother-to-be, oblivious to everyone else's pain? Eighteen months wasn't a long time, no matter what Jess thought. Veronica stared once more at the Cyrillic list before her. She tucked a few strands of hair behind her ear.

"By the way, I love your haircut," Jess said. "It's a statement. I know what it means. You're ready to move on." She reached across the table and took Veronica's hand gently in hers. "What if I give Michael your office number?"

"Is there any way I can stop you?"

Jess grinned and rolled her eyes upward. She gave Veronica's hand a squeeze.

"Fine," Veronica said. "My office number. And you owe me for this."

"No, you owe me, Professor." Jess flashed Veronica a triumphant smile. "You'll see."

"You're up for tenure in January." Regina Brack, dean of Alameda University's College of Arts and Sciences, repositioned herself on her plush throne of an office chair. "That's only four months away, and you haven't completed your monograph?"

Veronica felt a pinching at the base of her skull, like someone squeezing her nerves with a pair of pliers. The office décor didn't help matters any. A row of colorful butterfly specimens were displayed in a glass-fronted box on the wall behind Dr. Brack. Pins impaled their delicate abdomens, as if they'd displeased some medieval despot.

"I'll admit, I don't understand the attraction," Dr. Brack said. "Nicholas and Alexandra Romanov are the most spectacular failures in Western political history. Why devote an entire book to the woman?"

Veronica tried to read Dr. Brack's stoic expression. Was she suggesting Veronica would fail spectacularly as well? "I guess I'm just a sucker for history's losers."

Dr. Brack frowned. Not that she'd really been smiling in the first place. "With a subject this well known you need to find a unique angle. Some of your colleagues feel you haven't yet refined your argument well enough to claim such an angle."

A quiver of panic bristled in Veronica's chest. Still, she knew better than to let this woman see her rattled. Regina Brack collected information as methodically as she collected butterflies. Any change in Veronica's demeanor would be noted, logged, and no doubt passed on to key members of her tenure review committee.

Dr. Brack formed a steeple underneath her chin and tapped her index fingers together. Veronica once watched her make this same gesture in a seminar, right before she publicly decimated an untalented student. "You want me to be honest, right?"

Veronica's fingers clawed the sides of her chair and she scanned her brain for something diplomatic to say. "Sure."

"If the committee voted today, you wouldn't make tenure."

Veronica's panic morphed into a shimmering wave. If she failed to make tenure, her career was over. Russian historians were like three-legged puppies, pitied but seldom adopted because the upkeep was too expensive. She imagined standing under the freeway with a sign: *Will explain the dynamics of imperial Russian court politics for food.*

"Can we discuss this, at least?" Veronica managed.

Dr. Brack nodded toward a sturdy duffel bag and a glass jar propped beside it. "Maybe next week. I'm headed out the door. I'm collecting specimens in the Mojave this weekend." Her eyes momentarily brightened. "Have you ever been?"

Dr. Brack would spend the weekend tramping around the desert on her skinny little legs, trapping butterflies for her ghoulish collection. Meanwhile, Veronica would retreat to the darkest recesses of the library trying to resuscitate a career that might already be over. "I'm not much of an outdoorswoman."

"How unfortunate." Dr. Brack began to shut down her computer. "In the meantime, keep an eye out for job postings. That's all I have to say about that."

The last twelve years of her life—*poof*—into thin air. Veronica's career was in shambles and not one strand of Regina Brack's helmet of a bob had fallen out of place. Veronica slipped into a sloppy Southern accent. "And that's all I have to say about that."

Dr. Brack looked at Veronica like she was from outer space.

"It's how Forrest Gump ended his stories," Veronica explained.

"Oh. I don't watch films like that."

Veronica slung her bag over her shoulder and eyed Dr. Brack's skewered butterflies for a last time. Once full of life, now useless. Veronica could relate.

"I only need access to the right materials. I'll finish my monograph." Even as Veronica articulated the thought, she heard the off-putting tentativeness in her voice. She felt the dull ache of tears and blinked them back, refusing to give this woman the satisfaction. "I'll find a publisher."

"I hope so. From what I understand, university presses aren't as indulgent with junior scholars as they once were." Dr. Brack gave her a prim smile.

As Veronica walked down the stairs, back to her office, the clean lines of the administrative suite gave way to disorder: vintage travel posters clumsily tacked to walls, bulletin boards overflowing with flyers for study-abroad programs, outdated political cartoons taped to office doors. For a flashing moment, the bohemian chaos of her department inspired her. She would jump-start her brain with strong coffee and lots of sugar. If she determined what to write next, a sentence even, surely the rest of the chapters would flow.

At this hint of blossoming confidence, the voices in Veronica's head began to hiss. They had snakes for tongues, mythological beasts. *You're an academic fraud. What makes you think you can publish a book?*

Veronica hummed to drown out the voices. She reached her office and fumbled for her key. When she turned it in the lock, the door gave way too easily. Veronica shared her office with an adjunct professor, but he should have left by now. She kept her hand on the knob, confused, and peered inside.

Her officemate had pinned five new pages from his graphic novel-in-progress to the back wall, zombie knight crusaders in chain mail and bloodied tunics. A man stood before the pictures, bending from the waist to examine each one.

Veronica felt her heart thump in her chest. She left the door open, in case she needed to scream for help. Clutching her bag tightly to her chest, she stepped inside. "May I help you?"

The man spun around. The curl in his lashes and the arch of his brows made his face look innocent and ironic at once. Flecks of gray speckled his dark, wavy hair. Veronica put him at six foot four, but then she was short and given to overestimating.

"Dr. Herrera? I'm sorry to startle you. A student at the front desk let me in."

Veronica made a mental note to speak to the student first thing on Monday.

"I'm Michael Karstadt, Jessica's friend." He drew his right leg back and bowed to her, his left hand over his heart. Like an imperial courtier. Veronica took in the French cuffs on his shirt. A pulse of nervous energy shot from her stomach to her throat.

"Who?" she heard herself ask.

Michael quickly straightened again to his full height. He looked a little full around the waist, but his shoulders were broad and his suit tailored so cleverly it didn't matter much. "Jessica told you I was coming, right?"

"There may have been a misunderstanding," Veronica said carefully. She set her book bag on the chair behind her desk.

"She gave me your office number." Michael motioned toward the numbers on the door. "She said you expected me to stop by."

What a sneaky cousin she had. "She should have given you my office *phone* number," Veronica told him. "I'm not accustomed to finding strange men in my office." She cringed. She hadn't meant to sound like a nineteenth-century spinster.

Michael gave a soft laugh and scratched the back of his neck. "So this is even more awkward than it should be." He spun on his heels and wagged his finger at the pictures on the back wall. "By the way, are these yours?"

"They belong to my officemate. He's a Medievalist. They're all nuts."

"If they were yours I'd need to reconsider this whole thing. You might be a serial killer." When he looked at her, his eyes danced. "You're not the only one who worries about these things, you know."

Veronica tried to laugh, but the noise got stuck in her throat. Jess had a big mouth, all right. "I might be a serial killer regard-less. You never know."

"I'll take that risk." He picked up an old postcard of Alexandra Romanov from the corner of Veronica's desk. As he looked at the picture, his expression pinched. "Tell me about your book. Why did you decide to write about the empress?"

"The empress?" The sudden reverence in his voice seemed odd. Instinctively, she took a step back and away from him. "You make it sound as though she's still alive."

"You evaded my question." Now he sounded playful again, more like one of Jess's attorney friends. "Why are you writing a book about Empress Alexandra?"

"I've never been a fan of happy endings."

Michael looked at her, brows raised. "That's it?"

Veronica glanced at the picture on the postcard. It had been taken at the height of Alexandra's celebrated beauty. Even so, Alexandra appeared ill at ease, her back too straight and her head too primly tilted. She may have been Empress of all the Russias, but she'd never mastered the art of posing for a camera. "She always looked so stiff and awkward," Veronica said. "I guess I can relate."

He turned the postcard over and examined the note on the other side. "The woman who wrote this had grandchildren in Moscow. She wants them to visit her."

"I know. I read Cyrillic. Kind of goes with the job."

"Sorry," he said. "There's just something exciting about that alphabet."

The back of Veronica's ears tingled. She wished she hadn't been so quick to sound like a pompous twit. She couldn't seem to strike quite the right note around this man. "I feel the same way, actually."

Michael set the postcard down and swung his hands behind his back. Veronica had known him for all of five minutes and had yet to see him stand still. "I know it's early," he said, "but maybe we can get dinner."

She focused on his gold tie clip, glittering in the early evening light. The words sputtered forth. "Jess may have given you the wrong idea. I'm not really dating now."

His smile collapsed.

"I've had a horrible day," she added, remembering how deeply romantic rejection stung. "I wouldn't be good company." Her vision clouded with brown spots.

"Hey . . ." she heard Michael say. "Are you okay?"

Her eyes started to burn. "I'm fine." She'd get fired. She'd return to her grandmother's house in Bakersfield with nothing to show for twelve years in Los Angeles except a mountain of debt. She could hear Abuela already. *Oh mija, what happened? You're such a clever girl.*

Veronica shuddered. Before she could say anything, Michael stepped forward. He didn't exactly sweep her into his arms, but somehow her head pressed lightly against his chest. A pleasant scent clung to his jacket. It reminded her of sunshine on an autumn day.

Still, she wasn't in the habit of falling into strangers' arms. She pulled away. A little wet pool of tears stained his jacket. Humiliation complete.

Michael reached into his pocket and fumbled for something. She expected a tissue. Instead, he withdrew a monogrammed handkerchief and handed it to her.

Veronica hesitated. "Are you kidding?"

"It's pristine." She still didn't take it, but he kept his arm extended. "I promise."

She accepted the handkerchief and dabbed her eyes, avoiding the elaborately intertwined *M* and *K* on the corner of the fabric. "Do you think I'm a freak?"

"I think something's bothering you. Maybe I can help."

Veronica twisted the handkerchief in her hands. "Can you fly me to the state archives of the Russian Federation in Moscow?"

"I don't have a pilot's license." He dipped his head, so that despite the difference in their height, he seemed to look up at her. "But I collect books on the Romanovs."

"No offense, but I doubt your home library rivals the state archives."

"I didn't mean to imply it did. You saw the list though, right? The one I wrote for Jess? Maybe you're curious? Why don't you let me take you to dinner?"

Veronica met his gaze. His eyes were hazel and far prettier than she first realized. "Will you ask me more questions about 'the empress'?"

Michael raised his hands, palms forward. "Probably."

"So is this dinner for business or pleasure?"

The curve of his mouth was crooked and sweet at once. She wondered if it was meant to provoke her. "I'm not sure. It might be fun to find out."

Despite everything, Veronica had to admit going out with him held more appeal than going home and obsessing over her grim tenure prospects. The bar for the night had been set damn low.

She decided to let Michael Karstadt distract her from her problems. Not charm her or seduce her, just distract her.

Bright murals and tapestries draped the walls of Electric Lotus, the luscious scents of cumin and coriander drifting from the kitchen to the dining room. Yet the fluttering in Veronica's stomach tempered her appetite. Michael Karstadt didn't eat either, just pushed potatoes smothered in curry around his plate. He kept looking over his shoulder like he thought they'd been followed.

She craned her neck to look as well, but saw nothing of concern. "All clear?"

He turned back in her direction, almost startled, like he'd forgotten they were on a date. Or were they? Veronica realized she wasn't sure.

"Why don't you tell me more about your books," she said. "You mentioned they belonged to your grandmother. Was she nobility? Is that why you call Alexandra 'the empress'"—Veronica made air quotes—"and talk about her as if she's alive?"

Michael placed his fork on his plate and smiled. She noticed a small gap between his front teeth. It lent an off-kilter charm to his features. "You get straight to the point."

"I'm no good at small talk, or so I've been told."

"Give it a try. You might acquire a taste for it. How about 'What do you do?'"

"You're an attorney. Jess already told me about you."

"I'll try, then." He was still smiling, but his jaw tensed. "Why do you study history? Did you start by looking into your own family's past?"

Veronica sliced into a samosa with a greater degree of intensity than the flaky pastry warranted. "Hardly. I see history as cheap time travel. I delve into other people's problems so I don't have to think about my own."

"Tell me a story about a dead Russian celebrity. Peter the Great perhaps?"

She had to admit, it felt good to share space with a history geek. "When Peter first set out to westernize Russia, he invited the Muscovy *boyars* to dine with a group of European ambassadors. The *boyars* wore smelly fur coats and beards down to their knees. They slurped borscht straight from bowls. Peter was so angry he grabbed a knife and lopped their beards off." She paused for a sip of beer. "A little Freudian, don't you think? Not that you can blame Peter. Rude manners should be suitably punished."

Michael's features relaxed again. "You must love your job. What a cushy gig."

She choked on her beer. "I'm writing a four-hundred-page book with a fifty-page bibliography. That's your idea of a cushy gig?"

He laughed softly. "I only meant you get to study Russian history. Nicholas and Alexandra are fascinating characters. They represent the final standoff between autocratic monarchy and constitutional democracy."

Veronica reached for a piece of fluffy naan, liking his nimble mind. Without thinking, she touched his arm. "I wish you'd talk to my dean, this battleax named Regina Brack. She doesn't get their appeal at all."

Michael studied Veronica, his hand on his mouth. "Your eyes take on a gold tint in this light." He moved his hand to emphasize the point. "And your face is shaped like a heart. You're very striking."

Tiny goose bumps rippled across her shoulders. Veronica ran her fingers along the rim of her glass, her mind reeling. She needed to watch herself. She'd been burned before by semi-glamorous men.

If she refused to look at Michael, she couldn't fall under his spell. Instead, she watched the hostess lead a couple to the table directly behind them. The girl could have passed for Angelina Jolie's kid sister and the guy had the doe-eyed soap star look. The part of Veronica that devoured *Entertainment Weekly* was captivated by their effortless beauty. Another part of her resented always feeling like a hobbit in a land of lithe elves.

The guy ignored his date, talking on his phone instead. He cursed loudly, spewing misogynist nonsense that would have made the crew on *Entourage* blush. A mother at a nearby table scowled. Her little girl had black hair gathered into the same type of pink ponytail holder Veronica used when she was a kid. The little girl started to giggle. For some reason, this made Veronica sad. Life shouldn't turn coarse so early.

The guy took a seat directly behind Veronica and pushed his chair back so he was practically shouting in her ear.

At least now Veronica had an excuse to change the subject of conversation. "Speaking of rude behavior," she told Michael. "Even the Muscovy *boyars* couldn't compete with this."

Every muscle in Michael's face tightened, like he'd bitten into something sour. "Dr. Veronica Herrera," he said. "I'm disappointed."

"Why?" she cried, before realizing how pathetic she sounded. She lowered her voice. "What did I do?"

"It's what you won't do. Most people figure the past is the past and who cares. I think you immerse yourself in another time because the present is . . ." Michael rolled his eyes, as though the right word might drop from the ceiling. ". . . disheartening. We spend our days stuck in traffic or fretting over insurance or collecting friends we hardly know on the Internet. No one can tell this guy to watch his mouth around kids?"

"We're socialized to avoid confrontation," Veronica said. "It's a survival tactic."

The guy threw his elbow over his seat, jabbing Veronica's head. "Ow!"

"That's it." Michael tossed his napkin on his plate.

"Wait." She held up one hand and used the other to rub the back of her skull. "I don't want to cause trouble."

"What trouble? You can't eat in public without risking a concussion?" Michael reached across the table to tap the guy on the shoulder. Excitement bubbled in Veronica's chest. No one had ever stood up for her before.

"Hold on." The guy turned and glared at Michael. "What?"

"Will you keep it down?" Michael's voice had a tight edge.

"What are you, the FCC? Mind your own business."

"You hit my date in the head."

"Tell the bitch to put some ice on it."

The word rang in her ears, hard as any slap. Michael jumped to his feet. The guy set his phone on his table and the two of them scowled at each other like a pair of roosters ready to tear one another to pieces. The room stilled; even the waitress who'd come to clear their plates hesitated. The techno-sitar music, which blended so smoothly with the cacophony of voices a moment before, now blasted over the speakers. Michael's gaze locked with Veronica's. He looked scared. This seemed unreasonable, given his size, but then the other guy did have youth on his side. Veronica's shoulders slumped.

As soon as Michael saw her reaction, he spun around and snatched the guy's phone. He headed for the servers' station near the kitchen, where coffee hissed and dirty dishes were stacked in a plastic tub. Veronica heard a faint "hello?" from the other end of the line as Michael tossed the phone in the trash.

"That's my property," the guy screeched. "I'll sue."

Michael returned to the table. Veronica thought he could have stopped a charging cheetah in its tracks. "Try suing me. You'll have a countersuit on your hands, on her behalf, for assault and battery."

The guy's Adam's apple wobbled. His date, the mini-Jolie, suppressed a smirk. Veronica pivoted her head to gage the reaction of the room, expecting a cinematic chorus of approval. No such luck. The other diners averted their eyes. Even the little girl with the pink ponytail holder had returned to her meal. A manager in a clean white shirt and bow tie approached their table, his expansive forehead creased with concern. A voice inside Veronica's head hissed, *Do something*.

Veronica stumbled to her feet. She reached into her purse and flung a couple twenties on the table. "Don't worry. We're leaving." She took Michael's hand, and led him past the other diners to the front door.

Outside, the evening sky had deepened to velvety purple. Streaks of orange sunlight ignited the western horizon. The white dome of Griffith Park Observatory hovered in the hills above them like a Byzantine temple. Veronica drew in a deep breath, savoring the spicy-sweet scent of flowers and citrus trees mingled with bitter exhaust fumes. She had always preferred the vibrant east side of Los Angeles to the bourgeois western enclaves and she'd forgotten how pretty the city looked at dusk.

"Sorry to embarrass you," Michael muttered as they crossed Los Feliz Boulevard, heading to his new Prius and her well-loved Toyota. "And I think I owe you money."

"No. I mean . . ." What did she mean? She needed the money. Veronica lengthened her strides to keep pace with Michael. Maybe she should get home and call Jess: *What were you thinking with this guy?*

Except she didn't feel that way. She felt wonderfully exhilarated and sorry for the mere mortals shooting past them in sleek cars, going about the boring business of life.

"Most guys are so reserved," she blurted, "especially in L.A. You're different."

Michael stopped in front of the Prius. "You're serious?"

A gust of wind whipped tendrils of hair against Veronica's cheeks. She shivered, not unpleasantly. "Peter the Great would have been proud of what you did in there."

He dipped his head to meet her gaze. "Do you want to come over?" he asked.

Veronica froze. When she was ten, she had mounted the high diving board at her neighborhood pool. From the top, the pool stretched out before her, an endless sea of chlorinated crystal blue. She'd felt like Pelé, the Hawaiian volcano goddess. Then the voices in her head started to hum. It was too high. They'd scrape her remains off the bottom of the pool with one of the red nets hanging from the side of the lifeguard's station. The same onslaught of vertigo shook her now. Her head buzzed.

"For coffee," Michael added. "I'm only five minutes away in Silver Lake. I'm not trying to seduce you on the first date."

"You don't want to seduce me? How insulting."

He smiled, but looked at the ground.

When she was ten, Veronica had climbed down the ladder, wet toes curling around each rung. Her cousins' mocking laughter still rang in her ears. She'd always regretted not making the dive.

Michael's house was built in the cute Craftsman style so popular in the hills. In the yard, scraggly lemon trees clung to life and wild strands of ivy crisscrossed the fences. Shrill staccato barking greeted them as they approached the gate. Michael fiddled with the knob on the arched door. "That's Ariel. Watch out."

As soon as he unlocked the door, a furry golden chow charged them, panting wildly. Michael grabbed her and the dog strained at her collar like a half-trained Moscow circus bear. "It's okay," Veronica said. "I love animals."

"You asked for it." Michael let go and Ariel sprang on her, slobbering. Two gray-and-white cats balanced on either side of the sofa, glaring at the chow with jealous green eyes. The cats jumped down and set to work rubbing and threading themselves between her legs.

"That's Boris and Natasha. It's kind of a zoo, but make yourself at home." Michael moved into the kitchen, dog and cats close at his heels.

Veronica stood upright, her legs unsteady. "This place is amazing," she said. A beamed ceiling and huge fireplace dominated the front room, along with a thick Persian carpet, liberally scattered with cat and dog fur, which covered most of the hardwood floor. Modigliani prints, oblong female faces with eyes askance, hung from the walls.

Michael popped out of the kitchen. "I'll give you the grand tour in a minute."

He reached over and touched Veronica's hand. A surge of warmth shot through her. That touch had been meant to reassure, rather than seduce, and yet her limbs felt pliant. She supposed she could try to seduce him. Her heart raced. Ordinarily, she didn't think this way at all. Then again, perhaps a one-night stand was exactly what she needed to break out of her funk. She'd wake up next to him tomorrow morning and think, *Oops, I barely know this guy.* She'd call Jess and feign guilt while divulging every juicy detail.

Except she had no clue how to signal what she wanted. A hand on his knee? A sly wink? She wanted to feel sexy and wild. If only she had something sexy and wild to say.

"Where's your bathroom?" she asked.

"Downstairs." He hesitated. "Are you all right?"

She managed a contrite nod and Michael withdrew to the kitchen. Veronica didn't need to use the bathroom, but didn't want to play the fool either. She headed downstairs.

With every step, an ominous creak sounded. On the lower floor, one of the doors had been left ajar. Bookshelves ran along the walls of what looked like a home office.

Her lips twitched. Some people peeked into a stranger's medicine cabinet to learn secrets. Veronica looked at their books. She glanced at the stairs. No sign of Michael. She pushed the door open and stepped inside the room.

The evening breeze drifted in from an open window and Veronica huddled deeper into her black cardigan. Below her, trucks rumbled by on Hyperion Boulevard. Veronica rubbed her arms and looked around, noting the cluttered desk, file folders and legal pads scattered about. From upstairs, she heard the crackling grooves of a vinyl record. Michael Karstadt was an analog type of guy. She should have known. And he remembered her devotion to Joy Division. Ian Curtis's raw baritone soon barreled into "Love Will Tear Us Apart." God, she was a sucker for a baritone.

Veronica approached the shelves. Many of the books were bound in leather and stained. She breathed in deeply, taking in the scent of the decay, and traced the embossed lettering on their spines, careful not to damage the fragile stitching. Her hand came to rest on a thick, canvas-bound binder. She stood on her tiptoes to remove it from the shelf.

An elaborate reproduction of the symbol of Imperial Russia, the double-headed eagle, was imprinted in dark scarlet on the cover. The eagle's two heads guarded the ancient Crown of Monomakh, reptilian tongues lashing out at some unseen threat to the Russian land. Sharp talons grasped a long sword on one side and a round scepter on the other.

Pulse racing, Veronica flipped through the binder. Yellowing documents, faded at the edges and cluttered with typos, had been tucked between plastic leaves: birth certificates, marriage licenses, death records. On the last page, she found a family tree with neat geometric shapes framing the names. On top of the page, she read:

NICHOLAS I (1796–1855)

m. Charlotte of Prussia, 1817

Tsar of all the Russias

"What are you doing?"

Veronica fumbled the binder and almost dropped it. Michael stood in the doorway, a steaming cup of coffee in each hand.

"Oops." She tried to smile. "I found Bluebeard's secret room."

"But no dead wives, I hope."

She laughed, too loudly. He moved next to her. They didn't exactly touch, but he'd removed his jacket and Veronica felt keenly aware of his shoulders underneath the fabric of his shirt. Michael handed her one of the mugs, something from an arts and crafts festival. She didn't peg him for the arts and crafts type. Maybe the mug belonged to an ex-girlfriend. Maybe he brought women here all the time. But Russian history professors? When he kept a binder full of genealogical records? Her hand trembled as she lifted the cup to her lips. The coffee seared her tongue.

"Careful," he said.

Veronica ran her tongue along the roof of her mouth to ease the pain. It served her right for letting his shoulders distract her.

"Why don't you let me take that off your hands?" He reached for the binder, but she stepped back, set the mug down, and clutched it tighter.

She tried to sound playful, even with her heart banging in her chest. "So what's the deal with the Iron Tsar?" That had been Nicholas I's nickname.

Veronica saw a flash of panic in Michael's eyes. "You're not shocked?"

"I'm more thrilled than shocked."

He raised his hands in apology, but his shoulders rose and fell. "I just don't want you to get the wrong idea. I want to explain."

She shook her head, confused.

"You didn't see?" he asked.

"See what?"

Once again, he tried to snatch the binder from her hands. She dodged him and flipped it open to the page she had been reading before, the family tree. She scrutinized the other boxes on the chart. At the bottom of the page, in the last box, she spotted Michael's name.

Michael Karstadt had traced his own lineage through the male line of his family tree to a reigning tsar. Russian genealogy was charted this particular way for one reason.

To claim the Romanov throne.

Two

Empress Alexandra felt her shortcomings keenly: her inadequate upbringing in a small German province, her intense shyness, her propensity for bad luck. Worst of all, after nearly seven years on the throne, she'd failed to produce a male heir.
—VERONICA HERRERA, The Reluctant Romanov: Late Imperial Russian Court Politics and Alexandra of Hesse

PETERHOF ESTATE
JULY 1901

Lena was alone when the chambermaid came to share the news. Empress Alexandra suffered from a migraine and couldn't be disturbed. Lena bowed her head dutifully, focusing on the chambermaid's small hands and fidgeting thumbs. The maid gave Lena a quick curtsy. Lena nodded and returned to mending a tear in one of Grand Duchess Olga's velvet gowns.

Once the maid left the nursery, Lena stashed the dress in a cedar box and grabbed a sprig of lilacs she'd gathered from the garden. She gathered her long black skirt in her hand and tiptoed over dolls dressed in the latest fashions from Paris and miniature tea sets. Then she slipped out the back entrance to head upstairs.

Three weeks earlier, the empress had given birth to a fat and happy little girl named Anastasia, her fourth daughter. Since then, gossip ran rampant as a virus through the household. Alexandra had not spoken a word since the baby arrived. She refused to leave her bed. The thought of the poor woman trapped in her room made Lena's heart sink. The empress had always been kind to her. She had to see if she could help, or at least offer consolation.

Compared to other imperial residences, the Romanovs' modest house at Peterhof remained sparsely staffed. Over the summer months, the family wanted to relax. So the guard stationed outside Alexandra's boudoir caught Lena by surprise. When she spotted him, she ducked for cover behind a hanging cluster of potted ferns in the hall. She tapped her slippered feet against the parquet flooring, determining how best to approach.

Gold embroidery lined the edges of his scarlet waistcoat and black jacket, the dress uniform of the Honorary North African Regiment. Lena realized she had seen this guard before, standing tall and silent behind the tsar's chair at a state dinner for the Persian shah. Lena was helping the kitchen staff whisk away heavy porcelain plates when she noticed how the guard's stiff white dress shirt seemed to glow against his dark skin. Distracted, she'd let one of the plates slip from her hand. The head maid had caught the plate before it crashed to the floor, and ordered Lena out of the kitchen. She remembered her cheeks burning as she glanced back at the guard. He hadn't moved a muscle, yet she was convinced he'd taken in the entire scene.

Now, Lena made the sign of the cross over her chest with her thumb and two fingers, praying the guard didn't remember the incident. As she stepped forward, she forced a smile. She addressed the guard in English, hoping her familiarity with the private language of the tsar's family might impress him. "I've brought flowers for the empress," she said brightly. "Might I pass?"

The guard squinted straight ahead, as though trying to bring something at a distance into focus. His eyes were light brown and framed by a thick fringe of curling lashes. He refused to look at her. His indifference prickled Lena's ego. "I put flowers on the table next to the empress's bed every evening," she added.

"I hear you come from the woods up north, near the town of Archangel. Where did you learn to speak English?"

Lena took a quick step back. The guard spoke English in a deep, musical accent that put her own clipped cadence to shame. "How do you know where I'm from?"

"Empress Alexandra has mentioned you a time or two. She's fond of you."

Taking care not to crush the flowers, Lena folded her arms in front of her chest. "My brother taught me the language. He has been to university in Saint Petersburg."

"He's a student? He should watch himself. They say universities are full of . . ."

The guard spoke rapid English now, using words she didn't understand. Her foot tapped the floor again nervously.

He switched back to Russian. ". . . the university students are all terrorists now."

Lena's fingers twisted around the lilacs. A stray petal floated to the floor. She reminded herself this guard couldn't possibly know of her brother or his troubles.

"They say the students learn how to make fire bombs in class," the guard continued, his voice growing more animated. "We'll all lose our jobs if they have their way." He pointed to the lilacs. "If you're not careful, you'll ruin those flowers."

She waited, but he said nothing more of terrorists. The panic in her chest subsided. Perhaps he was the sort of man who spoke only for the pleasure of hearing his own voice. "I wish to perform my job now." Lena tried to move forward but he stepped in front of her, blocking her path once more.

"I'm sure you heard the orders. No one is allowed inside."

"You wouldn't want to be held accountable for any mistakes, would you?"

The guard's shoulders stiffened. "I wouldn't be here if I made mistakes. Besides, if you want to see the empress, shouldn't you change into fresh clothes?"

He pointed to her shirtwaist, where the Grand Duchess Tatiana had spilled grape juice. Lena's hand moved of its own volition to cover the stain. She wished she had at least thought to swipe a brush through her hair before she left the nursery. "I might ask for permission," she said.

"Is that my Lenichka?"

The voice from the boudoir, high and weak, startled the guard. Before he could respond, Lena called, "I've brought flowers, Your Majesty, only I'm not allowed inside."

"It's all right, Pavel," Alexandra replied. "Let this one pass."

At the sound of Empress Alexandra's frail voice, he opened the heavy bedroom door. He then turned at a more leisurely pace to examine Lena, regarding her now with grudging amusement. She tilted her chin to meet his gaze.

"My mistake, after all. Perhaps our paths will cross again." Pavel leaned in closer. "Next time I'll know better than to block your way."

"If we meet again, I can practice my English," she said.

"It opens doors in this place. And I enjoy speaking in my native tongue."

"I thought you were Abyssinian."

"I come from a place called Virginia. My given name is Paul. When we meet again, I will tell you more." Pavel stepped back so she could pass. "Until then, take care around the royal family. They say that when you speak out here, the sound travels all the way back to Saint Petersburg."

Lena opened her mouth to ask what he meant, but he only gifted her with a sly smile and shut the door soundlessly behind her.

Inside Alexandra's boudoir, a stout maid in a starched white cap clucked and fussed over the enormous canopied bed, fluffing pillows and smoothing the top sheets. The cretonne curtains on the windows had been unfastened to reveal Peterhof's lush gardens, forests of pine trees, and rolling gray waters crashing along the coastline below. The midsummer twilight cast Alexandra's oval face in a luminous glow, like the sad-eyed Virgin on the wooden icon above the headboard.

Lena dropped into a low curtsy. The humidity made her skirt cling to the back of her knees. As she struggled upright, she scanned the chaos of overstuffed chairs, framed portraits, and figurines. At last she spotted a crystal vase atop an end table draped in lace doilies. She moved to the table and arranged the lilacs in the vase, hoping their fragrance might alleviate the bitter aroma of bromide salts.

"Leave us," Alexandra ordered.

Lena stepped back and bumped a mahogany armoire. The slender silver drawer knobs rattled against the wood in protest. The maid placed her chubby hands on her hips and glared at Lena.

"Not you, Lenichka. But Anya, if you will."

The maid drew in a quick intake of breath and gave a lumbering curtsy before trudging out of the room. She shut the door so hard the windowpanes shook.

Lena hovered awkwardly in the corner, unsure of her next move.

"I knew you would visit me," Alexandra said gently. "Come closer."

Lena approached, but could not find satisfactory words. Congratulations for the new baby were in order and yet they were not.

"Please speak to me, Lenichka." Alexandra offered her hand. Lena kneeled and folded the long tapered fingers in her own. She detected the scent of rose water mingled with stale cigarette smoke. "My grandmother was Queen Victoria. My mother passed away when I was a girl and grandmama helped raise me. Now she's gone as well. I'm grateful you speak her language. I wish to hear it more often. I miss her so."

"Grand Duchess Anastasia is beautiful. Everyone says so. She pleases her father." Lena thought it important to include this last bit.

"Nicky loves all his girls." Alexandra sighed and leaned back into her pillows. "But four daughters and no heir? If only you had been present when the child was born."

Despite the humidity, a chill passed over Lena. "Why would you want me?"

"You told me your mother is a midwife. Perhaps you know secrets to help a woman conceive a boy." Alexandra's voice faded. Lena leaned forward to catch the last words. "Perhaps with your help, I would have delivered a son. An heir to the throne."

On the other side of the bedroom window, a breeze ruffled the

English rose petals and the delphinium blossoms. Lena wished she was strolling through the gardens now, gulping in the fresh air gusting in from the Gulf of Finland. "Only God can grant what you wish," she whispered.

Alexandra clamped her hand tightly around Lena's wrist, her palm hot and slick. "Are you suggesting God doesn't hear my prayers?"

With her free hand, Lena twisted a lock of hair around her finger. Usually, Alexandra treated her as tenderly as a newborn kitten. "I only meant you have the best doctors at your disposal."

"Everyone hates me. I hear the gossip. I'm called the German bitch. They say I'm useless. They say I'm cursed."

Lena wished she could deny it. But only yesterday she'd overheard a smug cow of a royal cousin whisper that the tsar should have married Matilda Kshesinskaya, the ballerina he'd kept as a mistress for many years, rather than Alexandra. At least then, the woman hinted, the empire might enjoy the stability of an heir.

"Your mother must have passed knowledge on to you," Alexandra insisted. "Please. My grandmother is gone. My sister is childless. I have no one."

Lena could smell the empress's desperation. She longed to lift Alexandra out of despair, yet it wasn't her place to give advice. If she helped and something went wrong, what a convenient scapegoat she would make. She could find herself suddenly under police surveillance, seized in the dead of night, and thrown into the darkest dungeon of Peter and Paul Fortress.

"I will continue to pray for you and the holy tsar." The words were cotton in Lena's mouth.

Alexandra dropped Lena's hand and drew a crocheted coverlet over her shoulders. Her voice shifted to the icy tone she used when a clumsy maid dropped a vase. "I have already prayed for help. I asked only for loyalty. You're excused."

Lena rose to her feet, curtsied, and backed out of the room gradually, not daring to give further offense. Alexandra buried her head in a pillow and let out a muffled gasp. Lena grasped the doorknob. A tremor rolled down the back of her neck. For a moment, she was no longer in the presence of the Empress of all the Russias, but back in the dingy cabin in the northern woods where she'd been raised.

"You want something." Alexandra sprang upright in bed. "I see it in your eyes. Something troubles you."

Lena bowed her head and thrust her hand into her skirt pocket, feeling for the paper, making sure it was still there. She closed her fingers over the crumpled letter.

Her mother had written with news of Lena's brother, Anton. After university, he'd been unable to find work. He'd returned home to Archangel and had grown involved with a group of boys too radical even for the local union. They reeked of alcohol, advocated violence, and viewed jail time as a soldier would a medal of honor. One of them had been arrested. Under duress, her mother feared, he might reveal other names.

Images of her brother's face raced through Lena's mind, the ruddy cheeks and perpetually startled high eyebrows. A solution began to take shape, like random stars assuming the form of a constellation. Alexandra was the last person with whom she would have thought to share Anton's problems. But now she had an opportunity she couldn't let pass. She only needed to summon the courage to ask.

Lena took care with her words. "My mother wrote. There is trouble at home."

"I can help," Alexandra insisted. "Whatever it is. We can help each other."

"I worry about my brother. He is a good boy. His friends are not."

Alexandra clenched her pillow, gaze fixed on Lena. "I understand wayward brothers. I have one, Ernest, back home in Hesse. He hasn't been the same since his wife left him. If you help me, I can protect your brother."

Lena drew in a quick breath. Simple advice could do the empress no harm.

"The women in Archangel needed sons to please their husbands," Lena said. "This is what my mother told them to do . . ."

PARIS

OCTOBER 1941

Horns blared. Try as she might Charlotte could not tear her gaze from the clock on her kitchen wall. The slim hour and minute hands had aligned, pointing upward to indicate noon. Right on schedule, the soldiers assembled along the boulevard, rifles angled on their shoulders, dark green uniforms drab but spotless. They started to advance. She closed her eyes, listening to their heavy boots thump cobblestones in time to a monotonous military march. The tune rattled through makeshift loudspeakers that now lined the city's streets.

Charlotte remembered the way people spoke of the soldiers at the beginning. The rumors kept the entire city in a state of terror. Occupying Huns came in the dark of night. They used spiked clubs to knock doors from hinges. The soldiers seized children and cut off little boys' hands, so they couldn't grow up to hold guns. Charlotte knew she shouldn't believe such stories. And yet, at the beginning of the occupation, whenever the soldiers marched, her pulse quickened. She'd grabbed her son and run to the bedroom. She'd shut the door and held him close until the heavy sound of boots and the crackle of music grew faint in the distance.

As the months of occupation progressed, Charlotte forced the fear to harden in her stomach, an irritating but benign tumor. Now, she opened her eyes and tried to focus on the tasks at hand: pinning her auburn hair into a neat bun at the nape of her neck, using the last of her long matches to light the gas on the stove and heat the watery substance passing for soup. She made a mental review of the exercises she meant to teach later that afternoon with her class at Matilda Kshesinskaya's ballet studio.

Charlotte stepped away from the stove and peeked into the parlor to check on her son, Laurent. Kshesinskaya had offered to watch him while Charlotte was in class. The two of them stood together at the front window. Kshesinskaya tried to distract Laurent with a stuffed monkey, but he slipped out of her arms and clapped for the soldiers, as though watching a Punch and Judy puppet show at Luxembourg Gardens.

"Be still," Kshesinskaya scolded. She looked up and saw Charlotte watching them. "He needs to understand," she explained.

Charlotte's fingers flexed irritably. Of course Laurent needed to avoid the soldiers, like automobiles on the street or a scalding pot of hot water on the stove. But he was only three. Charlotte moved toward them. She kissed the top of her son's head and then gently tilted his face up. He'd had a bad nosebleed yesterday and dry flakes of clotted blood still clung to his nostrils. She wiped them away with the back of her hand.

"The soldiers may need to march." Kshesinskaya pulled up the sleeves on her silk blouse and rubbed her slender wrists as she pointed at the windows. "But we needn't give them an audience."

"You're right." Charlotte made the rounds of her flat, drawing all the thick blackout curtains closed. It felt good to move her legs, to shut out the soldiers on foot and the officers on their fine stallions as they passed. Kshesinskaya understood how to handle this situation. She'd dealt with occupation before, when the Bolsheviks seized control of Saint Petersburg in 1917, forcing Kshesinskaya to flee her country with nothing more than a pocketful of jewels. "We'll listen to Madame."

Laurent's features scrunched into a frown. The horses were his favorite part of the parade. The back of Charlotte's neck ached. As she twisted to massage it, her gaze traveled to her rolltop desk in the corner of the room, where she'd stashed the latest postcard from her mother. Postcards were all the Germans allowed now, so they could read what people had to say without the trouble of ripping open and resealing envelopes.

Her mother had written diligently, scrunching her words to fit them on the small card. She begged them to return home to the Dordogne, to stay in the little cottage next to the vineyards, where they could help Charlotte's father tend the grapes. Her parents never wanted her to move to Paris in the first place and still refused to consider it her home.

Charlotte meant to respond to her mother, but every time she started, Laurent bruised his knee and started to cry. Or she had to take yet another call from one of her students' parents, informing her they were sorry but their family had to leave the city.

"The Germans can't stay forever," she heard Kshesinskaya say.

Charlotte wished she could believe her. And yet so many new

soldiers arrived in the city every day, each batch more fresh-faced than the last. On her way to class, she saw them strut along the streets with cameras strapped around their thick necks, snapping pictures like privileged tourists. She passed sidewalk cafés where they laughed and gorged themselves on foul-smelling schnapps.

A steady pounding at the front door sliced through her thoughts. A deep voice boomed from the other side of the door, in French, but with a halting German accent. "Madame? Open this door."

Laurent grabbed her hand. She tried to give him a reassuring smile, but her muscles cramped. She couldn't move, couldn't curl her fingers around his. This was what everyone said would happen. The soldiers may not have come under cover of night, but one of them had finally arrived at her door.

Laurent's small hand grew moist with sweat. Charlotte slid her feet together, heels flat to toes, in a perfect fifth position. She always felt better in fifth position. The stories about the German soldiers had to be false. Perhaps this one only needed to use the facilities. Perhaps he was looking for someone else entirely.

"Madame Marchand?" the soldier called.

Charlotte's stomach lurched. She didn't understand. She took care to avoid the soldiers, averting her eyes and crossing to the other side of the street when they passed.

Kshesinskaya's concerned face came into focus, her voice grave as death. "Charlotte, that soldier knows your name."

She shook her head. The pummeling at the door continued, obscuring the fading marching music from the street. Charlotte tried to swallow her panic, but she remembered more of the stories now. When soldiers came to your door, shouting your name, they sent you east to nowhere. That's what people called it now.

East to nowhere and never heard from again. Charlotte imagined one of the fat young Germans she saw on the street bursting into her flat and pointing a machine gun at her son.

"This door is opening one way or another," the soldier called.

She couldn't let him near Laurent. She couldn't let the soldier even see she had a son. Charlotte took Laurent by the arm. He stumbled in front of her as she pushed him to the bedroom. "Stay here." She kissed the top of his head, taking in the leafy scent of his hair and drawing strength from it. "Don't let them see you. Like hide-and-seek."

Charlotte tried to pull Kshesinskaya into the bedroom after Laurent, but she jerked Charlotte sideways, gold bangles jangling around her wrists. "What are you doing?" she demanded.

"Please. I don't know what else to do." Charlotte only knew it felt right to keep moving. "Avoid them. Isn't that what you were saying to Laurent?"

"Come in here with us then."

"If I don't answer, he might force his way inside. I'll see what he wants."

Charlotte shook Kshesinskaya's hand off her arm and pushed her into the bedroom. Laurent gave her one last pleading look before Charlotte shut the door.

She stood alone in the living room. The pounding at the door continued, more insistent now. In the kitchen, the soup had bubbled over in a foamy mess. Charlotte flipped the gas off on the stove. Then she rolled her shoulders back, as she used to when she prepared to take the stage. She strode to the door and unhooked the thin metal latch.

Behind her, she heard the jingling of bracelets. Kshesinskaya clamped her almond-scented hand firmly over Charlotte's mouth.

"Madame Marchand is not here," Kshesinskaya called, her voice a falsely merry singsong.

The pounding stopped. The German lowered his voice. "When will she return?"

What was Kshesinskaya doing? Charlotte couldn't breathe. She struggled against her grip, but the older woman wouldn't let go. "I'm not sure," Kshesinskaya said. "Some days, she stays out all hours, let me tell you. Why did you say you were here again?"

The soldier's tone changed, became almost flirtatious. "Pardon me, madame. Of course. My name is Herr Krause and I wish to speak to Charlotte Marchand. She used to dance with the Opera Ballet, did she not? Now she works for that old Russian prima donna Matilda Kshesinskaya?"

Charlotte wanted to scream, wanted to run for Laurent. It wasn't just her name. He knew all about her. But Kshesinskaya pressed her hand even tighter against Charlotte's lips.

"She may also be known as a grand duchess," the German said sweetly. "Is this familiar? Have you heard her use the title?"

Kshesinskaya spun Charlotte around. She touched her fingers to her lips. Charlotte nodded. Kshesinskaya lowered her hand, breathing heavily. Charlotte realized she'd never seen Kshesinskaya frightened before, not even when the German tanks rolled down the boulevards. Kshesinskaya motioned for Charlotte to take her handbag, which hung on a hook near the door.

"What happens to you when I don't come back?" Charlotte whispered.

"I'll take care of it."

"But where will we go?"

Kshesinskaya released Charlotte and flew across the room. She snatched the handbag from its hook. Then she moved to the rolltop desk, opening drawers, removing all of the postcards from Charlotte's mother and stuffing them deep inside the handbag. She tossed the bag to Charlotte.

"Go to your parents. They'll explain everything. Take Laurent to the Métro. Leave out the back door. Now!"

The force of her voice propelled Charlotte back toward her bedroom. She groped for the knob and stumbled inside, searching for Laurent. The door to the back garden had been opened and she spotted him outside, crouched and shivering in his thin coat near the remains of the rhododendrons Charlotte planted last spring. Frantically, Charlotte searched her room for anything of value she might snatch and take with them.

"It could be hours before Madame returns," she heard Kshesinskaya say.

"I've waited a long time to find her," Herr Krause replied smoothly. "I can wait a little longer."

Then she heard Kshesinskaya's calm but grumpy reply: "Fine. Fine."

Charlotte flung open a heart-shaped wooden box. Her jewelry collection consisted mostly of costume pieces. She was wearing a necklace from her mother and owned one diamond pendant and matching earrings, a gift from an admirer many years back. Charlotte thrust the diamonds in her handbag and bolted outside. She grabbed Laurent and started to run, stomping on the rhododendrons and pushing them both through the back gate and out to the boulevard.

The midday sun slipped behind puffy gray rainclouds. As she ran to the Métro, she noticed the drawn curtains in the flats and the thick iron locks on the doors of the shops. When Charlotte first moved to Paris, she couldn't sleep for all the noise. She'd come to the city because she was so sick of the quiet in the countryside. Now she heard only the patter of the wooden soles of her shoes, the snapping of twigs as a squirrel dashed up a tree trunk, and the dying notes of the military march crackling through speakers on the opposite end of the boulevard.

She dodged a bicyclist and descended into the dark Métro station, cradling the back of Laurent's head in her hand. His ribs felt sharp and thin against her body. She imagined Kshesinskaya facing the German soldier at the front door. When Charlotte never materialized, what then? He might send Kshesinskaya east to nowhere. And somehow it was all connected to Charlotte.

Charlotte moved faster, trying to shake the guilt. She would help Kshesinskaya. But first, she needed to find a safe place for Laurent to stay. Juggling him to one side, Charlotte thrust her hand in her pocket. She shook a few coins from her handbag and offered them to the attendant.

Once she stood on the deserted station platform, catching her breath, holding her son, Charlotte realized how isolated she'd become. She didn't have enough money for a hotel. She didn't know where to sell the diamonds. All of her friends, save Kshesinskaya, who insisted she had enough of fleeing soldiers for one lifetime, had left the city long ago. Paris was no longer the dream world she'd entered, as a starry-eyed provincial girl, twenty years earlier.

Kshesinskaya had said to go to her parents. She said they would explain. Explain what? Her words made no sense. But Charlotte realized now how much she ached to hear her father's gruff voice and the endless barking of his retrievers, how desperately she wanted to draw in the crisp scent of clean country air. Most of all, she wanted her mother's arms around her. She wanted to feel protected and safe. She wanted someone to help her keep Laurent safe.

The Nazis had established checkpoints all around the city. To leave, she needed help. Who else would be stubborn enough to stay in Paris? Only one person came to mind.

A horn blasted. A gust of gassy exhaust fumes assaulted them as a train rumbled into the station and then ground to a halt. Through the gray film of dust on the window, she caught a glimpse of the passengers: a man with broken glasses bent over a newspaper and a woman in an old housedress clutching a small, shivering dog.

She couldn't become like these people, hunched and scared, trying not to be noticed. She would take Laurent to her parents' house, just as Kshesinskaya had said to. She only needed somewhere to stay for a night or two, to strategize how to get past the Germans' checkpoints.

The train's doors slid open before them. Charlotte saw no other choice. She needed to find her husband.

Three

LOS ANGELES

PRESENT DAY

MICHAEL KARSTADT (1969–)
Heir Apparent

Veronica set the binder down on the desk, staring at Michael's name. Earlier this week, she'd stated her goal in dating: don't get killed by a serial killer. Sure, Michael wasn't hiding any bodies in his closet, but she took a step back and away from him nevertheless. Why hadn't he wanted her to see his family tree?

Michael drummed his fingers on the edge of the desk, not quite in time to Ian Curtis's brooding baritone, still blasting in all its analog glory from the stereo upstairs. She felt flustered. Whenever she felt flustered, she had one defense. Sarcasm. "So what's the proper protocol here? Should I fall down on one knee, Tsar Mikhail?"

He choked on a laugh. It emboldened her. "Why didn't you want me to see this?"

"You caught me off guard. I wasn't planning to mention it."

"You invited a Russian history professor into your home," she said. "Somehow I think you wanted to slip this little detail into the conversation."

"Look, it's not a big deal."

"This says you're a grand duke and heir to the largest country on earth."

"According to that family tree, I'm not a grand duke, only a prince."

"Only a prince. How modest."

He rubbed the back of his neck. "I only keep these records because they're important to my mother. They were extremely important to my grandmother. That's why they're important to me."

His voice faltered. Veronica didn't know what did it, the note of sadness when he spoke of his grandmother or the gentleness with which he passed his hand over his mouth. But she suddenly found it difficult to summon any more flip remarks.

Veronica tried to view Michael through new eyes. She saw no resemblance to the last tsar, Alexandra's adored but incompetent husband Nicky. Still, Michael didn't claim to be a direct descendant of Nicholas II, but of the nineteenth-century Iron Tsar, Nicholas I. Michael fit that genetic template well enough. Even his behavior earlier at Electric Lotus was a sort of contemporary noblesse oblige. "If this is accurate, your claim to the Romanov throne is strong," she said. "Have you thought about this at least?"

He dipped his head so it seemed he was looking up at her. His shoulders moved back. She still found it hard not to look at his shoulders. "Thought about what?"

"You know." She extended her hands and mimed placing a crown on his head.

"It's difficult to claim a nonexistent throne," Michael said.

"Besides, laws of succession are never foolproof, as I'm sure you know. If a rogue nation launched a nuclear attack on the United States, and the president, vice president, and speaker of the house didn't make it to the bunker, what would we do?"

"The president pro tempore of the Senate assumes the presidency," Veronica said, "and then the secretary of state, and then—"

"Okay. I get the idea." Michael smiled. "The Romanov chain of command is far less organized, as I'm sure you know. And that's assuming the dynasty will ever be restored, which is a long shot at best."

"You have a two-fold claim and a sentimental link to Nicholas and Alexandra." Veronica tapped the genealogical chart. "Grand Duke Alexander Mikhailovich? Your great-great-grandfather? He married one of Nicholas II's sisters. You're the great-grandnephew of the tsar."

"It doesn't matter," Michael said. "Russians shouldn't restore the monarchy."

"You think too much like an American. You assume monarchies are anti-democratic. I've read quite a bit on this topic. Monarchies can be progressive and help construct a common cultural landscape."

"Cultural landscape? You think too much like an academic."

She did think like an academic. How could she help it? Her brain was trained to doubt and question. She closed the binder and stroked the embossed double eagle on the cover. "Did you figure I'd help you prove your claim?" She tried to sound nonchalant, but caught herself babbling. "Keep in mind I'm an untenured history professor. No one pays any attention to me except my students. Scratch that. No one pays any attention to me, especially my students."

"You're the one who started snooping around my office."

"Some coincidence, though. The Romanov heir happens to meet my cousin who happens to mention I'm writing a book on Alexandra."

"Jessica said she'd thought we'd get along. She said you were lonely."

Michael clamped his lips shut. Veronica's heart sank. Maybe he wasn't a con artist or a predator or anything of the sort. Just a nice guy. Too nice. Somehow, that was even worse. "So you felt sorry for me."

"I don't agree to meet women out of pity, thank you. I have more respect for everyone's time, including my own. I agree to meet women who sound interesting." He placed his hand on hers. Every one of Veronica's nerve endings rose to immediate, thrilled attention. "Anyway, there's nothing wrong with being lonely," he added. "Not that you are lonely."

"Tell me the truth," she said. "That's all I ask. Do you want something from me? Do you want me to help you somehow? I won't hold it against you."

Michael turned her palms over. Veronica sucked in a quick breath and looked away, worried about her ragged nails and short, clumsy fingers. He brushed his lips across the inside of her wrist and she shivered. His mouth inclined to her ear, not quite touching it. She felt the soft rush of his breath on her neck.

"You're gorgeous, smart, funny, and your skin feels like silk." He touched her cheek with his nose. "That's why I want to spend time with you."

He kissed her cheeks and then kissed her softly on the lips. A lock of Veronica's hair fell forward, tickling the bridge of her nose. He pushed it out of the way and stroked the back of her ear. "Do you believe me?"

She nodded, spinning with desire. He leaned in to kiss her again, but the clacking of claws against the hardwood floor distracted him. The furry chow poked her nose in the room, panting in their general direction.

"Impeccable timing, Ariel." Michael's arms remained around Veronica's waist.

What was she doing? Veronica pulled away, smoothing out her skirt and blouse. Her lips were tingling and she was convinced he had noticed somehow.

"I should get going," she told him. "I have a pile of essays to grade. I can see the rest of your books on the Romanovs next time." Her cheeks warmed. "If you want there to be a next time. I mean, that's up to you."

"Is tomorrow too soon?"

Ariel's big wet nose nudged Veronica's leg. Veronica ruffled the silky fur on the back of the dog's neck and the chow gave a low grunt of appreciation, absurdly content.

"I'd like to take you to dinner, but we should do something else as well," he said. "I know you're into alt rock, but how about swing? Have you ever tried swing dancing?"

"Swing dancing?" she said. "You're on the cutting edge of 1996."

"Cutting edge of 1946, actually. I'd like to take a lesson. What do you think?"

He took her hand in his and started a few impromptu steps. Veronica had to admit, he twisted his body around with a certain bulky grace. Few men, at least in her admittedly limited experience, let themselves look so vulnerable in front of a woman.

"I should have known," she said. "All the Romanovs loved to dance. Unfortunately, I'm no Romanov."

Michael's grin buckled and his grip on her hand loosened abruptly. Veronica stepped back, sudden cold washing over her. She had a flashback to her fiancé dropping her hand. It always seemed like he let go first, like he couldn't wait to get away from her. She tried to imagine letting her aching humpty dumpty of a heart free again. If it fell this time it would shatter beyond repair.

But she couldn't be the only one taking a risk. You couldn't get to a certain age without having the humpty dumpty pulled on your heart a time or two. Michael must have been hurt before. Perhaps he was wary of starting over as well, of risking getting hurt again.

"You're serious about all this?" she asked tentatively.

Michael ran his hand back through his hair. "Veronica, I like you. I want to get to know you better."

"I meant the genealogy," she said. "You really believe you're the heir?"

He bent down to scratch Ariel's ears. Veronica decided to drop the subject, at least for now. She knew better than to try to talk him into making a play for the Russian throne, at least not this evening.

When the phone rang, lingering images from Veronica's dreams fluttered away like butterflies. Bright North Hollywood sunshine seeped through the blinds, illuminating a crack in the ceiling her landlord assured her would be fixed one of these days. She groaned and pressed the pillow to her ears.

At last, the answering machine picked up. "Not out of bed yet, *mija*?"

Her grandmother's dramatic voice roused Veronica to full,

guilty attention. She grabbed the phone and cradled the receiver between her shoulder and ear. "Hello?"

"You sound sleepy." It came out as an accusation.

Veronica adjusted her body on the mattress. "It's Saturday."

"I didn't hear from you this week. I started to worry. How is your writing? We're all wondering when we'll see your book."

Veronica felt the first pangs of a headache. Abuela took credit for Veronica's Ph.D. and her special interest in history. History books filled the house while Veronica was growing up, and Abuela took her to the library whenever she asked. Abuela had been especially supportive when Veronica decided to focus on Russian history, and always encouraged her, even when she didn't understand the mechanisms of academic life.

So Veronica knew it was a shame to dampen her grandmother's enthusiasm. But she didn't want to give her false hope either, not after her latest conversation with Regina Brack. "I don't think my monograph will hit the shelves anytime soon." She remembered the neat squares on Michael's family tree and smiled. "You never know, though," she added. "There might be renewed interest in the Romanovs."

"That's the spirit!" Abuela gushed. "Why don't you come home this weekend so we can chat? We'll get dinner tonight. I'll invite your cousin Nina and her family."

The prospect of a visit home ran through Veronica's head like a bad sitcom. They'd pile into someone's SUV and head for Applebee's. Maybe Chili's if Abuela felt wild. Thank God she had an excuse to skip this weekend. "I can't. I made plans."

"Plans?" Her grandmother stretched the word to three syllables.

Veronica didn't respond. That was all Abuela needed.

"You met a man."

She imagined her grandmother on the other end of the line, tapping her neatly manicured nails against the yellow paint on the kitchen table. Veronica waited.

"I hope this man appreciates your accomplishments," Abuela said at last. "You inherited your mind from your mother. She would have finished school except—"

She got pregnant with you and that ended that. Now her grandmother would regale her with stories of Veronica's white father and his numerous failings. In the extended version of the story, Veronica should beware of all men. Why did a smart girl like her need a man anyway? She could lead an independent life, a life of the mind. Such opportunities weren't available to women in Abuela's day.

But dinner and dancing with Michael Karstadt hardly jeopardized her scholarly agenda. Veronica was capable of screwing that up all on her own. "I'll be careful."

"I'd like to see you happy," Abuela said, "but I'd hate to see you hurt again. After what happened with your fiancé, I worry."

Veronica rubbed her bare left ring finger, silently imploring God. *Don't let her bring him up. I can't handle it now.* Not when this was the first morning she'd managed to wake up and not miss the warmth of him next to her in bed. She glanced at the alarm clock on her dresser, calculating how much more time she needed to devote to this conversation before she might gracefully bring it to a close.

"You'll come home in three weeks though," her grandmother purred. "Nina's daughter is having her *quinceañera*. Then we'll sit down and talk. I miss that."

"I'll be at the *quinceañera*." Veronica hoped to end the discussion on a high note.

"This is an important year," Abuela said. "Your tenure review is in January, right? You won't let this man distract you from your work?"

Little red spots swarmed in her mind. She didn't have enough votes for tenure. Her research was a joke. She should start to look for other jobs. Veronica squeezed her eyes shut, trying to generate more pleasant thoughts. She remembered the way she had to quicken her steps to keep pace with Michael. Last night, she'd dreamt of riding a golden barge down the Neva River, crowds of happy Russians lining the banks, waving imperial flags emblazoned with the double-headed eagle in their direction.

Veronica opened her eyes and leaned across the bed. She reached for the laptop she kept at the bottom of her nightstand. A side research project couldn't make matters worse. Maybe it would be just the thing to kick her into action. "Don't worry," she told her grandmother. "Actually, I feel newly inspired. Let me tell you what I found out about his family."

A light from the ceiling played on Michael's hair, bringing out the gray highlights. It worked for him somehow. He had taken her to a Cuban restaurant on Hyperion Boulevard before the promised swing dancing lesson. He'd also ditched the tailored suit she'd admired the night before, though he still looked plenty dashing in jeans, an olive green shirt that complemented his hazel eyes, and a dark blazer. She sensed he was the kind of guy who wouldn't dream of stepping out of the house without a blazer. "Why the Mona Lisa smile?" he asked.

Veronica nudged the grapes nestled on the bottom of her glass of sangria with a straw. "I conducted a little research today."

"A-ha!" He tried to sound lighthearted, but she heard a tremor in his voice. "And what did you discover?"

Veronica released her grip on the straw, pushed the sangria away, and folded her hands before her on the table. She looked Michael squarely in the eye. "Are you affiliated with any neo-monarchist clubs?"

Michael poked his fork into a small bowl filled with fried plantains. "Clubs for the nobility? Filled with sad old men? No way. Those are strictly for right-wing nut jobs. Why?"

"I'm curious. That's all. I shot out an e-mail or two, just to ask questions." Veronica felt her bottom lip twitch and tried to steady it. "Some of the clubs have questionable political views, but not all of them lack substance. After all, the Russian government reinstated the Zemsky Sobor. The Assembly of the Nobility. Legislators!"

Michael hunched forward. "I know. I went to Saint Petersburg last Christmas for a family reunion. My mother still keeps in touch with relatives there . . ."

As Michael spoke, a flourish of horns and maracas blasted over the speakers. The music made Veronica think of Havana in the fifties, before Fidel Castro. Men in Panama hats and women in slinky dresses enjoying decadent lives before Communism's proverbial hammer swung down. Just like tsarist Russia. For a moment, Veronica was back in the Russian dream world of ornate palaces and complicated love affairs.

". . . and believe me, no one is listening to any Zemsky Sobor." Michael's pragmatic tone shook Veronica out of the dream. "The fall of the monarchy is a sad fairy tale, but that's all. Russia is a capitalist oligarchy now. It's not a very romantic form of governance, but as long as more people get a piece of the financial pie, it will remain."

"This is Russia's gilded age, I get that," she said. "Still, there's also something to be said for salvaging national honor. That's why many Russians support restoration."

"God, your eyes are gorgeous. Have I mentioned you can see flecks of gold in them in the right light?"

Pulsing waves of pleasure shot down the back of Veronica's neck, but she was on a roll now. "Based on your genealogy, you qualify for the Assembly of Nobility."

"You're a closet monarchist? And here I had you pegged for a Libertarian."

"Humor me," Veronica said. "Let's say this could happen and Russians restore the monarchy. A popular tsar could act as an ambassador of goodwill. God knows we need that right now. You could be the male Princess Diana. What do you say to that, Tsar Mikhail?"

He looked down at his hands. "Last night, you questioned my motivations. Now I have to ask: Did you agree to go out with me so you could play kingmaker?"

"Tsar-maker." She sensed the wall rising between them and her defenses mounted in response. "I'm not sure."

Michael's laugh had a defeated ring to it. He polished off his beer. "If that's what you're after, you'll need to find someone with far greater delusions of grandeur."

The familiar, crippling anxiety washed over her. Perhaps she shouldn't be here. She had a monograph to finish. Four hundred pages. Abuela was right. She didn't need distractions. "Wait." Veronica forged through the doubt. She touched his arm. "If that's all there was to it, I'd tell you up front. I wouldn't ply you with sangria to extract information. I like you. I really do. I'm also curious about your claim. Frankly, I could use the distraction."

He frowned. "Distraction from what?"

Veronica arranged the salt and pepper shakers with the other condiments on the edge of the table, lining them up like dutiful soldiers. "I don't think I'm getting tenure. I don't have the votes. I'm behind on my research and my argumentation isn't consistent. I took out too many student loans. I'm in debt to my ears. If I don't make tenure, I'll have to move back in with my grandmother. She lives in Bakersfield."

"Is that where you grew up?"

"Yes. I couldn't wait to get away." Veronica tucked some loose strands of hair behind her ear. "Where are you from?"

"Brooklyn."

Brooklyn was yet another faraway place Veronica romanticized, a hipsters' paradise of novelists and indie rock bands. "Why don't you have a New York accent?"

"I moved to California after my parents divorced. I lost it."

"You wouldn't understand. You grew up somewhere interesting. You probably spent weekends at Coney Island and the Botanical Garden."

"My childhood wasn't quite that idyllic," he responded quietly.

"Oh." She felt like dirt. "I'm sorry."

He shook his head, dismissing the topic. "Tell me more about your book."

Veronica sighed. "Personally, I like Alexandra and argue she was the victim of misogyny from all sides. Yet I can't escape the fact she came down on the wrong side of history because she loved her husband too much. Love led to disaster. It did for my parents. It sounds like it did for your parents. Let's face it, love usually does."

He ducked his head to look up at her. It was adorable. She wished she could ask him to not be quite so adorable. "You really believe that?"

"I'm cautious," she said. "I've had my heart flattened."

"I want to spend more time with you, Veronica, but you can't assume I'll lead you to disaster. I need to know I have a chance here."

"That's an intense question considering I've known you all of twenty-four hours."

"I'm an intense guy."

Her gaze wandered to the bright oil mural covering the opposite wall, depicting Columbus's landing in Hispaniola. A slender young woman extended long strands of beads as a gift for the approaching conquistadors. *Don't do it!* Veronica wanted to scream. *Don't trust them. More will come. They have gunpowder and they'll line your blankets with smallpox.*

Veronica drew in a breath and counted to three in Spanish, Russian, and English. That usually calmed her. She leaned forward, until their noses almost touched.

"I said cautious, Tsar Mikhail, not dead," Veronica told him. "Not yet."

The halls of the History Department were deserted, as usual. Historians weren't known for their sociability. In that respect, at least, Veronica fit right in with her colleagues. Another beautiful Los Angeles morning, and here she sat inert, attempting to edit a tricky chapter about Alexandra's early days in the Romanov court.

For ten minutes straight, Veronica stared at a blank page on her computer, trying to will words to spring forth like Phoenix from the ashes. But the snakelike voices in her head had returned, hissing at full speed, undermining every sentence she attempted to construct.

Outside the window, Alameda University's quaint brick buildings and lush foliage called to her. Veronica wished she could go outside. She wanted to sit with the sun on her face, touch her lips, and think about Michael. She'd kissed him impulsively last night, right under the collar of his shirt.

Like a hypochondriac with an intriguing new illness, Veronica kept a close eye on her symptoms. She still knew so little. How had Michael managed to compile the records of birth certificates and supposedly royal marriages? If he didn't want to join any of those . . . how had he put it? Clubs for sad old noblemen? If he wasn't interested in any of that, then why bother to keep those records?

A sharp knock rattled her office door. Veronica exhaled, grateful for the distraction. "Yes?" she called out.

Regina Brack stepped into Veronica's office. Automatically, Veronica shot to attention. Dr. Brack's cheeks were red, no doubt from her weekend in the desert. Veronica imagined the woman tramping through the Mojave, squinting in the sun, trapping butterflies in her kill jar, not a strand of her helmet-hair out of place.

"This came for you." Dr. Brack tossed an express mail packet onto Veronica's desk and then hovered in the doorway. "Overnight mail. I figured it must be important." She lowered her voice. "Dr. Herrera, I've been thinking over our talk last Friday. I'm sure you want to discuss your options going forward."

Veronica heard Dr. Brack, but eyed the New York postmark. She nodded absently in Dr. Brack's direction while opening the express mail envelope. Inside, she found yet another envelope, cream colored and a perfect square, with ornate curlicues framing each letter of her name, like on a wedding invitation. But she didn't know anyone getting married. She frowned.

"Sometimes difficult decisions must be made," Dr. Brack said. "I know that's hard to understand when you're trying to start a career."

Veronica's breath caught as she noticed the Russian imperial double-headed eagle, scepter clutched in one claw, orb in the other, imprinted on the left-hand corner of the square envelope. Her heart did a flip-flop.

"It comes down to focus," Dr. Brack said. "Have you considered honing a more substantial subfield? Perhaps it's time to incorporate Marxist theory into your research."

Veronica tapped her pencil against the side of her desk absentmindedly. Out of the corner of her eye, she saw Dr. Brack press her thin lips together. "What is that, anyway?" Dr. Brack asked.

"I'm not sure. An invitation to a Romanov ball?" Veronica shook her head. "I'm sorry. It's distracting me. Could we talk this afternoon?"

"Consider what I've said," Dr. Brack told her. "I'm trying to help."

She gave a contrite nod. Regina Brack finally took the hint and left her in peace.

Veronica grabbed a letter opener, a souvenir from one of Abuela's Royal Caribbean cruises, and slit the envelope's seal. She withdrew a thin sheet of paper.

Dear Dr. Herrera:

After receiving your inquiry, I wish to formally introduce myself. My name is Grand Duke Alexei Romanov and I write on behalf of the Romanov Guardsmen, the only true representatives of the Russian Imperial House in Exile.

Thank you for your interest in my organization and our involvement in the reconvening of Russia's Zemsky Sobor. Our ultimate goal is Restoration of the Romanov Throne. We believe this new legislative body will engage the Russian people with the idea of restoration in a way we had not previously imagined possible.

You briefly mentioned your scholarship on the royal martyr Alexandra Feodorovna. Our organization identifies and cultivates young scholars dedicated to the more agreeable aspects of our blessed dynasty. Supporters in the current government recently granted us access to exclusive files hidden by the Bolsheviks for nearly one hundred years. Several of them concern Empress Alexandra. Would such documents be of interest?

To achieve our goals, it is imperative that we protect the memory of the Holy Family. It is equally necessary to root out Romanov imposters. In your correspondence, you mentioned your acquaintance with the notorious pretender Mikhail Karstadt. Take caution. We believe he is using you for his own dark purposes.

We will happily provide you with access to our files on the empress in exchange for information regarding the current activities of the False Mikhail. Under these conditions, we extend a warm invitation for you to visit our archives in Manhattan at our expense. You will hear from us again soon.

Highest Regards,
Grand Duke Alexei
His Imperial Highness and Heir Presumptive
The Romanov Guardsmen
Keepers of the Russian Throne

Veronica's throat constricted, as if she'd gulped water down the wrong pipe. The historical Alexei Romanov had been the hemophiliac heir to the throne, born in 1904 and murdered along with the rest of his family. She had never heard of this

Grand Duke Alexei, although she had contacted the Romanov Guardsmen after finding references to them in Russian papers and blogs.

Small, biting questions nagged. If Michael was a "notorious pretender," as claimed, why did he downplay his claim? Of course, maybe that was all part of his plan, she thought skeptically. Veronica opened a new message window in her Outlook account, typed in the e-mail address she found on the letterhead, and started to respond.

Your Highness

She grimaced, deleted the opening, and started again.

Dear Mr. Romanov:
    Thank you for writing. I'm intrigued by your information regarding Alexandra. Is it possible you might send photocopies of your files? As far as Michael Karstadt is concerned, I can't help. On a related note, why do you refer to him as a "notorious pretender"? He isn't even interested in pursuing his claim.
    Best,
    Veronica Herrera
    Assistant Professor of History, Alameda University

The instant she hit Send, another knock rattled her door. Veronica jumped back in her chair, banging her shin against the desk. She rolled her shoulders, expecting to face a horde of crazed neo-Cossacks, sabers rattling at their sides. "Come in."

Michael stepped inside, smiling broadly, shirt freshly pressed. He smelled like expensive soap and immaculate grooming.

"Oh," she said. "Hi."

He turned back to the door. "You were expecting someone else?"

"No. No." That didn't come out right. The second no made it sound as though she had something to hide. She swallowed, shin throbbing. Michael leaned against the corner of her desk, his hand near the letter from Alexei Romanov.

"Look." She pointed toward a new storyboard posted on the wall for her officemate's graphic novel. "What do you think of the latest installment? He introduced werewolf adversaries. How original! I told you all Medievalists were nuts."

While Michael examined the new pictures on the wall, Veronica slid the letter and the envelope underneath a stack of student essays on her desk.

"Right." Michael turned back to her. "My deposition was canceled and I have the afternoon free. Would you like to grab lunch?"

Veronica sensed she was on the verge of failing some sort of test. If she believed the letter from Alexei Romanov, she would order Michael out of her office. Then she would congratulate herself for getting rid of a scheming man. She would head home, stare at the cracks in the ceiling, and refuse to think about the shape of his lips. That's what she would have done when she still lived at home and allowed all of her grandmother's warnings about men to run through her head like a scrolling news ticker.

She didn't want to be that woman anymore. "I know a great Japanese place in Pasadena," Veronica said. "They don't allow cell phones so everyone can eat in peace. You'll like that." She reached for her purse.

"Veronica, you're talking a mile a minute." Michael took her hand and held it aloft, like a doctor checking her pulse. "And you're trembling. What's wrong?"

The words nearly bubbled to her lips, but Alexei Romanov's warnings about the "False Mikhail" buzzed like a distress signal. Veronica blurted out the only thing she could think of. "One of my cousins is having her *quinceañera* next Saturday. Have you ever been to a *quinceañera*? It's a big party for her fifteenth birthday. I get shy at parties. And it's in Bakersfield. My grandmother's coming. It will be hell."

Michael gave the crooked smile she remembered from when she first saw him. "Are you inviting me or looking for sympathy?"

"Inviting you."

"You're doing a great job selling me on it."

"If it's too soon . . . the family thing and all."

"Oh." His expression changed. "I see." He gave a courtly little bow. She thought he might go down on one knee. "Of course it's not too soon. I'd love to go."

Her heart soared. But then she didn't want to look too eager so she tempered her smile with a shrug. When she moved her shoulder, a pain shot down her back. Perhaps she'd fallen asleep in an awkward position last night. Perhaps she felt guilty for not telling Michael about the letter from Grand Duke Alexei. Or perhaps Abuela kept a voodoo doll at home and had poked pins in it to warn Veronica men were more trouble than they were worth.

Four

Four little girls hadn't endeared Alexandra to the Russian people,
the aristocracy, or her mother-in-law, the Dowager Empress Marie.
Life at court continued to trouble Alexandra, particularly since,
when it came to political intrigue, Marie and Alexandra
were as different as a tiger and a mouse.
—VERONICA HERRERA, The Reluctant Romanov

PETERHOF ESTATE
NOVEMBER 1901

When Lena knocked on the door to Alexandra's study, Grand Duchess Olga greeted her, squeezing a fluffy white puppy tightly to her chest. Lena smiled at Olga, but waited. No one was allowed to speak to a member of the royal family, even a five-year-old girl, unless spoken to first.

"What have you brought for me?" Olga's high voice brimmed with authority. She was the eldest of the tsar's daughters, after all.

"Vanilla wafers for you and special treats for your mama." Lena scanned the light snacks that accompanied the tea service: pretzels, thin slices of ham, and bananas. For the past few months, this had been Alexandra's standard fare. Sodium and potassium were said to help women conceive a boy. Lena suggested avoiding calcium as well, just as the old wives in Archangel advised, and now Alexandra refused even to take milk with her tea.

Lena modulated her voice to make it sound playfully grand. "Now may I enter?"

Olga swept aside to allow Lena to pass. She released the squirming white ball of fluff from her arms and ran around her mother's lemonwood desk, chasing the puppy.

Alexandra sat at her desk. She looked tired, but more content than Lena had seen her in weeks. When she saw Lena, she set her pen down on a stack of thick lilac stationery and smiled kindly. Lena placed the silver tray on a side table and poured hot water from the bubbling samovar over loose Earl Grey tea leaves. Alexandra once confided in Lena that Earl Grey tea reminded her of the summers she spent at Balmoral Castle in Scotland, with her grandmother, Queen Victoria.

After setting out the tea service, Lena hesitated. Sweet ferns and flowering plants graced the windowsills of the study, alongside sepia portraits of the tsar and grand duchesses. Lena ran her finger along the intricate wood carvings of ivy and berries on the side of the desk. Sometimes she wished she could curl up in one of the overstuffed chairs and rest for the night here. The servants' quarters were so impersonal and cold.

Olga stopped running. Lena dropped her hand, afraid that somehow the little girl could read her thoughts. But Olga wasn't paying her any mind. The dog yelped at the doorway. Lena turned to look.

The African guard, Pavel, stood silently at the door.

Automatically, Lena shifted her gaze to the geometric patterns on the carpet beneath her feet. She stole a glance at Pavel's black-and-crimson uniform, trimmed with gold braiding, and then up at his face as he stared blankly ahead. A strange twitching strummed her chest. Surely Pavel remembered her. He said their paths would cross again. He'd promised to tell her about his home in Virginia.

Another moment passed. He didn't take notice of her at all. Etiquette dictated that Pavel not speak. His mere presence signaled the arrival of a royal guest. Still, could he not spare a look or even a gesture?

Alexandra gave Pavel a serene nod. Once he left, she fingered the lace at her high collar and surveyed the cheery room. Lena sensed she didn't want it violated. Alexandra approached a mirror and began to fuss with her hair. "Lenichka, I know this isn't part of your normal routine, but can you assist me?"

Forcing thoughts of Pavel from her head, Lena joined the empress before the long oval mirror, wondering what she was meant to do. As she smoothed the folds of appliqué work on Alexandra's afternoon dress, she couldn't help but notice her own reflection. Next to her elegant mistress, she looked short and dumpy. Her hair was a shade somewhere between blond and brown with none of the highlights of either color. And her eyes were large, but too round, the lashes sparse. Still, she supposed, if one took the time they might notice a wide-open, pleasing aspect to her face.

Once more, the door burst open. This time the tsar's mother, Dowager Empress Marie, strode into Alexandra's study.

Lena had never seen the dowager in person before, but knew her well by reputation. Marie was over fifty years old, ancient by provincial standards. Lena had expected an older, graying woman, hunched over a cane. Yet despite her advanced years, Marie remained petite, trim, and pretty as a schoolgirl. A black fringe of bangs curled high on her forehead.

"Good afternoon, Mama." Alexandra's voice was a shrill squeak. Remembering herself, Lena dropped into a low curtsy.

A pair of female attendants trailed Marie into the study. They wore matching light green dresses with diaphanous outer skirts that reminded Lena of sea foam, at least the way it was rendered in the mermaid stories Olga enjoyed. The attendants approached Alexandra and gave perfunctory curtsies. One of them wore long ostrich feathers in her hat. The feathers swept across Alexandra's face and the empress stifled a sneeze.

The attendants then set to work on Marie, removing her feather-strewn hat and shaking a light dusting of snow from her wrap. Underneath, Marie wore a dark red gown with tiny cloth roses sewn into the bodice. Alexandra's conservatively tailored afternoon dress, so striking a moment before, looked prudish in comparison.

Marie turned to her servants. "Leave us." Her voice sounded oddly husky, given her small frame. "I'll ring presently."

Heads bowed, the ladies withdrew. Lena lingered in the corner, wondering if she should follow them out of the room. Olga sat on a cushion, struggling with the whimpering puppy and scowling. Marie headed for her granddaughter and Alexandra stepped to the side, a clumsy bear trying to outmaneuver a fox.

Marie took Olga's broad face in her hands. "She's not chubby yet," Marie declared, her long dark brows slanting. "But if you're not careful she will be."

Lena tried not to gasp. She'd never heard anyone so much as raise their voice to a grand duchess.

Alexandra withdrew a linen handkerchief from a drawer of her desk and laced it between her fingers. "Would you care for tea, Mama?"

"Only if it's not that dreadful English concoction you insist on serving." Marie turned to Lena and fluttered her small hands. "And she will leave us."

Lena glanced at Olga, whose happy features had twisted. Lena stepped closer to Alexandra. "Perhaps the grand duchess might be excused as well," she said quietly.

Alexandra nodded. "Olga, you may go. But Lena will stay."

Olga shot Lena a grateful glance before scooting off the cushion. She hugged her mother and scurried away, the yelping puppy at her heels. Lena wished she could follow Olga. Instead, she retreated to the side table. She located Ceylon in the carefully organized wooden tea box and prepared a cup for Marie.

"You've cultivated such reliance on your servants, Alix." Marie eased herself into a wicker armchair. "If you paid as much attention to the ladies of Saint Petersburg you'd find your time at court less trying. Didn't you call Princess Zenaida Yusopov by her mother's name last season?"

Blotches of color spread across Alexandra's cheekbones. "Nicky told you that?"

"Why shouldn't he confide in his mother? He needs to talk to someone who understands the pressures of his position and can advise him properly."

Lena approached Marie cautiously, taking care no liquid should splash out of the china cup. She caught a whiff of Marie's heavy floral perfume, so different than Alexandra's light rose water. "I know how you detest chitchat so I'll get straight to the point." Marie took a cautious sip of tea and curled her lips. "I understand you convinced my Nicky to try for another child already."

Lena's lips parted in shock.

"Get that simple look off your face." Lena wondered how Marie had seen her expression, for Marie's gaze had not yet strayed from Alexandra's face. "These matters concern the empire and the stability of this government. If you find the topic disturbing, take your leave of us."

Alexandra clenched her handkerchief. "We continue to pray for an heir."

"You're no longer a young woman," Marie said. "Successive births take a toll."

"I put faith in God. He will see us through. And Lena Ivanovna has helped me."

"This silly girl? When the best doctors will tell you it's no use?"

"Lenichka is a good Russian woman," Alexandra stammered, "from the northern heart of our empire. Her mother was a midwife. She has advised me."

Lena bowed her head as she maneuvered a tiny ham sandwich onto Marie's plate, trying to conceal her distress. At times Alexandra's blind faith felt too intense.

"Did you tell her to cast a spell?" Marie asked. "Something about the moon? Have you drawn up an astrological chart? Speak up, young lady."

Lena almost dropped the serving plate. Marie spotted her for what she was, a scared and inexperienced girl. "I only wish to help."

"Help? To what end?" Marie narrowed her eyes. "What were you promised?"

Lena's mouth went dry. Her brother needed her help. She couldn't let him go to jail for some foolishness with his friends. To protect him, she needed Alexandra. Now the empress was wilting before her eyes. Lena's foot tapped the floor and she could not will it to stop.

"This is the person you entrust with your future?" Marie said.

Alexandra straightened her back and for the first time Lena noticed how the empress towered over her mother-in-law. "I requested her advice."

"Anyone with a modicum of sense would have fled the room the moment you did so. It's too great a pressure. Either this girl has no brains or she wants something." Marie leaned forward and Lena caught another stifling gasp of her perfume. "Surely you've heard of her welcoming attitude toward charlatans. You took advantage."

Alexandra's hands balled into fists. "She's not like the women in Saint Petersburg."

"If you believe every bit of nonsense passed on by a peasant, we're all doomed."

"If I believed every bit of nonsense bandied about by aristocrats, I'd think myself already doomed," Alexandra snapped. "They say now that Grandmamma Victoria has passed to the other world, I lack protection. That the throne is in danger."

Lena lowered her gaze once more, but saw Marie flinch, the first crack in the dowager empress's composure. "Sounds like nonsense to me," she heard Marie say.

Lena raised her head. Alexandra had angled her chin upward, so the difference in height between her and Marie seemed even more pronounced. Marie arched one of her long black brows.

"I do not believe the Queen of England would have countenanced such talk in her own palace," Alexandra said. "Why should I?"

"If you must confront such talk, do so," Marie replied. "If you must try again for an heir, do so. Only don't raise Nicky's hopes. Don't disappoint him."

"Nicky's not disappointed. He's exuberant. I am with child again. And this time we are having a boy."

Lena's heart pitched like a bucking horse. She stared at Alexandra, whose hands had come to rest gently on her stomach. The empress's shoulders rose and fell with each deep breath, betraying her anxiety, but her lips curved into a smile. Lena supposed it was possible her advice had helped Alexandra conceive. It was even possible the empress had conceived a boy.

"I see . . ." Marie deigned to take a dainty bite from the sandwich Lena had served. "And how do you know it's a son?"

"A mother always knows."

Lena waited for another snarky comment from Marie. Instead, she saw a hint of a smile on the dowager's face. "I suppose congratulations are in order then."

Lena's spirits soared. The empress had done it. At last, she'd stood up to her mother-in-law. Lena wished she could hug her mistress.

Alexandra took Lena's hand and squeezed it softly. "Congratulations are in order, yes. And gratitude as well. For Lena. For the wisdom and goodness of her family."

Lena shifted her weight and rocked back on her heels. Archangel was blocked in by ice nearly half the year. During that time, Lena's father used to behave like a caged wolf. He paced the length of their small central room, taking swallows from a flask of cheap vodka, staring blankly at sheets of snow while the wind screamed outside.

"Useless," Lena's mother would say as potatoes boiled on the stovetop. "And to think of the life I might have had."

After supper, Lena's mother would bundle up in her warmest furs, grab her bulging black bag, and take off into the freezing night to attend to a woman in labor. Lena once admired her mother's dedication. Now she realized her mother had only been eager to escape that stifling cottage.

On those cold winter nights, when their mother ran off and their father drank, Anton used to play chess with Lena in front of the fire, on a set he'd constructed from scraps of discarded wood. "Get out of here as soon as you can," he told her, as she twisted her hair in her hand and tried to determine how best to protect her lopsided queen. Though the words were dead serious, Anton smiled when he said them. She remembered his dimples. "Don't end up like one of them. I'll teach you English. That will take you anywhere in the world you want to go."

Everyone else in Archangel accepted poverty, drunkenness, and cruelty without question. Anton had encouraged her to seek a better life. In return, she would protect him.

Nothing could hurt Anton, certainly not the careless accusations of local boys. The Empress of all the Russias had promised his safety. This knowledge made Lena feel buoyant, like a life ring bobbing in the waves, safely distant from a sinking ship.

PARIS

OCTOBER 1941

By the time they reached her husband's building, Charlotte's arms ached. Her hair, so carefully rolled that morning, lay wet and flat against her cheeks. She hesitated before the door, every muscle taut, and lowered Laurent to the ground.

"I'm not supposed to see Papa yet," he complained.

"What does it matter? Papa will be glad to see you." Stress hardened Charlotte's voice. She kissed the top of Laurent's head and took his hand in hers. She tried to soften her tone. "Let's see if he's home."

The gold numbers on Luc's door were ornately cut, but rusted and crooked. Just as she remembered. It had been easy enough to get inside the building. The bell was always broken. She couldn't even blame the Germans for that. With her free hand, Charlotte rapped on the door. The thick wood hurt her knuckles.

Nothing happened. Charlotte felt faint. She was about to tell Laurent they would need to take another ride on the Métro, when she heard movement on the other side. Metal clicked against metal as the lock unlatched. Charlotte tightened her grip on Laurent's hand.

Luc opened the door. Her breath caught. He wore loose trousers and a flannel shirt with the sleeves rolled to his elbows. For a moment, it was all too familiar, as though she'd suddenly traveled backward in time. She recognized his shirt. She'd always thought it brought out his eyes. She recognized his expression as well. He'd come to the door annoyed, prepared to launch into a speech about how he'd been disrupted.

Charlotte pushed past him, pulling their son behind her. "See," she told Laurent brightly. "I told you Papa would be happy to see us."

Once safely inside, she stopped. She eased Laurent down and took a moment to appraise the flat. Their flat. Luc's flat. He had always kept things sparse, but now she noticed the bare patches on the walls and shelves where her things had once been. Oil stains blotted the carpet near the kitchen. She'd stood in this very spot once, watching the movement of Luc's shoulders as he prepared supper, wondering how to tell him she'd missed her period when he'd been so adamant about his career and not having children. At the time, she'd thought her situation so hopeless. How petty it all seemed now.

Reluctantly, she turned to face Luc. He glanced furtively down the hall and then shut the door behind them. Now that she was closer to him, she saw his features were harsher than she remembered. He'd lost weight. But loose strands of light brown hair fell into his eyes, much like before.

Laurent ran to Luc, hugging his knees. Luc's anger melted as he swung his son into his arms. He may not have planned on Laurent, but he never held that against him. So close, their resemblance was pronounced, though Laurent was fairer in coloring. They shared the same high cheekbones and lush brows, even the slight hooding around their lids, like they both needed a nap.

She tried to smile, but seeing them together, Charlotte felt a deep pang of regret. She saw for a moment the way it all might have been.

He carried Laurent to the window. Rain dripped off the sloping eaves of his building, where doves nested and cooed. Luc still wouldn't look at her. He acted as though she weren't there, as though she didn't exist. She remembered that all too well. She hated it when he behaved this way, as though she weren't even worth the effort it took to speak. He constantly forced her to guess what she'd done wrong.

"Laurent's not supposed to be here for another two weeks," Luc said.

"I didn't have time to prepare you. It's an emergency." Charlotte straightened her spine. There was a subtle difference in their height and she intended to use it to her advantage. "A German soldier came to my flat looking for me."

"What?" Luc's voice rose, and she heard the accusation in it, as though she'd asked for any of this. "Why would a German soldier want to see you? What did he say?"

"I don't know. I didn't ask. I didn't want him near Laurent." The words lodged in the back of Charlotte's throat.

At last, Luc turned back to her, Laurent still in his arms. His gaze was intense, but in a different way than she remembered, hardly the smoldering Valentino stare he used to cultivate. She had a strange notion if she touched him she might turn to stone. "Why didn't you find out what he wanted?" Luc demanded.

"I was with Matilda Kshesinskaya. She told me to go. It seemed like the right thing to do."

"That woman always did have a hold on you." Luc shook his head. His shoulders sagged. "I can manage Laurent, but we agreed it was better for us to remain apart."

Charlotte had expected these words. They stung nonetheless. "I don't have any friends left in the city." Except Kshesinskaya. The guilt pressed at her chest again. What had happened to her after the soldier discovered Charlotte wasn't there? Charlotte tried to put it out of her mind. She rummaged in her handbag for the flat, square card she used for bread. "I'll sleep on the floor. I'll get more ration cards. I'll wait in line. I'll tell them I'm pregnant to get extra milk."

"Then the soldiers will find you. I thought that's what you're trying to avoid."

"Two nights. Even one. Then I'll leave you alone." Charlotte desperately pressed on. She remembered the diamonds. She removed them and extended her hand. "And you can take these."

"That's all you left with?" Luc said.

"Please take them. I'll feel better."

Luc looked away again. He kissed Laurent's cheek and then stared at his son's face, frowning. "Laurent's bleeding. What happened?"

Charlotte reached over and wiped a few drops of blood from Laurent's nose.

"Did the German hurt him?"

Charlotte decided to say nothing and let Luc draw his own conclusions. That might strengthen her case.

Luc's lip twitched. He never made decisions quickly. If she wanted his help she needed to give him space. Charlotte tried to swallow her impatience.

"Put the diamonds away, Charlotte." Luc spoke softly now. He lowered Laurent to the floor. "You know where the toys are," he told him. "Why don't you play for a little while so I can talk to your mama."

Laurent nodded and headed upstairs. Charlotte started to follow.

"Let him go," Luc said.

"Up those stairs by himself?"

"The stairs were repaired. Do you think I would let my son get hurt?"

Charlotte clenched her fists. She remembered the terrible night when she told Luc she was pregnant. He'd looked at her like he wanted her to sink into a hole in the earth and disappear. Now he played the protective father. Somehow, it didn't seem fair.

"He's looking thin," Luc added.

"I'm doing my best."

"Like you did with our marriage?"

"You made me leave. It was unbearable." Charlotte's teeth sliced into her tongue. She was becoming the shrew he'd made her feel like toward the end. But she'd promised herself she would hold her anger inside for Laurent's sake. "Anyway, that was a long time ago. I'm desperate now. We need you."

"Even if I let you stay a night or two, what then?"

"I'm taking Laurent away from the city. We'll stay with my parents. Kshesinskaya told me they could explain everything."

"Charlotte, what's wrong with you?" Luc grabbed an open pack of cigarettes on his table and shook one out of the box. "You materialize out of nowhere thinking I'll welcome you with open arms. Now you want to take my son away? Your parents live in the Dordogne. The south isn't under Nazi control, but the Vichy government is as bad."

"It's safer there than here."

"You don't know that. Besides, the Germans set up checkpoints around the perimeter of the city and in every train station." Luc shoved a cigarette in his mouth and raised his eyebrows, as though such a thought never would have occurred to Charlotte.

His lack of faith scared her, but the memory of the soldier pounding at her door scared her even more. "I don't know what else to do."

"Forget it. If you want to run off, fine, but leave Laurent here with me."

"I am not abandoning my son."

"Leaving him with his father is not abandonment."

"The soldier knew my name. My married name. Your last name. He knew I was a dancer. He knew I worked for Kshesinskaya."

Luc froze, the cigarette still between his lips, his lighter hovering in midair. "Why would a German soldier care about any of that?"

"I don't know." Charlotte paced the room, past the worn cushions on his sofa. The movement relaxed her. She heard Laurent drag something that sounded like wooden blocks out of the closet upstairs. "But you know what they do to people. They make them disappear. God knows what they could do to Laurent."

"Can't you just call your parents?"

"Someone might be listening on the line. Besides, I want to see my parents. Kshesinskaya was clear. She said to go to them and they would explain everything."

Luc lit his cigarette. The rich, musky scent of it caught her off guard. With tobacco strictly rationed, most people used foul and verdant substitutes, rolling dried grasses and herbs. Luc had an actual cigarette. Charlotte pointed an accusing finger at the box. "Where did you get those?"

"A friend."

Charlotte's mind raced through the possibilities. Luc was no collaborator. He must have purchased the cigarettes on the black market. The back of her neck bristled. "You're a smuggler. Or at least you know someone who is?"

Luc didn't answer. He glanced nervously at the front door, as though he expected soldiers to barge in at any moment and arrest them.

"You were a journalist," she said. "You knew so many people."

She saw the anger flare once more, but this time it wasn't directed at her. "The Germans shut down the paper. That doesn't mean my professional life is over."

"You are a journalist," she amended. "You still have connections, I'm sure. Think about it, Luc. You must know someone who can help get the right papers, fake an identification pass. Then I can get past the checkpoint. You can help us leave Paris."

"It's hardly that simple. I can't clap my hands and it's done."

"Luc, I need you. Laurent needs you."

He looked her in the eye. That had never been easy for him. He'd grown accustomed to maintaining a distance and didn't talk easily about his emotions. Now, the pain was right on the surface, so tangible it hurt Charlotte to look at him. Despite the wreck of their marriage, she never doubted his love for his son. In a strange way, she never doubted his love for her. Even now.

"I'll do what I can," he said at last. "But I can't make any promises."

Five

"This is our coming-of-age party." Veronica raised her voice above the blaring pop music and flurry of chitchat around them and tried a sip of her margarita. It tasted sickly sweet, but then this was a party for a fifteen-year-old girl. Someone had thrown a bone to spinster cousins like herself, who needed alcohol to make it through nights with her family. At least the margarita did the trick and helped steady her nerves. Michael had insisted he was game, but somehow she doubted a *quinceañera* was his first choice for a Saturday night date. And in a rented church hall in Bakersfield no less.

Veronica glanced at her cousin Inez on the other side of the hall, resplendent in a white satin gown, tiara, and pink lip gloss, surrounded by a giggling entourage in matching lavender dresses. They floated from table to table while a smiling videographer recorded every move. "I know it looks like a wedding, but Inez gets to wear that pretty dress without the trouble of a groom."

"The groom's more of an afterthought anyway, right?" Michael shifted Jessica's new baby to his other arm. Jess had cornered them earlier and practically thrust the baby into his arms. Michael wiggled his finger. Carlos gurgled approvingly, a sliver of drool running from his chin.

Jess glowed with the pride of new motherhood and successful matchmaking.

"He looks good with a baby," she gushed. "Don't you think so, Veronica?"

Of course Michael looked good with a baby. What man didn't? Veronica hardly needed further convincing. Michael had removed his jacket and she kept eying his shoulders, imagining what his arms looked like underneath the shirt.

"He likes you." Jess put her hand on Michael's arm. "And he doesn't like just anybody."

Jess was happily married and a knee-jerk flirt. Still, Veronica eyed her hand.

"Why don't you take Carlos for a while, Veronica?" Jess chirped.

"No thanks."

"Come on. You won't drop him."

"I think I'm coming down with something."

Jess rattled the hand sanitizer she made everyone use before they held Carlos.

Michael turned to Jess, smiling mischievously. His smile reminded Veronica of the pictures of satyrs in the big book of mythology Abuela gave her on her eighth birthday. An *uh-oh* rang automatically in her head, along with the sound of her grandmother's voice. *Watch yourself.*

"Did Veronica have a *quinceañera*?" Michael asked.

"Of course," Jess said. "She let her grandmother talk her into wearing a hideous dress. It made her look like a fluffy white bird. We teased her all night."

Michael grinned. "I bet you looked stunning," he told Veronica.

"I was fifteen. And it was hardly my scene."

"Understatement!" Jess cried. "You wore glasses the size of bread plates and a retainer. Don't you remember?"

Veronica fiddled uncomfortably with one of the favors on the table, a purple butterfly made from tulle. Not that she felt particularly traumatized by the memory of her *quinceañera*. Her long white satin gloves were itchy, she needed help to get her dress undone to go to the bathroom, and she'd flubbed one of the lines in her speech. But Abuela had dabbed tears from her eyes with a handkerchief and beamed proudly. Veronica had no regrets.

No, it was the other memories that haunted her now, the same ones that returned whenever she visited family. Memories of long summer days, time alone in the library, prettier cousins, and her reputation as the smart, but weird one. As long as she remained in Los Angeles, she was Abuela's precocious granddaughter the professor. Back home, she reverted once again to poor, strange little Veronica.

"I've always had a fetish for glasses and braces," Michael added. "That Jan Brady thing."

He squeezed Veronica's hand. Guilt simmered in her chest. Once again, he was being adorable. He was making her happy. How long had it been since she'd actually felt happy? And here she was keeping a secret. She kept intending to tell him about the letter from Alexei Romanov and the Romanov Guardsmen, Keepers of the Russian Throne, but then he said something funny or cute and she didn't want to ruin the moment.

Carlos whimpered ominously.

"I think he's wet." Michael passed him back to Jess, who splayed a hand on her chest and gave a motherly sigh of concern.

"I'd better take care of this." Jess gathered her son in her arms and patted his back. "The two of you should come and visit Carlos and me and Antonio sometime though. We could all get dinner."

"You'll tell Michael more stories about me?" Veronica asked.

"Come on. It will be fun."

Despite the teasing, Veronica liked Jess better than her other cousins. Even as adults, most of them barely spoke to Veronica, like it had been hammered into them not to distress the so-called genius of the family. Jess wasn't so easily intimidated. "I'll give you a call soon," Veronica promised.

When Jess left, Michael glanced at his trousers.

"Did he get you?" she asked.

"Nothing an expensive dry cleaning bill won't take care of." Michael reached into his pocket and withdrew his handkerchief. He began to scrub his leg.

"Sorry about that. You can't say I didn't warn you, though."

The music stopped and then abruptly switched tempo. After Inez's mariachi serenade, the deejay had catered to the musical choices of fifteen-year-old girls. Strictly Radio Disney. But now Veronica heard the thrilling opening notes of "Shadowplay."

Michael stopped scrubbing his leg and turned to her, smiling.

"Wait a minute." She pointed a finger at him. "They must take requests. You requested Joy Division for me."

"So let's dance."

This wasn't everyone's idea of danceable music. Still, Veronica imagined sweeping across the room hand in hand with Michael as her cousins appraised her, eyebrows arched. She was about to take his hand in hers and show him off when she spotted a round figure in a pale pink dress moving with surprising speed toward their table. Veronica felt her smile collapse.

Michael scanned the room, suddenly on red alert. "What? What did you see?"

"*Mija*. I'm so glad you came."

Abuela swept Veronica into a tight hug, smelling of fresh lipstick and face powder. She'd arranged her black hair in a puffy French twist bedecked with her favorite pearls. At family occasions, Abuela liked to fashion herself like an aging Broadway star, not quite ready to bow gracefully off the stage.

Michael rose to his feet to greet her. Abuela offered her hand. "I'm Ginger Herrera. I thought I should meet the man my granddaughter's presently seeing. She may be a professor, but I still get to keep tabs on her."

Veronica pressed her lips into an impenetrable seal.

"I'm Michael Karstadt." He gave one of his courtly bows and they all sat down. So far so good.

"Veronica told me about your family," Abuela said. "Intriguing coincidence." She raised her eyebrows and threw her arms up in the air with dramatic flair. "The heir to the Russian throne meets a Russian history expert."

Veronica bent over her margarita, avoiding her grandmother's eyes. "She mentioned that to you?" she heard Michael say.

"How could she not? Didn't Veronica tell you? I like to take credit for her interest in Russian history because I left an old copy of *Nicholas and Alexandra* out one night. I have a predilection for family dramas myself."

Veronica peeked at Michael. He looked scared, but then that was a normal reaction to Abuela. "Anything intriguing in your family history?" he asked.

"Every family is intriguing. No Aztec princesses though, if that's what you want to know." Abuela brushed against Michael's arm. Really, was there any member of her family who wasn't planning to flirt with her date tonight? "Although, according to legend, one of my aunts dated Leon Trotsky when he lived in Mexico."

"I bet she made Frida Kahlo jealous. Didn't Trotsky run around with her crowd for a while?"

Abuela laughed. "Maybe women in our family lose our heads over Russian men. What is it you do for a living, Mr. Karstadt?"

"I'm an immigration attorney. Many of my clients are Russian families in West Hollywood, since I speak the language."

Abuela cast a sly smile in Veronica's direction, like a secretary privy to the boss's secret bank account. She'd worked as a paralegal for years and found the law a far more stable profession than the one Veronica had chosen. Veronica felt the familiar sting. After she left home for graduate school, her grandmother couldn't wait to turn her old bedroom into a sewing room. But she tried to preserve Veronica's personality and their relationship just as it had been when Veronica was sixteen and in danger of instant impregnation by any guy who talked sweetly to her.

"I'm sorry if I sound old-fashioned." Abuela patted Michael's arm. "It's a wonderful act, the bowing and all, what with your imperial status. It's a fantastic story." She raised her chin to Michael and narrowed her eyes. "Fantastical perhaps?"

Abuela loved to throw around words she'd heard Veronica use a time or two, to mixed results. It was never a good sign.

"I understand why my granddaughter finds it all so attractive," Abuela continued. "It's just that I've learned to see through that type of thing."

Michael rubbed the back of his neck. Veronica saw the hurt in his eyes. Her grandmother's thoughtless words had hit a mark somewhere. Anger rose in her throat. "Don't talk to him that way."

"He's an attorney. I'm sure he's heard worse."

"It's the way you said it. You've just met him and you start off by insulting him? We drove a long way for this."

"Well, I'm sorry if you were inconvenienced." A familiar strain of martyrdom blunted her grandmother's inflections.

Before she moved to Los Angeles, there had been no awkwardness between Veronica and her grandmother. They went shopping together. They watched movies and *telenovelas* at night. As she earned her doctorate, Veronica's world had grown larger and somehow Abuela had been left behind. But surely that hadn't all been Veronica's fault. "When's the last time you drove down to see me?"

Michael grasped Veronica's upper arm. He stood and gently pulled her out of her seat. "I see someone I know. Let's say hello."

"Who would you know here?"

"Oh, you'd be surprised."

"It's all right. I need to move on myself. Good luck claiming the Russian throne. I'm sure you'll keep my granddaughter enchanted." Abuela took a napkin and handed it to Veronica. "Wipe your chin, *mija*. You hit the margarita too fast."

Veronica watched as Abuela floated to another table, unfazed. Without thinking, she dabbed at her chin. "You don't know anyone here," she told Michael.

"I needed to get you out of your grandmother's face before one of you said something you'd regret. By the way, I don't see anything on your chin."

She sank back down and put her forehead in her hands. "Shadowplay" had ended and the awful pop music resumed. Veronica sensed the impending headache, the red spots. "Leave if you want. I won't make you deal with my family anymore."

Michael laughed softly. "They're not so bad."

"Not so bad? Did you catch any of that?"

"All right, your grandmother's not exactly taken with me."

"She's trying to protect me, I suppose," Veronica said.

"I wouldn't expect anything less."

His good humor was contagious. "She's never had the greatest taste in men," Veronica said. "In fact she hates most of them."

Michael's foot tapped the floor. He looked all around the room. Always it seemed he had his eye out for something. "She raised you? What happened to your parents?"

Veronica began to tear the napkin in her hands. "My mother contracted meningitis and died when I was two. My grandmother calls it the Virgin's miracle I didn't get sick."

"I'm sorry. Do you remember your mother?"

"I don't know." Inez and her attendants neared their table. Hopefully, they'd get to them in time to distract Michael from this line of questioning.

"What about your father?"

The remains of the napkin fell to pieces in Veronica's lap. "He was older than my mom. She studied abroad for a year and he was one of her professors. I don't think they knew each other that well. I don't care. We managed fine without him."

"Sometimes it's not much better when your father's around," Michael offered. "My father's idea of discipline was grabbing me by the shoulders and shaking me until my brain felt like jelly. He never even bothered to say what I did wrong."

Veronica was shocked. Michael seemed so well-adjusted. "I'm sorry."

"He was older too," Michael told her, "and a traditional man."

He said nothing more. Veronica remained silent, looking at him. He met her gaze and smiled. A touch of color brightened his cheeks. "What?"

"I love it that you help immigrants. Maybe you're secretly Batman, too."

"I'm glad you see there's more to me than my family tree."

"You just seem a man of many parts, all of them intriguing. Anything else I should know?"

Michael passed his hand over his mouth. "I was married before."

Veronica smoothed her skirt. Why should this upset her? Why should it bother her to think he once looked at someone else the way he looked at her now? "Any kids?"

"When it got to that point, it was already over. I found Ariel at a rescue shelter and decided a dog was right for me instead." He ducked his head. "It's been several years. I gave myself the time I needed to recover."

"It's your business."

"Trust me," he said.

Veronica wanted to trust him. Desperately. But she still felt like an invisible hand was pushing her beneath the surface of the ocean. She could stare up and see the sun shining. Then she thought of how badly she'd reacted to her failed engagement, the wasted days in bed, choking on her own tears. She felt herself fall back in the ocean, water filling her lungs, and she was suffocating once more.

Alexei Romanov's warnings floated in her head as well, his accusations that Michael was a "notorious pretender." She would tell Michael about Alexei Romanov. But not here. Not in front of her family.

"My past is more in the past than yours," he said. "That's all."

She pressed his lips gently with her fingertip. He told her he'd fallen off monkey bars when he was little, splitting his bottom lip, and that accounted for the slight swelling.

"I'm not perfect," he said. "But I would never break anyone's heart. I couldn't live with myself. Trust me."

"I'll try," she said softly. "Believe me, I'm trying."

On Monday morning, Veronica received another message from Alexei Romanov. It arrived in her department e-mail account, along with a deluge of messages from students griping about poor grades on the first essays. Judging from their tone, Veronica didn't think her next crop of evaluations would exactly help her tenure chances.

Veronica sighed, letting the complaints fade into the background like white noise, and clicked on the message from Alexei Romanov.

Dear Dr. Herrera,

First of all, thank you for your prompt response. With regret, I must inform you I am not authorized to make either electronic

*or hard copies of the files on the Empress. These documents are
highly classified and deal with the underexplored period of her
life between the birth of the child martyrs Anastasia and Tsarevich Alexei. Nevertheless, I hope you will accept the invitation
to visit our archives. I would be honored to provide for your
airfare and accommodations, as I am anxious to hear your
scholarly evaluation of these materials.*

*I continue to advise you to take caution around Michael
Karstadt, the False Mikhail.*

Highest Regards,

Grand Duke Alexei Romanov

Her mind drifted to thoughts of Michael, holding the door for
her, dancing, the shape of his lips. He was clouding her judgment.
She squeezed her eyes shut and pinched the bridge of her nose,
trying to think of something unromantic. Brezhnev in a Speedo.
Good enough. Veronica opened her eyes and began to type.

Dear Mr. Romanov,

*I accept the offer to visit your archives. Please let me know
what dates and times would be convenient so that I may make
the proper arrangements for coverage of my classes.*

Veronica hesitated for a moment, and then added:

*If you have specific information regarding Michael Karstadt,
keep me apprised.*

Sincerely,

Veronica Herrera

She hit Send. Needles of self-reproach bristled in her chest. She needed to share this with Michael. She couldn't put it off any longer.

"You've got that Mona Lisa look again." Michael intertwined his fingers with hers. "What's the matter?"

Veronica shook her head and took another sip of pinot. Flickering candlelight cast dancing shadows on the Modigliani prints. Ariel had curled up around Michael's feet, snoring happily. One of the cats, Boris, watched them from the top of the stereo cabinet, paws tucked under his chest, calm as the Sphinx. Earlier, Veronica had scanned Michael's music collection and commented on Arcade Fire and the National. She wanted him to know her taste in music hadn't stagnated since the 1980s. Now, Matt Berninger's matter-of-fact baritone rolled through "Terrible Love."

She ran a hand through Michael's hair. She wished she could stare at him, undisturbed, burning every last detail of his face into her memory. Between the music, the candlelight, and the perfectly pitched buzz in her head, she wanted to forget the folded paper in her pocket. She wanted to roll onto Michael's body and drown in him.

But then Alexei Romanov's comments would continue to haunt her. She straightened her back, and refilled her glass, setting the empty pinot bottle down on the end table. Immediately, Michael picked up the bottle and moved to the blue recycling bin near the door. Veronica smiled. In Russia, empty bottles were considered bad luck. She hadn't seen this superstitious side of him until now.

After he tossed the bottle, he asked: "What's wrong?"

Veronica took a deep breath. "Have you heard of the Romanov Guardsmen?"

Michael stood before her, rocking back and forth. His voice sounded a shade too calm. "Why?"

Veronica examined her cuticles. "Given your family's lineage, they might want to speak with you."

Michael turned to the stereo. With what struck her as tremendous effort, he steadied his hand and tenderly lifted the needle from the vinyl record. "Veronica, tell me the truth. Have these people contacted you?"

"I sent them a quick question about their participation in the Zemsky Sobor. They invited me to see their archives in New York and offered to pay my way. They have access to documents on Alexandra." She took a quick breath. Now that she'd opened the door, she had to keep going. "And they seem to know about you."

He pivoted toward her, finger jabbing the air. "What did they say? No, let me guess. Don't believe anything he says? I'm an imposter? A fraud?"

Boris leapt off the cabinet and landed on the floor with a graceful thud. Ariel sprang to life as well, panting heavily. Veronica hesitated, still hazy from the pinot. "Something along those lines."

"They discredit everyone with a claim. They helped destroy Anna Anderson."

Veronica's fingers began to flex. Anna Anderson was the most famous Romanov imposter: the woman who claimed to be the tsar's fourth daughter Anastasia and inspired all the movies. She wasn't sure why talking about Anna Anderson made Michael so upset. But his sudden burst of temper made her feel strangely calm. "They were right," Veronica said.

Michael tapped his foot impatiently.

"Anna Anderson was a fraud. DNA proved it."

"That's not the point. They didn't have DNA tests in the

1920s. The point is the Romanov Guardsmen refuse to investigate evidence that contradicts the claims of their members. Their claimant doesn't want rivals. I don't trust him." Michael thrust his hands behind his back, kneading his fingers furiously. "What did they say about me?"

Veronica reached into her pocket and offered him a print copy of the e-mail from Alexei Romanov. Michael scanned it quickly. "Unbelievable." He crumpled the paper and threw it across the room. His other cat, Natasha, jumped out from under the dining room table and pounced. Ariel whimpered and approached Veronica. She stroked the dog's bushy fur, wishing she could soothe Michael as easily.

"Their heir apparent?" he said. "This aging playboy who calls himself Grand Duke Alexei? He's Kyril Romanov's grandson. Do you know what Kyril did?"

Kyril Romanov had been the eldest cousin of the last tsar, Nicholas II, and next in line to the throne after the tsar's brother and the tsar's son. "During the Revolution, Kyril raised a banner to support the Revolution," she said. "Some people in the family thought he was ready to join the Bolsheviks. After that, some of them considered him a traitor."

"Well put, Professor. And later, after most of the rest of the Romanovs were shot, Kyril declared himself 'Tsar of all the Russias.'" Michael lowered his voice. "Did Alexei Romanov tell you he's met with Vladimir Putin?"

A shiver darted down Veronica's spine. Putin wasn't Ivan the Terrible, but she wouldn't want to get on his bad side either. "For someone who claims to have little interest, you've kept close track of the Romanov Guardsmen. Besides, this Alexei Romanov might have good information."

"You're not taking him up on this foolishness, are you?"

Veronica's cheeks warmed with agitation. "They have papers on Alexandra and are willing to pay my way to New York. My tenure review is in January. I need something to show my committee or they'll cut me loose. I told you, I can't wind up back in Bakersfield with my grandmother."

"I know. I know." Michael knelt in front of her and took her hand. "I'm just afraid this man will feed you lies."

"If Alexei Romanov is as bad as you say, confront him."

Michael took a seat next to her and leaned back on the sofa. He rubbed his forehead, focusing on some distant point on the cciling.

"Everything you told me only intrigues me more," Veronica said. "First they send a creepy letter, then this e-mail . . ."

"They sent you a letter before?" Michael said. "When?"

Veronica looked down at her cuticles again. "Two weeks ago."

"And you didn't bother to tell me?"

"How do I know what they say isn't true?"

"What did they say?" he asked.

"They called you the 'False Mikhail.' They said you're using me."

He pulled away from her, looking crushed.

"All I mean is how would I know for sure?" she said.

"I don't know either, Veronica. You could be using me."

A wave of cool reasoning warred with her rising panic. Veronica felt frozen and powerless to act. Once again, she felt the wall rising between them. "If Alexei Romanov can help with my research, I need to see him. I don't feel like I have a choice."

"Fine. Then go." Michael leaned down and his lips brushed her neck. "But I want to come with you."

Veronica pulled away. "That's it? Now it's all right."

"If I come with you. I have a light caseload this month. I can afford a few days."

Knots of anxiety welled in Veronica's stomach.

"Don't you think it will be fun?" he asked.

Ariel's furry head butted up against her leg. She tried to stall. "What about Ariel and the cats?"

"One of the clerks from my office takes care of them when I travel."

"What about . . ." She searched for the right words. ". . . the hotel room?"

"Sleeping arrangements per your suggestion."

Veronica bit her bottom lip. "There's still a problem."

"What? What's wrong?"

Veronica leaned in close. She felt dizzy. "Nothing."

He tried to kiss her, but she pulled back. "I'm serious. That's the problem." She made a sweeping gesture with her hand. "You own an awesome house. You have incredible taste in music. Your cats are cute. Your dog is adorable." She paused to catch her breath. "You're from New York. You probably know all the great bars in SoHo. I don't even know what SoHo means, but it sounds cool. I don't trust myself around you."

Michael nodded. "What if I shared my problem? Will that help?"

Her shoulders stiffened. "All right."

He beckoned for her to come closer. She inclined her ear to his mouth.

"Your eyes are gorgeous. When you consider something, you bite your lip and all I can think about is when you're going to let me kiss you again. You're funny, smart, down-to-earth. You're a California girl with East Coast neuroses. I could go on."

His leg brushed hers, sending waves of pleasure cascading though her. The lump in her stomach began to melt. She touched his jaw and pushed him back onto the couch, straddling her legs around his waist, kissing his neck. His finger trailed her stockings, from her ankle to the back of her knee.

She knew she'd been beat. She was taking Michael to New York.

Veronica waved her index finger. Carlos stared back with big brown eyes and kicked Jessica's arm with his little feet.

Jess looked exhausted. Only her curly black hair hinted at her former vitality. She shifted Carlos onto the other side of her lap and kissed the top of his head. "He says thank you for coming. He didn't get to spend enough time with you at the *quinceañera*. Would you like to hold him?"

"I don't know."

"Go on. He doesn't bite. Much."

Before Veronica could protest further, Jess thrust Carlos into her arms. As she did, a police helicopter flew low over the house, shaking the toys and bottles strewn over the floors and shelves. Veronica went rigid, terrified at the prospect of dropping him. "What about his head? I'm supposed to support his head, right?"

"You're fine." Jess guided Veronica's hand underneath his soft skull. Veronica tried to relax her arms. Carlos smelled like freshly laundered sheets.

"So how does it feel to be a mom?"

"Great." Doubt lingered in her cousin's voice. Jess touched her son's forehead. "I love being a mom. But I took so much for granted: movies, nice dinners, sleep. Appreciate that stuff while you can. That's all." Her tone brightened. "It looks like you're enjoying yourself plenty. I told you! Whenever you talk about Michael I see little hearts in your eyes."

"Sure." Veronica rocked Carlos. How could she possibly explain her concerns without sounding crazy herself? "We're going to New York together."

"Didn't he grow up there? He'll show you around."

"You don't think it's too soon?"

"You're both adults. I thought you liked him." Jess narrowed her eyes, the district attorney once more. "What's the real problem?"

"Do I have to spell it out?" Veronica said.

Carlos opened his little pink mouth and began to cry. Veronica tensed and passed him back to Jess. Carlos hiccupped and Jess turned him over, patting his back, frowning. After a moment, she said, "I'm sorry. I guess I wanted it to work out because I set you up. I mean he named his dog after some character in Shakespeare."

"Ariel. From *The Tempest.*"

"See?" Jess said. "At the *quinceañera,* he told me you're the first girl who didn't ask him why he named his dog after a font or the Little Mermaid. But if you're not attracted to him . . ."

Veronica stared down at the letter blocks scattered at their feet.

"You *are* attracted to him," Jess said. "I thought so."

"Stop looking at me like I'm a hostile witness."

"Has Michael been cruel or something?"

"No!" Veronica said. "He's a sweetheart."

"Exactly." Carlos began to cry. Jess tugged at the buttons on her blouse. "So why not go for it?"

"He was married before."

"What did you expect? The forty-year-old virgin?"

"He should have told me sooner."

"Did you ask?" Veronica shook her head. "Then so what?"

I want to know everything he did and everyone he loved before he met me. I'm turning into a crazy woman because I like the shape of his lips. Veronica placed a block with a yellow *B* for bananas between a red apple *A* and a white coconut *C*.

"You're organizing," Jess said. "What's wrong?"

"It makes me wonder what else he's not telling me."

"Like what?"

"I think he may be delusional," she blurted. "He thinks he's the heir to the Russian throne."

Jess rocked Carlos back and forth thoughtfully. "That does sound delusional."

"He makes a strong case though," Veronica amended.

"Wonderful! You'll become queen of Russia."

"Not queen. Tsarina. Or empress. It doesn't matter. It's doubtful."

"I don't get it. Is he crazy or not?"

Veronica shook her head.

"Maybe you're crazy. Don't you want to be happy?"

Jess pulled up her blouse. Veronica averted her eyes and fiddled with more of the blocks. She heard soft, suckling sounds and looked again. Jess seemed so peaceful and content. She hadn't gotten this way by analyzing every move. Veronica had always tried to be supportive, but privately shook her head and wondered how her cousin could be so rash and impulsive.

Jess met her husband two years ago and they were like matching salt and pepper shakers. Now look at her, beatific and happy. Veronica, on the other hand, who prided herself on control, couldn't even maintain her grip on a yellow block designed for children. It tumbled to the ground.

"So you think I'm right, Professor?" Jess said. "Don't you deserve to let your heart do the talking and give your big brain a rest?"

"I should go to New York?" Veronica asked. "No worries?"

"You like him? You think you'll enjoy yourself?"

Cinematic images of couples gliding across the Rockefeller Plaza ice-skating rink and romantic rendezvous at the top of the Empire State Building filled Veronica's mind. No one could accuse Michael of not being fun. "Absolutely."

"Then go, and see what happens," Jess said.

"No worries?" Veronica asked.

"No more than the usual worries," Jess said. "Let's put it that way."

Six

After a few months, Alexandra summoned a mystic named Phillipe
Vachot from the South of France to help her with her next pregnancy.
Palace gossip buzzed about the charlatan, but Alexandra's optimism
remained intact. She believed everything Vachot said because he told
her only what she wanted to hear.

—VERONICA HERRERA, The Reluctant Romanov

SAINT PETERSBURG
JANUARY 1902

Lena's fingers trembled as she mended the silver brocade trimming on Grand Duchess Olga's woolen cape. No one had thought to start a fire in the empty room. Even so, she felt grateful for the rare moment of peace.

At the turn of the year, the royal family returned to the Winter Palace, the official imperial residence in the capital. Lena found the marble staircases, cold-eyed statues, and enormous crystal chandeliers too cold and imposing for day-to-day life. Despite the palace's grand dimensions, she could scarcely take three steps on the polished floors without slipping and bumping into a stern footman in a red-and-gold uniform ornamented with the double-headed eagle, or plump chambermaids giggling with one another under stiffly starched white caps.

When she tried to take refuge in the family's private apartments, Alexandra found her, grabbed her by the wrist, and asked impossible questions. Should she start eating red meat again? Should she wear a copper bracelet during the first trimester of her pregnancy? Lena grew to fear the sound of Alexandra's leather heels clacking against the tile, and so she sought refuge in deserted rooms in the farthest corners of the palace.

The latch on the parlor door clicked. Lena braced herself, ready for Alexandra to enter unannounced and ask Lena if she should track the phases of the moon.

"There you are! I've been looking all over for you." A new chambermaid named Masha flopped down on a divan across from Lena. Masha smelled of damp fur and perspiration, thinly veiled by cheap vanilla perfume. While Lena dressed in a plain black skirt and white shirtwaist, Masha wore Siberian fur, one of the regional costumes worn so that the grand duchesses might better understand the people of their country. Masha had been assigned to share sleeping quarters with Lena and had taken to following her around during idle moments.

"So is it true you met Empress Alexandra's mystery man, Monsieur Vachot?" Masha asked. "Is he as peculiar as everyone says? I hear he uses stones shaped like pentagrams to communicate with the dead."

Given the rumors, Lena had expected Monsieur Vachot to be a wild-eyed giant. Earlier that morning, when she came to collect dirty linens from the boudoir, Lena found Alexandra on her knees before a short, fleshy gentleman with a tender gaze and receding hairline. He murmured to the empress in an impenetrable

French accent. As she watched his small hand caress the top of Alexandra's head, Lena had been surprised by his tenderness.

"I only caught a glimpse of him," Lena said. "He didn't ask me if I wanted to communicate with my babushka from the great beyond or anything like that."

"He's not a real doctor, you know," Masha said. "Once it's known the empress dabbles in the occult it's only a matter of time."

"A matter of time until what?"

Masha eyed the doorway before she spoke. "They say if the next one's not a boy, her dependence on this quack gives a perfect excuse."

"Who says this? Excuse for what? No one can harm the empress."

"They say Vachot works for one of the tsar's cousins, to make Alexandra look delusional."

Lena missed the next seam and stabbed her index finger. A dark blob of blood appeared on her skin and she dropped the cape, terrified she'd stain it. She stuck her finger between her lips to stanch the blood.

"You should use a thimble," Masha said.

Lena took her finger out of her mouth and stroked the small welt where the needle had pricked her skin. "The empress may be eccentric, but she's not delusional."

"You see how she mopes around here."

"She hasn't moped lately. Not since she started seeing Dr. Vachot."

"Exactly." Masha loosened her belt and began to scratch furiously underneath her furs. "If she's dependent on a quack, she can be set aside for someone else. Haven't you heard? They say

Dowager Empress Marie wants her darling son Nicky to take a new wife, a healthy, younger woman who will give the tsar boys."

Lena's finger throbbed with pain. "I don't think so. Besides, that will never happen. The tsar loves the empress too much."

Masha inclined her head curiously. "What's that?"

Lena followed Masha's gaze. A corner of the letter from her mother, telling of her brother Anton's troubles, stuck out from underneath a velvet cushion on the chaise longue.

"Who's writing you letters?" Masha demanded. "Why are you blushing?"

Lena heard her brother's laughter ringing in her head. She'd brought her mother's letter with her to reread once she finished her stitching. Lena focused on a watercolor landscape suspended from a cord on the opposite wall. She touched two fingers to her forehead. "Perhaps I've taken fever."

"What a terrible liar you are." Masha narrowed her eyes, as though trying to discern the contents of the paper from Lena's expression. "It's a love letter!" she concluded triumphantly. "And I've never seen you so much as flirt with one of the Cossack guards."

Lena tried to smile, but her lips locked in a downward trajectory. The broad-shouldered palace guards looked handsome in their formal kaftans with the bright blue-and-red sashes, but they were loud and chewed tobacco. She either watched from a distance or avoided them entirely.

"You could have a love affair," Masha mused, "if you took more care with your appearance."

"I wouldn't know about that." The more she denied an affair, the more Masha might suspect one. A secret lover made as good a cover story as any.

"You better watch yourself though," Masha said. "I hear your idol Alexandra is a prude. If she knew you kept a lover, she'd dismiss you at once. And jobs are hard to come by these days. If you know what's best—"

Masha stopped abruptly. Her pale brows curled and she turned to the door. Pavel stood at attention, still as one of the granite statues in the garden. He wore a white jacket decorated with colorful embroidery, and an emerald sparkled atop his fez. The outfit was so elaborate it might have looked comical on another man, but Lena thought it complemented his dark skin tone and the amber flecks of color in his eyes. His voice was deep and melodious, as she remembered from their first encounter. "That garment is too small for you, don't you think?"

"At least I'm making good use of my time." Lena gathered Olga's cape from where it had fallen on the floor. Butterflies began to dance in her stomach. "Not scaring defenseless women."

"I doubt you're as defenseless as you look, seamstress."

Lena cast a cautious glance in Masha's direction. The girl probably didn't understand a word of English, but her open mouth conveyed shock well enough. Lena wondered what surprised Masha more, that Pavel spoke or Lena dared to answer.

Pavel kept his gaze on Lena, but addressed Masha in Russian. "Please leave now. The empress wishes to see Lena Ivanovna alone."

Masha gave a hoarse laugh, betraying the cigarettes she snuck while walking in the gardens. She turned to Lena. "Has she discovered your beau already?"

Lena grabbed the letter from under the cushion and thrust it deep into the pocket of her skirt for safekeeping, resolved not to let it out of her sight again.

Masha ambled toward the door. "Don't let it slip about the

Cossack, Lena. Secrets have a way of revealing themselves, you know."

Lena bit back her angry response. After all, Masha was just a silly girl, cranky from the itchy furs.

Once Masha left, Lena told Pavel, "You shouldn't sneak up on me like that."

"The Winter Palace is worse than Peterhof. There are no secrets. You are close to the Empress Alexandra? Then you could do with the practice."

She tried to imagine Pavel with the other bodyguards and footmen, chewing tobacco in the garden, but she couldn't picture him joining in the gossip. Even so, he knew of her growing intimacy with Alexandra. Everyone must know.

"Are you in love with a Cossack, as the girl said?" Pavel's jaw tightened. "If so, perhaps you should watch what you say with the empress. That girl's right. The empress doesn't care for love affairs among the staff."

Despite the cold air in the room, Lena felt warmth spread across her cheeks. Still, the hint of annoyance in Pavel's tone pleased her. Perhaps he was jealous. "I'm sure Empress Alexandra has more pressing concerns than my romantic life."

"She's not the empress that concerns you." He put his hand on his heart and bowed his head. "Forgive me, seamstress. I misled you. I was instructed to keep this meeting confidential. I've been reassigned to the dowager. She's here to see you."

The butterfly wings in her stomach flapped so quickly now that Lena grew queasy. "Why does Marie want to see me?"

"I don't know. But the dowager doesn't usually call on servants." Pavel's tone grew serious. "Watch yourself. Remember, she doesn't care for disagreement." He threw a quick glance over his shoulder, eying the doorway the same way Masha had earlier. "Of course when it comes to the topic of Phillipe Vachot, I agree with the dowager. You care for the welfare of Empress Alexandra? Convince her to dismiss him. He's causing more harm to her reputation."

"You give my persuasive abilities more credit than they deserve."

"I have a good sense of people. I have a good sense of how to protect myself. I learned that skill as a boxer. It's the only way to keep the blows from destroying you. I think it's a skill you possess as well, little seamstress."

Lena now took note of Pavel's large and nimble hands. She could easily imagine those hands curled into fists, and Pavel bare-chested, within the boundary of a chalk outline ring, like the men used in Archangel. She lowered her head, trying to appear modest despite her thoughts. "You were a boxer?"

Pavel smiled. It was genuine, not a smirk or even a flirtatious grin. It changed his entire face, made him seem more vulnerable. "The sport got me out of Virginia."

He hesitated and their eyes met. Lena didn't look away. Pavel leaned in closer, inclining toward her ear so he could speak in a whisper. She drew in the scent of something woodsy and comforting. "Until she produces a son, your mistress is in a precarious position. You can be a friend to her, only don't turn the dowager against you."

Lena nodded. Pavel withdrew. At once, she missed his scent and his lips so close to her ear. He bowed to Lena one more time as he backed out of the room.

Marie appeared a moment later, dressed in an ivory gown and delicate wrap that made the tiny garment in Lena's hands seem fit only for a rag doll. Lena stood to curtsy.

"Sit down," Marie commanded in her husky voice, flapping her hands. "I'm on my way to meet Nicky and the girls at a reception for the Serbian ambassador. I don't have much time."

Lena wished the dowager didn't move so quickly. It made her feel clumsy and stupid. She lowered herself back into the chair, set the sewing aside, and folded her hands in her lap.

"So my daughter-in-law trusts her servants more than her own family." Marie fingered a crystal paperweight on the desk. "But then I've always found the Germans an odd race. Apparently, they can't even keep their rooms warmed to a civil temperature." Marie pulled her lace wrap tighter around her shoulders. "I'll get straight to the point. When we last saw one another, Alix began to talk about your family. I'd like to hear more from you. Tell me about them."

Lena remembered the letter from her mother. She willed herself not to feel for it in her pockets. She felt certain Marie could hear the beating of her heart. "We are good, simple, patriotic country folk—"

Marie raised her hand. "Not your prepared speech. I meant about your mother, the midwife."

Lena nodded miserably. "What would you like to know?"

"You must have the highest regard for your mother's skills. After all, you have promised the Empress of Russia an heir. You truly believe you helped Alix conceive a boy? I'm listening, if you wish to explain."

"That's not true. I never promised an heir," Lena sputtered. "Empress Alexandra begged for my advice. She wants a son so badly. I only shared a few things I'd heard from my mother and other women."

"Your advice is probably more sensible than the claptrap Vachot feeds her." Marie's dark brows slanted. "Alix is convinced the child is a boy. What if she's wrong and bears another girl? A fifth daughter?" Marie's gaze ran up and down Lena's form, evaluating her as though she were a serf to be sent out to the fields. "Surely you understand the danger if Alix fails again. I don't expect you to fully comprehend the consequences, but I expect you to behave as a patriotic subject should."

"I've done everything the empress asked."

"*I'm* asking now. I want you present at the birth."

"I've never delivered a child," Lena said. "I never claimed I could do so."

"I'm not asking you to play court physician, but seeing as how Alix trusts you implicitly it's only natural for you to be with her at such a momentous occasion."

Lena moved her shoulders uncertainly. For an instant, the sharpness in the dowager's eyes reminded Lena of her mother's. She checked the impulse to shrink away.

"I know you trust Alix. You think she can protect you," Marie said. "I don't know what you need protecting from, but I can help you far more than poor Alix."

Lena didn't care for the dowager's tone on that last phrase, *poor Alix*. Lena often felt sorry for Alexandra as well, but she still merited her respect. Lena remembered what Masha had told her earlier. Perhaps the dowager wanted to replace Alexandra. Lena tried not to put faith in palace rumors, but the cold seed of suspicion had already taken root.

"My only wish is to help the empress," Lena said. "I know I'm only her servant, but sometimes I think she would like a friend. I only want to make her happy." In a smaller voice, she added, "That is what we all want, I should think."

Marie patted her fringed bangs, looking thoughtful. Then she took Lena's hand. Her skin felt smooth and cool to touch.

"Alix needs a friend desperately," Marie said. "You can help her. You can be that friend. Stay at her bedside during the birth. And do exactly as I say."

PARIS

OCTOBER 1941

Judging from the frail autumn sunlight, Charlotte guessed it was late morning. She had hardly slept the night before. She pulled the bed linens tighter around her shoulders, not caring yet to face the day. She stared up at the ceiling, where patches of peeling paint clung to plaster. Then she stretched her arm out to where Laurent had cuddled alongside her back all night. When at last she'd fallen asleep, it was to the gentle rise and fall of his breathing.

Her son's voice cooed from downstairs. "Which one," she heard him ask, "the chicken or the egg?"

"No one knows, *mon petit*. That's the mystery."

Luc's voice sounded calm, smooth, almost seductive, the voice she fell in love with. Charlotte half-expected Luc to bound up the rickety old stairs, ready to caress her shoulder and drag her back under the sheets. The warm smell of melting butter brought back memories of better times. Once, she'd carved thick slices of butter from creamy wheels and used it to cook chanterelle mushrooms and delicate crepes. Now she couldn't remember the last time she'd prepared anything more exciting than rutabaga and dry boiled potatoes.

A familiar pain made her stomach clamor for food. Charlotte

closed her eyes. Despite her hunger, she wanted to remain in bed, thinking of those days when food was plentiful, and she danced on stage, and Luc still loved her.

She heard Laurent's strangely raspy laugh. Charlotte realized she hadn't heard her son laugh properly in months. Her shoulders relaxed and she managed to find her way out of bed.

Charlotte dressed quickly, shivering in the chilly room. She smoothed the pleats of the skirt she'd worn yesterday and ran her fingers through her hair to work out the tangles. She lifted her hair to clasp her necklace, and then splashed water on her face, balking at the pale image reflected in the cracked mirror above Luc's sink. Tiny lines creased the edges of her eyes. She grabbed a sliver of soap and scrubbed her cheeks.

She stopped. She wouldn't scrub so hard at home. Charlotte set the soap back on the cold basin, patted her face dry, and headed downstairs.

Laurent sat at the table, swinging his legs, staring at Luc as he cracked eggs and they sizzled in the frying pan. Charlotte kissed the top of Laurent's head and gently tilted his face up. One eye gave off a watery discharge and his skin felt too warm. Still, he seemed happy. He'd emptied his pockets, which he kept filled with string, rocks, and old coins. The contents had been spread out on the table for Luc to admire.

"Where did you find eggs?" Charlotte asked.

Luc glanced over his shoulder, a cigarette dangling in his mouth. The tobacco smelled as good as the eggs. He gave her a lazy smile. "Good morning to you too."

"Thanks for letting me sleep in." She ruffled Laurent's hair.

"You looked as though you could use a good night's rest."

Charlotte's fingers clenched. "How kind of you to say so."

"As for these . . ." Luc reached for salt and shook it over the pan. "I got lucky."

He scooped scrambled eggs onto three chipped plates and set them down on the table. Then he poured boiling water over the coffee grounds in his press. The powerful smell shocked her. Real coffee, not the hickory shavings that passed for it these days.

Luc stamped his cigarette out in a metal ashtray. "*Bon appétit.* Such as it is."

They ate silently. Laurent's lips moved determinedly over every bite. Charlotte wracked her mind for something to say. Outside, the previous night's rain had given way to sunshine. Droplets of water clung to violets in the courtyard. "Look, Laurent," she said. "The garden is sparkling, like in a fairy tale."

Luc jabbed at the eggs with his fork. "Really? That's what you see?"

She waited, ready for him to tell her what she'd said wrong.

"The landlord grew pinot noir grapes. Don't you remember? You're the daughter of a farmer—I'd expect you to notice. The Hun soldiers ripped the vines out. The Nazis control everything now, even our wine."

Charlotte stared at one of the misshapen rocks Laurent had placed on the table. When she last heard from her father, he said the Germans hadn't come to them yet because they were too busy destroying vineyards in Bordeaux. He'd guessed it was only a matter of time. She couldn't bear the thought of soldiers trouncing through her father's vineyards in their hobnailed boots. The retrievers would bark at the soldiers, they might even try to nip their ankles. The soldiers would shoot the dogs. Her heart froze.

Luc wiped his mouth with a soiled cotton napkin. "I want to

show your mother something," he told Laurent. "It's rolled up on top of my desk in the other room. Will you fetch it for me?"

Instantly, her son obeyed. She'd never seen him move so quickly for her. Jealousy pricked her heart.

Luc also watched Laurent as he ran from the kitchen, his backbone sticking out against the flimsy fabric of his shirt. "He's too thin."

The next bite of egg stuck in her throat. Charlotte set her fork down and clasped her fingers together. Like so many other children, Laurent had experienced a dangerous drop in his weight over the last year. Did Luc really think that was her fault? "I tried to get nutritional supplements," she said. "There's none to be had."

"If this winter is as cold as the last, he'll get sick."

"All the more reason to get him to my parents' house as quickly as possible."

"It's my fault, too," Luc admitted. "I don't see him as much as I should. From now on, he'll stay with me more often."

Charlotte imagined her entire body staggering back. She choked back tears. "We're leaving the city. I told you."

"Yes. I want to talk to you about that."

Laurent returned to the kitchen and solemnly handed Luc a rolled-up map.

"Look what I have for you." Luc reached under his chair and withdrew a brightly illustrated field guide of birds. Laurent smiled shyly and gathered his things off the table, shoving the string and coins and rocks back in his pocket. He accepted the book and moved to the living room, curling up under a worn patchwork quilt.

"You've probably seen this before." Luc moved the plates to the cluttered sink and spread the map out on the table, flattening it with the base of his palm.

Charlotte stared at the faded map, its thick black line of demarcation dividing the curving northwestern region of the country, directly under Nazi control, and the southeastern region under the Vichy regime. She wrapped her hands around the mug of coffee, taking some comfort in its warmth, and tried to ignore Luc's disapproving stare.

"Look at Sainte-Foy-la-Grande," he said. "That's the nearest town to your parents' farm. It's on the border of the occupied zone."

"There's a direct train from Paris to Bordeaux," Charlotte replied. "And then I only need to travel east. They can't guard the entire perimeter."

"They don't need to. They've established checkpoints all along the rail lines."

"How do you know that?"

He lowered his gaze again. Charlotte thought it best to leave the topic alone. For now. "What if we had a car?" she asked.

"The Germans took all the cars. You'll be lucky to find an old horse and buggy."

His voice remained steady, but Charlotte saw uncertainty in his eyes. Luc could be talked into helping her. She only needed to grant him the illusion he'd arrived at this conclusion himself.

"You're right," she admitted. "All the cars are gone. But then I thought they'd taken all the tobacco and coffee and eggs as well. Or are you raising chickens? And now you seem to know where the German checkpoints are located as well."

Luc didn't reply, but his lower lip twitched. Charlotte almost smiled. Laurent had the same tic when he was about to give in.

"Without the right connections," she said carefully, "how could I possibly find a car on my own, or gasoline for that matter?"

"You couldn't," Luc said.

He never failed to point out what she couldn't do. Charlotte bit her lip to keep from fighting back. "Perhaps you know someone. Perhaps the person that provides you with cigarettes and eggs, someone in the Maquis, the Resistance."

His lip quivered. "The less you know about that, the better."

"But you could help us leave?"

"Charlotte, be realistic." He switched tactics, just as she'd done with him. Now Luc used his cajoling, seductive tone. "If the Germans are looking for you, you can't go. Stay here with me."

How could she make Luc understand? She needed to get home. She needed her mother to hug her and tell her she would be all right. She saw Laurent peep out from over his book, worry clouding his gaze. She gave him a subtle wink. It's just a game, she wanted to tell him. Something for adults. Nothing to make you worry.

"A soldier came to my flat," she told Luc, with as much firmness as she could muster and not scare Laurent. "He knew my name. He knew all about me. Why?"

Luc's face paled. Without thinking, Charlotte set the mug of coffee down on the table and pressed the back of her hand against his forehead. Luc's skin felt firm and enticing. Despite everything, a familiar longing gripped her.

He gave a wan smile. "Do I have a temperature?"

She knew that smile too well. It acted as a talisman, robbing her of reason. Charlotte stumbled over her words. "Something came over you. You looked sick."

Luc's smile crumbled. "You told me once that your parents emigrated to Sainte-Foy-la-Grande from Denmark. Do you know why?"

"My father wanted to grow Muscadelle grapes," she said.

"You were adopted. What do you know about your biological parents?"

Charlotte turned her feet out, toes to opposite heels, in fifth position. She could handle anything as long as she maintained fifth position. "Nothing."

"The Germans just completed a census of Jews in the occupied zone," Luc said. "Is it possible your biological family was Jewish?"

She felt the cool metal hanging around her throat. Charlotte held the chain out so Luc could see the cross on her necklace. Three bars sliced through the cross, the third bar angled down. Her mother had given it to her before she moved to Paris. Since she and Luc separated, she had worn it every day. It made her feel less lonely. "What about this?"

"I've never seen one like that before." Luc regarded the crucifix with mild interest. "Is your family religious?"

Charlotte hesitated. "No."

"Why did your mother give it to you then?"

She realized she couldn't answer. Not that Luc bothered to wait for an answer anyway. "If they have something they call proof you're Jewish, no German officer will care about what's around your neck. They might think it's a ruse or just not care. You know what the Nazis are. You should consider the possibility."

Charlotte's chest constricted. Shortly after the Germans seized control of the city, she'd taken Laurent out for a new pair of shoes. While they walked the Champs-Elysees, three adolescent boys in black boots and black berets began to smash the window of a jewelry shop. Charlotte knew the shop well. Luc had purchased her wedding ring there. She'd sold the ring back to the store after they separated, to help pay the first months of rent on her new flat. Charlotte remembered the man who owned the shop had spoken so softly she had to incline her head forward to hear him.

When she saw the looting, she expected to hear German. But the boys smashing the shop windows shouted to one another in perfect French. Charlotte remembered how young they looked, no more than children really. And yet their faces were so cruel. She'd tried to cover Laurent's eyes, but he kept pushing her hand away. The employees ran out to the street, pleading for help. A pair of soldiers were posted on the corner. The soldiers only laughed. The collaborators dragged the owners out to the street, their wrists roped together, a graying middle-aged couple.

The next day the shop was boarded. She knew the Jewish owners had been sent east. East to nowhere. That's what people said.

Charlotte wanted to find a dark room, where no one could see in or out, and sit, undisturbed, rock her body back and forth, and think. Surely her parents wouldn't have kept something so important from her, especially not when the occupation put both her and Laurent in danger.

"The Spanish border isn't far from your parents' house." Luc jolted her back to the present. "Some Catalans are sympathetic to the Maquis. I think they will help us."

"Now you think we should leave the country? Before you didn't think we should even leave the city."

"If you're determined to leave, you must do it the right way."

"You're convinced I can't do it right."

Luc glanced behind him at Laurent, still on the armchair, still ostensibly examining the brightly colored birds in the book. Every few seconds he looked up at them, brows furled.

"I want what's best for Laurent." Luc made an effort to brighten his voice. "I know a courier who might lend us his car."

"I knew it!" Charlotte said. And then she realized he'd said "us." She didn't like the implication. "You needn't come."

"He'll only lend us the car if I give him something in return. I'll offer to make a drop for him in Vichy territory. Then we can cross over to Spain."

Charlotte felt exhausted. She glanced at Laurent, snuggled like a kitten in Luc's quilt, and wanted to join him. An idea flickered in her mind. "You can come on one condition. My friend Matilda Kshesinskaya. I need to make sure she's all right."

Luc frowned and stared out the window. She couldn't read him, but she had never been good at that.

"Fine," he said at last. "Just get Laurent out of the country."

Charlotte began to pace the living room. Resting her hand lightly on the worn fabric of the sofa, she slid her feet into fifth position, and extended her leg in a series of *battement tendus*.

"Well?" Luc asked.

Charlotte drew in a deep breath, feeling the fullness of the air in her chest. "I guess it's time we learn Spanish."

Seven

Veronica lengthened her stride to keep pace with Michael as they pushed their way through the lunchtime bustle on Fifth Avenue. Strangers brushed her coat with their elbows and car horns blared. She'd never been to New York City before, yet it seemed familiar, gritty and polished at once, like an enormous soundstage. It was a place she could call home. A little swagger made its way into her steps.

"I guess that's part of growing up in California," she was telling Michael. "At least in the Central Valley, you grow accustomed to cars. You don't think about the confinement and the isolation. You don't realize what you're missing. All the energy."

"You don't find this claustrophobic?" Michael said.

"It's exhilarating."

When Michael stopped at a crosswalk, Veronica gulped in the chilly air, catching her breath. The light turned. She stepped off the curb. Michael grabbed her elbow. She almost lost her balance, but he held on tight. He pulled her back just in time. An angry cabdriver honked as he screeched past. Hot, putrid exhaust blew in her face.

"Watch it." Michael's cheeks had paled. "Don't get too exhilarated. I know everyone jaywalks, but remember, pedestrians don't have the right of way here."

Veronica's life didn't exactly flash before her eyes, but she had a quick vision of her death. Her body cold on the street. Strangers kicking her purse aside.

"I get that now." The backs of her calves throbbed. She'd worn a pair of black boots with heels because she wanted to look like a cosmopolitan Carrie Bradshaw type, not some yokel from Bakersfield. She kept walking, slower this time and swagger somewhat mitigated.

Michael stopped at a gray building with four Corinthian columns and two giant American flags waving in the wind. The place looked more like a bank than a museum.

"This is what I 'had' to see?" Veronica commented.

"I know it doesn't look like much from the outside, but there's a gallery on the ground floor. Malcolm Forbes was a major league monarchist. He owned the largest collection of Fabergé eggs outside the Kremlin, along with some other Romanov relics." Michael pivoted, frowning. "I don't understand. My grandmother took me here all the time when I was little. They kept Nicholas and Alexandra outside."

"Stuffed?"

"Good one. No. Life-size pictures. Let's take a look."

"Fine with me." Veronica shivered. Now that they'd stopped moving, the cold air had started to seep through her thin coat.

She wanted to linger in the foyer, underneath the rumbling

heating vent. But Michael wandered into the narrow, mazelike interior and she followed. They passed toy boats, old violins, framed presidential letters. Still, she didn't see Fabergé eggs.

They reached the last room, filled with toy soldiers assembled to re-create famous battles. Despite the militaristic overtones, Veronica found the dioramas pleasing, like history books come to life. She bent to examine a miniature Alexander the Great charging Hannibal's elephants.

"What happened?" Michael made another circle. The top of his head brushed precariously close to the low ceiling. He looked like Gulliver surrounded by Lilliputians. "Forbes owned at least five Fabergé eggs, Alexandra's coronation crown . . ."

Veronica's lip twitched. Nicholas II's father had died suddenly and the ceremony had been a tense affair. She imagined Nicholas's sweaty palms and trembling fingers as he placed the jeweled diadem on his wife's head. Suddenly, Veronica had to see that crown. "Why don't you go up front and ask? I'll wait in here."

Michael swung his hands behind his back. Even in jeans and a black overcoat he looked dashing. Still, he was acting strange, even for him.

"Come with me," he said.

"Why?"

He shook his head and looked at the floor.

"This side of you concerns me," she said. "I'm an adult. I can manage."

Michael backed away reluctantly, hands in the air, palms forward. "Just don't talk to strangers."

"I learned that in kindergarten, but thanks." Veronica moved away from Hannibal and Alexander the Great to a display of jousting knights.

"I'll only be a few minutes," Michael said.

"Great. Go."

Veronica bent down to gaze at the little cheering spectators in Tudor-era costumes. One of the tiny brunettes looked like Anne Boleyn. She wondered who arranged these exhibits. Now that was a cushy gig. Come up with a new formation every month or so. No pressure to publish. No tenure committee ready to send you packing.

As she peered through the glass, she caught the milky reflection of a man on the other side of the room. He must have slipped in while she was examining Anne Boleyn. Only he wasn't walking from exhibit to exhibit. He just stood there staring at her.

She tried to concentrate on the jousting match, but couldn't focus anymore. She'd probably attracted a garden-variety weirdo. It's not like it would be the first time that happened. But she couldn't let him stare at her.

Veronica spun around. The man stood with his back turned to the Battle of Little Bighorn. Sioux and Cheyenne warriors in feathered headdresses circled U.S. soldiers in blue uniforms. He had been watching her all right. He didn't even care that she'd caught him. He was nearly as tall as Michael, but with lean and wiry musculature and reddish brown hair that gave him an air of sleek cunning, like a Machiavellian fox. On his left cheek he bore a deep purplish, acorn-shaped scar.

"Can I help you?" She folded her arms across her chest.

The man had a trench coat slung over one arm. He held it out to her. "You will take this?"

She sucked in a deep breath. The man had a thick Russian accent, the kind that smashed vowels to dust. "What are you talking about?"

"Is it you work here? You will take coat then."

"I don't work here."

Now he folded his arms across his chest, mirroring her stance. Mocking it as well, she felt sure of that. "Why say 'can I help you'?"

"You were staring at me."

He gave a big shrug. "I think perhaps I know you. Now I think no."

"I've never seen you before in my life."

"Such a shame then, no? But you are here with friend?" His mouth curled when he spoke. Amazing how Russians could laugh in your face without laughing at all. "More than friend, I think."

"They sold the Fabergé eggs, along with everything else. A Ukrainian oil oligarch bought them all!" Michael strode back into the gallery. "That's what I get for not keeping up with *The New York Times*." When he saw the man, he stopped dead in his tracks.

"And here he is coming," the Russian man commented. "The Cossack in all his glory on the search for Romanov relics."

Michael threw the Russian a look that would have made Ivan the Terrible quake in his ermine-lined boots. The Russian ignored him, still directing his comments to Veronica. "Maybe I am disappointed like you. They no longer carry the holy artifacts of the blessed family. Not that I am so surprised. It is not in American nature to appreciate history. So sad for historian, no?"

An alarm rose steadily in pitch in Veronica's head. This man knew she was a historian. He used archaic language, the "blessed family" and so forth. Veronica stepped forward, close enough to catch a whiff of the Russian's astringent cologne. Michael tried to clasp her wrist, but she waved him back.

"Are you Alexei Romanov?" she asked.

"The tsarevich? You think I am one of these that say bullets bounce off royalty by magic? One of these desperate for attention, claiming I am someone I am not?" The Russian looked straight at Michael when he said that, waved his hand three times in a circular motion, and bent into a mockery of a bow.

Veronica's heart hammered in her chest. Michael stepped between Veronica and the Russian. "What do you want?"

"I want nothing. And if I did, that would be between myself and the lady, I think. Move away please." The Russian made a dismissive gesture, like he wanted to pass and was accustomed to those around him responding immediately to his requests.

Michael's fists clenched. Veronica squeezed his hand. "It's okay. Let's go."

"Try to follow us and I'll call the cops," Michael said.

"Why would I follow? Why would I care where you go? Perhaps you are following me."

Veronica tugged on Michael's hand, her stomach churning. She didn't want this man provoking Michael. "Seriously."

Michael backed out of the room, holding her hand, and then turned abruptly to lead her to the exit and through the narrow maze of a hall. Veronica trailed, pulse pounding in her ears. She remembered Orpheus, from another story in the book of mythology Abuela had bought her long ago. Orpheus was allowed to bring his wife back from Hades, but the gods warned that if she looked behind her, she'd have to return for good. Veronica held Michael's hand tight. She wanted to look back, but didn't dare.

Once they were outside of the gallery and back on the street, the icy wind kicked up. Michael walked in front of her at an even quicker pace. "What did that guy say to you? What did he want?"

"Nothing. He was staring at me. It began to get on my nerves." She hesitated to catch her breath as they walked. His legs were so much longer than hers. "When I confronted him he said he thought he knew me. Do you think he's connected to the Romanov Guardsmen? Of course I'm sure this city is full of random perverts."

"With Russian accents?" Michael squinted thoughtfully. "Okay, probably. But in the Forbes Gallery on a Wednesday afternoon? Making sarcastic comments about heirs to the throne? Bowing to me? I don't think so."

They passed a gothic church tower and a low iron gate embellished with metal crosses. Michael opened the gate, pulling her behind him, and ducked under the awning in front of the sanctuary. "I want to make sure he's not following us."

Veronica stood on her tiptoes to peer over Michael's shoulder. She bit her lower lip, which had started to crack from the cold.

Then she recognized the spark of red in the Russian's hair, a stark contrast to the gray sky. She almost let out a cry. Michael shook his head and she kept quiet, just watching. The Russian threw his trench coat over his shoulder, daring the East Coast cold to touch his hearty bones. Then he crossed Fifth Avenue against the traffic, artfully dodging several taxis and even a city bus. Veronica almost let out another little cry, but he made it safely across the street and headed in the opposite direction, toward the Midtown skyscrapers.

"By the way, don't try crossing any streets like that," Michael told her.

"Don't worry." Veronica watched the Russian disappear into the sea of pedestrians farther down Fifth Avenue. She started to miss her cozy office at Alameda University, where the worst thing to fear was one of Dr. Brack's nastygrams about poor attendance at faculty meetings. Still, it seemed her fifth-grade Nancy Drew fantasies had finally come to life. It wasn't an entirely unpleasant sensation.

"Do you see the park?" Michael spun her around in the other direction. Veronica recognized the ornate and massive marble arch at Washington Square, several blocks away. She'd seen pictures in her tour book. "It's a nice place to walk."

"Shouldn't we go to the cops?" Veronica asked. "Something?"

"What will you tell the cops?"

"That guy was bothering us."

"Was he?"

Veronica opened her mouth, but found she didn't really have an answer. "We have to do something. He was following us."

"You can't prove that. Besides, we are doing something. You're being careful and calling for me if there's any problem. In the meantime, you asked me to show you the city. Let's go."

She let him tug her hand and drag her behind him once more down Fifth Avenue. When they got to the park, Michael led her past the arch and the statues of George Washington to a small, sand-covered area within the square. Dogs ran loose while their owners drank coffee and chatted. Michael pointed to a fluffy chow, alternately chasing and being chased by a friendly yellow Lab.

"Look!" he said. "I miss Ariel already."

The blare of taxis and construction permeated the air, but now she heard birds rustling tree branches and squirrels scampering in the bushes. They leaned against the railing and watched the chow try to catch a fat pigeon. The bird flew off, its heavy wings flapping in disgust.

"Oh, look at his eyes," Veronica said. "Just like Ariel's. He looks crushed, poor thing. But I'm glad the bird escaped."

She turned to Michael. His body remained still, his eyes intensely focused on her face. An inner jolt rocked and then warmed her chest, like the first time she'd tried a shot of vodka. "What is it?" she asked.

"I don't know how to explain it," he said. "I'm not sure the time is right."

Veronica stood on her tiptoes once more, threw her hands around Michael's neck, and kissed him. His lips warmed under hers. She pressed her nose against his.

He didn't open his eyes after they kissed. His forehead remained pressed against hers, soft and warm. "I'm sorry if I've been overprotective. It's just that if anything happened to you . . ."

Veronica knew. She'd seen it in his eyes. One of the reasons she liked Michael so much was that she could talk to him without censoring herself. He always understood what she meant. Now, however, her mouth felt dry and the words would not come easily.

As she wracked her mind for the right response, she thought about Alexandra, the young and beautiful Princess Alix, beaming with joy and optimism, ready to marry her soul mate Nicholas. Veronica often wondered what it felt like to let a man love you that desperately. She wondered if it scared Alix a little. Yet she knew Alexandra wouldn't have changed anything about her life, even her horrifying death screaming for mercy at gunpoint, if it meant giving up that love.

Veronica still felt as though she were just beneath the ocean's surface, gazing at the sun, but drowning in bad memories, fearing she wasn't worthy of anyone's love. But the pressure didn't hold her down as firmly anymore. She could struggle against it.

Glittering rows of bottles sparkled underneath the dim bar lights. Nat King Cole gently crooned "Nature Boy." Every so often, the hum of voices in the bar softened, and she heard only the tinkling piano notes. A stale cigarette scent clung to the leather bar stools. Michael and Veronica had finished their drinks. Veronica felt wonderfully disoriented, as though she'd accidentally stepped onto the set of a romantic old movie or an episode of *Mad Men*.

She fumbled in her purse. "You lost your key?" Michael asked.

Veronica wished she had lost the key. Michael had booked adjacent rooms, as she'd requested. A lost key might give her an excuse to stay with him instead. But she didn't have it in her to lie. She withdrew the small plastic card from her wallet and rose slowly, hoping to prolong the moment. "This hotel is cute."

"Faded grandeur, granted." Michael took her hand and led her to the iron-and-brass cage elevator, adorned with art deco metalwork flowers. "Somehow I thought you'd like it all the more for that."

"That does seem to be my style," she said. "Let's get breakfast tomorrow. Take me somewhere you like. Then I'll head over to meet Alexei Romanov."

"I can't change your mind about that meeting?"

She slapped his chest. "That's the whole reason I'm here."

The cage door snapped shut and the elevator rumbled upward. It was a cozy fit. She had to arch her neck to look up at him. It made her a little dizzy. "I have a book to complete. Remember the whole tenure thing? My financial and professional future? Alexei Romanov promised I could look at their archives and—"

Michael bent down. She closed her eyes and took in the tantalizingly gentle pressure of his lips on hers. His hand caressed the front of her blouse and the curve of her waist. She relaxed and eased into him.

The elevator came to an abrupt halt and buzzed to announce

they'd reached their floor. Michael pulled away first. Their rooms were right across from the elevator. He unlocked her door. "Give me a minute." He walked in the room, looked all around, and then held the door open for her.

"All clear?" she asked.

"Remember, if anything worries you, anything bothers you, anything doesn't feel right, yell. I'm here."

She gave him a coy smile and stepped into her room, expecting him to follow.

"Good night," he said, smiling back. He shut the door and the latch clicked.

Stunned, Veronica stared at the closed door like an idiot. She wasn't sure what she'd expected.

Fine. She stepped into the bathroom, started the hot water, and undressed. She lingered in the shower stall, letting the jets of water soothe her sore muscles. She almost forgot about the Russian man at the Forbes Gallery. Michael was next door. He wouldn't let anything happen to her. She felt as secure as a fairytale princess in the highest turret of a castle. And every bit as restless.

As she toweled off her hair, Veronica gazed at her reflection in the steamy mirror. Most of her makeup had washed off, but she looked alert and happy. She pulled on a new robe and took satisfaction in the feel of silky fabric against her clean skin. She plopped down on the bed and stretched her limbs out. From her window, she could see the top of the Empire State Building in all its art deco majesty. The iconic image taunted her. *Do something.*

Pipes creaked and churned next door. Veronica thought of Michael on the other side of the wall, brushing his teeth, shaving, changing. She remembered the scent of his skin, like salt and pine. She turned over and bit her pillow. She had a sense of Michael's body, but curiosity burned every thought. What did his chest look like? His arms? His shoulders? Did he have a tattoo? A little bit of stomach? She wouldn't mind if he did. She liked strong arms and legs, but a perfectly chiseled abdomen had always struck her as somehow inhuman.

Again, she glanced at the mirror. Not bad. The green robe brought out the gold tint in her eyes. Michael would notice that. Why waste the effect?

She hopped off the bed and tapped on the door that connected their adjoining rooms. She called his name.

He answered at once, opening the door. "What is it? What's the matter?"

He wore only a white T-shirt and jeans. She'd never seen him in short sleeves before. His arms were gorgeous, muscular but not overly so. A dark Celtic tattoo, like barbed wire, encircled his left bicep. "My shower drain's clogged. Can you take a look?"

He touched her cheek. "You scared me."

She felt awkward, but she'd come too far to turn back now. Veronica beckoned to him and he followed into her room. He stepped into the bathroom. She shut the door. The lock clicked. She waited, pulse racing.

Michael emerged a few seconds later. "Nothing's wrong. Why did you . . . ?" His voice trailed off. She couldn't keep her eyes off the shape of his lips as he started to smile. She could drown in his smile. "Why didn't you just invite me in?"

"I don't know." Veronica raised herself onto her tiptoes and placed an open palm on his warm cheek. She was about to kiss him, but stopped abruptly.

She saw confusion and a hint of sadness flickering in his eyes, a reflection of her own battered, mixed-up emotions. She wondered then about Michael's ex-wife. Perhaps he was afraid to let this happen. He held her gaze and hesitated, giving her an out.

From the night they'd met, she'd maintained control. Now she wanted to relent. She wanted the knight in shining armor, the bodyguard, the fledgling tsar, or whatever role Michael Karstadt cared to play.

Veronica leaned back against the wall, cast-off clothes scattered about her feet. Michael closed the space, putting his hand on the wall next to her, his arm outstretched, and she shivered with anticipation.

He caressed the back of her neck. The brush of his fingers on her skin made every nerve ending come alive and she trembled. She caught his scent once more, comforting and powerfully arousing, calling to her as strongly as his touch.

He leaned down to kiss her. She tilted her head back, gasping for a second at the lack of air, and then giving in to the dizzying sensation. His tongue explored her entire mouth, urgent and deep, yet his hands skimmed her body with the lightest touch, sliding across the thin silk of her gown. She pulled away from his mouth and let out a sharp little cry as his finger trailed down the length of her sternum. She still hadn't touched him. She felt moist and supple, yet couldn't move. The warm scent of their arousal filled the air. His cheek lay flat against hers. She felt the rhythm of his breathing.

His lips covered her mouth. She stepped back long enough to pull his shirt over his head. It stuck and she wondered if this was a sign that this was a mistake after all, another doomed relationship fated to collapse. She waited, scared for wanting him so much. Then he tugged at the shirt and miraculously pulled it free.

They laughed, nerves still taut. She watched his face and recognized the lust in his eyes, as demanding and desperate as her own.

He scooped her up into his arms and her robe fell to the floor. He carried her to the bed and she tumbled down on her back, pulling him on top of her, kissing him and biting his lower lip, ready to explode. Every defense melted at his touch.

Eight

Perhaps Alexandra kept her next pregnancy secret to control the inevitable court gossip. Deep inside, she may have suspected something was wrong. Perhaps she thought it better to be called a liar than a victim of wishful thinking.

—VERONICA HERRERA, The Reluctant Romanov

SAINT PETERSBURG
MAY 1902

"You do have a secret lover. I knew it!" Masha took a sugar cube from the silver-plated dish on Alexandra's desk and popped it in her mouth, slurping like a serf. Her gaze flickered over the neatly arranged stacks of stationery and steel pens. "And writing a love letter on an imperial desk," she added playfully. "For shame."

"I asked permission." In truth, Lena was only transcribing English letters for practice. She didn't dare write anything more important in public. Still, the elegance of the desk, even the smooth, solid nib of the pen felt unnerving. The few nice items her family owned were never used, but stowed away in a trunk, as though to emphasize that life in Archangel was hardly worth the trouble.

"What kind of man pleases you, Lenichka?" Masha asked as she circled the desk. "A fair Ukrainian or swarthy Tatar?"

Lena snickered.

"It's the latter then," Masha said triumphantly. "A dark stranger with eyes like coal. Does he have a mustache? Does it tickle when you kiss?"

Lena caught the rancid smell of wet fur and cheap vanilla perfume as Masha peered over her shoulder. "That's not a love letter, just English nonsense. How can anyone understand those funny shapes?"

"Lower your voices, ladies. You never know who might sneak in and overhear your secrets."

Lena dropped her pen. Pavel stood at the door. Once again, he'd caught her off guard. "Have you heard of knocking? It's a custom we've developed a taste for in this country. Perhaps you don't have doors in Virginia?"

"You've acquired a lady's wit, little seamstress," he told her.

"And you've acquired a tongue, prizefighter," Lena replied. "For the longest time, I doubted you had one."

Pavel smiled playfully, a stark contrast to the formality of his black-and-gold tunic. A surge of warmth simmered in Lena's stomach. He switched to English. "The dowager prefers a silent, captive audience. Remember what I told you about boxing? Self-protection first."

At the mention of the dowager, Lena turned to the door and waited, holding her breath, half-expecting Marie to materialize out of thin air. When this failed to happen, her shoulders relaxed. Pavel had come only to see her.

"I shall keep your words in mind when next I see the dowager." She picked up the pen once more, hoping he'd summon an excuse to remain.

He gave Masha a sideways glance. Pavel knew better than to push his luck. "I will let you return to your tasks, ladies." He gave a little bow and exited.

Lena watched him, twisting a lock of hair in her fingers. She almost wished Marie would come to the palace more often, bringing Pavel with her, but then did she really wish that on Alexandra? She wondered if there weren't some way that she might see him sooner, perhaps a task she could run between Alexandra and the dowager empress.

"What has come over you?" Masha's voice startled Lena. Masha crinkled her lips as though she'd smelled something foul. "I thought you had a Cossack lover."

Lena folded the paper with the English letters. She tried to make a sharp crease in the middle, but found her hand moved with difficulty.

"This is the second time I've seen you together now. He is no Cossack."

"You're making wild assumptions. You don't even understand English."

"Don't think I haven't noticed the changes in you over the past few months." Strands of pale blond hair slipped out of Masha's hat and curled down her forehead. "Everyone figures you're in love. He's the one?"

"Your imagination has gotten the best of you."

"I don't think so. I know you're from up north in the middle of nowhere. Maybe you don't understand what could happen if you two were caught together."

Lena's foot tapped the floor. Did Masha really think she knew nothing of the terrible things that happened to people because they were different? If anything, it was worse back home, where superstition governed action. She had worked hard to separate herself from that place. The last thing she needed was a silly chambermaid spreading idle rumors. "In Archangel, we have a saying about these matters."

Masha leaned forward, her features more relaxed now. "Oh! I love country talk."

"They say a dog should make sure its own ass is clean before it sticks its nose where it doesn't belong."

Lena held her breath. She had no idea whether or not Masha had her own secrets to protect, but it stood to reason. Sure enough, Masha's cheeks puffed out in response.

"Don't presume to guess what the empress thinks," Lena added. "That's blasphemy."

Masha released the air in her cheeks. Then she burst into a fit of high laughter. She gave Lena a playful slap on the shoulder and collapsed on the chaise longue.

"I've underestimated you," Masha said. "I should have known. It's always the quiet ones. Fine. To each his own I always say. Just be careful. Strange things happen around this place. I feel it. I wouldn't want you to get caught in the middle."

"He's showing, isn't he?" Alexandra patted her abdomen, swollen underneath a violet kimono. "It's so wearying this time around, so different. The shifts in my mood, the way I walk. Not that I'm complaining. Quite the contrary."

Lena nodded vaguely and tugged an ivory brush through Alexandra's loose curls. Alexandra took another puff on her cigarette and patted her cheeks, appraising her reflection in the low electric lamplight. "I look tired. Perhaps I shouldn't appear in public at all. But our friend Dr. Vachot thought it best I stick to a normal routine."

Every day, Lena overheard some new and increasingly out-landish story about Phillipe Vachot. He'd made ghosts material-ize or hypnotized young women so they would consent to sleep with him. Deep in her heart, she knew Pavel was correct about Vachot. She should try to convince Alexandra to dismiss him, but couldn't quite summon the words to do so.

"You've always been good to me, Lenichka," Alexandra con-tinued. "I confess I didn't summon you here for hairdressing. I must take you into my confidence once more."

Lena removed a long string of silky pearls from an enameled jewelry box and strung them around Alexandra's pale neck. She remembered Marie's cool hands and her dark brows slanting. *Do exactly as I say.*

"What are people saying about me?" Alexandra asked. "And my condition?"

"Everyone rejoiced at the good news." The flattery came easily to Lena's lips, as it did for everyone in the royal family's service. She smiled at Alexandra's reflection in the long mirror. "People sense your joy. They see you're radiant."

Alexandra's lips were taut, her tone smooth as ice. "I asked for the truth."

Lena fumbled with the pearls and they fell on the vanity with a loud clatter.

"I'm sorry." Alexandra closed her eyes and touched her fore-head. "My migraines are worrying me again. I haven't slept well. But I haven't forgotten your help and I haven't forgotten what you told me of your brother and his troubles."

Lena stared at the patterns of gray wreaths on the mauve carpet. She'd received another letter from her mother. Anton's friend
had been released from jail, no further questions asked and no
further suspects taken into custody. Alexandra was as good as her
word, but Lena hadn't thanked her directly. She sensed this wasn't
how these matters were best handled.

"I understand." Alexandra tilted her long cigarette holder onto
the edge of a crystal tray. "I would do anything for my brother,
Ernest. I suppose you've heard. His fickle wife abandoned him for
Nicky's cousin, Kyril."

Lena took a moment to recall the right words in English. "It is
an unfortunate situation," she said carefully.

"It's shameful. Grandmama would never have stood for this.
He can't marry her. The fool and the adulteress deserve perma-
nent exile." Alexandra reached for Lena's wrist and squeezed. "I
won't let the corruption of Saint Petersburg touch you. Terrible
things happen in this city. You wouldn't know, coming from the
north where life is clean and simple."

Most of the things Lena saw as a girl were neither clean nor
simple. She'd once watched a bear, frenzied from baiting, tear
half the scalp off a screaming child.

"As long as your brother is under your influence, I can't imagine he will do anything but repent," Alexandra said, releasing
Lena's hand.

Lena nodded and reached for Alexandra's evening gown, a
pale pink brocade studded with tiny diamonds. Alexandra stamped
the remains of her cigarette into dust in the ashtray and stood so
Lena could drape the gown over her head and shoulders. "This is
my dilemma. I must remain vigilant and constantly on alert. I
must know what people say about me. I notice, even when they

think I don't. Their voices draw to a sudden hush when I walk into the room. Servants. Guests. Nicky's family. They're the worst. I can't trust my own husband's family. I can't sleep for worrying."

That explained the dark semicircles shadowing Alexandra's eyes and the thin lines that had appeared on her forehead, despite the heavy cream she applied faithfully every night. Lena smoothed the gown. Alexandra took a decanter of rose water and sprayed the scent about her neck. "I suppose there are some in Nicky's family who pray I never bear an heir to the throne. I know Cousin Kyril hopes I'll throw myself in the Neva River." Alexandra's gaze wandered to a sideboard, where one of Olga's French dolls had been left out. "Sometimes I think my daughters are the only ones who love me."

"The tsar loves you beyond reason," Lena said.

"Yes." A faint smile played on Alexandra's lips. "But what good does it do me to be loved by my husband when the rest of the world is against me? Nicky will try to protect me, but I must help him as best I can. Delivering an heir will go a long way toward that end."

Lena hesitated, brush in hand. Pavel and Masha both believed the real power in Saint Petersburg resided in Marie's small frame. If she betrayed Marie's confidence, Lena would face the dowager's wrath. Yet she thought Alexandra had a right to know. "The dowager . . ."

Alexandra spun around and seized Lena by the shoulders. "What?"

"Dowager Empress Marie requested my presence in the birth room."

"That's wonderful news." Alexandra's long lashes beat furiously against her pale cheeks. "Mama knows how much I rely on you."

Lena began to fidget. "I helped my mother sometimes."

Alexandra delicately raised her eyebrows. When necessary, she could convey her power with precision. "Surely you did not mislead me regarding your credentials."

"I did not mislead you. Only I'm afraid I'll get in the doctors' way."

"Nonsense. You'll see me through the ordeal. I think of you as a friend now."

"The dowager fears you might not have a son," Lena blurted.

Alexandra watched Lena in the mirror. "I confess. I sympathize with her anxiety. Who can blame her after four girls? She thinks I'm bad luck. I used to think this way myself. But not anymore. Faith will see me through this ordeal. If I believe in my son, then all will be well. Monsieur Vachot said as much."

She patted her stomach gently. Lena's heart melted. The empress looked so protective of her unborn child, and yet so vulnerable.

"But I don't trust the court doctors," Alexandra said. "Stay with me when I go into labor. Promise you won't leave. No matter what."

Lena nodded. "I promise. I'll stay no matter what."

PARIS

OCTOBER 1941

Early in the morning, Charlotte had raised the blackout shades drawn over the windows in the front room. Luc lurked under the sloping eaves of the building across the street, huddled into a raincoat. She watched what happened next with her heart in her throat. When the stranger came, he had the hood of his jacket pulled low over his head. Charlotte could not make out his face. She supposed that was the way most members of the Maquis made their way across the city. She watched Luc slip a crumpled wad of bills into the stranger's hands. And then Luc walked in a little circle, waiting.

The car itself didn't impress Charlotte. It was just a beat-up sedan with broken taillights and deflating tires. Still, she'd grown accustomed to squeaking bicycles and tired horses yanked out of retirement. Charlotte worried over this now. They'd thought a car necessary, but the vehicle might arouse suspicion. Luc wouldn't tell her what the stranger had placed in the trunk of the car for them to smuggle across the border into Spain. At any moment, German soldiers in their drab green uniforms could have sprung out from behind the building and arrested Luc. She'd waited, clutching the cross around her neck, wondering what they would do if they caught him.

Fortunately, the soldiers hadn't materialized. Now Luc turned the vehicle onto a narrow dirt highway heading south. They were finally leaving the city, and yet a bubble of tension kept growing inside of her, threatening to pop.

She craned her neck to check on her son, curled into a fetal position and asleep in the backseat. Before they left, Luc had given him medicine to make him drowsy. He'd mentioned something about valerian root. He'd failed to mention how helpless it would make the boy look. Laurent's eyelids drooped and his head fell to his shoulder at an unnatural angle. "You're sure the medicine won't hurt him?" Charlotte asked.

"He'll sleep. That's all. Do you think I'd hurt . . . ?" Luc took another puff on his cigarette and blew the smoke out the window.

He didn't have to complete the thought. *Do you think I'd hurt my own son?*

"Anyway, I thought you wanted to find out what happened to your friend Kshesinskaya," he said. "You haven't asked after her."

Charlotte had been afraid to ask. "Did you learn anything?"

"She hasn't been arrested. At least no one thinks she has. Other than that, I don't know. I only had a minute with the courier, when he dropped off the car."

Relief coursed through her. "I'll write to her once we get to my parents' house."

"Don't do that. She risked herself to protect you. We've done all we can for now. Try to relax so you'll be ready at the checkpoint." Luc's lips twitched. If Charlotte didn't know better, she would have thought he was suppressing a laugh. "Now say it again."

"But I sound like a fool." Charlotte's fingers flexed with irritation. She held up the Spanish phrase book once more. *"Le puedes repeterez, por favor."*

"Puedes repetir, por favor," Luc insisted. "Please repeat that. Trust me. You'll need to know that one."

Charlotte lowered the book. "What's the use? I can't concentrate. I've lost my touch with languages. I guess I'm getting old. At least it will be easier for Laurent."

She sighed and gazed out the window. Husks of barns and cottages dotted the low hills on either side of the road, victims of the Germans' last bombing raid. Seeing the countryside this way tarnished the memories of better times, as if she had driven past the house in which she'd grown up only to find the current owners kept it in disrepair. Charlotte thought then of everything else she missed: amaretto liqueur, imported Billie Holiday and Glenn

Miller records, patent leather shoes dyed red. How had life become all dry potatoes and boorish Prussian military marches? She felt the weight of it pressing her chest, the sense that all her happiness was in the past.

Charlotte tried to focus on the route, not the landscape. She and Luc used to take this road when they went to Burgundy for the weekend, before they were married. They stayed in a cabin loaned to them by one of Luc's journalist friends. Luc brought along plenty of red wine and baguettes. At night, he tried to shave with a dull razor and no mirror. She used to touch the blobs of red on his face where his hand had slipped and he'd punctured the skin.

"What are you thinking about?" The orange tip of Luc's cigarette glowed in the dim daylight.

"Nothing." A lump stuck in her throat and she forced it down.

"We traveled this way before," Luc said, his voice warm as melted chocolate.

Charlotte tapped her fingers on the dashboard. It made a hollow sound. She hated the confinement of the car. She longed to be outside, moving.

Smoke curled around Luc's face. He laughed. "Remember the old shrew that sold me baguettes before we left? She called me a hooligan because I always paid in change. She never let me leave the shop without counting every last coin. If she had enlisted, we would have driven the Huns back over the Rhine."

"I remember." Being near him, it all came rushing back. His scent, his gaze, even the way he held his cigarette. Charlotte stared out the window. Luc fell silent again. She supposed it was his way of declaring the subject off-limits. She was grateful they were in agreement on that much at least.

A dark Daimler-Mercedes passed them on the right, rattling their windows. She watched the little red flags with black swastikas bat back and forth in the wind. The brake lights illuminated. They hadn't traveled but a few kilometers past the city limits and already they were approaching a checkpoint. The booth looked as sturdy as the German soldiers who'd erected it.

Luc pulled to a stop behind the Mercedes. In the booth ahead, a gendarme slid the thin glass window open and poked his head out. The men inside the vehicle cranked their window down and dutifully turned their travel passes over to him.

"You remember what to tell him if he asks?" Luc rolled the window down. It squeaked horribly. A blast of cold air made Charlotte shiver.

"*Bonjour.*" She heard the gendarme greet the car in front of them in a classic French singsong, so different from the staccato rhythm of the Germans.

"Is this why you took this route?" she said in a low voice. "He's not German."

Luc tossed his cigarette and rolled the window back up. "He's a collaborator. That's worse. Say as little as possible."

Charlotte wished Luc had said something more reassuring. She only hoped her lips would part when needed. She turned to place a hand on Laurent's shoulder.

"I know this guard, but I usually don't bring along a woman and a child," Luc said. "Hopefully he's feeling pliable today, but you can't arouse his suspicion. Do you understand?"

The Mercedes peeled out, spewing grimy exhaust fumes that irritated her throat, making her cough. Luc clutched the worn gearshift and pulled up to the booth.

The young gendarme had a pale complexion, ruddy cheeks,

and merry green eyes at odds with the severity of his black uniform. His light brown hair had been shorn close to his skull, as the Germans preferred. "Ah, monsieur. Good to see you again."

Luc shrugged, not in an unpleasant or disrespectful way, but no one could accuse him of fawning, either.

"And how are you, madame? This is your wife? Strange you have not mentioned her before." The gendarme addressed Luc, but didn't take his eyes off Charlotte.

"Sister," Luc said.

"Sister? And this young fellow in the back belongs to which one of you? No, let me guess. He is your nephew. He belongs to the lady."

"Correct," Luc said.

The gendarme knocked on the back window. "Sleepy this morning, isn't he?"

The gendarme's cheerful voice shredded Charlotte's last nerve. She'd expected harsh words, a probing stare, and careful examination of their documents. In the end, this friendly interest might prove more damning. It required more improvisation. "He stayed up late last night." Charlotte tried not to stumble on the words. "He's a sound sleeper."

"Lucky you." The gendarme winked. "Leaves your nights wide open, doesn't it?"

In better times, she'd have had something cutting to say in reply. Now she only gave the gendarme a curt whisper of a smile.

"You have your papers?" he asked.

Luc brushed Charlotte's arm as he reached into the glove compartment and fumbled with the crumpled travel passes. "Damn nuisance," he muttered.

"Perhaps, but they're deemed necessary."

Luc handed his papers over. The gendarme squinted. "Where are you heading?"

"The Dordogne," Luc replied. "We have family there. You can check."

"No need. Still, you wouldn't suppose so many people have family near the Spanish border." He handed Luc his papers. "And for you and the boy, madame."

Charlotte willed her hand not to shake as she passed her papers over. More than anything, the lack of control over her own body's motions scared her.

The gendarme flipped through the papers. Luc had told her that the travel pass for the occupied zone belonged to a woman who died in an Allied bombing raid, along with her three-year-old son. "You're thirty-nine?" The gendarme gave her the once-over, head to toe. "I'd never have guessed. Especially since you have such a young boy. And your birthday is in April, same as mine."

She had memorized every word of that document, in case any soldiers asked. The woman's birth date was closer to her own. "You misread. I was born in August."

"So you were." Still, he didn't return the papers. He didn't take his gaze off the picture. "Pardon me. I noticed the photograph . . . it is very strange. It may require more time on my part." He grabbed a small phone inside the booth.

Charlotte pressed her feet hard against the floorboard. If the gendarme detained them, the Germans would send them east to nowhere. They'd chop off Laurent's hands so he couldn't fight them.

Luc placed his hand gently on her wrist. He reached again into the glove compartment and withdrew a second envelope, this one stuffed with bills. Luc's tone grew exceedingly reasonable as he addressed the gendarme. "Not necessary."

The gendarme cradled the phone back on the receiver. He took the envelope from Luc's hands and made a show of counting the bills inside. "Times are difficult for the Maquis, I see."

Luc's voice remained steady. "The amount is fair."

The gendarme stuffed the bills back in the envelope and extended his arm, returning them to Luc. "Not everyone's resources are dwindling."

Charlotte stared at the gendarme's smooth, pale hand as it reached for the phone again. The movement seemed to happen in slow motion, like a film. She needed to do something, anything to stop the gendarme from making that call. She'd close her hands around his throat.

"I think it's her," she heard the gendarme say. "Very well."

"Luc . . ." she began.

He stared straight ahead. He'd withdrawn into his own world, with his own worries, where other people were only a nuisance.

"Move," she whispered. Charlotte reached down and shifted the gears.

That was enough. Luc slammed the accelerator down to the floor. Charlotte jolted out of her seat as the car sped forward.

Three shots fired. She screamed and put her hand on Laurent, who stirred in the backseat. Luc kept his hands on the wheel, trying to maintain control. Charlotte gripped the sides of her seat, feeling the rips in the leather and the bits of stuffing flaking around her legs. They might still make it. If she focused hard enough, if she pulled every reserve of strength and concentrated, she might will this into being. The engine would roar. They would speed off. The gendarme would choke and cough on the exhaust.

They would finally be free of the soldiers, free of the soul-crushing paperwork, free of the officers' questions about Charlotte and her family.

The car came to a shuddering halt. The acrid smell of burning rubber filled the air. The gendarme approached them, his gun drawn and pointed at Luc's head.

Nine

Rays of sunlight slashed through the slats in the window shades, promising a bright, chilly mid-Atlantic day. Veronica raised her arms high above her head, and then dropped them at her sides, safely cocooned from the outside world.

On the hotel room's desk, she spotted her research notebook. A wave of guilt washed over her. She'd intended to get more work done on this trip, at least strategize her visit with Alexei Romanov in advance. Abuela was right. She had let Michael distract her from her work. The heavy scent of sex still clung to the bed. The previous night had been intense, better than she expected. Her skin felt pliable and sensitive to the touch.

"Wake up, sleepyhead," Veronica said, and turned over, expecting to uncover Michael beneath the thick white comforter. She patted lumps on his side of the bed, but found only damp, twisted sheets. Her heart dropped to her stomach. Perhaps he'd packed up while she slept in. She would find a note on the door telling her he needed to return to Los Angeles unexpectedly. She pulled the comforter over her shoulders, trying to summon a shell to close around her heart.

The lock on the door unlatched. Michael walked in carrying a copy of *The New York Times* and a white paper bag. His hair was tousled and he wore the same rumpled shirt she remembered from the night before. He hadn't shaved. He looked perfect. She wanted to drag him back into bed.

Michael kissed her forehead and handed her the bag. Grease stains and rainbow-colored sprinkles stuck to the bottom.

"Donuts?"

He set the bag on the nightstand and plopped down next to her, bouncing the bed. Veronica ran her hand along his jawline, played with the rough bristles. She leaned into Michael and kissed the side of his neck.

He leaned on his elbow, head propped in one hand, the other lightly stroking her inner thigh. "So I have a question. Why now?"

Veronica nudged her nose against his forearm. "Because it felt wonderful."

"That's good to know." Michael arched his eyebrows mischievously, a satyr out to chase a wood nymph. She didn't think it would be so bad, the life of a wood nymph.

"But in Los Angeles you made it clear you needed time and wanted to take things slowly," he continued. "What made you change your mind?"

This wasn't exactly the pillow talk she'd expected. "You swept me off my feet."

"I think not. Remember, you lured me in here under false pretenses." He ran his hand through her hair, which stuck out in all directions. "By the way, I like this look. Very punk."

"Just trying to recapture my lost youth," she said.

He tickled her right on the curve of her waist until she squealed with delight. "Let's talk about this lost youth of yours," he said.

"Not much to tell, I'm afraid." She traced the edges of the dark Celtic band encircling his upper arm. "What's going on here? Are you an Irish prince as well?"

"What went on there was college," he said. "I thought it looked cool."

"You thought it looked cool." She sighed. "I wish I wanted to look cool in college. All I thought about was graduate school. I didn't party. I guess I've always preferred books to people. It sounds like you were wilder than me."

"My job was to keep wild people out," Michael said. "I worked as a bouncer at a club in Chelsea. That's how I paid for law school at NYU."

Veronica sat up. He may as well have said he was an astronaut. "Where did you work? Studio 54?"

Michael made a face. "How old do you think I am?"

"Sorry." She couldn't wipe the smile off her face. The Romanov heir working as a bouncer. The image appealed to her sense of irony. "Seriously, I'm impressed."

"It was Chelsea. Once I caught a guy urinating on the side of the building. He tried to take a swing at me. I told him I'd call the cops and he started to cry."

"I think you're holding out. I bet it got rougher than that."

He gave her a crooked smile.

"At least you enjoyed your youth," she added. "I never knew my mom, but I think she would have been a good influence in that respect."

His expression changed abruptly, grew more serious. Suddenly, she wished she hadn't mentioned her mother. "What do you mean?"

Veronica looked at her cuticles. Maybe she had been waiting for the right person to tell. She wasn't sure. "Abuela says my mom loved history and novels and art and all that. She always made books available to me while I was growing up. I guess it was her way of keeping me and my mother connected. But Abuela also says my mom refused to stay home and study every night. Abuela makes it sound like a character flaw. Did I tell you my mother went to Madrid for her junior year abroad?"

Michael shook his head, focus still intense.

"From what I can gather, it sounds like my mom had to beg Abuela to let her go. You can probably figure out the rest of that story." Veronica stared at the white bumps of plaster on the ceiling above. Her hands felt clammy. "A literature professor knocked her up and nine months later I popped out. My mother dropped out of university."

Michael understood how to listen. He didn't pat her hand. He made sure she was finished before he asked, "Did you ever try to find your father?"

"It upset me too much. Why torture myself? I'd rather focus my energy on other people's problems, historical problems, where I can remain objective."

"It makes more sense now. Why your grandmother is so protective of you. She's worried you'll repeat your mother's mistake."

"I already made that mistake." Veronica's head throbbed. She rubbed her bare left ring finger. "I was pregnant. That's why I was engaged. At least I'm pretty sure that's why he finally asked me to marry him. I didn't let myself think about it. Then I had a miscarriage."

Michael enveloped her in his arms. Still, his touch felt remote. She was stuck in the tiny bathroom of that shabby apartment in Redondo Beach, doubled over. The cramping pain wrapped around her middle as she stared at the dark brown blood clotted in the toilet. She'd curled into a fetal position, her cheek resting on the cold white tile. She'd felt empty inside, but it was more than the baby. Something else was gone. She didn't know how to explain the sense of foreboding, like this was only the beginning.

Her fiancé had knocked on the bathroom door. She couldn't answer. He wasn't the right person to tell. Maybe then she should have known it wouldn't end well. He barged in anyway and saw for himself.

"We carried on, but I made all the wedding plans," Veronica said. "Whenever I asked his opinion about anything, he said he didn't care. He didn't talk to anyone, not my family, not his own family. The night before, an hour before the rehearsal, he called it off. I was drying my hair when the phone rang. I went back to the bathroom and sat on the toilet. I didn't tell anyone for an hour."

She paused, the physical nature of the release taking her by surprise.

"I thought you should know," she said quietly.

"God, Veronica." Michael tightened his grip. "What's wrong with this guy?"

She caressed the back of his neck, just below the hairline where the skin felt softest. Now that the doors of her past had swung open, she felt compelled to look into his. "What about you? What happened with you and your ex?"

He shrugged. "Apparently, I wasn't a challenge anymore."

Veronica smoothed his hair back away from his face. "I don't think so. She made that up to feel better. She just couldn't handle you."

Michael snuggled his lips into her neck, every kiss an aftershock of pleasure. She wanted to stay in his arms, her legs intertwined with his, not facing reality. She wanted to believe every word he said.

By the time they emerged from the subway station, on an unassuming uptown side street, the bright morning sunshine had faded.

The office of the Romanov Guardsmen was located in a residential building with exposed brick and zigzagging fire escapes. Flowerpots, murals, and air-conditioning units lined the windows of the residences on the upper floors. Veronica doublechecked the address in her notebook.

"I know. It's not exactly the Winter Palace." Michael regarded the building with a skeptical eye. "'Keepers of the Russian Throne' indeed. I wish you'd reconsider this. When they start saying terrible things about me—"

"I'll tell them they're wrong." She jabbed her finger in his chest, harder than she intended. "We've been through all of this. Why don't you come in with me?"

"Romanov wants to protect his claim. He won't allow for other possibilities."

"I don't get it. Yesterday, you were desperate to protect me."

Michael's shoulders slumped. She was about to apologize when he reached into the front pocket of his coat, withdrew a small brown bag, and gave it to her. She opened it and saw a small canister.

"Is this pepper spray?" she asked.

"Mace. I picked it up this morning with the paper and donuts."

"I don't want this. I don't know what to do with Mace."

Michael reached for her purse and undid the clasp in front. "You press the button. Keep it in here. Just in case."

"This is ridiculous."

"Come on. It'll make me feel better."

"Fine." She dropped the canister into her purse.

"I'll wait for you right there." He flipped his thumb back to indicate a park across the street. "If you need anything, yell. I'll keep an eye on the door. Remember, I used to do that for a living." He kissed her cheek.

Veronica watched him as he withdrew to the park. He settled on a bench with a clear view of the front door, her personal bodyguard whether she liked it or not. She straightened her back, turned, and pressed the buzzer on the intercom.

A fuzzy voice crackled on the other side. "May I help you?"

She leaned into the speaker. "This is Veronica Herrera. I made an appointment."

The buzzer screeched and she stepped into the building's lobby. Crumbling crown moldings of fleur-de-lis graced the corners of the ceiling. A spiral staircase led to the second floor, as did a tiny elevator. The overhead lights flickered brightly for a minute or two, and then made a hissing sound and went dim. Veronica decided to take the stairs.

The apartment wasn't difficult to locate. The imperial double-headed eagle had been posted on the door. As she approached, a frail-looking older man stuck his head out to greet her. He had a round face and a neatly trimmed white beard, Santa Claus after Weight Watchers. Underneath thin-rimmed glasses the man's eyes were a startling shade of light blue. The color of his suit jacket matched his eyes. "Dr. Herrera! What a pleasure. I'm Alexei

Romanov." He planted a quick peck on her fingertips and ushered her inside.

Inside, the apartment looked like a special episode of *Hoarders* for slavophiles. Pendants of the four grand duchesses were suspended from rusted chains along the ceiling. A collection of Nicholas and Alexandra postage stamps hung on the wall, next to icons of the royal family dressed in robes, with halos of light emanating from their heads. She took in the strangely intoxicating scent of the decaying books stacked around the room.

As Alexei Romanov helped her out of her coat, Veronica stared at a lavishly framed portrait of the royal family that dominated the back wall. She guessed the photograph had been taken around 1910. Nicholas and Alexandra sat with the heir, little Alexei, posed cross-legged, the four beautiful girls forming a semicircle around them. Veronica could never look at the grand duchesses without imagining the way they died, screaming, white dresses splattered with blood. She'd read of that night so often. Sometimes she felt she had been right there with the family. Even with the heat blasting, she shivered at the thought.

"Isn't it gorgeous?" Romanov hung her coat on a wobbly knob by the front door, underneath a Russian flag. "It's a miracle the Bolsheviks didn't take a bayonet to it during the Revolution. We purchased it for a song in the nineties."

Veronica turned her attention to Nicholas and Alexandra. Nicholas looked clear-eyed and untroubled, immune to the difficulties ahead. But the pressure of caring for her hemophiliac son had already taken a toll on Alexandra. Despite her elegant gown and strands of pearls, her features looked slack, her eyes haunted. She was thick around the waist, no longer the famous beauty of her youth. Even over the hundred-year gap, it saddened Veronica to see another woman so emotionally drained.

Romanov made a clicking sound with his tongue. "Such a tragedy. Restoration is the least we can do for them."

"I suppose that's one way of looking at it," Veronica responded primly. "Of course, the best interests of the country should be the primary concern."

"The interests of the ruler and the country are one and the same," Romanov replied easily.

"A constitutional monarchy isn't to your liking?"

"I never said that. But as you know, Russians demand strong leaders. Please have a seat."

He moved a stack of books aside to clear a path to his desk, and gestured to an antique rosewood armchair with an embroidered cushion. When Veronica sat down, bits of hardened thread poked through her skirt and black tights and into her legs. She shifted on the cushion, wishing she'd worn jeans instead.

"You share your name with the tsarevich, the heir to the throne," she said.

"My family deemed it appropriate." Alexei Romanov straightened his tie and took a seat opposite her, behind a mahogany desk. For an instant, his bright eyes reminded her of the tsar in the photograph.

Veronica withdrew a pen from her purse for notes. "And you have information about Alexandra that might be useful to me?"

"Oh, yes. We'll get to all of that soon enough. We were delighted to find an academic who favors restoration."

"Wait a second." Veronica's eyes widened. "Is that a joke?"

Alexei Romanov shook his head, looking suddenly troubled.

"First of all, I never said I supported restoration," she said. "But let's say I did. What would it matter? The public doesn't care what academics say about anything. And even if they did, I'm not some BBC-ready, sonorous-voiced Oxford lad."

"You told us you're writing a biography of the empress," Romanov said. "We expect you will treat the empress with honor in your work. That's rare."

"I try. But either way, I work at an unranked university. And they don't even want me. If you're looking for sanction from the academic community, look elsewhere." Veronica took stock of the room once more. "You keep saying 'we.' Who is this 'we'? I only see you. Where are the other Romanov Guardsmen?"

"As the heir apparent I run the organization. But our membership just surpassed three hundred, all individuals of documented royal or noble descent living across the world. At least for now. With restoration, the Romanov Diaspora will soon end."

Veronica moved uncomfortably in her seat. "I heard you met with Vladimir Putin," she said. "Did he endorse your claim?"

Romanov held her gaze for a moment. She wondered if she had made a mistake to raise the topic. Then he let out a light smattering of a laugh. "Vlad is smarter than that. Endorsing a claimant would hardly be the most politic course of action. Still, he's a fascinating man. For all his KGB bona fides, a traditional aristocrat through and through. Besides, who needs Vlad when I have this?" Romanov indicated a photograph on his desk. He looked twenty years younger and debonair in a white tuxedo. He stood next to the Queen of England in her signature pillbox hat.

"You met the Queen of England," Veronica said. "That's fun, I suppose. But she meets many people. She met the Spice Girls."

"She stood for me when I entered the room. Do you know what that means?"

Veronica was quiet for a moment. "The Queen of England only stands for other monarchs. That's the protocol."

"Precisely." Romanov grinned. She caught another glimpse of this man's faint resemblance to Nicholas II, something about the line of his cheeks. "My grandfather and father would have disapproved. They hated the British for abandoning the tsar and the family to their murderers after the Revolution. But I felt it was important."

"It seems as though you've garnered at least implicit support for your title."

Romanov's smile disappeared. "The Romanov Guardsmen stand ready to embrace sublime destiny: the restoration of the throne. But there's still the matter of your friend, the False Mikhail."

"You don't believe his genealogy is accurate?"

"I have come to believe he is a false man," Romanov said carefully.

"He poses no threat, not if the Queen of England stands for you."

"You believe him, though, don't you?"

Veronica tried to laugh, but it came out more as a snort. "What does it matter? He has no interest in pursuing his claim."

"Is that what he said? I wouldn't believe a word of his nonsense. Tell me, how much do you know about this gentleman?"

"He's an attorney . . ." Veronica heard her voice trail off.

"Still helping the poor Russian émigrés open art galleries and espresso bars in West Hollywood, is he? Let me guess. Despite this professed disinterest in his claim, he accompanied you on this trip? No doubt he's waiting somewhere outside?"

Veronica's pulse jumped. "How did you know that?"

"We've tracked Mikhail's actions for several years now. The community of Russian émigrés in Los Angeles is strong and many of them sympathize with our cause. Many more than you might think. They help when we require help."

Like the Russian man who had followed them into the Forbes Gallery. Veronica glanced at the door, calculating how quickly she could escape. "You had us followed here in New York as well?"

"For your protection, Dr. Herrera, I assure you."

"Why do I need protection? I don't need some creep following me."

"Creep? I'll tell Grigori to tone down his affectations."

"You didn't answer my question," she said. "Why do you think I need protection?"

Romanov swiveled in his chair to face the portrait of the royal family, looking up at the tsar as though for inspiration. "You said Mikhail shows no interest in his claim. Did he tell you about the time he spent here in college? When he was a young man he spent hours poring over our records."

A thin spike of panic pounded a nerve in Veronica's head. Why hadn't Michael mentioned this detail before? Still, she felt compelled to defend him. "Why are you trying to turn me against Michael? Why do you hate him?"

"I don't hate anyone." Romanov sounded vaguely offended. "I don't trust Mikhail. That much is true. I wish to support the true heir to the Russian throne. Not anyone can step in and fill that role. I can't stake the reputation of this organization on a man who is perpetuating a wild hoax."

"Or you don't want any rival claimants."

"Dr. Herrera, it is most important you understand my personal quest." Romanov leaned forward, his fragile, blue-veined hands splayed on the table. "The Guardsmen want the closest living Romanov relative recognized as the rightful heir. It is the cause dearest to my heart. If Mikhail's claim is true, I'll relinquish my claim. Willingly." Romanov began to fidget in his chair now. It made him look less sincere and more like an impatient schoolboy. "But there are many complications to his tall tale. First of all, there's the matter of his convenient memory lapses. He'd mention something his mother or his grandmother said. When we asked for specifics like times and dates, he wouldn't provide them. Why is he so secretive?"

"He has documents to back up his genealogy."

"We've seen some of those documents," Romanov admitted, "enough to get him through the door and to our records in the first place, anyway. Still, documents can be forged. Why hasn't he agreed to a DNA test?"

Her head throbbed now, the pain sharp little pulses. Why hadn't she thought of this? Had she been afraid of ruining the dream? "I'm sure if he were asked he would agree."

"I already asked. As a personal favor. He refused. Perhaps Mikhail is afraid of getting trapped in his own . . . delusions? I don't know the technical term. Then again, if he has the wherewithal not to take a DNA test, he must know exactly what he's doing. He's a con artist. It's the only explanation." Romanov released a sad little sigh. "We're worried for your sake, Dr. Herrera. If he has no interest in staking a claim to the throne, ask yourself why he's suddenly expressed interest in an academic? A professor of Russian history no less?"

Veronica's heart sank. She had asked herself the very same questions when she first met Michael. "Maybe he enjoys my company."

Romanov gave a wisp of a smile and a gallant nod. "Of course. Your charms are numerous, I'm sure. But Mikhail's timing concerns us. These are volatile political times in Russia. We think he's using you for his own personal gain. Surely you understand our concerns, given the trouble over these past elections. A new tsar would be a useful distraction, a smokescreen for the powerful." Romanov drew his hands to his heart. "I am prepared for that environment. I've been preparing all my life. I speak four languages, though like most of the Russian nobility I admit a bias toward French. You see, I know the Russian culture and land inside out, Dr. Herrera. A flimflam man like Mikhail Karstadt in my place? *Quelle horreur.*"

Veronica would confront Michael about the DNA test. First, she needed to bring this conversation to an amicable close. "I think you're imagining dragons to slay. Even if restoration is possible, even if Michael is a con man or delusional or whatever else you think, what's the likelihood that anything would come of his claim anyway?"

"Russian history is that of sane and noble leadership?"

"Fair point." Veronica raised her hands up, palms forward, and then realized she was unconsciously mimicking Michael's gesture for surrender. She lowered her hands abruptly. "Still, I think you're overreacting."

"You must understand our concerns given the ludicrous nature of his claim."

"His family's genealogical records trace a direct line from the Iron Tsar Nicholas I. He's also a great-grandnephew of Nicholas II."

Romanov started to shake his head, looked confused.

She paused. "You've seen his family tree, haven't you?"

"I suppose you're referring to when Mikhail still traced his descent through Alexander Mikhailovich and the tsar's sister Xenia. Not that the twice-fold claim means anything. Matrilineal descent doesn't count, and my grandfather was far closer to the succession than his great-grandfather." Romanov raised a bushy white eyebrow. "He hasn't told you the other story? He hasn't told you who he thinks he is?"

Veronica's vision spotted and the room seemed to close in around her. "What other story?"

"His family believes there was a cover-up of some sort and the tsar himself was actually his great-grandfather."

She focused above Romanov's head, making out the picture of the royal family through the brown spots in her vision, Alexandra's sad eyes and Nicholas's tight, wry smile. "You're joking," was all she could manage.

"On this subject, I do not joke," Romanov said flatly. "That's the story we've tried to investigate further, what we hoped you could help us disprove. Or prove, I suppose. I'll still allow for that possibility."

"You're wrong," Veronica said. "Michael's not some nut who thinks Anastasia or Alexei escaped the carnage the night their family was murdered."

"Oh no." Romanov shook his head. "I see now he hasn't been forthright with you, Dr. Herrera. His tale is far more creative than that."

Ten

At the end of August, the family gathered at Peterhof, awaiting the birth of the fifth child. Alexandra complained of migraines and stomach pains, supposedly brought on by pregnancy but no doubt due to the probing stares of her husband's family.
—VERONICA HERRERA, The Reluctant Romanov

PETERHOF ESTATE
AUGUST 1902

Lena huddled with Masha at the window. They had traveled to the Upper Palace for the morning, volunteering to polish the black lacquer wall panels in the Chinese Wing. From this vantage point, Masha assured her, they'd get a clear view of the Romanovs as they descended on the summer residence.

While Lena dusted a decorative golden dragon hidden in a panel's crevice, Masha shared all the best gossip. The tsar's cousin, Alexander Mikhailovich, wished to divorce the tsar's sister. The tsar's other sister was about to run away with a common soldier. A powerful friend of the family demanded a certain nobleman be exiled to Turkey, all because the man had disappointed him in lovemaking. With all the family trouble, was it a wonder the tsar had so little time to spare for affairs of state?

Lena covered her mouth and laughed softly.

"Look." Masha touched Lena's arm and pointed out the window. A shiny red touring car had pulled into the paved turnaround. Lena spotted Marie in the back of the vehicle. She should have known the dowager and her entourage would be the first to arrive. Lena lengthened her neck to see over Masha's wide shoulder.

"Look at how she makes her people dress." Masha loosened the furry belt on her shirtwaist to scratch. "Even in the summer."

Marie's footmen wore moleskin driving caps, flowing scarves, and huge goggles, reminding Lena of characters in the Jules Verne novels her brother loved so much. One of the footmen set down thick pallets of wool carpet, forging a path for Marie as she made her way across the muddy footpath to the front door. Lena bit her lip and scanned their faces as they approached the palace. If Pavel were to join them at Peterhof, he would accompany Marie. Lena thought it might be fun to know of his presence in advance, to catch him by surprise, since he usually snuck up on her.

Slowly, the footmen unwrapped their scarves, and removed their goggles and caps. She didn't see Pavel.

She felt a sharp jab in her side. "He might come later," Masha whispered.

She eyed Masha, who shrugged and pushed a strand of pale blond hair behind her ear. "Maybe I'll find a Cossack for myself while we're here," Masha added. "Oh! Look at those two in the black Daimler. What have they done to that poor vehicle?"

A new automobile had pulled into the turnaround. The Russian flag was affixed to long poles that stuck out crookedly from each side of the car, like an insect's antennae. A silver-plated double-headed eagle crest had been embossed on the driver's door.

"That's the tsar's cousin Kyril," Masha said. "And Victoria Melita, the woman they call Ducky. I should have known. What showboats!"

Lena expected to see a chauffeur, but the tsar's cousin had driven himself. Kyril stretched his long legs and exited the vehicle. He was third in line to the throne, behind Nicholas's younger brother. He looked so stately and stern, even in his long driving coat and goggles, that Lena easily pictured him as tsar. A blasphemous thought, but she couldn't get the image out of her mind.

"Ducky is the one who divorced Alexandra's brother," Lena said, even as she wondered why Pavel hadn't accompanied Marie to Peterhof. "The empress hates them both." At least she had something to add to the conversation.

"Everyone knows that," Masha said, clearly disappointed. "They've been lovers for years. Though God knows what he sees in a dull Englishwoman."

Lena watched Kyril open the door for his companion. Ducky was tall and angular with sharp blue eyes. Given her sour expression, she struck Lena as the type of woman who would find difficulty inspiring affection in anyone, but then she didn't pretend to understand the minds of men. "Why do they call her Ducky?"

"Who knows," Masha replied. "She's English. They're full of nonsense. But don't be fooled by the silly name. She's all business. I hear these two are the ones who hired Phillipe Vachot, with his potions and magic spells, to discredit the empress. They'll faint dead away if she actually does push out a boy."

Lena twisted a lock of hair between her fingers. "Does the whole family expect a boy?"

"Of course they do. There will be big trouble if the baby isn't the heir."

"No one can hurt the empress," Lena said, forcing a confidence she didn't feel. "Too many people protect her."

Masha narrowed her eyes. "Including you?"

"I was thinking of the tsar."

"Maybe you're right," Masha admitted. "They say Kyril and Ducky will do anything to get nearer the throne, but I'm not sold on them. What a pair of cold fish!"

Lena cupped her hand over her mouth but didn't bother to stifle the giggle. "They do both look like they're sucking lemons," she said.

Masha suddenly bolted upright, knocking her head against a petal-shaped lantern dangling from the ceiling. She rubbed her skull with one hand and yanked the drapes shut with the other. Then she grabbed a dry cloth from their bucket of cleaning supplies and began to dust Alexandra's collection of porcelain vases and plates from the Orient.

Lena spun around. Marie stood at the door, absent her usual fanfare, staring right at Lena but addressing Masha. "You—look at me when I'm talking to you. Surely you have more pressing matters than dust on a few old vases."

Masha responded with a clumsy curtsy. Marie lifted the skirts on her tailored black traveling suit and approached the windows. She drew the drapes back. Outside, Ducky made elaborate motions to indicate that the house servants should fetch her traveling cases from the back of the car.

"I told them not to come." Marie arched her dark brows. "You girls don't be so hard on Kyril's adulterous lover, though. She is as beautiful on the inside as she is on the outside. And that's the truth."

Marie's eyes met Lena's and twinkled. Everyone said the tsar had kind eyes, and now Lena saw that kindness reflected in his mother's. Lena realized that with regard to Kyril and Ducky at least, Marie was on Alexandra's side.

All night, a storm lashed the coast. A clap of thunder jolted Lena awake from an already fitful sleep. She checked the clock on the wall and saw it was two in the morning. Then she leaned back onto her thin mattress, gathering her bearings in the hot, humid sleeping quarters. Someone was pounding on the thin door.

In the next bed, Masha stirred. "Not now," she muttered, pulling a sheet over her eyes. "What does the German woman want with you at this time of night?"

Lena felt her way around in the dark, knowing Masha would fuss if she switched on the light. She changed into her uniform and smoothed the long skirt. Even before she looked into the terrified eyes of the maid waiting on the other side of the door, she knew why Alexandra wanted her. The contractions had started.

When she arrived in the master suite, all of the electric lights were turned on. Lena's eyes strained against the artificial brightness. She focused on the family photographs lining the mantel, alongside the icons of long-faced saints.

On the other side of the room, Tsar Nicholas smoked and paced. At the sight of him, Lena's pulse quickened. He wore a white silk bathrobe and a monogrammed nightshirt. Sweat speckled his brow. His cigarette smelled strongly of cloves. "Thank God," he said gruffly. "I didn't know how long we'd have to wait for help."

Lena gave a quick curtsy and moved to the bed. Out of the corner of her eye, she watched the icons. Even as she moved across the room, the gaze of the saints followed her. She shivered.

Damp spots stained the ivory sheets and lace-trimmed pillow-
cases around Alexandra's head. Despite the elegant trappings of
this room, Alexandra's body gave off a familiar scent, sweet and
metallic, like menstrual blood.

She grasped Lena by the wrist. "Is so much pain normal with
a boy?"

Her eyes had the defeated, frightened look of the small animals Lena's father used to catch in his traps. Lena gave her hand
a reassuring squeeze. "It is a new sensation, I'm sure," Lena said.

"Nicky called for our friend Dr. Vachot," she gasped. "He'll be
here any minute."

"I'm not leaving." The tsar straightened himself and rolled his
shoulders back. "Until he arrives."

"Dr. Vachot warned me," Alexandra said. "There are those
among us who want something to go wrong. I must stay alert
during the labor. They have plans."

Lena shook her head. "Who? What plans?"

"You must help keep them away from my room."

"Try to relax, Alicky. You're letting your nerves get the best of
you." Lena recognized the dowager's husky voice as Marie entered the room. "She'll be fine, Nicky. Now wait outside."

Gently, the tsar touched Alexandra's cheek. "Don't worry," he
whispered. "Mama will take good care of you." As Lena watched
in amazement, the Tsar of all the Russias obeyed his mother and
left his wife alone in the room with them.

Marie placed the back of her hand on Alexandra's forehead.
"She feels feverish. She should take something."

"She doesn't want to risk the baby's health," Lena said. She
wished the tsar would come back. She needed someone else in the
room to take Alexandra's side.

"And you?" Marie's eyes bored into her. "You wish the same? That your mistress should suffer so greatly?"

"My mother felt women were too often overmedicated during labor," Lena said. "Sometimes they can't push properly."

Alexandra winced in pain. "Where is Dr. Vachot?"

"He has not yet arrived," Marie said, impatience speeding her voice. "You look like death. Consent to an analgesic. You took medication during your other labors and look what happened. Four healthy girls." Marie shut her mouth abruptly. The last word hung in the air, unwelcome. "If you wear yourself to exhaustion you're no use to anyone," Marie added quickly. "Ask your maid. You value her opinion over mine."

Alexandra focused her gaze on Lena. "What do you think?"

"Perhaps you could walk around a while," Lena suggested. "Gravity helps bring the baby quicker."

"Don't be silly," Marie snapped. "Alix is not some common peasant woman. Tell her she needs medicine."

Given Alexandra's agony, perhaps drugs were the kindest option. "If pain causes the woman to lapse into shock then medication is safer," Lena advised.

Alexandra sank back into the pillows. "Very well."

"I know you're tired, but don't worry, Alicky. We'll take good care of you."

Marie lifted her heavy skirts and indicated Lena should open the door. Reluctantly, Lena drew away from the bed and followed her out to the hall. Lena scanned the hall for the tsar, but he was nowhere to be found.

"Not another soul is to come in this room without my permission," Marie said.

"The empress asked about Monsieur Vachot."

"Alix doesn't know what's best for her right now."

Lena sucked in her breath. "It's best for her to see whomever she wants. It will help the baby as well if the mother is content."

Marie frowned, but sounded more sad than angry. "You have no idea what is best." Her eyes darted back and forth, as though she expected spies to jump out from behind the curtains. She lowered her voice to a whisper. "If Alix delivers a boy, the cannons from Peter and Paul Fortress will shoot off three hundred blank rounds. You'll help your mistress care for the little tsarevich."

When the Grand Duchess Anastasia's birth had been announced the previous year, Lena remembered the disappointed sighs and anxious faces, the subsequent rumors about the empress's mental state. She'd only wanted to make sure Empress Alexandra was all right. That impulse was what had gotten her involved in all of this in the first place. "And if the baby is a girl?" she asked quietly.

"You'll follow my orders," Marie said. "And not ask so many questions."

PARIS

OCTOBER 1941

Charlotte clung tightly to Laurent, trying to still his trembling shoulders. Shafts of weak light drifted into their cell through gaps in the wooden planks haphazardly nailed across the window. Wilted bags of flour and sugar lined splintering shelves, along with empty bottles of wine. Charlotte spotted a cockroach scurrying along the wall. Her throat clenched. She averted her eyes, hoping not to see another.

Laurent stared at the roach, his eyes glazed over. Gently, Charlotte cupped her son's chin in her hand and turned his head.

"Look at me," she said. "Only look at me."

The gendarme had brought them to an abandoned casino. Charlotte had shielded Laurent's eyes as they were marched down to the cellar. She'd caught glimpses of roulette tables, their ghostly green covers stained with patches of blood. She couldn't shield Laurent from the stench of unwashed bodies and urine. The French army had used casinos as temporary hospitals before they abandoned Paris. She tried not to think about amputated limbs and the cries of the dying that had once filled the place.

They sat on the floor together now, in sawdust, Laurent on her lap. He scratched the crusty discharge around his nose. It started to bleed again. Charlotte dabbed at the blood frantically with the end of her shirt. Luc had given each of them one of his old corduroy jackets before they left Paris. It wasn't much, but she spread a jacket around Laurent's thin shoulders now.

"Where's Papa?"

Charlotte shook her head. The gendarme had taken Luc to a different room. Charlotte couldn't bring herself to ask why. She needed to focus on Laurent, and distract him so he wouldn't talk about Luc. "When we get to your grandparents' house, you'll sleep in your own room. There's a huge yard and a garden in the back. You'll play every day with their dogs, two giant yellow retrievers." She longed to see their tails thump the floor in greeting.

"Once the grapes are ripe, we will press them and turn them into wine," Charlotte continued. "Would you like to learn how to do that?"

"Why are you talking so fast? Why are we here?"

If only she could make him understand without scaring him. "It's just for a short while, *mon petit*. Soon we'll be on our way."

"Then we're going home?"

Charlotte heard the thud of heavy boots on wood from the hall outside. She gulped the stale air of the cellar, wishing she could walk, move, pace, do anything but sit there helplessly. "If the soldier asks you questions, hide your head in my shoulder." She stroked the cross around her neck. "I'll talk."

The door swung open and the young gendarme strode in, beaming. A German officer followed, tall and slender, perhaps in his mid-forties. She saw at once that he ranked higher than most. He wore a black leather overcoat with a gold swastika affixed to the upper right-hand sleeve. He had a distinct profile, like a Roman senator. Under different circumstances, she might have found him attractive. He carried a large wooden box, yellowing with age, before him like a Christmas gift.

The German officer smiled politely and carefully set the box on the floor, near her. Then he drew his right leg back and placed his left hand over his heart. A red welt scarred his hand. He gave a curt bow.

"Madame Marchand? How terrible and cramped is this room. How unfortunate."

Charlotte recognized his voice, the same formal and belabored French of the man who'd been at her flat three days earlier. Instinctively, she hugged Laurent closer. She focused on the officer's large, flat ears, which pressed in closely to the sides of his head. "There must be some mistake."

"There is no mistake, madame. You are not to run away this time."

Laurent trembled underneath her. She caressed his hair to calm him. She forced her voice to stay strong. "What have you done with my brother?"

"He is safe enough for now." The German made a slight wave to indicate he found this a small matter. Then to the gendarme, "Leave us."

The gendarme gave a stiff nod and obeyed. Charlotte found herself staring after him. She wanted as many people in that cell as possible, no matter how hostile.

"I am Herr Krause," the officer said. "This is my assignment to deal with the matter of your family."

She didn't answer. After another moment, she felt the full weight of his stare. But it wasn't directed at her. He was looking curiously at Laurent.

"This handsome young man. I wish to see his face." Herr Krause bent for a closer look, but Laurent had buried his face in her shoulder, as instructed. "You have a boy. What a wonderful surprise. This is your son? Where is his father?"

She and Luc had discussed the cover story before they left. "He died defending the Maginot Line."

"Anything else I should know? Any other stories?"

Charlotte remained silent.

Herr Krause switched from French to Danish, a language that ran far more smoothly from his lips. "I wish you would be honest with me. Perhaps speaking in your native tongue will help? You are not French, not by birth anyway. Charlotte Marchand? That is your married name. But your papers say you were born in Copenhagen and your given name is Charlotte Pedersen. Be truthful, madame. I have a soft spot for the Danes."

Charlotte stared at the polished steel toes of the officer's boots, trying to catch her breath. How could he have known she was from Denmark? Maybe he had found her parents and hurt them. She felt tears threatening and pushed them back. "You seem to know me well." She hadn't used Danish in years, but it flowed naturally. She only wished she hadn't been forced to use her family's language in front of the German officer.

"I'm sorry, I could not hear?" He leaned closer.

"Why bother with these questions?"

"I am in the middle of an investigation. You are a guest of the SS."

"These aren't the quarters of someone you consider a guest."

"I can change your situation. I can make life better." He stepped closer. "Let me show you something. This might help."

Herr Krause crouched, opened the box, and spread its contents out before her on the floor. None of the items seemed noteworthy: tattered bits of lace and linen, an ivory-backed hairbrush, a porcelain teacup with a large chip in it, tarnished metal toy soldiers.

"Does any of this look familiar?"

She shook her head.

"Our army found this in one of your churches, when we began the liberation of your country. It belonged to the White Army of Imperial Russia at one point. Thank God it has come under our care. We can offer it the proper respect and due diligence. You're sure none of the items look familiar?"

"Why should they? What is this?"

"The box was taken from a house in Siberia in 1918. The Bolsheviks called it the House of Special Purpose. Didn't your friend Matilda Kshesinskaya tell you about this?"

When Charlotte didn't answer, Herr Krause shoved the contents back inside the box and slammed the lid. Then he rose to full height. "The conditions in this city are deplorable. How can you feed this boy? He is too thin. Think this through, madame. Nothing is changing anytime soon. The orders from above are one thousand calories per day. That is not enough for a growing child."

"Perhaps now you'll work to change that policy," Charlotte said.

"If I were in charge, everything would be different. But I don't have that power. Not now. Still, I can make life better for you and the boy. He is too important to languish this way." He placed two fingers on Charlotte's chin and she flinched as he forced her to look up at him. "Think about this. How long has it been since you have eaten steak? Smoked an actual cigarette? Slept through the night? All of this is within your reach."

Unwillingly, Charlotte felt her mouth water. Laurent couldn't resist looking at the officer. Herr Krause smiled down at him. "You like the sound of that, don't you?"

Gently, Charlotte lowered Laurent's head. "Don't talk to him." Turn away. Don't look at them. Don't acknowledge their existence. The practiced disdain seemed to come naturally to native Parisians, but she had struggled. She had been afraid.

Herr Krause's voice cracked with anger. "We are here to help, to liberate you people. Don't you understand? Look at what's happened to your son because of your weak government. He is sick. He needs medicine. I can get that for him. I can send him to live with a fat family on a farm in the Ukraine. He'll be happy there."

Panic swelled in Charlotte's chest. The Ukraine. The east. East to nowhere.

"He will have everything he wants. He will be healthy again. You can make this happen. You can go with him. We want you to go with him."

Charlotte shuddered, but even through her fear she pictured

Laurent at a table piled high with food. She felt faint. "I should like to talk to a lawyer."

Herr Krause smirked. "No lawyers are involved, nor will they be." He looked again at Laurent. Tears streamed from her son's eyes, but he kept the sound of his crying to a minimum, just little sniffles. She was proud of him.

"You are a very important young man," Herr Krause said. "Do you know that? You will make a fine leader for your country." He extended his hand, as though he expected Laurent to shake it in friendship. The gesture was a knife to her heart.

"Don't touch him." She scarcely recognized her voice. The low growl seemed to originate outside her body and yet the terror burned so fiercely she thought it might kill her. It took all her strength not to strike the man's hand away from her son. "If you touch him, you'll die. I don't know how or when, but so help me God I'll see you dead."

Herr Krause jerked her to her feet. Laurent let out a cry and grabbed her leg. "You people expect the worst of us. You think I would hurt a helpless child? You and your boy are vital to our interests. We will give you all the respect you deserve."

Charlotte's heart beat so rapidly she could barely focus. A sharp pain pressed upon her chest. She wanted to stop talking and gasp for air, but she didn't want the German officer to witness the extent of her panic. Her fingers flexed and curled. She kept her voice as calm as she possibly could. "Why are we important to you? Why do you need a little boy? Why?"

"We will treat you far better than the Red Army if they get their hands on you. I can assure you of that."

Herr Krause whistled and a minute later the gendarme reappeared, dragging Luc by the shoulders. Charlotte choked out a gasp. Luc's nose bled and a purplish, waxy swelling marred his left eye. The gendarme flung him in her direction. Laurent released her leg and Charlotte stumbled back as Luc landed in her arms. He went limp and she braced her legs to support his weight.

"This is your brother?" Herr Krause demanded. "You're lying. He is the boy's father, isn't he? They look exactly alike."

"Why do you care?" she cried. "What do you want from us?"

Herr Krause frowned and addressed the gendarme. "I asked you to take care with him. He looks bad." He turned back to Charlotte. "This man is a courier for the Maquis as well. A traitor to the Reich. Do you know what we found in the trunk of your car, madame? Does your boy?"

She looked at Luc and bit her lip to keep from crying out. He lowered himself to the ground, and stopped when he was bent down on his knees. But he managed to shake his head. Charlotte rolled her shoulders back, centered herself. "We don't know."

"We can kill the three of you on the spot. The evidence is damning."

The fear, cold and clammy, slithered down her throat. Charlotte's fingers balled into fists. If he wanted to kill them, he would have. She still had a chance. "What do you want from me?"

"You and your son will join us," Herr Krause said. "We require full cooperation."

"You can't take him," Charlotte said evenly. "I'll go with you if you leave my son and let the two of them go."

"You expect this man to take care of your son?" The German kicked Luc in the ribs and Luc slumped to the ground. Charlotte screamed. Laurent touched Luc's shoulder and began to whimper.

"He seems a sorry excuse for a father to me," Herr Krause said. "But if you and your son help us, we will let him free."

"No." Charlotte doubled over with agony. She could no longer fight the tears. "This is blackmail. A game. I understand. I have diamonds. I'll give them to you. My flat, my savings, anything you want."

It seemed impossible. Everything around her turned surreal, a nightmare. She heard a small laugh and then another. Herr Krause approached her and she could see, just barely through the fog of tears, his terrible smile. The gendarme stood smirking behind him and his smile was even worse because she could tell he didn't care about her at all.

Her stomach twisted. She lowered her face.

"We're not interested in any of that." Herr Krause entered her field of vision once more, as he bent to pick the wooden box up off the floor. "We need you and your son. I am a reasonable man, madame. You will find that we are all reasonable people. I don't wish to start our regime change in the Ukraine on a sour note. You have twenty minutes to get your thoughts in order and accept your destiny. Cooperate and we'll let the boy's father live."

Eleven

NEW YORK CITY

PRESENT DAY

Veronica dashed down the stairs of Alexei Romanov's building, clutching her coat tightly to her chest, gulping gas-laden fumes from the ancient heating system. Her pulse thudded in her ears in time to the shaky rhythm of her breathing. She burst out the lobby door, determined to confront Michael at once.

She spotted him on the bench in the park across the street, waiting for her, as he promised, still the loyal bodyguard. He'd pulled his wool hat over his ears, his cheeks were flushed red, and his breath was steaming in the chilly air. Behind him, laughing children in scarves and mittens played on a swing set.

A rubber ball landed in the bushes behind Michael and he bent to retrieve it. The shrubs rustled and he emerged a second later, dirt on his cheeks. He threw the ball back to a kid on the playground and wiped the dirt away. Veronica felt a catch in her throat. She remembered her dream the first night after she met Michael. All those happy Russians lined up along the banks of the Neva River, flags waving. The reptilian voices in her head began to hiss again. *You can't trust him.*

Then Michael spotted her and rushed forward to greet her. "What happened?" He paused to catch his breath. "Did you meet Alexei Romanov? What did he say?"

Veronica pulled the hood of her coat down over her ears to protect them from the wind. She stared at Michael, at a loss for how to begin.

"He called me a liar, right?" She heard a tremor in his voice. "I told you he'd say that. What else?"

"I can't believe it," she said.

"I knew it." Michael snorted and began to pace in front of the bench.

Veronica remembered all the accounts she'd read of the Romanovs under house arrest. The tsar had spent his last days in captivity marching back and forth across the cramped living room of the Ipatiev House in Siberia. She saw the same restlessness in Michael now. And Alexandra . . . she saw a resemblance there as well, despite the generations that had passed since. The height, the steady gaze, even the hint of sadness in his eyes.

"Why didn't you tell me?" she blurted. One of the little boys on the playground turned to look at her. "Alexei Romanov doesn't trust you," she said, quieter now. "I don't think he knows what to make of it all. I can't believe you didn't tell me."

Michael took a moment to study her face. "Can't believe I didn't tell you what?" he asked carefully.

"About the missing fifth daughter of the tsar."

Michael grasped the back of the bench for support. "He told you."

"You think Alexandra is your great-grandmother? Nicholas is your great-grandfather?"

"Wait." Michael held his hand up. "He told you that?"

"Why didn't you tell me? If this is true, no one else in his little club would have a prayer of crowning themselves tsar."

She watched the movement of Michael's shoulders as he drew in a deep breath. "I didn't tell you because it's nothing more than a family rumor. Something I looked into when I was younger. I'm surprised he mentioned it at all."

The headache still thudded, jabs of pain tightening her skull. The wind blew her hair into her eyes. Michael touched her forehead and brushed the strands aside. Veronica stepped away. She couldn't let him confuse her with his touch. "You know I'm writing a biography of Alexandra. You know I'd be interested, even if it is just a rumor. Besides, you told me you keep all those genealogical records around because they're important to your mother and they were important to your grandmother. Right? If you want to honor them, you'll learn the truth. There's a simple way to know for sure."

He scratched the back of his neck. "If you were seeing it from my perspective, you'd know it's not simple."

"It is," she insisted. "Get your DNA tested. A swab from the inside of your mouth. A museum in Japan has Nicholas II's blood on file. Some crazy policeman attacked him while he was visiting the country and split his head open. They saved the handkerchief he used to mop up the blood. It's in a museum. Test against that."

Michael touched his hand to his forehead. "DNA that's over a hundred years old? That's Alexei Romanov's solution?"

"There are other relatives," she said, frustration building. "Living relatives, plenty of other ways to have DNA tested. It will take seventy-two hours. And then you'll at least be able to prove you're a Romanov."

Michael looked at the ground.

"I don't understand. Why won't you do it?"

"Veronica, these people are dangerous. I've been trying to tell you all along."

"Alexei Romanov? That guy must be seventy."

"I'm trying to protect you," Michael insisted.

That's what Romanov had said to her as well. She gave Michael the same answer she'd given earlier. "Protect me from what?"

"Alexei Romanov wants to be the tsar. He's wanted that all his life. It concerns me that he's suddenly so interested in you. You're a professor of Russian history."

Veronica threw her arms up in frustration. "You're repeating his words. Romanov said they're trying to protect me from you. He said they're suspicious because I'm a professor. And then he gave me some nonsense about how dangerous it is in Russia now. Who should I believe?"

Michael kicked a stray rock. Veronica no longer saw the tall, proud descendant of Nicholas and Alexandra Romanov before her. Instead, she noticed Michael's graying temples and the slight paunch around his belly.

"Look." Veronica tried to reach a truce. "I don't get it. I'm sorry. I don't see why a DNA test is a problem. And it concerns me. Maybe I should give you some time alone. I'll take some time alone as well. We just need space."

She pivoted, but Michael grabbed her hand. "Don't leave like this."

Veronica realized she was becoming the person she hated in any relationship, the person who walked away. But to think straight, to feel some relief from the hammering of her headache, she needed to distance herself from him. "I only want time to think."

He released her and she headed down First Avenue toward the subway. She wanted to go back to Midtown, where she could disappear into a crowd and be alone with her thoughts. But Michael moved quickly and soon kept pace with her. "At least tell me where you're going."

"I can take care of myself."

"I'll stay three steps behind you," Michael said. "I won't even talk to you."

He'd follow her around like a stray dog if she let him. She almost relented, but the rational side of her returned. "Why did you spend so much time looking at their records when you were younger?"

Michael stopped cold. "He told you that too?"

"You don't deny it, then?"

He looked in her eyes and then shook his head. "No," he said quietly.

"Did you want to pursue your claim back then? Do you want to pursue it now?"

He shook his head again. "No."

"Then taking the DNA test shouldn't matter one way or another. You can find out if you're a relative. If you're not, so be it. Who cares? But there are those of us who might be interested in finding out if the story about the fifth daughter is true." She pointed to herself.

"I don't think that's a good idea," he said softly. "Not now."

"Why not?"

He said nothing. He gave her nothing. Perhaps Alexei Romanov was right. Michael didn't want to take a DNA test because he knew the results would be negative. If he cared, that meant he wanted to pursue his claim all along. He'd lied to her.

The shell started to close around her heart. She walked toward the subway station, not daring to look back. She couldn't bear to see the crushed look on Michael's face.

Veronica didn't want to return to the hotel. Michael would find her. Besides, she felt too depressed to go back alone. She'd taken the subway back toward Midtown. Now that she was aboveground once more, she tried to blend in with the other pedestrians. The crowd, the anonymity of it, helped clear her head. She felt apart from herself, like she could disappear.

As she approached Forty-second Street, she recognized the stone lions, cold sentries at the top of the steps leading to the public library. Businesspeople in suits and student tourists with bulging backpacks sat on the massive steps, an oasis from the commotion of the busy street below. Veronica plopped down next to a girl with burgundy hair who was smoking and reading a paperback.

Veronica bent to peek at the cover of the book. *One Hundred Years of Solitude.* Despite everything, she smiled. Márquez had been one of her mother's favorite authors, or so Abuela said. She could picture her mother sitting on stairs like this in Madrid, smoking a cigarette and reading a paperback. It made her want to stay on the steps. It was freezing, but she liked the proximity of strangers, particularly ones who read Márquez. It distracted her from thinking that she was in Manhattan, the center of the universe, and yet had nothing more to show for this trip than an undefined relationship with some guy who was what? A liar? Delusional? Both?

And what would happen when she made it back to her safe little cubbyhole at Alameda University? She imagined the smug look on Regina Brack's drab face. At this point, Dr. Brack may as well stuff Veronica's career into one of the kill jars she used for her doomed butterflies.

Slowly, Veronica's saving grace, rationality, returned. She had new information about Alexandra to consider. Michael was clearly a liar, but perhaps there was something to what Alexei Romanov said about this missing fifth daughter, some kernel of truth. When Romanov had first written her, hadn't he promised access to files on Alexandra? New information? Veronica might yet salvage this trip. She might not return home in disgrace after all.

Besides, Abuela would be horrified if Veronica squandered an opportunity because she was upset over a man. Veronica was horrified at herself.

She reached inside her purse, found her phone, and punched in the number Alexei Romanov had given her.

He answered after only one ring. "Romanov Guardsmen." He made it sound as though she'd reached a customer service center.

"This is Veronica Herrera."

"Dr. Herrera! I'm glad to hear from you again. You bolted out the door, so eager to confront the pretender, and I didn't even have a chance to say good-bye."

"Michael won't submit to a DNA test. I don't understand why not." She hesitated. "I guess I do understand. You were right. He's not the heir to the throne."

The girl with burgundy hair looked up from *One Hundred Years of Solitude* and shot Veronica a puzzled look. Veronica shrugged. On the other end of the line, Romanov clicked his teeth against his tongue. "Is Mikhail with you now?"

"No. I wanted time alone to consider everything you said."

"Oh." It was a simple syllable, but Romanov sounded pleased.

"I'm calling because I'd like to come back and look at your archives on Alexandra, as we discussed in the first place," Veronica said. "You said you had new information. I'd still like the opportunity to see the files."

"Splendid! But I have an even better idea. Beforehand, why don't you let me introduce you to a lovely woman of my acquaintance? Her mother worked for the royal family. I think you'll want to hear what she has to say about Mikhail's story."

Veronica felt a quick pitch of excitement. "About the fifth daughter of the tsar?"

"Related to that tale, yes. I'm sure she would like to meet you. She doesn't make her way out of her home much anymore, though, I'm afraid. Perhaps we can arrange to visit her this afternoon. Would you like that?"

"Should I come back to your office?" Veronica asked.

"Where are you?"

"At the library on Forty-second Street. By the lions."

"Ah!" he said. "You're with the lions called Patience and Fortitude. How à propos. I retain a car service. Let me fetch you. I'll be there as soon as I can."

Once they ended the conversation, Veronica rubbed the back of her shoulders, trying to relieve the tension. She fumbled in her purse for her iPod. For a few minutes, she would disappear into the Strokes' "Heart in a Cage," fast and chaotic. It relaxed her more than a massage ever could. Luckily, she had an entire playlist just like it. The music helped drown out thoughts of Michael while she waited for Alexei Romanov.

Ten minutes later, a long black sedan double-parked in front of the library. One of the tinted windows in back rolled down. Alexei Romanov stuck his head out the window and mouthed something. Veronica removed her earbuds.

"Dr. Herrera." He shouted to be heard above the traffic, but kept his voice polished as a debutante. "Thank you for agreeing to this on such short notice."

Veronica turned off her iPod and rose to her feet. Alexei Romanov stepped out of the car in a long overcoat trimmed with black fur. He held a file folder, overlaid with plastic sheeting, in his hand. Cars and taxis honked at his sedan, but nothing broke his concentration. "I'm glad you agreed to meet Ms. Rubalov. We have reason to believe something remarkable happened between the births of Anastasia and Tsarevich Alexei. She will provide further insight."

"Wait." Veronica tried to organize her thoughts. She glanced back at the steps. The girl with the burgundy hair had stashed her book in her purse and was smoking now as she watched Veronica and Alexei Romanov. "You called Michael 'a notorious pretender.'" Veronica lowered her voice. "Do you believe him or not?"

"Our organization is determined to uncover the truth. We need your help."

"My help?" Veronica said. "Why me?"

"My joints don't do well in the cold air anymore," Romanov said. "It's an old man's curse. Why don't you join me inside the car?"

It seemed he wasn't going to answer any of her questions. She decided to try one last time. "Uncover the truth about what?"

With tremendous care, Romanov removed the plastic sheeting from around the manila folder and withdrew a thin, curling piece of white paper.

"This is what I wanted to show you," he said. "It may be a missing link in the story of the fifth daughter."

A tingle of delight coursed through Veronica as he stepped closer. Even on the pale copy of a copy she recognized Alexandra's neat, slanted penmanship. She gasped.

Romanov smiled broadly, handing Veronica the letter.

5 September 1902

Dearest Lena,

How sorry I was to hear of your parents' sudden illness. I miss you so and cry in my pillow to think I couldn't even bid you good-bye. I wish we had time to speak. I beg your forgiveness for the tardiness of this letter.

When I walk through the palace now, I see the looks on the faces of the servants and of those in Nicky's family who still bother to visit. They think I'm hysterical and that I would fool my own body into maintaining such an illusion.

The empress wrote not in Cyrillic, but in English, the same language she used with her husband and daughters. Veronica heard Alexandra's desperation, recognized her phrasing. If someone had forged this letter, they did an expert job. She pictured Alexandra holding a piece of stationery between her long fingers and blowing softly on the ink.

But who was Lena?

Veronica strummed her fingernails against the sedan's immaculate paint job, too excited to remain still. "You'll need a paleographer to date the original copy," she said, "and to verify the handwriting isn't a forgery."

"We were hoping you could do that. Ms. Rubalov is a friend to our association, though not a member, I'm afraid. Her lineage doesn't warrant it. But she is devoted to the cause and is willing to show you the original letter in its entirety. What do you make of the portion you've seen so far?"

"It sounds like Alexandra," Veronica admitted. "I would like to see the original."

"Ms. Rubalov has the original." Romanov indicated the open car door and gracefully stepped aside to let her in. "Let's pay her a call."

Curiosity churned inside as she slid into the backseat, taking in the scent of newly upholstered leather. Warm air blasted in through vents. A panel separated the backseat from the chauffeur.

Romanov tapped the panel at the back of the driver's seat. "We can go now."

The driver started the engine, flicked on his turn signal, and then accelerated into the farthest left-hand turn lane, nearly side-swiping a bike messenger in the process. Veronica twisted around to watch the bearded hipster on the bike wobble to the side of the road, shake his fist, and then recede into the distance.

"What's the hurry?" Veronica asked uncertainly.

As she turned again, the panel before her lowered. Veronica saw the driver's reddish hair and his knobby knuckles gripping the steering wheel. He adjusted the rearview mirror. She caught a glimpse of the acorn-shaped scar on his left cheek, below his eye. At once, the harsh scent of his cologne registered. The driver was the man who had followed her into the Forbes Gallery.

Veronica felt the fear again, so intense it clawed at the lining of her stomach. She heard her own voice, but it sounded more like a croak. "Where are we going?"

"Brighton Beach," the driver said, in his brusque Russian accent. "I'll make sure Mikhail knows where to find us."

Twelve

Historians find it odd no one noted much of that night. After all, the palace buzzed with suspicion. Alexandra failed to call any of the court doctors to her room. This made the family and the servants question the true nature of her condition.

—VERONICA HERRERA, The Reluctant Romanov

PETERHOF ESTATE

AUGUST 1902

Lena struggled to keep her eyes open. Her shoulders slumped. All of the windows in the master suite were tightly shut and the room stunk of a metallic, medicinal odor. She patted another damp towel on Alexandra's white forehead and nodded at the skinny parlor maid in the corner. The maid had been standing in the same spot for ten minutes now, scratching at a mole on her chin, trained to receive permission before leaving the presence of a royal. Unfortunately, Alexandra was in no condition to grant anything of the sort now. Lena's nod would have to do.

The maid straightened her back, mouthed a thank-you, and gave a sloppy curtsy before scurrying out of the room. Lena felt sure ugly gossip would follow. Where were the doctors? Why wasn't word sent to the waiting family members as to Alexandra's health? Lena wished she had an answer. She wanted to leave.

Marie entered the room, brows knit in disapproval. "Who was that girl? I ordered the servants to stay outside. What did she want?"

"Nothing. She probably didn't hear the orders. She was just going about her normal routine."

"No one else is to come inside. I don't care about their normal routine."

Marie opened the door a crack and gestured to someone on the other side. A man in a long white coat entered the room. He was balding and short, with wispy whiskers sprouting from layers of fat under his chin. Lena flashed back to the morning in Alexandra's boudoir when she'd watched Monsieur Vachot murmur to Alexandra and caress her head.

Lena covered her mouth. Her skin felt clammy and smelled like salt. She couldn't believe Marie would let Vachot anywhere near the empress. Yet he hovered over the bed now. He withdrew a stethoscope from his thick leather bag and pressed it gently against Alexandra's still chest.

Lena was too exhausted to take care with her tone. "Where are the court doctors?"

Marie shot her a dirty look. "Hush."

"I'll take good care of our little mother." Vachot patted Alexandra's hand.

This wasn't right. Lena's mind raced. At least five doctors should attend to Alexandra. She didn't think the tsar would agree to this arrangement. He'd call for the others at once. The tsar loved his wife beyond reason, certainly enough to defy his mother's shrill demands. Maybe he had called for more doctors, but somehow Marie intercepted his orders. They were in the palace somewhere. Lena only needed to find them.

Then she remembered what Pavel told her about the time he spent boxing and the need for self-protection, how such skills were valuable when dealing with the imperial family. If she planned to defy Marie, she needed to do so with subtlety. Lena bowed her head as she approached the dowager. "Forgive me. May I leave the room for a moment?"

Marie regarded Lena as though she were a mosquito in need of swatting. "Why?"

"I wouldn't ask if it weren't urgent." Lena shifted her weight from foot to foot.

Marie sighed. "Very well. Don't dawdle."

Once outside the stifling room, Lena drew in a deep breath, ridding her lungs of the sickly smell from Alexandra's boudoir. The storm had passed and weak rays of early daybreak filtered into the palace through the bay windows. Even the flimsy light was enough to revive her senses and strengthened her resolve. Lena balled her skirt in her hands and rushed toward the stairs.

Before she could descend, she heard the patter of footsteps from one of the bedrooms at the end of the hall. Lena stopped short. The door creaked open and a woman's head stuck out. She had her hair covered in a turban and wore a scarlet kimono with a bright yellow dragon scampering up one shoulder.

"Girl," the woman called. "Girl!"

Lena turned and recognized the shrewd blue eyes and thin lips of Grand Duke Kyril's lover, Ducky.

"No one has brought fresh water this morning," Ducky said in clipped and precise English. "Could you attend to it?" And then in a lower voice, "If you hear any word of the tsarina's condition, we would like to know about that as well." Ducky grasped a twenty-ruble note between her manicured fingers.

Lena's foot tapped the floor, beyond her control. She couldn't risk offending Ducky since she was such a high-ranking visitor.

But then she realized Ducky had spoken in English. Why would this woman assume she spoke the language? Lena squinted and offered a pallid smile. She shrugged with her entire upper body, palms upward, and responded in Russian. "What is this?"

"Oh . . ." Ducky must have communicated to Kyril in English, just as Alexandra did with the tsar. *"Voda."* Ducky pantomimed drinking a glass of water.

Lena put a finger up to indicate she understood, gave an exaggerated sigh of relief, curtsied quickly, and turned to head off.

"No, wait. *Nyet.*" Ducky grabbed Lena's arm to drag her back. "There's more. The empress . . ." Now Ducky released Lena's arm so she could pantomime a full stomach and rocking a baby.

"Ah!" Lena said. And then in heavy English, "Water. You. Water. For empress."

"No! Damn. Kyril!" she cried, turning over one shoulder, but Lena had already taken off. She rushed down the stairs, taking them two at a time.

Gray tendrils of smoke seeped from the crack at the bottom of an arched door downstairs, near the entrance to the gardens. The door led into the tsar's private study, yet no guard stood watch outside. The tsar must not be there. Someone else in the room might help her though. She heard a faint hum of voices and laughter.

Lena glanced over her shoulder to make sure Ducky wasn't watching, then placed her hand lightly on the knob, and tugged.

Through the haze of smoke, Lena saw photographs of Alexandra and the grand duchesses hanging on the walls alongside mounted heads of reindeer and bears, souvenirs from the royal hunts. Lena averted her eyes to avoid the vacant stare of a dead elk. The trophies reminded her of late summer in Archangel. Her father hunted and trapped while her mother cured and salted the meat. The fetid smell of fresh carcasses made Lena nauseous. Her mother always scolded her for her weak constitution.

Near the center of the room, four men gathered around a circular table, cigars clenched between their teeth. They lounged in chairs upholstered in dark leather that squeaked whenever they shifted their weight. Each of them held a hand of cards.

"Well played, Konstantin," one of the men said as the others laughed. "You'll be the ruin of us all."

The man sitting nearest the door sensed Lena's presence and turned. A cloud of fresh smoke from his cigar irritated her throat and she coughed. All of the men swiveled to face her.

"What do you want?" The man who spoke was younger than the others. His hair hung in lanky strands along the sides of his face. He looked more like one of her brother's friends than a court doctor, yet his voice bore the unmistakable cadence of the privileged class. He swept a pile of bills from the middle of the table to a larger pile directly in front of him.

Lena's foot tapped the floor in a furious rhythm. She thought about Alexandra alone in her bedroom, at the mercy of Marie and Vachot.

"Shame on you," she sputtered. The words came out louder than she anticipated. "Playing cards when your sovereign needs you." For good measure she repeated the words in English. Lena knew Alexandra preferred English doctors.

At first they sat in stony silence. Then the men began to laugh and that scared Lena even more. "I thought all young people were radicals now," one of them said.

Lena scanned the table for a familiar face, her gaze finally resting on the gentle brown eyes of the court physician, Dr. Ott. He regarded her kindly, like a teacher waiting for a struggling student to sound out a difficult word in a spelling book.

She appealed to him directly. "The empress lies unconscious with only one physician and her mother-in-law."

"Why worry your pretty head about it?" another man said. He had a deep, booming voice and a birthmark the size of a kopeck on his neck. "Do you know how to play poker? Konstantin learned in America and he wouldn't mind teaching one more."

Lena bristled at the suggestion. The men started to laugh again. "Please."

Dr. Ott rose and placed his long, delicate surgeon's fingers on her shoulders. It was an overly familiar gesture, yet executed with great tenderness. "There's nothing we can do." He guided her gently away from the others, lowered his voice, and spoke in English. "The dowager empress doesn't want us in the room."

"The dowager has no right to keep you away."

Lena waited, hardly daring to breathe. The men exchanged glances. Lena imagined the hard face of the policeman who would come to arrest her for speaking against a member of the royal family, and the metal handcuffs slicing her wrists. Still, no one stood to arrest her. These men were no government spies.

"Talk to the tsar," she pleaded. "He'll let you into the room. At least look in on the empress and make sure everything is all right."

Dr. Ott shook his head and dropped his hands. "We have to follow the family's orders, just as you do."

"I don't believe the tsar understands the gravity of this situation," Lena said.

"But the dowager understands," Dr. Ott replied sadly, "and she's in control of the family's affairs now."

Lena lurked in the back of the room, twisting the ends of her skirt in her hands. The orange glow of sunrise revealed the deathly pallor of Alexandra's face. Whatever Vachot had injected knocked the empress unconscious. She couldn't communicate and her body's natural contractions had weakened.

Vachot mopped his broad forehead with a handkerchief already soaked with sweat. "Don't worry, little mother. All is well."

"You said you delivered many babies," Marie snapped. The corners of her eyes looked pinched and in the morning light she appeared to have aged ten years overnight.

Vachot fumbled through his bag. "She's older than most of my patients."

"She's hardly thirty. I was past thirty when I bore my youngest children and had no difficulties. Perhaps I was blessed with more competent hands at my bedside."

"She's dilated five centimeters with little cervical thinning. A caesarean section—"

"You want to get paid, don't you?" Marie shot back. "Or have you decided at long last to tell your wife of your gambling debts."

Vachot and the dowager glared at each other. Then Vachot removed his spectacles, cleaning them with the end of his shirt. "The longer this takes, the greater the risk. If forceps become necessary . . . if you could bring in the other doctors . . ."

"We can't do that." Marie touched her fingers to her forehead, and then added quickly, "This girl worked as a midwife. Will she do?"

Lena's knees felt weak. She stumbled over her words, trying to form a coherent sentence. "I helped my mother. That's all."

"No one expects you to deliver the baby," Marie said abruptly, "only to assist as needed." She turned to Vachot. "You want her help, don't you?"

He nodded wearily. "An extra pair of hands would be invaluable. Yes."

"Wash up," Marie told her.

Lena moved to the free-standing marble sink in the opposite corner of the room. Her hands shook as she turned the lever. Water rushed over them, so hot her skin turned red, yet the pain scarcely registered. She soaped three times. An image of her mother's face, scowling in disapproval, was locked in Lena's mind. The room started to spin around her. Lena grabbed hold of the cold basin for support. Marie eyed her wearily.

"I must speak with you," Lena whispered.

The dowager nodded sharply and tilted her head to the door. Lena followed her into the hall. She looked down at the tiles lining the floor. She might swoon. She might vomit all over Marie's tiny satin shoes.

"I can't help." The words spilled out before Lena could determine how best to arrange them. "When I assisted my mother . . ."

Lena felt Marie's hand, soft but cold, on her shoulder. For the first time, the dowager regarded Lena with something other than contempt. Her eyes widened like a little girl's. "What is it?"

"A breech birth." Lena's corset pinched her waist. She gasped for breath, water from the basin still dribbling down her arms. "My mother turned the baby inside the mother's womb." The words came faster now, like purging her body of a virus. "It took too long. There was too much blood."

Marie fingered the fichu lace on her collar. Underneath, Lena spotted a delicate chain with a simple silver cross hanging at its end. She tried to focus on the cross. But Marie began to fade into the distance and then disappeared altogether.

Lena was back home in the northern woods. Perspiration trickled, salty and hot, down the sides of her face, but she didn't dare move her hands away from her mother's bulging black bag of instruments and ointments. She remembered the oppressive stench of the fields mingled with the heaviness of body odor. The father had been drinking all morning and shouting at them. He called Lena's mother a slut and told her he'd kill her if anything happened to his son. Her mother's hands shook as she pointed to a spatula-shaped instrument. "Come on. Come on," she hissed in Lena's face, her breath stale.

"The woman was in agony the entire time," Lena told Marie. "When the baby came, he had physical strength, but was addled in the mind. It was my fault. I took too long to hand my mother the instruments she needed. He didn't receive a proper flow of oxygen during delivery. His brain was damaged."

Marie rested her small white hand on the moldings along the edge of the wall. Lena watched the rise and fall of her slim shoulders. "How old were you?"

Lena bowed her head. "Eight."

"I see." Marie touched the fringe of bangs on her forehead. "All right. I don't have time to put this delicately so I'll say it straight out. Look at me." Wearily, Lena obeyed. "Your mother is a fool. No child should be given such responsibility. She only wanted someone to blame for her own mistakes."

Deep in her soul, Lena knew Marie was right. A part of her had always known. How could her mother have expected a young girl to handle the pressures of a difficult birth? Why had she taken her frustrations out on her daughter? Lena only needed to hear someone else say it.

"Put this out of your mind now," Marie said. "You must have confidence."

Lena knew she should feel better. Still, her stomach coiled like a knotted rope.

"The empress requires your confidence," Marie said. "I require it." Lena felt the gentle pressure of Marie's hands pressing into her shoulders. "Ready?"

For the first time, Lena realized, she felt something other than fear in Marie's presence. The feeling almost resembled gratitude. She nodded and stepped forward to open the door. The dowager stopped her. "Keep your hands clean. I'll open the door."

Back in the room, Lena shook her hands until the beads of water evaporated, and then wiped them down with a clean towel.

"I'll remind the dowager empress that a caesarean section is advisable in these cases," Vachot told Marie. "Especially when the mother is past thirty."

Marie shook her head. "Lena, what do you think?"

Lena regarded her mistress's still body. She didn't want to think about her mother right now, but she needed to utilize the midwife's expertise. She thought back to what her mother told her about doctors, how eager they were to cut a woman open and mangle the newborn with forceps when patience often produced better results. She tried to remember what her mother gathered to help speed the birth. Clean rags and towels. Lubricants from her bag. An icon of the Virgin.

"Let's get more oils and towels and keep going," Lena said. "This will take time."

PARIS

OCTOBER 1941

The officer's timeline swung like a pendulum through Charlotte's mind. She bent over, banging the sides of her head with her fists, and still came no closer to a plan. Another roach, fat as her thumb, scuttled past them and through a crack in the wall. She looked down at Laurent, nestled against her thigh, asleep once more.

Doubt wormed its way into her every thought. Every decision she'd made had been wrong. She should have followed Luc's original advice and remained in his flat. They could have waited for the occupation to end. And now what would happen to Luc? The swelling around his cheeks had forced his left eye almost completely shut. Underneath his torn shirt, dark purple bruises splattered his chest. In the German's eyes, he was expendable. Luc remained alive only to force her hand and make her cooperate.

"I'm sorry," she whispered. "I'm so sorry."

Luc opened his eyes as best he could manage. He blinked twice and straightened his back against the wall. Once he sat upright, he winced in pain. She wanted to brush his hair back from his eyes, stroke his cheek gently. But she could scarcely look at him; the guilt was too much to bear.

"What happened, rose petal?" he asked.

The tenderness of the old endearment brought back the tears. He'd begun to call Charlotte rose petal after she devised a dance by that name for a recital she'd planned. It reminded her that once the world had been right. Everything had once made sense and she'd felt something other than hopelessness. She bit her lip and a hot burst of tears flowed, streaming down her cheeks.

Luc waited patiently, touching her hand softly. Stress brought out the worst in him, but trauma the best. She stared at the crumpled bags of sugar and flour on the shelves, the threads of cobweb behind them. "This is my fault," she said at last. She tried to wipe her face, but her hands shook. "You were right. We should have stayed in Paris."

"We don't know it would have made any difference."

She rubbed her fingers back and forth over the sleeves of the old corduroy jacket Luc had given her. Soon, it would be all she'd have left of him. She drew it tighter around her shoulders, caressing the patches at the elbows. "If we stayed in the city, I could have found a way to keep Laurent safe. I shouldn't have listened to Kshesinskaya. I shouldn't have brought you into this. Now they've hurt you."

"What did they tell you?" His voice remained strangely calm. His expression was intense underneath the bruising, his gaze steady.

"They want Laurent and me." Charlotte stroked Laurent's lower back, making small circles with her fists. "I don't know why. That's why he brought us here. I'm so sorry they hurt you, Luc. But I don't think they're going to hurt Laurent after all. The officer wants me to go with him willingly. That's all. He said he'll keep Laurent safe."

"Go willingly? Where?"

"They'll take him to the Ukraine," Charlotte said. "I don't know why. He said they'll take good care of Laurent."

Luc withdrew his hand from hers. "You think the German army will take good care of our son? In the Ukraine?"

The calm had vanished. His condescending tone had returned, making Charlotte's face burn even more than the heat of her tears. She knew how this conversation would proceed. Luc would criticize her, but ultimately leave the decision in her hands. Then her decision would remain subject to even more criticism. "You were the one who told me I wasn't taking good care of him," she shot back, "that he looked sick. If the Germans can take better care of him, maybe we should go. They'll make sure he gets enough food."

Charlotte lowered her head, inhaling the mold and sawdust surrounding them in the cellar. She couldn't take care of her own son. Luc touched her arm, but now Charlotte scarcely felt the pressure, as though a thick layer of insulation protected her skin. Laurent stirred, his head making little bobbing motions, but he didn't waken.

"You're exhausted and hungry," Luc told her. "You're not thinking straight."

"Look at Laurent! I can't care for him properly. You said so yourself."

Luc shook her gently. "Don't let them take him. Do you hear me?"

The effort to speak made Luc choke. He leaned over and coughed abruptly into his sleeve. When he raised his head again, she saw spots of blood dotting the spittle on his arm. She'd loved him so much once. He was the father of her child. And she'd reduced him to this. "I don't have a choice," she said.

Luc covered his mouth before he spoke again. "Is it me? Did they threaten me? Try not to think about that. Neither one of you can go with that officer. They'll use Laurent. They'll use you."

Waves of nausea roiled in and out, clouding Charlotte's concentration. "What happened in the other room?" she asked. "What did they tell you?"

"I didn't want to scare you. I wanted to wait until we found your parents."

Her parents? "What do you know?" Charlotte cried, louder than she intended.

Luc sighed, his face sunken from exhaustion. "The man I got the car from this morning is part of the Maquis. Many members of the resistance follow Soviet politics closely. Half of them are Communists, you know. They believe Hitler made a grave miscalculation when he broke the pact with Stalin."

She gave a hoarse laugh. "I've seen no evidence of that."

"Now that the Eastern Front has opened, the Nazis are lost."

"They're fine." Charlotte shook her head, defeated. "We're lost."

"I know you listen to the broadcasts from London. The Russians will suffer, but there are so many of them."

She forced the fear and the sickness to harden inside of her so she could think straight. "The officer mentioned the Red Army. He told me Laurent would be treated badly if they took him. Why would the Red Army want a little boy?"

"What if the Nazis found a way to withdraw from Russia and save face?"

"They would never do that." Her words were sure, but somehow they came out sounding more like a question.

"What if the Germans were backing a new government?"

Luc slumped back against the wall and closed his eyes. Charlotte took his hand. She was shocked at how cold it felt in hers, but she couldn't let him see her reaction. She squeezed his fingers. "Stay with me, Luc. I need to know what's happening."

He opened his eyes once more. "The Maquis believe the Nazis want to destabilize the Soviet government from the inside." His voice dropped. Charlotte inclined her ear closer to his lips to hear. "The Nazis want to restore the Russian monarchy as a puppet regime. They think they can do that from the Ukraine."

Charlotte's limbs began to numb. "But the Russian royal family was murdered."

"Not everyone believes it. They never found bodies."

The gears in Charlotte's mind began to turn once more. "The officer brought a box in with him. He showed me lace and linen and toys and teapots. He asked me if I recognized anything. He mentioned Madame Kshesinskaya again."

"How did you come to work at her studio?" Luc asked. "You never talk about her much."

"She approached me one day after a performance of *Coppélia*. I'd heard of her, of course. Everyone had." Charlotte remembered that cold and wet winter morning, dreary as any. And yet she'd been entranced by the bright-eyed little woman before her.

"She took pity on me, I guess," Charlotte continued. "I was getting older. My performing days, even in the corps, were numbered. She likes to take in stray cats. I think she thought of me the same way. She rambled on, complaining about Nijinsky for nearly thirty minutes, and then offered me a position as a teacher at her studio. It was generous."

Luc stared at her intently. "Maybe Kshesinskaya sought you out. She's Russian. She had connections to the royal family, didn't she?"

Charlotte gave another sharp laugh. She hoped Luc might laugh as well, but his expression remained focused, his lips tilted down. "When the officer came to your door, did he say anything that would make you think you were connected to the royal family?"

"I'm some long-lost princess? That's your theory?" Charlotte twisted the thin chain of her necklace around and around in her hands, feeling the cool metal cross in her hands, remembering her mother hanging it around her neck on her tenth birthday. Her thoughts began to swim, and yet she heard Herr Krause's voice ringing clear, flirting with Kshesinskaya through the closed doors. "He asked Kshesinskaya if she knew me as Grand Duchess, if I used that title."

Luc paused to suck in his breath, blinking from the pain. "When the gendarme beat me, he said the German code word for you is 'the Lost Grand Duchess.'"

Charlotte's pulse raced. Laurent stirred beside her. She couldn't remain still. Gently, she maneuvered Laurent's head to Luc's lap, and then worked her way upright, her muscles cramped from sitting so long. She shook her legs to stretch them.

"It doesn't make sense," she said. "My parents would never have kept that secret from me."

"Whether it's true or not doesn't matter, at least not yet," he said, gazing up at her. "What matters is this German officer believes you're a Romanov. If the Russians seek a separate peace, the Nazis could withdraw from the Eastern Front completely. The British will face a German army twice the size it is now. Even if America joins the war, we won't stand a chance."

Charlotte began to pace. She could only take a few steps before hitting the opposite wall. "That's all speculation. I know for certain what will happen if I don't help them. Laurent is sick." She felt the tears roll silently down her cheeks once more. "He needs help. Where else am I going to find help for him?"

Luc straightened his back. "We'll protect our son," he said. "I promise. Please trust me on this."

Charlotte shook her head uncertainly. "You didn't want him. You didn't want a child. You didn't even want to be a husband, not really, let alone a father."

At first, Luc didn't respond at all. Then, slowly, she saw the corners of his lips quiver and the hurt in his eyes, so deep she couldn't stand it. She felt an arrow in her heart every time she thought of how badly they'd treated one another. Charlotte wished she could take back the words, but she had to know for sure. If he couldn't take the truth, how could she trust him with Laurent's safety?

"I know," he said. "I'm sorry. But you know how much I love him." All of his pain seemed to fade, as though by sheer force of will. "I'm here now. I'm going to help. We have to try to escape. If it doesn't work, I'll insist you had nothing to do with the planning. They'll still let you go with Laurent. But if we escape, we'll go straight to your parents' house."

"I thought you wanted us to go to Spain."

"We should see your parents first. Maybe they know more."

"So we need to figure out a way out of here." Charlotte raised her eyebrows, hoping for an answer. Luc looked down at the sawdust collecting on the ground.

"You haven't figured that part out," she said.

"Not yet," he admitted.

Charlotte bit her lip, thinking. Luc looked stronger now, but a moment before he had looked like death. Surely he could look that way again.

Luc gave one of his sleepy half smiles. It reminded her again of the time when they'd loved one another, when they thought they could accomplish anything together. "I know that look," he said. "You have an idea."

"They already know you're badly hurt," Charlotte said. "Maybe we can convince them you're in even worse shape than they think."

Thirteen

Veronica gazed out the sedan's tinted window, watching the sky darken as a storm approached. She had been in the car with Alexei Romanov and his driver for thirty minutes, a knot slowly twisting in her gut. She tried to focus on the route they'd taken in from the city and the area they were driving through now. The neighborhood reminded her of East Los Angeles, except all of the signs were in Cyrillic, not Spanish. Hand-painted cards in storefront windows advertised sales on produce, electronics, imported compact discs, and the immigrant's best friend: prepaid phone cards. A woman huddled in a brightly colored shawl sold canned caviar from a street cart. Behind the woman, dark waves crashed restlessly against the shore.

"That's all you know?" Alexei Romanov said.

Veronica glanced up front, at the driver's cold blue eyes framed by dark lashes, as he adjusted the rearview mirror. She lowered her voice. "I told you already. Alexandra may have been pregnant in 1902. No one knows for sure. She was desperate for a son."

"This was two years before the birth of the heir, my namesake, Alexei?"

His namesake. Veronica found that comment a tad pretentious, even if it happened to be true. Romanov's calm demeanor grated on her already frayed nerves. He was a well-groomed man, but she chose to focus on a few loose and unruly white strands of eyebrow hair. "Some historians think it was a false pregnancy. Others think a stillbirth."

Romanov rubbed his hands together. He'd been fidgeting the whole drive, but not the way Michael fidgeted. Michael acted as though he was being followed, as though some central casting gangster might sneak up behind him and stuff a chloroform-soaked handkerchief in his mouth. Romanov looked more like a little boy waiting to open birthday presents. "The family expected an heir. A fifth girl would have been . . ."

"A disappointment," Veronica said.

"Then Mikhail's story already has a ring of truth to it."

"I didn't say that." Veronica listened to the intermittent scraping of the windshield wipers against the front window and the patter of raindrops on top of the car as the storm clouds finally released. She wouldn't let herself believe it. And yet the images of the royal procession along the Neva River came rushing back to her mind.

"Did the empress ask for anyone's help when she tried to conceive a son?" Romanov said. "Besides Phillipe Vachot, I mean. A female servant perhaps?"

"I told you, I don't know."

"Ms. Rubalov does."

"Then why are you asking me?" Veronica asked, irritated.

"I hoped for validation. Regardless, I'm certain you'll want to hear her story."

A subway train rattled above them as they drove underneath elevated tracks. Romanov leaned forward and made a twirling motion with his index finger, signaling the driver to turn into a parking lot near the wooden boardwalk. Veronica peered out the front window, blurry from the beating rain. Across the parking lot, a bright neon sign blinked VALENTINA against the gray sky. "I thought you were taking me to this woman's house."

The driver parked and turned the engine off. Romanov hopped out, unconcerned with the rain and buttoning his fur-trimmed overcoat against the wind. He slid over to Veronica's side of the car, opened the door, and offered his arm, as though escorting her to a formal dinner party.

She didn't budge. "Where are we?"

"Brighton Beach. The cultural center for Russians in North America."

"I mean why a restaurant? I thought we were going to this woman's house. I thought you said she could talk to me today."

"How often do you get to eat authentic Russian cuisine when you're back home in California?" Romanov said proudly.

Veronica could eat Russian food whenever she wanted. There were places all over West Hollywood and even some in the Valley. She just wasn't a big fan of cabbage and borscht. "I'm not hungry. I want to talk to Ms. Rubalov."

Romanov reached into his pocket for his phone and checked it. "Not yet."

"We are not meeting old lady here?" The thick Russian accent boomed from the front seat. "What is this that takes so long?"

"Ms. Rubalov asked that we come to her home. But Mikhail hasn't received the message yet. I don't want to impose overly long on her hospitality. She's not a young woman anymore. We don't want to exhaust her. We should wait a while longer."

Despite the wind and chill blowing into the car, Veronica's hands went clammy. "What's really going on?"

The driver twisted in his seat and scowled at her. Romanov merely smiled and nodded as though everything were fine.

"Tell her!" the driver roared.

Romanov gave a timid laugh. Veronica realized this was the first time she'd seen him thrown off his game. And she found it strange he would let his chauffeur take that tone with him. "I'm afraid I've engaged you in something of a ruse," Romanov told her.

The knot in Veronica's gut grew into a sick lump of terror.

"Now that you're with us, we think Mikhail will see the sense of our request for his DNA," he added.

They didn't require her expertise or academic credentials. Alongside the terror, she felt a pang of injured pride. She was no more than bait on a hook. And not very strong bait at that. "You're using me to get Michael to talk to you? I don't know that I'll do you much good . . ." The driver was still scowling at her. Veronica realized it might not be a good idea to imply she'd out-lived her usefulness. ". . . because Michael made plans this afternoon to visit friends," she added quickly. "And he's not the type to check his phone every few seconds. It might take a while."

Romanov smiled, the charmer once more. "We are patient people, aren't we, Grigori?" He nodded at the driver and gave a nervous laugh. "We've already waited nearly a hundred years for the heir."

"You are patient man. I am man who knows value of time."

The driver, Grigori, jumped out of the car and slammed the door shut behind him. He threw his trench coat on over his jeans and black turtleneck sweater and then folded his arms in front of his chest.

Veronica decided to try a different tactic. She directed her comment to Grigori as he stood in the rain. "There are laws in this country that protect innocent citizens from being held against their will."

Immediately Romanov chimed in: "He's covered by diplomatic immunity."

A diplomat? This guy reeked of *mafiosi*. She was sure of it. He could have passed for Tony Soprano's Russian cousin. Veronica looked Grigori straight in the eye, trying not to stare at the purple acorn scar on his cheek. "You're a government representative?"

He smirked. "I know the right people. They give me proper credentials."

"What about you?" she asked Romanov. "You're American."

"A very old American," Romanov replied. "Besides, my citizenship was always more of a technicality anyway."

Pain throbbed at the base of Veronica's skull, like someone had taken a vise to her head and clamped down. She needed to contact Michael and warn him not to come. She still had the Mace, if she could figure out how to get to it without them noticing.

"Please." Alexei Romanov nodded toward the restaurant's front door. "You serve a great purpose here. You should feel honored."

Veronica shrank back in her seat and shook her head.

Grigori leaned down. Before she even realized what was happening, he had taken her by the shoulders. He wasn't rough. It didn't hurt. She didn't even think to resist. He pulled her out of the car, lifting her off the ground momentarily. Then he set her before Alexei Romanov, leaving no doubt as to who controlled the situation.

"Now, now," Romanov said, clicking his tongue against his teeth. He kept his voice even, but his brow wrinkled. "Really, that sort of thing isn't necessary."

The chill forced Veronica tighter into her thin coat. Droplets of rain brushed her cheek. She had Mace. She could disable Grigori and run. She reached for her purse, but Grigori grabbed her wrists, more roughly now, and put her hands behind her back, blocking any possible escape. She saw no choice but to follow Romanov.

Inside, Valentina had two levels. The top level, on the board-walk, was brightly lit and filled with Formica tabletops. As they passed the kitchen, thick Russian accents competed with running water and a blend of balalaika and techno pop blaring from an old radio. The scent of fried potatoes and onions filled the air. Veronica's stomach curdled.

Romanov led them down a steep flight of stairs to the restaurant's lower level. Grigori still held her hands tight behind her back. Either no one noticed or no one dared say anything. Downstairs, the main dining area was decorated in gold and silver tones that left no room for subtlety. Sound equipment had been shoved against the back wall and a dance floor roped off to the side. She imagined the bar picked up at night, crowded with Russian gangsters in expensive suits tinkering with smartphones—the kind of place where they brought in strippers.

Alexei Romanov led them to a booth in the back, where bottles of mineral water and the ubiquitous *zakuski*, small plates of pickles, boiled eggs, and sliced herring—the chips and salsa of Russian tables—awaited consumption. Romanov slid into the booth beside her and Grigori sat across from them, removing his trench coat. Veronica didn't dare meet his gaze.

Instead, she stared at the menu. All of the items were in Cyrillic. Silently, she translated: crab salad with soured cream, wild porcini mushroom soup, baked cod in a walnut sauce. It helped steady her thoughts.

"First, you try to convince me Michael's a fraud," she told Romanov in a low voice. "Now you believe his story?"

Romanov brought out a pair of reading glasses and perched them low on his nose. "Really, you should come to New York under more pleasant circumstances. I'm sure if you and I talked, we'd find we have much in common."

An hour earlier, when she still thought of Alexei Romanov as a courtly if eccentric old gentleman, Veronica would have agreed. Not anymore. "We have nothing in common. You're a liar. I think you believe Michael's claim and the story about the fifth daughter. He's a threat to you. You don't want anything from me. You just wanted to lure me out here to get to him."

Romanov lifted a slice of herring from the serving plate and began chewing irritably. His bites were dainty enough, but the sight of the fish in his mouth made her stomach turn again. "When Mikhail first came to us, we wanted to believe him," he snapped. "But his story was so outrageous. Now we will determine the truth once and for all. If Mikhail is the true heir, he'll need my help. Think about the current government in Russia and how they behave. It's an abomination. Not that this country is any better, what with all the foreign policy disasters. The U.S. could use a rival."

"You want a tsar to bring back the Cold War?"

Romanov compressed his lips. "Of course not. My parents were staunch monarchists. They dedicated themselves to the preservation of the glory of the old order. No one was more pleased to greet the demise of the Soviet Union than my family. But that doesn't mean Russia shouldn't remain a strong presence in the world."

"Let's say Michael is the rightful heir," Veronica said. "He doesn't strike me as the sort who wants to dominate the world outside a game of Risk. He doesn't even think Russia should restore the monarchy."

Romanov waved his fork in the air like a mad conductor. "He wants this more than I do. He has a plan. I know it."

Veronica stared back down at the menu: buttered pastries filled with shredded beef, carrots cooked in sugar. "Michael wouldn't cooperate with your organization. He warned me not to come to see you. Now I see why. I hope he stays far away."

Grigori slammed his fists on the table so hard their bottles of mineral water shook.

"Mikhail will come for her," Romanov assured him. "He's the sort."

"Maybe he will come. Maybe not. I give him extra motivation."

Grigori reached under the table. He retrieved a hard, flat smartphone and pointed it at Veronica. She heard the imitation click as he took her picture.

"Is that really necessary?" Romanov removed a handkerchief from the front pocket of his blazer and dabbed the corners of his mouth.

"He'll call the police." Veronica switched to Russian and raised her voice on the last word, hoping someone in the restaurant might hear her and come over.

Grigori shrugged and pressed some buttons on the phone. "Speak in English, like me," he said calmly. "Less people to understand." He nodded his head at Romanov and continued in a low voice. "I send this with message. He will not contact police. He will come. He will not want me to kill the girl here."

No emotional affectation. Just a simple statement. A choking sensation gripped the back of Veronica's throat.

A rosy-cheeked waiter with curly blond hair and a green apron approached their table. He gave Grigori a respectful nod, and then Grigori proceeded to order *blini* with caviar, borscht and black bread, salmon and trout. This gave Veronica time to gather her thoughts. She needed to stall. She had to find out who Grigori really was and what he wanted. Then she needed to contact Michael and warn him.

Grigori waved his hand and the waiter withdrew to the kitchen.

"Who are you?" She might as well start with the obvious.

"A chauffeur. Good way to make money. So many lazy people." Grigori waved his arm vaguely and then laughed a little, sounding pleased with himself.

"I mean who are you really?"

"I work for businessmen," he said smoothly, still in English. "I follow instructions. I collect money. Good way to live. They pay well. What more is to know?"

Veronica stared down at the menu again, but now all of the Cyrillic letters were a meaningless blur. "What type of 'business' do these men conduct?"

"A little of everything. Real estate. What does this matter?"

"I'm here against my will," Veronica said. "I want to know why."

"Americans. Always wanting to know why. Always wanting to

understand." He gave a big, petulant shrug. No one could shrug like a Russian. "Under old system, money was nothing. Success was about connections. Not anymore. I want money for little house in the country, a *dacha*. When I return to Russia, I grow turnips and spend winter nights reading our great authors." He tilted his head cunningly. "You like Alexander Pushkin?"

Veronica loved Pushkin, but she ignored the question. "You have no personal stake in all of this?"

"For this one"—he pointed at Romanov—"politics is passion. Not for me." He smiled at Veronica, almost fondly, like she was an unruly child who amused him. "But it pays well. Half of Russian people want Stalin back. Street vendors sell notebooks with his ugly face. He is rock star now. Maybe they bring tsar back instead. New rock star."

"Come, Grigori." Romanov gave a nervous chuckle. "I don't know that half of Russia wants Stalin back."

A spark of hope flickered at the back of her brain. She turned to Romanov. "You want to know the truth about Michael badly enough to involve your organization with someone like this? And these men he works for, these . . ." Veronica was about to say *mobsters*, then stopped herself. She started to say *nut jobs*, but caught herself again. ". . . businessmen."

"My loyalty is to Russia," Romanov said, his wrinkled face pink with agitation. "Now is the time to seize sublime destiny."

"Mikhail Karstadt is to help determine truth," Grigori said. "He would not come willingly, so here are you."

"I don't care what you told Michael. He'll go to the police."

Grigori tilted his head again. "Tell me, does Mikhail love you?"

Veronica felt the pain deep inside, like a punch in the stomach.

"You are unsure," Grigori said smoothly. "That is response I expect from woman. You love him. I see it. I have done you magnificent favor then. I tell Mikhail everything bad that would happen if he goes to police. You will know soon if he is in love."

The waiter returned with their order. Veronica couldn't look at the black beads of caviar. Romanov didn't appear to have much of an appetite anymore either. They watched in silence as Grigori pushed his sleeves up and shoveled fish in his mouth. A bitter taste rose in Veronica's throat. She was going to be sick. She stumbled to her feet. Romanov stood as well, ready to grab her.

Veronica snatched her purse off the seat. She felt too shaky to risk the Mace. If she missed, who knew what Grigori would do? And would she even make it to the door? She remembered how respectfully the waiter had treated Grigori. They were still technically in the United States, but she felt as though they'd taken her to Russia. "Where is the bathroom?"

"What are you going to do in there?" Romanov demanded.

"What do you think?"

"Let her go." Grigori waved his hand benevolently and returned to his lunch. "I know place well. Windows barred."

Reluctantly, Romanov stood to let her pass. "Don't take long."

Clutching her purse as she walked, Veronica kept her gaze focused on the tiles on the floor in front of her. As she passed the stairs, she heard the laughing Russian dishwashers in the kitchen and caught the scent of fried onions once more. When she reached the restroom, she shut and locked the door. The bathroom smelled strongly of antiseptic and her stomach roiled. Hands shaking, she reached into her purse for her phone.

It wasn't there. Grigori must have taken it while he was fiddling under the table finding his own phone. She had no way of contacting Michael.

After lunch, they drove past bungalows with badly weathered roofs and half-finished paint jobs until Grigori parked in front of a gray cottage that stood in stark contrast to the sad neglect of the other houses. Neatly clipped hedges encircled the front porch and cherry red nasturtium spilled over brick planters on the window-sills. Flower-shaped pinwheels rippled in the breeze.

"Stay here," Romanov told Grigori. "Call me when Mikhail arrives."

"I think not. This one looks ready to bolt." Grigori indicated Veronica should open the car door. She obeyed and they walked to the cottage together, Romanov running two steps in front of them like a giddy schoolboy.

She heard a buzzing in Grigori's jacket pocket. He withdrew his phone and checked the message, frowning. Veronica wondered if it was Michael. She tried to move her hand subtly. Grigori had her phone, but somehow he'd missed the Mace. Now both he and Romanov were distracted . . .

Before she could think about it further, Grigori grabbed her arm. She bristled at his touch. He pressed her hand firmly back down to her side.

Veronica felt her breathing grow ragged and hard. Her hands clenched in and out, making fists. As soon as he let go, she shoved him. Grigori stumbled.

Romanov's voice shook. "Please. Let's handle this like adults."

Veronica expected Grigori to turn on her, but he just gave a stout laugh. "It is all right. I would do same."

Romanov expelled his breath and started babbling. "I apologize again for these unfortunate circumstances, Dr. Herrera, but I do think you will enjoy your visit. As I told you, Ms. Rubalov's mother was one of the empress's attendants at the turn of the century. She is magnificent." He pushed the doorbell and it chimed pleasantly in response.

"What do you want?" Veronica recognized the Russian words from the other side of the door. Russians weren't much for small talk.

"I've brought her to you," Romanov said.

The door swung open. A tall, trim, older woman waited on the other side. Her eyes retained an open, expectant expression at odds with the firm set of her lips.

"May I introduce Ms. Natalya Rubalov," Romanov said, sweeping his arm gallantly in the woman's direction. "And this is Dr. Veronica Herrera."

"A pleasure to meet you," Veronica replied in Russian, extending her hand.

At first her hand hovered awkwardly in midair. Natalya Rubalov gave Veronica a thorough inspection, starting at the top of her head, lingering on her eyes, and moving all the way down to the tips of her black boots. Veronica dropped her hand and returned the favor. Natalya Rubalov wore a cranberry-colored caftan, and small charms dangling from a slim silver bracelet made tinkling sounds as she moved. Her lipstick matched the caftan and her hair was pulled back in a neat white bun. Her bright blue eyes were all the more astonishing set against her dark olive complexion, so different than the Russian winter white Veronica had expected. And something about the shape of her face looked familiar.

All at once, Natalya Rubalov drew Veronica into a suffocating bear hug. Veronica struggled for air, but she liked how Natalya smelled, like powder and floral perfume. For a moment, Abuela's face flashed in Veronica's mind.

"I told Ms. Rubalov you're writing a book about Empress Alexandra," Romanov said. "Clearly, she wishes to express her appreciation."

"Who is this?" Natalya let go of Veronica and nodded her chin at Grigori. "You only told me you were bringing the professor."

"An associate," Romanov replied smoothly. "Please let us in, Ms. Rubalov."

Natalya stepped aside. Veronica was about to step inside, but before she could cross the threshold, Grigori flashed a malicious smile and pushed her through the door. She stumbled and would have fallen if Natalya hadn't taken her arm and steered her to the sofa with surprising strength.

"Shame on you," Natalya spat at Grigori. "And in my home. Mind your manners or you will wait outside."

Grigori's smile vanished. He gave Natalya a sheepish look before staking a corner of the room as his own. Such was the power of the elderly in Russian culture. They could even stare down a gangster.

The house appeared as neatly kept as Natalya herself. Brightly embroidered quilts covered the sofa and chairs and intricate lace doilies graced each end table. Warm scents of cinnamon and baking bread filled the small rooms. Natalya ambled off to the kitchen, where Veronica spotted a silver samovar waiting on the counter.

"Lovely home, isn't it?" Romanov said. "She is a true lady. Even if she is only the daughter of a servant."

Natalya returned with steaming hot tea in a china cup edged with flowers. She placed it on the coffee table, but Veronica didn't dare move.

"You look nervous," Natalya said.

"Wouldn't you be, in my place?"

Natalya sighed. "Here is the Russian cure."

"I thought vodka was the Russian cure," Veronica said.

"Some of us come from a more elegant upbringing."

Romanov positioned himself neatly on the sofa next to Vero-nica, holding his back erect, as though he'd already assumed the throne. Natalya settled easily into an armchair. Though seated to the side of them, her gaze never left Veronica. "What's the mat-ter? You don't like how the tea smells?"

"It smells great."

"Then drink. Drink."

Veronica blew the steam away and took a quick sip. She would have preferred coffee, but found comfort in the cinnamon-tinged tea, even if it was still too hot. Some of her vigor returned. "The tea is wonderful."

Natalya nodded.

"Your mother worked for Empress Alexandra?" Veronica said.

Natalya turned to a nearby shelf. She produced a gold photo album and spread it open in her lap. She gave her fingertip a dainty lick before turning the page. "The tsar's family rarely took pictures with their servants. See the special bond that Alexandra and my mother shared."

Veronica's nerves tingled. She thought she'd seen every photo of Alexandra in existence, or at least that the Russian government had released. Natalya turned the album around so Veronica could see, and pointed.

The photo had been shot from a low vantage point and the subjects were off center. Veronica wondered if one of the grand duchesses had taken the picture. Alexandra looked around thirty, still beautiful with those incredibly sad eyes. Next to her stood a young woman in a plain, starched white skirt and shirtwaist. The woman's features were small and indistinct, but Veronica thought she looked scared. "This is your mother?"

Natalya nodded. "Her name was Lena Ivanovna. She left the Romanovs' service before the Revolution, praise God. If she'd stayed, the Bolsheviks would have hunted her and killed her like an animal."

"Why did she leave the country?"

Natalya peered over her shoulder at Grigori. He was leaning against the wall opposite Veronica, near a small television set, his arms folded, staring out the window. He seemed unimpressed by Natalya's story of her mother.

Natalya shrugged and then turned her attention back to Romanov. "You're sure?"

Romanov nodded. "She will help us. I'm sure of it."

From the back of the photo album, Natalya withdrew a yellowing letter. Veronica recognized Alexandra's handwriting. This was not a copy of a copy, as Romanov had shown her earlier, but the genuine article. Veronica tried not to snatch the letter from Natalya's frail hand.

"Anastasia was born in 1901," Natalya told Veronica. "Everyone supposes that the heir, Alexei, who was born in 1904, was the next child. But between those two, Empress Alexandra also gave birth. It wasn't a hysterical pregnancy or a miscarriage. My mother knew the whole story."

Fourteen

The following day, the tsar's female relatives were summoned to the
room where the birth was to have taken place. By the time they
arrived, Alexandra lay prostrate and hysterical. Blood stained
the sheets. No one understood what had happened.
Or if they did understand, they never bothered to tell.
—VERONICA HERRERA, The Reluctant Romanov

PETERHOF ESTATE
AUGUST 1902

In the nursery adjoining the master suite, Lena rocked the sleeping newborn in her arms. The room had been set up for a tiny tsarevich: a crib filled with soft plush animals, a blue-and-white chest of drawers embellished with stencils of the imperial double-headed eagle, and a brand-new changing table, still spotless. Lena turned over the blue blanket, soft as lamb's wool, to examine the baby wrapped inside. The child was still slick and glistening, cheeks a healthy pink. Tiny buds of red hair shot off the baby's head and sparkled in the bright daylight. Toes and fingers curled up and out, flexing as though to test their newfound place in the world. Creases marred the fresh skin around the baby's eyes, but these marks would disappear after a few days. Perfect.

If only she'd been a boy.

At some point, Alexandra would demand an explanation. Why hadn't Lena's remedies ensured an heir? Once more, Lena would try to explain that these were only the tales of old women, that she never made any guarantees. But no matter what she said, she knew the empress would mutter and insist she was cursed, as she had after the birth of Anastasia. And Lena would feel sick at heart.

Right now, however, Alexandra remained unconscious, and so Lena could savor the moment. She'd brought a baby into the world. Her mother would have been astonished to see Lena holding a Romanov grand duchess in her arms. "I told you I could do it," she whispered.

"I never had any doubt," Marie said.

Lena shot to attention. The dowager had kept her distance and remained uncharacteristically silent. At last, she stepped into the nursery. "You'll be properly compensated for your service."

Lena tucked the blanket back around the baby's neck and shoulders. "Will you present the grand duchess to the tsar?"

"I will do no such thing," Marie snapped. "How can you even suggest it?"

Some of the black curls from Marie's upswept hair had spilled out and stuck to the thin layer of sweat on her neck and shoulders. Something about the disorder bothered Lena. She'd never seen Marie look anything but perfectly polished. Lena wondered if perhaps she was waiting to talk to her son, to gently break the news of another girl. This seemed unnecessary. Though she didn't presume intimacy with the tsar, Lena knew he adored all of his children. Nothing in the world could keep him from seeing his newborn.

Marie softened her tone. "Now put that poor creature down."

"I should stay. During the first few hours it's important to keep watch . . ."

"Have you lost your senses?" Marie's voice echoed in the small room.

"Where is the doctor?"

"He left. Of course." Marie's eyes widened. "What more could he do?"

Vachot should have remained at least until Alexandra awoke. He should have checked the child's vital signs. Lena may not have had much faith in the man's abilities, but she knew he would do that much. "Dr. Vachot left?"

"I sent him away. Can you blame me? I knew Alix shouldn't have let him anywhere near her."

Lena hesitated. "I saw other doctors. They were playing cards."

"All of them left." Marie reached into the front pocket of her voluminous skirt. Her hand moved slowly, as though the action caused her pain. She withdrew a long envelope. "Take this." She extended her hand. A stack of multicolored bills had been stuffed inside the thin envelope. "Your services are no longer required."

A shimmering wave obscured Lena's vision. She took a moment to process Marie's words. The baby cooed softly in her sleep. Lena pulled her closer to her chest. "You're dismissing me?"

"Surely you wouldn't want to remain in our employ. Alix will manage. I've given you enough money to last until you've found another position. If you need a reference I'll gladly provide one."

"I did everything you asked."

"Let me make this perfectly clear." Marie's expression remained set in stone. "Take the money and leave her with me. Speak to no one. Don't even look at anyone as you leave. I can see it will be too difficult for you to remain here."

Lena drew back. Her mother once told her evil spirits sometimes invaded the room after a birth, causing vulnerable new mothers to say strange things and commit unspeakable acts. Sometimes these mothers even killed their own babies. Much as Lena had fought to dismiss her mother's superstitions, she couldn't help but wonder if perhaps such a spirit had entered Marie's body, finding Alexandra's temporarily vacant. Lena placed her hand across the baby's forehead like a shield. "If Nicholas knew—"

Marie slapped her hard across the cheek. Sharp pain shot through Lena's face. Stunned, Lena reeled back, but the grand duchess remained safely tucked in her arms.

"Addressing the tsar by his Christian name? Who do you think you are?"

"I'm sorry," she stammered. "I don't know what I was thinking."

Marie touched her collar and fingered the chain around her neck protectively, like she thought Lena might lunge for her throat. "Do you think this brings me pleasure?"

Despite her severe tone, Lena believed Marie could be worn down, if only one found the courage to confront her. After all, Alexandra had managed it at least once. Lena took a tentative step forward. Marie glanced at her grandchild, in obvious distress. Lena's cheek still smarted from the slap, but she couldn't leave the grand duchess alone with this woman.

"The empress is not old," Lena said. "They can try again for a son, for the heir. I can help them. Please don't make me go. Let me stay and help."

Marie picked up a soft toy lamb from the crib and kneaded its stomach in her hands.

"You only need to approach the tsar. Perhaps there is the

possibility of an alternate succession to the throne that might include girls."

"Alternate succession? Is that what they told you to say?"

Lena stepped back, hating herself for the miscalculation. She shouldn't have presumed to give Marie political advice. "No one told me to say anything."

"Don't give me that look," Marie said. "You know who I'm talking about. I asked you before about your family and you tried to be coy. You didn't think I knew about your brother, Anton Ivanovich?"

Lena's vision faltered. Marie's small figure seemed to advance and then retreat before her. "He's done nothing wrong."

"Perhaps not in the last twenty-four hours, no," Marie said dryly. "Poor Alix is so incompetent when it comes to these matters. Or perhaps she does know about him. She would sympathize. She has a miscreant brother of her own. I should never have allowed Nicky to marry into a family of deviants." Marie stepped closer. "Your brother is one of them. One of the radicals who'd see my son's throat slit and this country plunged into anarchy. He taught you English? What else did he teach you? Did he send you here to hurt my family?"

The words struck worse than any physical blow. Lena struggled to remain upright. She tried to remember Pavel's advice, though now the words were a jumble in her mind. He'd spoken before of self-protection, the skill he'd learned as a boxer. She'd seen boxing rings back home on the streets of Archangel, circles chalked haphazardly into the dust around two men beating one another. Dark blood flew into the gathered crowd of shouting men as the faces of the fighters grew swollen and then turned to pulp.

Lena tried to imagine herself inside a boxing ring, holding her fists up to protect her face. "My brother has done nothing wrong and neither have I."

"Can you prove that?" Marie said.

"I helped the empress. I was a friend to her when she needed one. I gave her advice when she asked." Lena heard her voice crack. She backed away from Marie again, bumping into a wall. "I helped deliver her child."

"Do you know what happened to my father-in-law?" Marie said.

Lena ran her tongue along her dry lower lip.

"He was blown to pieces," Marie said flatly.

Lena remembered the stories. Marie's father-in-law was the tsar-liberator, Alexander II. The day after he signed the document emancipating the serfs, a young man threw a grenade at his carriage. The first one missed him, but when Alexander went to check on his coachmen, the second grenade hit its mark. Lena had heard all of the gruesome details. The tsar, his limbs mangled or gone, asked to be brought back to his palace, where he died slowly, in agonizing pain. Marie's late husband had been crowned tsar on an act of terror.

"I watched him die." Marie leaned in close. "Since that day, I've never known a moment of peace. When my husband was alive I kept him safe. Now I must do the same for my son."

"It is what we all want," Lena whispered.

"I said tell me. Tell me what you will report to them. Did they give you a grenade to throw at the tsar when the time is right?"

"My brother is not a terrorist," Lena cried. "He has a troubled past, it's true, but he's a good boy. His politics . . . it's a phase he'll outgrow. And I have nothing to do with it. I would never hurt the tsar or the empress."

"Your brother, this good boy, could spend time in prison in Archangel," Marie said. "The death rates in the prisons up north are the worst in the country."

A sharp pain rocked Lena's body. She imagined her brother, poor Anton who had always treated her so gently, languishing in a dank prison cell. Alexandra's promises would mean nothing. She'd failed him.

"You must know what happens to handsome young men in jail," Marie said. "He'll wish he was dead. I shall write the warrant for his arrest myself. They will torture him until he screams for mercy."

The walls of the room seemed to close in around her, choking Lena until she wanted to scream. Instead, she dropped to her knees, cradling the grand duchess's tender skull. The baby mewled softly. Lena stroked her forehead, hot tears streaming down her face. With her free hand, she groped for Marie's skirts. She clutched a bit of cloth in her hand and kissed it desperately. "I beg you. Find it in your heart to spare him."

Marie thrust the envelope forward. Lena just made out the outline of the bills.

"Give me that poor child," she said. "And leave here at once."

PARIS

OCTOBER 1941

Twenty minutes later, as promised, Herr Krause returned to their cell. The gendarme followed, grumpily finishing a cigarette, his cheeks pink from the cold air outside. Herr Krause stopped in front of Charlotte. He smiled at her, smug as a snake. "Well? You have reached a decision? You are prepared to leave with us?"

He spoke in Danish again, the language of her parents. It made her thoughts shudder and spin, when she most needed to focus.

Charlotte looked down. Luc lay motionless in her arms, eyes closed and head slumped. Laurent remained still as best he could, though every few minutes his shoulders trembled. She had forced him awake, afraid that if he woke of his own volition, terror would overcome him. But he followed her instructions and stayed quiet. She was proud of him.

She closed her eyes, steadying her breath. She couldn't confront Herr Krause yet. They'd agreed to get as much information as possible before attempting to escape. Hopefully, Charlotte would learn something to help piece together her past. "How did you do it?" she asked quietly.

"How did I do what?" Herr Krause said.

"How did you find me?" she muttered.

Herr Krause put his hand on his heart and bowed to her once more. "So you acknowledge your title, Grand Duchess? You accept your destiny?"

Charlotte remained rigid. She couldn't bring herself to nod. She lifted her head slightly, redirecting her gaze from Laurent's soft blond hair to the dark scar, like a child's drawing of a sunburst, on Herr Krause's tanned left hand.

"Say it," Herr Krause said pleasantly. "Say you accept. And then I will tell you how I found you."

"I accept."

Herr Krause stooped over, grabbed her hand, and kissed it, his lips moist. She tried not to show her repulsion, forced herself not to pull away. "I have searched for you for many years, ever since I met with your grandmamma in Denmark," he said, his voice quivering with pleasure. "But finally your friend the dancer, Matilda Kshesinskaya, led me to you."

Charlotte gulped in a pungent lungful of the secondhand smoke that clung to the air. As far as she knew, her grandparents were all dead. She'd never met them. He was lying. He had to be lying about Kshesinskaya as well. "She wouldn't do that to me."

"Best to know who your true friends are. You'll need to hone your diplomatic skills when you assume the throne." Herr Krause tilted his head. "We had her son. He had joined that sad excuse for a resistance group, the Maquis. Didn't she mention any of this? After she learned of her son's imprisonment, she told us where you were."

Charlotte saw red spots. Kshesinskaya. How could she?

"She was intimate with the tsar once, was she not? Perhaps I shall find a position for her once I'm charged with the Ukraine." Herr Krause seemed oblivious to Charlotte's rising temper. He let go of her hand. "You see, I am to serve as your prime minister."

The anger flashed so intensely it blinded Charlotte as to what she was supposed to do or say next. She rolled her shoulders back, as she did before going onstage. Push the nerves back down your throat. Forget yourself. Focus. "What is wrong in the Ukraine? Why do you want us there? I thought the Germans held it fast. That's what the papers say."

Herr Krause's gaze shifted, no longer projecting reptilian watchfulness. Instead, his eyes fixed on hers, steady as a hypnotist's. Unwillingly, Charlotte found herself spellbound. "The people there must have a government that inspires loyalty," he said. "Your time has come, Grand Duchess. Reclaim your birthright."

Charlotte heard only the steady rhythm of her own breathing. She wanted it all to end, her life to return to what it had been. Without control, life meant little. Even Laurent's life, she realized with a shudder, could become worthless.

"I won't be of much use to you," she said.

Herr Krause reddened. "I've made the consequences clear."

She eased Luc onto the ground, next to Laurent, and rose, sliding her feet together until they locked into a perfect fifth position. Charlotte looked down at Luc. Herr Krause followed suit, as did the grumpy gendarme, who peered over Herr Krause's shoulders to see what was happening. The gendarme's expression changed at once.

When Herr Krause spoke now, his elegant Danish sounded rattled. "He's out. So what? He had a rough afternoon."

Charlotte summoned the emotion, all the fear and anger she'd been forced to bottle inside. "You killed him," she growled.

Herr Krause attempted to retain his practiced composure, but his lips trembled as he stared at Luc. Behind him, the gendarme dropped his cigarette. It hit the damp cell floor with a sizzle.

"You bastard!" Charlotte curled her hands into tight balls and lunged at Herr Krause. He easily caught her and grabbed her swinging fists. Charlotte fell into the cold folds of his jacket. Perspiration and heavy cologne clung to the leather.

"Control yourself," he hissed.

She clutched his hand, the one with the red welt, as though she needed someone, anyone, to lean on for support. His muscles stiffened under her grasp, but he didn't let go.

"What is this?" Herr Krause addressed the gendarme, his

voice edged with indignant anger. "You were only supposed to make him look bad, not really hurt him."

Charlotte continued to scream and pound at his chest. He had to use the full force of his weight to control her.

"It can't be," the gendarme sputtered. "I was careful."

"He had a weak heart."

Herr Krause took her by the arms and shook her until her vision blurred.

Charlotte allowed a small note of triumph in her voice, through the hysteria. "You killed him for nothing. I won't cooperate."

"If you think I'm letting you go after all of this time—"

"It's impossible." The gendarme approached the corner of the cell where Luc and Laurent lay still. "Even if he had a weak heart."

"Stay away from him," Charlotte cried.

The gendarme ignored her and leaned in close to Luc. "You must be mistaken. You see? He was only knocked unconscious."

Luc's eyes opened. He punched the gendarme flush in the jaw. The gendarme tumbled backward and fell. Luc scrambled for his holster.

Charlotte knew what she had to do next. She braced herself, willing herself not to miss. But she had done this a thousand times before, a quick, clean *grande jeté*. She landed a backward kick square in the German's groin. He cried out, let go, and crumpled inward.

Luc grabbed the revolver and pointed it down at Herr Krause's lowered head. He addressed the gendarme. "Empty your pockets."

The gendarme crossed his arms in front of his chest belligerently. But when he heard the click of the safety lock on the revolver, he thrust his hands in his pockets and removed a slim black wallet and a set of keys.

"Grab Laurent," Luc told her. "Go." He tossed the keys to her and she caught them in midair. "Hurry."

Charlotte gathered Laurent in her arms. She glanced at Herr Krause, who was starting to recover and right himself. "Luc . . ."

"Go!"

She held Laurent close and ran up the metal stairs. The sour scents of blood and decay lingered in the casino. She ran past the bloodstained roulette wheels, feet thumping on the padded carpet, until she reached the revolving doors.

Outside, in the metallic autumn light, she tried to gather her bearings. She spotted the glass booth where the gendarme had stopped them earlier and about sixty meters beyond that, Luc's beat-up car. They'd shot out the tires. She stared at the keys in her hand. They were unfamiliar: black, sleek, and clean. Then she noticed an unmarked black Mercedes, like the Germans drove, parked at the crest of a low hill behind the casino. She ran, shifting Laurent to her left arm, and then stopped to fiddle with the unfamiliar lock on the door. "Come on," she muttered.

She heard a gunshot and jumped, every sense alert. "Come on!"

At last the lock gave way. She lowered Laurent onto the clean passenger seat, and then moved to the driver's side in front. The car smelled of antiseptic. She curled her nose and jammed the key in the ignition. The engine rumbled to attention. Her hands shook as she grasped the steering wheel.

Where was Luc? She adjusted the polished rearview mirror so she could see behind them.

Luc was coming, hobbling on one leg. A dark red trail of blood streamed down the other. She tried to coax the unfamiliar gearshift into reverse.

The gendarme stood behind Luc. He'd recovered from the

blow and taken out another gun, which he pointed at Luc's head.

Time seemed to slow. She drew in her breath. She could practically feel the hot stage lights on her face, as she did right as a performance began. Charlotte turned the steering wheel around until the car was facing the other direction, aimed at the gendarme.

She hesitated. She was about to kill a man. She would burn in hell forever. But it was either that or let him shoot Luc. She'd take her chances with God. She pressed her foot down hard on the accelerator.

The gendarme tried to turn his gun on Charlotte, but there wasn't time. He hopped out of the way to avoid being mowed down by his own Mercedes. Then he tumbled backward and started rolling down the low hill.

Charlotte slammed on the brake. Luc, still hobbling, opened the back door and hopped inside. "Go, go!"

She heard Laurent's cry and glanced down. His nose was bleeding. Huge tears slid down his cheeks.

"Keep going, Charlotte," Luc demanded. "I'll help him."

Luc reached over and squeezed Laurent's shoulders. Then he turned Laurent toward him and pinched his nostrils carefully, as Charlotte had taught him to do, to stop the bleeding. "It's all right," Luc said. "Breathe through your mouth. Breathe slowly."

"You're hurt," Laurent said.

She heard Luc's breath coming only in raspy gasps. The sound alone made her heart sink. Still, Luc managed to keep his tone reassuring. "We're going to be all right now," he told Laurent. "They can't hurt us anymore."

Charlotte worked up the courage to glance in the rearview

mirror. The color drained from Luc's face at an alarming rate. Blood seeped darkly down his leg, staining the pristine seat around him. She forced the rising panic back down her throat. "We'll stop somewhere," she said. "You need help. We'll get help."

"Don't stop." Luc was still pinching Laurent's nostrils. He couldn't free his other hand to apply pressure to his leg and stanch the bleeding. "I'll be fine."

"My parents' house is hours away."

"You can't stop. Keep going."

Charlotte worked her way out of his jacket, keeping one hand on the steering wheel. "Laurent, can you do it yourself?" she said gently. Laurent nodded and moved his hand to his nose so Luc could let go. "Here." She tossed Luc the jacket. He put it on and then closed his eyes in pain.

She pressed her foot down on the accelerator once more and headed south.

Fifteen

"When the dowager empress asked her to leave the nursery, my mother felt lost." Natalya Rubalov's voice had dropped to a hoarse whisper. She'd withdrawn Alexandra's letter from the manila envelope in the photo album. Veronica stared, mesmerized by the thin stationery; lightweight, yet somehow substantial in Natalya's frail hands. Veronica's fingers flexed. She was meant to hear this story, and hold that letter. After all of these years, somehow it had always been meant to pass from Alexandra's hands to her own.

"May I hold it?" The words sounded curt and overly abrupt, even to her own ears.

Natalya glanced up, took one look at Veronica's trembling fingers, and averted her gaze. "How could the dowager empress do this?" she said, as though Veronica hadn't spoken at all. "How could Marie ask my mother to leave the baby?"

Veronica supposed she wouldn't want that letter in a stranger's twitchy hands either. She told herself not to fixate on the letter, on some magical imagined connection between herself and Alexandra. Instead, she pictured the face from Natalya's photograph, Lena, come to life, clutching a banister, harboring Marie Romanov's secret.

"My mother then needed to make an agonizing choice," Natalya continued, "the safety of the child or of her brother."

As Veronica imagined this scene, her professionalized skepticism returned. With supporting evidence, she might believe Alexandra gave birth to a living baby in 1902. But this element of the story, where the dowager empress told Lena to abandon the baby, made Veronica balk. "What did your mother think Marie would do?" she asked Natalya.

Natalya narrowed her eyes and dropped her gaze.

"She thought Marie would kill her own granddaughter?" Veronica said. "If that's so, how could she possibly abandon the baby?"

"Wait, now." Alexei Romanov balanced one of Natalya's porcelain cup and saucer sets on his knee. The cinnamon scent of tea still clung to the air. "Let's not rush to judgment. Lena's brother was in danger. She was an uneducated, untested girl from the country in impossible circumstances. What more could you expect?"

Veronica bit her lip. "Still, even if her brother was in danger, maybe she could find a way."

Natalya sighed. "The professor makes a good point, Alyosha."

The teacup rattled on Romanov's knee. Veronica couldn't help but smile. Natalya used "Alyosha"—the diminutive, affectionate form of Alexei Romanov's first name. She may have "only" been the daughter of a servant, but the two of them were close, or had been at one time.

"This is what everyone in my family has wondered all of these years," Natalya said. "I was in Russia only this past winter and we still discuss it amongst ourselves. We wondered how my mother could even think about it."

As she listened to Natalya's story, Veronica's fear subsided to a dull ache. Nevertheless, she remained keenly aware of Grigori's presence. Even as she tried to fight the impulse, every few seconds her gaze jumped from Natalya's face, wracked with emotion as she told her mother's story, to Grigori's. He stood at the window, gazing blankly outside. At certain points during Natalya's story, his head tilted ever so slightly to the left. He was listening, but he took in this incredible story with little in the way of shock. He must have heard it before. Veronica wondered how many other people knew.

"From everything you've told me, it sounds as though your mother loved Alexandra," Veronica said. "She loved the family. She would never betray them."

Natalya turned to Romanov. "You assured me she is an expert in this time period. I thought she would be thrilled to hear the story."

"I am thrilled," Veronica began. "I just want to know—"

Romanov set his teacup down on the end table and placed his hand on Veronica's arm to quiet her. He addressed Natalya. "Now, my dear, remember this is so much to take in at one time. Remember how you felt when you first learned of the fifth daughter?"

"You know me so well, Alyosha." Natalya pressed the letter between the plastic sheeting that protected it and turned once more to Veronica. "You must understand the forces at work against Empress Alexandra. The pressure to produce a son."

"A fifth daughter would have been unpopular. I get that." Veronica saw Grigori check his watch. She wondered if Michael had received his message yet. Her fingers clawed the sides of her chair. She tried to keep her voice steady. "But I still don't understand. Did your mother really believe Marie would hurt her own granddaughter?"

"Maybe Marie only meant to spirit her away somewhere. Either way, my mother worried for the child's safety."

Natalya pointed to the letter. When she moved her hand, the charms on her thin silver bracelet tinkled. "We know something happened to Alexandra, something sinister."

Now that the letter was safely protected behind the plastic, Natalya placed it gently on the coffee table in front of Veronica. Once again, Veronica gazed at Alexandra's elegant handwriting.

5 September 1902

Dearest Lena,

How sorry I was to hear of your parents' sudden illness. I miss you so and cry in my pillow to think I couldn't even bid you good-bye. I wish we had time to speak. I beg your forgiveness for the tardiness of this letter.

When I walk through the palace now, I see the looks on the faces of the servants and of those in Nicky's family who still bother to visit. They think I'm hysterical and that I would fool my own body into maintaining such an illusion.

I remember waking afterward, sore and spent. I'd hemorrhaged and lost so much blood. Marie was at my side looking like death. I cried for the baby. I wanted to see the body. They kept telling me it was gone, dead before born, and long since buried. Even Nicky. He said I was upset and needed rest. He patted my hand and assured me this was nothing but a minor setback. He told me it was better if people didn't know, if we insisted I had never been pregnant at all.

I must know what happened. I so need your dear little face at

*my side, if only in spirit. And I trust only you with the answer
to my next question. What happened to my baby?*

Veronica's heart beat furiously. Still, the letter alone proved
nothing, only suggested something "sinister" had happened, as
Natalya had put it. Besides, something else bothered her. "Marie
escaped to Denmark after the Revolution," Veronica said. "She
lived for years after that. If she knew she had a surviving grandchild, why didn't she try to find her?"

Natalya's lips parted into a sad smile. Romanov raised his
brows in sympathy.

"The Revolution ruined Marie," Natalya said. "Her mind went
soft. She never accepted that her son and his family were killed.
She lost touch with reality."

"What happened to your mother after the birth?"

Natalya opened her mouth to answer, but the mechanized
ringtone of Tchaikovsky's First Piano Concerto cut her short.
Romanov checked his phone and smiled. "Good news. Mikhail
received our message. He's almost here."

Grigori straightened his back. His eyes grew strangely merry,
as if he was watching a movie he'd seen before and had finally
gotten to the best part. He adjusted his belt and Veronica caught
a glimpse of his gun.

The terror came rushing back, choking her. Grigori would do
something terrible to Michael. And it was all her fault. She hadn't
believed him when he said Alexei Romanov was dangerous. She
had gotten in the car with Romanov because she couldn't resist
that damn letter. She didn't even want to look at the letter anymore. She rubbed her bare left ring finger. The guilt was far worse
than the fear.

Natalya fiddled with a small silver rose dangling from her charm bracelet. "Mikhail Karstadt claims to be the descendant? Do you believe him?"

Romanov rubbed his hands together. "We'll soon see."

Panic drummed inside Veronica's head in an urgent, steady rhythm. *Don't let him come in here.* She would run outside before they could catch her. She'd cry out, wave her arms, anything to keep him from coming in. She rose to her feet.

Too late. Michael didn't knock, just burst through Natalya's front door. He swept her into his arms, so quickly she didn't even get a good look at his face. But as she felt his body press into her, relief coursed through her. She drew in his incredible scent, the salt of his skin now mingled with the remnants of the rain shower clinging to his coat.

His voice shook when he spoke. "I came as quickly as I could." He pulled back and clasped his hands on either side of her face, searching for signs of injury. "What happened? Did anyone hurt you?"

"I'm okay." She saw the shadows of worry under his hazel eyes, but his gaze was steely and determined as that of any Romanov autocrat. "I'm sorry," Veronica whispered. "I should have trusted you. But I'm not hurt."

Natalya leaned forward. "Why would anyone hurt this young woman?"

Romanov coughed abruptly into his fist. "We needed to persuade Mikhail to give us information he's been reluctant to part with thus far."

"What?" Natalya cried. "Alyosha, what did you do?"

Romanov's voice rose in pitch as he pleaded with Natalya. "Please understand. This was all harmless in the end, I assure you."

Michael's chest rose and fell, heavy with labored breathing. He spun around to face Romanov, his hands forming fists. "How could you stoop this low?"

"You don't really think I'd feed your lady friend to that hungry Russian wolf, do you?" Romanov said. "That was his idea. It was a bluff and it worked."

Grigori turned to Veronica with a lecherous smile. "You never know though. Things happen. If your boyfriend hadn't come, who knows what might have passed between us. Perhaps you can help with my garden when I get my *dacha*."

Michael sprang forward. In an instant he had Grigori by the throat and thrust against the wall.

"What makes you think you can get away with this?" Michael shouted. "Do you know what I can do to you?"

Veronica rushed to Michael's side. The sight of Grigori throttled against that wall was intensely satisfying, but she was frightened to think of the kind of friends Grigori had back in Russia, or even here in Brighton Beach.

"He didn't do anything," she said frantically. "He didn't hurt me. He's just trying to make you angry." Gurgling noises bubbled up from Grigori's throat. He seemed older and faintly ridiculous as his head bobbed in time to Veronica's words. "He's trying to provoke you. He's an asshole, but he's not worth it."

"I don't ever want to hear from you again. If you come near her—"

"He won't come near me," Veronica said. "Please, Michael."

"Mikhail." Natalya stood up. She spoke softly. "Stop."

At the sound of Natalya's voice, Michael instantly obeyed. He shook his shoulders, like he only now realized what he was doing. He freed Grigori, who coughed twice before spewing out venomous Russian curses. Veronica followed just enough to get the picture: sheep, unusual sex acts, Michael's mother, etc.

Michael touched his fingers to his head. Veronica remembered when he'd told her about his father, how he used to shake Michael until his brain felt like jelly. She could practically see the thoughts running through his mind. He was afraid he would turn out that way as well.

Romanov took Natalya by the elbow and guided her back down into her chair. He addressed Veronica. "Ask yourself, Dr. Herrera, is this the man for you?" Romanov jerked his chin at Michael while Grigori wiped his face with one of Natalya's cloth napkins. "Has he brought you anything but trouble?"

Veronica looped her arm around Michael's waist protectively.

"I see. Well, your loyalty is admirable, if misplaced." Romanov turned to Michael. "We had an agreement. I take it you brought what we need?"

"Wait a minute . . . what they need?" Veronica wiggled her arm out from around Michael's waist. "He said they needed a DNA test. You couldn't run one that quickly."

Michael didn't look at her. He rocked silently back and forth on his heels. That couldn't be a good sign.

"Oh, you don't know then?" Romanov let out an exaggerated sigh. "Well, I guess no one should be shocked by that anymore. Mikhail is a man of many secrets."

Veronica suddenly felt hollow and stupid.

"As it turns out, he had the test run several years ago," Romanov said. "He's known the truth for a while now. He simply hasn't chosen to share."

"Is that true?" she asked Michael hesitantly.

Alexei Romanov extended his hand. "Come now. Let's see."

Michael dug his heel into Natalya's thick area rug. She couldn't read anything in his eyes. She'd seen that look on men's faces before, the coldness. It made her want to lock her heart in a box.

Slowly, Michael turned to Natalya. She gave a slight nod. Michael reached into his coat pocket and retrieved an envelope. Veronica's inner voices began to hiss. *This won't be good.* Michael's jaw remained rigid as he handed the envelope to Alexei Romanov, who immediately ripped the envelope open and scanned the results.

At first, Romanov's expression didn't change. He tucked the envelope away in the inside pocket of his jacket, approached Natalya, and folded her small hand into his.

"You're a faithful servant, just like your mother," he told Natalya, his voice measured and elegant. "But your assistance is no longer required. I have exactly what I need. *Merci beaucoup.*"

A terrible sensation wrapped around Veronica's middle, squeezing and strangling her. It slithered to the pit of her stomach, making her sicker and sicker. She didn't need to ask. She didn't dare look at Michael.

And yet she had to ask. Her voice was so small she scarcely recognized it as her own. "What are the results?"

"None of the DNA units correspond with any Romanov. This man is not related to anyone in the Russian royal family." And then Romanov couldn't stop smiling.

"The letter . . . this story . . ."

"Is just that. A story. My grandfather, Kyril, told me about it, even before the lovely Natalya came into my life. Kyril and his wife heard it from some alcoholic French doctor after the Revolution. This doctor claimed a daughter survived, a missing fifth daughter of the tsar. Apparently, this lunatic raved for hours. I didn't believe a word until Ms. Rubalov was kind enough to contact us." Romanov bowed in Natalya's direction. "I am sorry to disappoint you, dear lady. We tried. We went to Europe to determine the where-abouts of this lost grand duchess. Our motives were pure."

"Pure?" Veronica said. "You're working with . . ." She mo-tioned indefinitely in Grigori's direction. "You call that pure?"

"I said our motives were pure. I said nothing of our associates. Sometimes strong measures must be taken for the greater good. It is our sacred duty. The Romanov Guardsmen wish to locate the true heir. Restore the glory of our past to secure a greater future. Do you like it?" He turned to Michael, his face lined with anger once more. "It could have been your campaign slogan."

Michael had moved behind Natalya's sofa and gripped the back of it for support. Veronica waited. She needed Michael to say something in his own defense.

Romanov faced Veronica again. "With the recent upheaval in the Russian government, the time is right. We will convince the Russian people to vote on a referendum to institute a constitutional monarchy. First, we needed to know if Mikhail was related, if he was connected to this story of the fifth daughter. Clearly not."

The color had drained from Michael's face and he kept flinching, reminding Veronica of a tired lion trapped in a zoo. "There must be some mistake," Veronica insisted. "The results could be wrong."

"It's not the best scenario for you either, is it? You've been fol-lowing this imposter around like an impressionable baby duck." Romanov clicked his teeth with his tongue. "Now that we know Mikhail is a fraud, we intend to dismiss this tall tale."

A growl erupted from the back of Natalya's throat. "You are calling my mother a liar?"

"No. I am calling this man a liar." Romanov strode right up to Michael, his chest puffed. He wagged an accusing finger in

Michael's face. "What did you think would happen? How long do you think Anna Anderson, the false Anastasia, would have lasted in the era of DNA testing? Not a month, I can assure you."

Romanov continued on along the same lines. His voice faded in Veronica's ears. She reviewed the last few months in her head, all the time she'd spent with Michael. Everything made more sense now, like some grotesque puzzle, the meaning of which she could only now decipher. Michael had overheard Jessica talk about her at a party. No doubt Jess played up her poor cousin's desperate romantic state and Michael had found the perfect opportunity. He must have known she couldn't resist antiquated gallantry.

Veronica thought she had found an ally in her ongoing battle with the rest of the world. In reality, Michael had taken her in an emotional stranglehold. Her heart had failed her once more.

"Let's just say I've tired of the foolishness of imposters and confidence men," Romanov berated Michael, his voice shaking with indignation. "We thought you were the one. But then, as always, proof to the contrary."

Michael tried to take her hand again, but she shifted away. Veronica wanted to put as much distance between them as possible. She stepped toward the door.

Grigori stepped in front of her, blocking her path. Instinctively, Veronica backed away. Romanov gave a polite wave in Veronica's direction. "Sorry to have detained you. Have a pleasant flight back to California." Then he told Grigori, "This poor creature has been through enough. Let her go."

Grigori folded his arms in front of his chest. "I still have a *dacha* to buy."

"We have what we need," Romanov insisted.

Grigori shrugged. "So you say. She is not going anywhere."

Romanov looked wobbly. He spoke to Grigori as though trying to reason with a toddler. "We have the proof to counter Mikhail's claim. The test is negative. We don't need her. Your people want a tsar. They have the tsar now." He took a step back and pulled his hands dramatically to his own chest.

"I cannot return to Russia with the empty hands," Grigori said.

"If you want to detain Mikhail, that's understandable. He's certainly caused us enough trouble to warrant it. But you can't detain Dr. Herrera. Not any longer."

Michael edged slowly to Romanov's side. Some of his healthy color had returned. He stepped forward, to move between Veronica and Grigori, but no longer had the element of surprise on his side. Grigori lifted his arm and aimed his gun at Veronica's head. Grigori's eyes locked with Veronica's, the shrewd Slavic features betraying no emotion. Her stomach clenched. Michael stopped cold.

"My employers need a tsar the people will want," Grigori said. "And I need a down payment for my *dacha*."

"You can't mean Mikhail?" Romanov sputtered. "He's not even family. No one will believe it. No one will want the imposter to play tsar."

"They'll believe the old woman's story about her mother," Grigori said calmly, unclicking the safety on his gun. "And then this American woman can explain to the Russian people why Mikhail Karstadt is the true Romanov heir."

Sixteen

The court doctors were finally admitted to the room to examine
Alexandra, who appeared broken by the loss. Her heart was set on
a son, and when there was no baby at all, she buried her head in
a pillow and sobbed for hours.

—VERONICA HERRERA, The Reluctant Romanov

PETERHOF ESTATE

AUGUST 1902

Lena walked noiselessly through the deserted hall outside the master suite. She descended the staircase and stopped in front of the tsar's study, bending down for a quick peek. No smoke seeped under the crack at the bottom of the door. All of the doctors had disappeared. Only Lena, Marie, and Phillipe Vachot knew about the baby girl. Even Alexandra, knocked insensible by sedatives, didn't know about her daughter.

The lack of food and sleep started to play queer tricks with Lena's head. At first the hallway seemed interminably large. Then it closed in all around her. She leaned against one of the huge balustrades for support, tilted her head back, and gulped a few hasty breaths, staring at the plaster cornices on the ceiling. Her uniform stuck to her arms and the backs of her legs. She could smell her body's odor, rank and heavy.

Think . . . think . . . think . . . the word became a mantra in her head, more urgent with each step. She had options. She must have options, if only she could will them into her head. She could sneak back into the boudoir and hide in the closet. When Alexandra awoke, Lena might blurt the truth before Marie managed a word. If that didn't work, she'd find the tsar. He was a good man, a father before a ruler. Surely he would protect his own daughter.

In her head, she heard Anton's low, rollicking laugh and soft, encouraging words. His hands made little chopping gestures in the air when he spoke about a new book or a new friend he'd met. *I'll teach you English. That will take you anywhere in the world you want to go.*

If it weren't for her brother's kindness and attention, she would have remained a prisoner in their cabin in the northern forest, caring for aging parents and slowly rotting away. Or perhaps she would have married a local boy and lived in a different cabin, avoiding a groping father-in-law and a husband who beat her for his own amusement. Such was the fate of most girls in Archangel.

Lena continued to walk, hating herself more with each step. She was abandoning an innocent child for the safety of her brother Anton, a grown man who'd brought on his own troubles. She only imagined the penance she'd serve to make everything right with God.

Even that, however, seemed a small matter compared with the agony of the coming years, living with what she'd let happen.

Tears gathered in Lena's eyes and she wiped them away with her sleeve. She tried to decide if she should return to her room and pack her belongings. She didn't have any pictures or mementos, only the scrawled letters from her mother and her dresses and shirtwaists, all stained with juice and none worth saving. Her hand folded over the bills in her pocket. Marie had given her enough money to replace everything she owned.

And then she thought of Pavel and the pleasure in his eyes when he made her laugh. She remembered the curve of his lips and the beautiful contrast between his white shirt and his dark skin the first time she saw him. He had felt something as well, hadn't he? He'd sought out her companionship. He'd tried to help her.

Lena tripped on her own feet and almost fell. What was the point of dwelling on it? Yet she kept seeing Pavel's face.

She turned her attention to the arched windows lining the hall, beyond which were Peterhof's lavish gardens and gilded fountains. The gardens were open to the public during the summer. Hansom cabs lined the gates. She could step into any one and hand the driver a bill from the envelope. As simple as that. Alexandra would ask after her, of course, and maybe Masha. Pavel might wonder about her, at least she liked to think so. No one else would even notice she had left.

After she secured a ride, then what? The unfamiliar sensation of choice stalled her, made her feel adrift and without direction. She had enough money to start over anywhere she wanted. But where? She rubbed her temples.

Anywhere.

The thought hovered uncertainly and she teetered on her feet. The solution came to her then in a stroke of gleaming light. She might still save the young grand duchess and protect her brother at the same time.

Lena lifted her skirts and ran all the way back upstairs to the master suite. Her feet slipped on the polished floor and she extended her arms to regain her balance.

As she reached for the knob, she heard feet pattering. The door swung open. Marie stood before her, hair unfurled from the velvet ribbons she used to keep it in a chignon at the top of her head. Lena took a tiny step back, fearing the gleam in Marie's dark eyes. Marie looked as though the slightest irritation might provoke her, and then she would pounce and tear Lena apart.

But there, tucked away in her grandmother's arms, the baby peacefully slept.

"I couldn't leave her." The words came out in a rush. Lena didn't want to lose her nerve. "Let me take her away from Saint Petersburg. I'll hide her. No one will ever know."

"Leave the country?" Marie's voice sounded fierce and almost mocking. "I thought you and your family were patriotic subjects."

Lena bowed her head, but her gaze stayed focused on the sleeping baby. "If what you say is true, I can serve Russia better by taking her away. I speak English. I'll go to England. I could find work in a shop or as a nanny."

"Won't you miss your family? You'll never see them again."

Her mother's face loomed large in her mind, still disapproving. Lena shook the memory away. She had forgiven her mother. She no longer had power over her. She'd miss Anton, of course, but then he'd left her no other options. "They'll understand."

Marie glanced at the child. Lena wanted to pry the baby from her arms, but she knew better than to try to force Marie's hand. "What if you need money? You'll be tempted to reveal her identity."

"Not if it meant endangering the empress and—" Lena almost said her brother's name, but stopped herself in time. She couldn't bear to hear Marie threaten him again.

The grand duchess awoke and Marie shifted the baby in her arms. The tiny girl looked at Lena for a moment, her blue eyes clear. Then, as though grasping the dire nature of her situation, she squeezed her eyes shut and began to whimper.

Marie thrust the child into Lena's arms. "Thank God you volunteered," she whispered. "I thought I might have to force you. Take her before she starts crying and someone hears."

Lena swept the baby into her arms and pressed her to her chest. The grand duchess's heart beat strong. Lena followed Marie as she dashed down the hall, her gaze darting to and fro, as though someone would stop them at any moment.

"Neither the tsar nor the empress will care the child is a girl," Lena said, still dazed. "I don't understand why this is necessary."

"Greater forces are in play here. My son's advisors. The family. Kyril and his shameful lover. Getting rid of Nicky and Alix would put them so close to the throne. A fifth daughter gives them an excuse."

"No one would stand for it."

"If Alix hadn't been so foolish in court, then perhaps that would be so," Marie said dryly. "As matters stand, she has few supporters. Other than you and that quack Vachot, she has no friends."

Though adrenaline kept her blood pumping and her steps sure, Lena's head spun. "What you said before in the nursery . . ."

"I had to get you out of there. Kyril and that brittle woman he keeps are already asking questions. They've paid off some of the servants for information. I hadn't time to check the nursery for spies. I wasn't sure I could speak freely. I needed to make them think you were delusional."

Lena remembered what Masha had told her, the gossip about

plans to unseat the empress. Of course Masha had assumed Marie was behind it all.

"I've made it known there was a stillbirth, and we're still determining how best to tell Alix. And I wanted anyone listening to think you'd gone mad and couldn't accept the child's death."

"Who did you think was listening?" Lena paused. "Ducky?"

"Ducky's a shrewd bird, I'll give her that. Nicky is blocking her marriage to Kyril because of Alix. The best way to get rid of Nicky is to get rid of Alix. Then they're free to marry and Kyril has a clearer shot to the throne. They win on two counts." Deftly Marie maneuvered Lena past empty parlors and servants' quarters. "They've been plotting. I assigned the guard Pavel to listen. He overheard them in Saint Petersburg, before they left to come here. The fools assumed he couldn't understand English."

"But he speaks fluent English."

Marie gave her a sideways glance. "I know. That's why he had the assignment."

Lena nodded, probably too quickly. Hearing Pavel's name gave her a twinge of regret. She was leaving someone behind after all. Lena looked down at her feet as they pressed forward. "What did they say?"

"They wish to prove Alexandra unfit. Another daughter gives them an excuse."

"Surely Kyril and Ducky aren't so powerful," Lena said.

"Not alone," Marie replied. "But the ministers and other members of the family are frustrated as well. If Alix left, they'd be rid of my son. He would never willingly divorce her. He'd sooner abdicate." Marie pursed her lips. "I will not let that happen."

Lena pulled the baby closer, already feeling the weight of her responsibility. "What about Monsieur Vachot? Can you trust him?"

Marie snorted. "The good doctor is so far in debt he will do whatever I ask. As long as the money keeps flowing in his direction. He'll return to France and stay there."

"And what should I do?" Lena asked.

"You will take the grand duchess to a ferry. One of my men will escort you to Copenhagen. That's where I grew up." Wistfulness misted her eyes. Lena caught a glimpse of Marie as a young girl, strolling the seaside without a care.

"It's all been arranged," Marie added briskly. "You will take her to a young couple who work for my family. I've even given them a name for her, a good Danish name, after my own grandmother, Charlotte of Denmark. It was the name of my husband's grandmother as well, Charlotte of Prussia. I believe it will suit her well."

Grand Duchess Charlotte. "What will you tell the empress?"

The reverie playing on Marie's features passed. Now her little face appeared pinched. "I'll tell her she suffered a stillbirth. The doctors will confirm. But we'll issue an official statement saying it was a false pregnancy. Better that than news of a failure."

Lena bit her lip. It was such a cruel thing to do to a mother. "Can't you tell her?"

"The country needs an heir. She can't get depressed. She must keep trying."

"But when everything is more settled. After she's had a son."

Marie sighed. "I know what you must think of me. I've thought all the same things myself. But I believe if Alix had to choose between another daughter and Nicky's security, my Nicky would win the battle. I'm saving Alix the pain."

Deep down, Lena suspected this was true. "She'll have a boy soon."

"I hope you're right."

They burst through the back doors and into the bright and windy morning, making their way through the gardens and down a flight of marble steps. Lena shifted the grand duchess to one arm and lifted her hand to her forehead to shield her eyes from the sun's early glare.

"I can't let you take a car, it would attract too much attention," Marie told her. "One of the hansoms will have to do."

Lena followed Marie to an unmarked coach, its curtains drawn. The driver's velvet cap was pulled so low Lena couldn't see his eyes. The carriage may have been ordinary enough, but the horse up front was a jet-black gelding that looked like he came directly from the imperial stables. His front hoof pawed the ground impatiently, kicking up a puff of dirt.

The wind whipped her hair into her face, nearly blinding her. The driver helped Lena with the baby, shifting her to Marie's arms. Lena accepted the driver's gloved hand and hopped into the back of the coach. Inside, it smelled of oil and fresh leather.

She reached again for the baby. For an instant, she saw Marie's lips curl into a frown. She wasn't certain Marie would release the child, but the dowager empress thrust the baby back into Lena's arms.

"Wait!" Marie tapped the driver's shoulder so he wouldn't shut the door. "I found this in one of Olga's albums." She pulled a folded paper out of her pocket. It was a photograph of Lena with Alexandra taken last winter, after the tsar had requested a picture of the empress with her new favorite.

"You should have it." Marie placed the photo flat on the seat next to Lena.

"My brother . . ."

"As long as you say nothing, your brother is safe. You have my word."

The morning sunlight dimpled the flowers and grass and the fluttering leaves of the birch trees. Lena wished she could stay longer and memorize every detail. This would be the last time she ever saw the palace and the gardens.

"My man will care for you as long as you need. I've given him plenty of money as well. He'll set you up in a shop or something similarly suitable." Marie hesitated. "What will you do then? Will you continue to work or will you look for a husband?"

The thought made Lena's heart jump like a startled rabbit. But she had started from scratch before, when she left Archangel to seek employment at the palace. "I'll think of something."

"I'm sure you will. You've coped with worse." Marie hesitated again. "I can't leave her without at least a token of her birthright." Marie's eyes suddenly brightened. She reached around her neck and tugged on a clasp. She removed her necklace and pressed the cool metal in Lena's free hand. Lena gazed at the silver cross with three bars, the third bar slanting downward.

"She should have some relic of her family," Marie said, "even if she can't know them. Give it to my people. They'll let her have it when she's old enough."

Lena nodded. Marie seemed to age before her eyes. Her dark hair wilted and her delicate features scrunched. Even her erect shoulders fell. She no longer looked like the Dowager Empress of all the Russias, the pretty and vivacious woman so full of life, but like any other brokenhearted grandmother.

"Now off with you," Marie said.

The driver shut the door. Marie tapped the carriage before stepping away. They shot off and Lena was forced back against the warm leather seat. She only had time to look briefly at the dowager through the back window. As they retreated, Marie's determined figure grew smaller and somehow less substantial, the train of her dress flapping in the harsh summer wind.

SAINTE-FOY-LE-GRANDE

OCTOBER 1941

They were nearing her parents' house. Charlotte could tell from the dark stillness of the country roads, empty barns, and rows of stripped wooden crosses that should have been entangled with gnarly grapevines. Even the low hills in the distance seemed devoid of life. The stillness had always bothered her. This evening, she felt like she'd been stuffed prematurely into a coffin.

She heard a shallow snore and peeked behind her. Laurent had moved into the backseat and fallen into blissful sleep, his head in his father's lap. Luc stared blankly out the window. His leg had stopped bleeding, but his lips were an alarming shade of gray. And a strange calm settled his features, different than what she'd seen before in the cellar, as though all the fight in him was gone.

As she turned back to face the road, she tried to keep her voice strong. "We're almost there."

When she glanced in the rearview mirror, she saw Luc close his eyes.

"Don't do that." She reached behind her to shake his knee and then stopped abruptly. She shouldn't risk further damage to his leg. "Don't fall asleep."

Charlotte grappled in the dark for the handle and rolled down the window. Cold air and the sharp odor of fields flooded the car. She hoped it was enough to keep Luc awake.

In the speckled provincial darkness, Charlotte distinguished the three bright stars of Orion's belt, and then the great hunter himself hovering in the horizon. As a little girl, she would go out at night with her father and throw her head back to watch the night sky. The rest of the countryside was too still for her taste, but the sky always struck her as full of life. Her father would take her small hand in his, point out and name the constellations, and tell her the myths that explained their names. Her mother would then come outside with a mug of hot chocolate and chide him for keeping her out so long in the cold. But she never insisted they come back in.

She wanted to hear her father's gruff voice. She wanted him to take Laurent outside and discuss the constellations. She wanted to share the stories with him over hot chocolate.

"Mama will care for your leg," Charlotte told Luc. The sound of her voice broke the stillness at least. She turned off the main road and onto the dirt tracks that led to her parents' house. "Then we'll get rid of this car."

Luc nodded miserably. Charlotte spotted the plain, sturdy form of her parents' two-story farmhouse at the end of the narrow road. She stuck her head out the window, oblivious to the cold. Normally when she approached home she could smell her mother's bread baking. Not this evening. Dogs kept in a nearby barn barked and howled as they drove past. She waited to hear her father's retrievers respond in kind, and her father telling them to hush. But she heard only crickets.

She slammed on the brakes and yanked the key out of the ignition.

"What is it?" Luc said.

"I'm too late," Charlotte muttered. "I'm too late."

She bolted out of the car and ran toward the house, making out its simple silhouette even in the darkness. Overgrowth from trees and bushes obscured her mother's carefully tended flower beds and she tripped on a stray branch. Charlotte righted herself and ran up the steps to the front door. By now, the retrievers should have been barking and pawing at the door to greet her.

The door was unlocked. Charlotte burst inside, shouting for her parents in the dark. She felt her way around the walls to the main kitchen window and tugged on the cords and sashes. Light from the moon and stars spilled into the room. A fresh white cloth covered the kitchen table. The lacy curtains on the window were drawn. Everything looked tidy, as though they had only gone out for the evening. But Charlotte knew her parents were far too cautious to leave the door unlocked. Even in the safety of the countryside, even with the dogs, they bolted and latched the locks religiously each night.

Outside, the car door slammed. She peered out the window and watched Luc try to gather Laurent in his arms. He stumbled on his bad leg and fell back against the car. Charlotte ran back out. She took his hand and helped him upright, but he looked ready to crumple to the ground again at any moment.

"Your parents aren't home?" Luc said softly.

"No." She looked at the left side of the house, by the dog runs, where her father usually parked his battered red pickup truck. It wasn't there either.

"If your parents aren't here, we should turn around," he said. "It could be a trap."

Luc was right. Still, Charlotte couldn't leave without trying to determine what had happened. "Stay here," she said quietly. "I'll look around the house before you come inside. If it's all clear, I'll tell you. If not I'll scream. Then you take Laurent and go somewhere safe."

Luc opened his mouth, but lacked the strength to protest. He sat down once more in the backseat next to Laurent and gave a nod. Charlotte ran back to the house.

Once inside, she wandered back and forth between the living room and the kitchen, fiddling with the cross on the chain around her neck, making little kicks with her feet, perfect *jetés*. Perhaps her parents had been tipped off that soldiers were coming after them and had left.

She collapsed on the worn love seat in the living room and pulled one of her mother's quilts close. She breathed in her mother's clean domestic scent, a mixture of baking powder and the earthy scent of gardening. Charlotte put her head in her hands.

She couldn't get past that unlocked door. Even if her parents had left quickly, they would have locked it. If soldiers had come and forced them out, she would have seen more signs of a struggle.

Charlotte sat up straight and stared at the coat hooks by the front door. Her father kept leashes there for the retrievers, to use when he decided to take them into town with him. The leashes were gone. That meant her parents had left of their own volition. The dogs were with them. They'd left the door unlocked because they expected Charlotte and Laurent to come. Her parents must have left a message somewhere.

The safe.

Charlotte sprang to her feet and went out to tell Luc. He'd left the car door open for her and was shivering in the cold night air,

Laurent cuddled at his side. When Luc looked up at her, his eyes betrayed the pain in his leg. She forced a smile.

"It's all right. I don't think the soldiers came here. There's a safe in the kitchen. Maybe my parents left something for me." She looked down at the dark blood still staining Luc's trousers. "And we need to tend to your leg. I don't think we have much choice but to stay here for a while."

Charlotte made Laurent walk next to her to the house while she slung Luc's arm around her shoulder and helped him through the front door. Once she'd settled them both on the love seat she moved to the kitchen. She bent down to reach the cabinet doors under the stove, moving clanging pots and pans aside to reveal the small metal safe where her parents kept important documents. She twisted the black dial to the right numbers until the lock clicked.

Frantically, Charlotte rifled through the old papers, family letters, and bank notes. Her parents' travel passes and the deed to the farm were gone. In their place, Charlotte found a yellowing envelope and a large leather photo album. Charlotte and her mother had spent many hours bent over it, using a pot of glue to paste family pictures onto its pages. But her mother usually kept the album on one of the bookshelves. Charlotte was surprised her mother hadn't brought that with her as well.

Charlotte gathered everything in her arms. She brought the papers, along with the photo album and envelope, into the living room. Laurent had fallen back asleep on the flowered quilt, the sedative still overwhelming his system. Luc stared at her, pale. She shouldn't waste time with the papers in the safe, not when he looked this way. "I need to take care of your leg. My mother usually keeps medicine upstairs."

"It can wait a few more minutes. What is that?"

"Our family pictures. Some paperwork." Her voice trembled. She felt her hands shake under the weight of the heavy album. She dropped the papers to the floor and they scattered at her feet.

"Luc, you do it. I want to see if they left clues to where they went, but I can't focus." She handed him the photo album and began to pace the living room, stepping carefully over the fallen papers, biting her lower lip. Luc frowned and flipped through the pages of the photo album, his face a mask of concentration. Then he stopped abruptly. Charlotte rushed to his side to see.

He was staring at a page filled with pictures of Charlotte taken before performances. She wore all manner of costumes: a short tutu and a tiara in one picture, a flowered cape and tightly bound corset in another. A faint smile played on Luc's lips. "You were always a looker."

"So you're not focused either."

"I'm not focused? What's in your hand? What's in the envelope?"

Charlotte looked down. She was still clutching the yellowing envelope from the safe. She broke the seal. Inside, there was a sepia postcard of four girls in identical white sundresses. They had gathered around a handsome boy of about twelve. Charlotte held the picture up to the moonlight streaming through the window. She didn't recognize any of the faces.

"Let me see," Luc said.

Charlotte handed him the postcard. Luc took a moment to examine the picture, and then tapped the card triumphantly.

"I've seen them in books," he told her. "Those are the tsar's children. Your parents are definitely trying to tell you something."

Charlotte felt a cold chill. She stroked the chain around her neck and the three bars slicing through the cross. Then she saw it

in the photograph, small and fuzzy. The same type of cross hung
from a chain around the neck of one of the girls.

"That must be the Russian Orthodox crucifix," Luc said.
"Maybe the German officer was right about you."

Charlotte's thoughts scattered once more. She sat down, hard,
on the arm of the love seat. If everything Herr Krause had said
was true, how could her parents have kept this secret? Her pulse
started to race. She would turn forty next year and they still
treated her as a child who couldn't be trusted with important information. She gulped in a deep breath. "I need to talk to them."

"I know." Luc reached up and squeezed her shoulder. "They'll
come back. Or else you'll find them. You'll see them again."

Charlotte nodded desperately. If she believed, perhaps it would
be true. She had to see them again.

"For now, let's concentrate on what they left you," he said.

Luc sounded so calm, so sure of himself. Charlotte tried to
concentrate. She looked again at the postcard. One of the older
girls in the back row captured her attention, the same one wearing the cross. The girl leaned forward on one elbow and looked
solemnly at the camera. She was tall and slim with an elegant
neck, a long nose, and thin but pretty lips. The photograph was
black and white, but Charlotte wondered if the girl had auburn
hair, like her own. Her lips trembled.

Luc stared at the photo and then at Charlotte. "That could be
your sister," he said. "She looks just like you."

"Doesn't she?"

At the sound of the low female voice, Charlotte spun around.
Someone was on the staircase, watching them. The woman took a
few steps down, but her face remained shrouded in darkness.

"Who's there?" Luc called, his voice still rasping.

The sound of the voices startled Laurent awake. His eyes blinked slowly open as he gazed up at Luc and then looked at the staircase. He frowned, still blinking. Then his lips parted suddenly into a huge smile. He jumped off the sofa, running toward the figure in the dark and hugging her knees.

"Madame Kshesinskaya," he cried. "You found us."

"Yes," Kshesinskaya said, stepping into the light, stroking Laurent's hair. "I thought your mother might want to hear more about her four sisters."

Seventeen

Veronica tried to still her fingers. They kept twitching at the sight of the small black revolver Grigori was pointing at her head, a sleek Glock pistol. He'd be surprised she knew enough about guns to name it. She'd even seen one before. All of Jess's brothers worked for the sheriff's department.

Her gaze moved to Grigori's face. His cold glower seemed overly practiced. He'd seen plenty of Scorsese movies, she'd give him that. Or maybe he was more of a Tarantino style gangster, all chatter and swagger and stifling cologne. His affectations were hopelessly out of place among Natalya Rubalov's doilies and the comforting smell of cinnamon tea. Without the Glock in his hand, Veronica would have been more irritated than frightened.

Veronica's thoughts continued to zip around uncontrollably, little pulses of subatomic energy. She drew in a deep breath, counting silently to three in Spanish, Russian, and English. Then she gazed imploringly in Michael's direction. She needed him to come up with something, anything, to explain the results of the DNA test, to explain why he lied.

Michael had backed slowly away from Grigori. Now he stood next to Natalya, gaze still focused on the revolver. He didn't say a word.

"I certainly didn't agree to any of it," Romanov was huffing. "And besides, what is the point? Without proof, no one will believe a word of this tall tale."

Grigori chuckled. "In Russia, anything is possible."

"The proof is in the pudding. I should say it isn't there. Mikhail is not the one."

"We want who we want. Mikhail is our tsar. Not you." Grigori pointed to Romanov, then to Michael. "Who do you think?" he asked Veronica. "Who plays better on television? This is what my people want."

Romanov's shoulders sagged under the weight of his wounded pride. Veronica had to admit, she understood Grigori's point. Anyone with the slightest romantic inclination would prefer Michael as tsar. She felt sure Russian monarchists would prefer the direct descendant of a fifth Romanov daughter, even if it wasn't true.

"He's never declared his claim," Romanov said. "He's made my life unpleasant, I'll grant you that. Planting seeds of doubt in everyone's minds."

"He will have the backing now," Grigori replied calmly. "We tell the story."

Natalya straightened her back and fixed Grigori with a death stare. "It's not a story. It was my mother's life."

Grigori focused on Veronica. "What do you think? You want to believe, I see this. You can publish story, make you famous."

Veronica's thoughts were still buzzing. Her mouth felt dry. At last she found her voice. "I'll tell the story about the fifth daughter of the tsar, but I won't say Michael is the heir when he's obviously not."

"But that's the best part," Grigori purred. "Don't you think so, Mikhail?"

Michael held his hands straight in the air. Too straight. She wondered if he would explode again and lunge for Grigori, or grab Alexei Romanov's skinny neck and shake him until his teeth rattled. But Michael remained calm. He gave her a slight nod and then looked pointedly at Grigori. He wanted her to distract Grigori. "Can we put our hands down?" she heard herself ask.

Grigori motioned for her to lower her arms. An unpleasant tingling replaced the numbness as she rubbed her biceps.

"I won't agree to this either," Michael said.

"You will. You want to keep people you care for safe," Grigori replied easily.

Veronica shuddered, but she needed to keep him talking. "What does it matter if I publish any of this about the fifth daughter anyway? I'm not even tenured. I'm an academic fraud." As she babbled, she hopped between Russian and English and a little Spanish to find the right words. "My college is research level two. Do you know what that means? We're nothing. The best of the rest. I remember being excited when I saw Alameda University at the top of a list in *U.S. News and World Report,* and then I realized the list was in alphabetical order. We're not even ranked."

Grigori made a dismissive gesture.

"Never mind," Veronica said, settling back into English. "All that's important is no one will care about any article just because my name's on it."

"She's right," Romanov chimed in. "We only wanted her to get to Mikhail. No one in their right mind would care what she says."

Veronica shot him a dirty look. Romanov compressed his lips, not quite contritely enough for her taste.

"People believe what they believe." Grigori shrugged. "Pretty face will help."

"Restoration is a sketchy proposition at best," Veronica said, "even with a legitimate heir."

"That's true," Natalya said. "Why risk it all?" Veronica noticed when Natalya spoke, Michael stopped inching toward Grigori.

Grigori smiled, almost kindly, at Natalya, but ignored her question. "You could make money, you know." He gave Veronica a sly wink.

"Not as much money as you, I bet," Veronica snapped.

"I try to help. What is problem here?"

"The government will discover the truth eventually," she said.

"Exactly." Alexei Romanov had briefly retreated to a corner to pout, but now he pounced on Veronica's comment like a cat. "There's no point to this charade."

"You visit our country?" Grigori asked Veronica. "Perhaps you pay bribe or two? Get to front of line? Get cab before others? Buy tin of caviar on the cheap?"

"That's a far cry from perpetuating this type of hoax," Romanov blurted.

"A DNA sample can be faked," Grigori replied. "Easy to bribe technician. Some people think bones of blessed royal family are faked."

Romanov folded his arms in front of his chest. "That's ridiculous."

"Will it be so hard to taint a small portion of DNA for money? And not for harm, but for high purpose?"

Veronica tried to laugh again, but it came out as a snort. "What high purpose? Alexei Romanov is a true believer. You're just after cash."

"Common good, financial rewards . . . these two motivations can be reconciled."

"But why do your people need Michael? Why do they need a tsar at all?"

Grigori gave another one of his big Russian shrugs. "Property of Russian government should be in rightful hands of private citizens. Rightful owner is tsar. If tsar part of government, tsar decides who gets what."

"I can attend to those matters better than Mikhail is able," Romanov insisted. "Why, if that's the concern—"

"You think I'll help a few oligarchs make a little more money?" Michael cut in.

"It is hardly a little." Grigori sounded offended at the suggestion. "Real estate worthless in your country now, not ours. Not in Moscow and Saint Petersburg."

"Did you know about any of this?" Natalya asked Romanov sharply.

"We talked about restoration of real estate to rightful owners," Romanov said.

"And then there is public land. In your country, men make millions of dollars from oil. We do too. Worth fighting for. Worth keeping." Grigori struggled to maintain his game face. The shaded hollows under his eyes betrayed his exhaustion. He looked like he wanted this all to be over. "The people I work for believe tsar will smooth negotiations between Russia and U.S. Putin make mess.

But Americans make mistakes too. Afghanistan. Should have let Soviets have their way."

Romanov made a guttural sound. "True monarchists do not let the Soviets have their way. No one was gladder—"

"—for the demise of the Soviet Union than your family. I know." Grigori rolled his eyes. He'd done a pitch-perfect impersonation of Romanov. He turned back to Veronica. "If the Americans had worked with Soviets, everything different. No Taliban. No bin Laden."

"This marvelous new world order will come to pass if you prove that Michael is the Tsar of all the Russias?" Veronica said. "Forget it. He won't cooperate."

"I think he will. You are key. Watch."

Grigori stepped toward her, gun raised. He nudged the gun to her temple, cold and hard. Veronica jumped back, gasping for air, and covered her head with her hands. She closed her eyes and waited, struggling for breath.

Nothing happened. She opened her eyes. Michael had moved between them, jaw set, arms spread wide to shield her.

Grigori raised his eyebrows, looking supremely pleased with himself. "You see. Brave Cossack." He turned to Michael. "That will play well on television."

Romanov turned his accusing finger to Michael. "He's not a Romanov at all. He may not even be Russian."

"We want fantasy here," Grigori said. "This story is like fairy tale."

"In fairy tales, true blood triumphs." Romanov sounded haughty, even for him.

Grigori gave a foxlike smirk. "How many tsars descend from true bloodline? Your precious Romanovs—shaky fellows."

Romanov began to huff again. "Ridiculous," he muttered.

"You think I am buffoon?" Grigori said to him. "You think I do not know our history?" He turned to Natalya. "*Matushka*. Elegant place you keep. I think you have bottle of red wine in house. Not for you, of course, but for guests?"

"I have wine," Natalya said uncertainly.

"Indulge me," Grigori said. "Great poet Alexander Pushkin used to do trick at dinner parties, to sweet talk ladies. I will show you. I need wine, pitcher filled with water, and eight glasses."

Natalya nodded at Michael, who immediately headed for the kitchen. Veronica heard the clink of glass on glass and a rush of tap water from the sink. She frowned, confused. How did he know where everything was kept in the kitchen?

Michael returned quickly, keeping his eyes on her the entire time, as though he were afraid something might have happened while he was gone. When Michael passed Natalya, Veronica's breath caught. Their eyes were the same shape and nearly the same color. The resemblance crystallized in her mind now, not only their eyes, but the shape of their noses and the elegant span of their hands.

Michael set the wine bottle and a pitcher on Natalya's dining room table, atop a runner crocheted with songbirds. Then he went back and forth until he had eight wine glasses lined up.

"Fill one and hold it up," Grigori ordered.

"Why?" Michael said.

"Do it," Natalya told him.

"Yes, please." Grigori seemed to be enjoying this. "Soon you will have all servants you desire. This will teach humility."

Michael glared at him, but splashed the wine into a glass.

"This glass of wine represents Peter the Great." Grigori assumed a professorial tone. Under different circumstances, he would have fit right in at Alameda University. "The great Romanov. Pure Russian blood. Who did he marry?"

"His second wife was Lithuanian," Veronica offered. "Of course we're not exactly sure of her origins, since she was a peasant. Some people think—"

"Wonderful," Grigori said, cutting her off. "So Russian bloodline weakens. Mikhail, pour half of that glass into the next glass."

Michael held up the second glass, its color pinkish and weak.

"Keep going. Fill half water and half glass before. Get to last. See what happens."

Michael did so sloppily, keeping one eye on Grigori and the gun.

"Last glass represents tsar of blessed memory, Nicholas II. How does he look?"

Michael held up the glass, filled mostly with water. The remaining wine gave the liquid only the faintest hint of a blush.

"So who cares?" Grigori concluded. "Mikhail will do as well as any other."

Romanov looked like a little boy who'd had his favorite toy crushed to pieces in front of him. "It is my birthright," he whispered.

Veronica found herself unwillingly sympathizing with Alexei Romanov. He'd dedicated his entire life to this goal and now that it was actually within his grasp, he couldn't have it. Like her academic career. All that work all those years, for nothing.

"It is not for you anymore." Grigori spoke to Romanov, but took another step toward Veronica. Michael cut between them. Grigori pointed the gun to her head. Michael went pale and stopped.

"Stop threatening the girl." Natalya reached, grabbing Michael's hand.

Grigori gave a quick, regretful glance in Natalya's direction. "It can't be helped, little mother. We need Mikhail to cooperate."

"This isn't Russia." Veronica couldn't stop looking at the gun. Each tortured beat of her heart must have shaved another year off her life. "You can't get away with this."

"You people make it easy," Grigori said calmly. "You all act as little children, think nothing bad can happen. You want open society? We find anyone we want."

Veronica thought of Abuela bustling around her little yellow kitchen in Bakersfield. She never remembered to lock her doors, no matter how many times Veronica reminded her. She'd put Abuela in danger. A soft gurgling noise escaped her as she gasped for air, a choking sensation rising in her throat.

"You make it easy for man to do what he wants," Grigori said.

"You are not a man," Natalya told him. "You are only a bully."

Veronica watched Grigori move toward Natalya, the gun no longer pointed in her direction. If Michael was quick about it, he could jump Grigori. He only had to move. Then she realized Grigori had one hand on Natalya, the gun close to her neck. If Michael moved, Grigori could shoot her.

"Think about this," Grigori told Natalya. He bent down near her ear, the red undertones in his hair glinting in the light. "Your mother loyal to empress. Why let effort go to waste?"

Veronica cringed. She couldn't bear to watch Grigori's eagle talon fingers clutching Natalya's delicate shoulder. Still she clung to faint hope. The fierce look on Michael's face made it easy to imagine him as a younger man, grabbing drunken frat boys by the collar and tossing them out of the bar.

"Bolsheviks kill the empress, kill the children," Grigori said. "Little girls. Your mother devoted. She made sacrifices. She would want revenge. Restoration of tsar is revenge."

"Not this way," Natalya insisted.

"Do it for her," Grigori said. "Take back what Bolsheviks took away."

Natalya's head collapsed into her hands. Veronica saw red spots dance before her eyes. She couldn't stand it anymore, couldn't stand to watch Grigori try to push this woman around. She would have made a deal with the devil to make it end. "This is your glorious restoration?" she demanded, turning to Alexei Romanov. "You will let this happen? You'll betray everything you worked to build all these years?"

"I have tried and tried." He gestured toward Grigori. "I don't know what happened. I thought we had an agreement."

"Then maybe you don't deserve the title or the throne," Veronica said. "Maybe you never did."

That roused him. Romanov had the look of a man trying to hold himself together when everything was falling to pieces, blurry around the edges. "I've been groomed from birth. I've been educated in Russian culture and history. I speak four languages. I remain steadfast and true, waiting for sublime destiny."

"Then seize your destiny," Veronica said. "Put a stop to this. You were the one who hired this man? Or did he approach you?"

"I suppose we courted one another," Romanov said.

"I think you can put a stop to all of this," Veronica said. "You're smart. Smarter, I think, than this one realizes." She jutted her chin at Grigori. "I know what this means to you, how you want to accomplish restoration the right way."

Grigori rolled his head to the side and repositioned the gun, pointing it at Veronica. His voice rose an octave. "Don't be fool, Alyosha."

The term of endearment sounded far different on Grigori's tongue than it had earlier when Natasha used it. Veronica tasted the fear in her mouth, but pressed on. "I don't think you would have associated with him unless you could hold your own."

"If I put a stop to this madness," Romanov said, "what will I get in return?"

Veronica opened her mouth, but then dropped her gaze. She realized she had nothing to offer. She watched Natalya rub the silver rose on her charm bracelet.

"Mikhail will publicly renounce his claim," Natalya said.

Romanov raised an eyebrow. "And why should I believe you?"

"He will do it because I ask him."

"She's my mother," Michael said quietly.

Veronica stifled a gasp. She'd been right about the resemblance.

"You have my word of honor as well as his," Natalya said. "We will make no further claims on behalf of our family."

Romanov stared at Natalya, a pained look in his eyes. "How could you?" he cried. "Why not tell me? Why create a fake line? Why falsify a claim?"

"We needed access to your files," Natalya said. "We wanted to see if you had any evidence to support my mother's story. You only allow those of noble birth near them."

Romanov allowed a hint of triumph in his voice. "Mikhail was lying all along?"

Veronica stared at Michael. He looked at her, his eyes pleading for forgiveness, but said nothing more.

A ghost of a smile played on Romanov's lips. "The grandson of a servant. I should have known." Romanov rubbed his hands together. Veronica saw a glimmer of his old vigor return as he turned to Michael. "You'll publicly admit you're a fraud?"

"That would be for fool, Mikhail," Grigori rumbled. "Think about offer, whatever you desire in reach."

"I will publicly admit that I falsified my claim," Michael said. "Now who is he? Who does he work for? What do you know?"

Alexei Romanov straightened his blue blazer. When she'd first met him, Veronica sensed dignity about the man. Some measure of that dignity returned now. He strode toward Grigori, puffy as a rooster. "Grigori Ilyich Yurovsky is known to the authorities in Moscow, Kiev, and New York as a dealer in heroin and methamphetamine."

"You wouldn't dare," Grigori roared. He turned his gun to Romanov.

Romanov put his hands in the air, but his voice remained clear. "I send an e-mail to other members of our organization every day at five, with updates. If I don't send one today, the Guardsmen are under instructions to call the police and tell them everything we know about you."

Grigori's expression crumbled, his dreams of the *dacha* evaporating before his eyes. "We find your family."

"I don't have a family," Romanov said curtly. "I don't have children and my parents are dead. My only mission now is to preserve the sanctity of my family's memory. I'd rather die than see you put an imposter on the throne." He reached into his jacket pocket to retrieve his phone and began pressing buttons. "This will all be very embarrassing for you, I think. It makes you look sloppy."

"I am a Russian citizen. Americans can't hold me."

"So what? They extradite you? To Russia? Where you'll be taken into custody and asked to give names of associates." Romanov clicked his tongue between his teeth. "Of course those associates will make sure you're shut up."

Grigori stepped back. "So what do you want me to do?"

"Leave us," Romanov instructed.

"And tell my people what? Mikhail escaped? I failed?"

"This is not my problem," Romanov said coolly.

"They do not want you as the claimant."

"I'm sure you'll think of something to change their mind. After all, everyone will know Mikhail is an imposter." A slow smile spread across Romanov's face. "*Quelle dommage.* But we can work together. All I ask in return is that your people back my claim. I assure you it is valid. My grandfather kept impeccable records, as did my parents. I'm the one."

Veronica saw the anger churn in Grigori. His eyes grew fierce, the acorn-shaped scar on his cheek flaring. He raised his black Glock again, but pointed it at Romanov.

Michael lunged toward Grigori and in one swift, sure movement wrestled his arm to his side and then behind his back. He shook the gun out of Grigori's hand and it tumbled to the floor with a thud.

"Let me take care of him," Grigori cried. "Just the old man."

Heart hammering, Veronica stared at the gun. It was too far away. Michael couldn't possibly retrieve it. She'd never touched a gun before, but she had seen her cousins at the firing range once. With the adrenaline pumping, she supposed she could handle one well enough.

Romanov was blinking, confused, as though he hadn't expected to still be there. He was staring at the gun as well. Before Veronica could react, he scrambled to the floor. She followed, but he had a head start. His hand folded over the handle.

Michael and Grigori stopped struggling. Romanov pointed the gun at Grigori. His breath came in loud gulps. Then he turned the gun on Michael.

Veronica grabbed her purse from the floor and reached inside. Romanov pivoted slightly. "What are you . . . ?"

She felt the canister at once. She lifted it and sprayed in Romanov's direction. He screamed in agony and the gun fell to the floor. Michael grabbed it.

Romanov stumbled to a chair, crying out like a yowling tomcat, hands splayed over his face. "I wasn't going to shoot him," Romanov cried. "Why would I shoot him?"

"I'm sorry," Veronica sputtered. "I wasn't sure. I had to do something."

Natalya rose to her feet and moved swiftly to the kitchen. She reappeared a minute later with a wet towel and handed it to Romanov, who pressed the towel to his eyes, still howling.

"You'll live," Natalya said soothingly. "It wasn't even a direct hit."

Veronica swung around to fire the Mace at Grigori, but then turned in a full circle. Grigori's trench coat had been slung over a chair near the door. Now it was gone. He was gone. A car engine roared to life outside. She ran to the window in time to watch his sedan peel out and disappear around the corner.

Michael opened the gun's chamber and shook it until the bullets fell with a clatter to the floor. Then he passed his hand over his mouth.

As she watched him, a bit of the old spell returned. Despite the shadows under his eyes and his sickly pallor, she saw the man who'd stood up to the jackass at Electric Lotus and twirled her around dance floors and held her in his arms as she finally let go of her past. Michael looked like he belonged in the Winter Palace. She still longed for him to say something to put all that had transpired this afternoon in a new light.

Michael started to walk toward her, ready to sweep her in his arms again. But he said nothing, still gave no explanation for what had happened. She drew in a deep, painful breath. "You kept telling me to trust you, but you were lying all along."

Michael's lips moved, trying to find the right word.

"At least tell me why. Why go to all this trouble?"

He began to sway, his eyes rimmed in red.

She saw Michael for who he truly was now, a muddled man with delusions of grandeur. Michael had lied and she'd been a willing and starry-eyed target, eager to play Cinderella at some fake Romanov court. How gullible she'd been. She wanted to freeze and turn to stone. Nothing could hurt her then, it would all be superficial static.

Michael extended his hand. She raised her own hand with resignation. "Don't."

Michael's face looked ashen. "I failed you," he said. "I'm sorry."

Veronica's stomach felt like lead. She'd indulged a ridiculous fantasy, been drunk on romantic stories. She wouldn't parade him through Saint Petersburg or anywhere else, for that matter. How much time had she wasted only to be made a fool?

She tried to visualize a layer of armor enfolding her heart to protect her, but the trick didn't work anymore. She felt a pricking sensation at the back of her eyes. Another minute and she'd turn into a blubbering mess. Slowly, she picked her purse up from the floor. "Thank you for sharing the letter with me," she said, nodding in Natalya's direction. She wanted to say something to Romanov, but his head remained between his knees, the towel still pressed to his eyes.

"Perhaps you could wait a few minutes, dear," Natalya said gently.

Veronica shook her head. "Not this time." She headed for the door.

Michael didn't try to stop her.

Eighteen

After the initial shock had passed, the dowager empress spoke with Alexandra of Phillipe Vachot, but the empress wouldn't listen. Vachot had promised Alexandra he'd reappear in the form of another man. Alexandra would remember these words later when she met a mystic from the East named Rasputin.

—VERONICA HERRERA, The Reluctant Romanov

THE GULF OF FINLAND
AUGUST 1902

Lena tried to close her ears to the sound of Alexandra's agonized scream. It did no good. She watched the empress turn and writhe and bury her face in the lace-trimmed pillow, crying for her missing child. Heat rose in Lena's chest until she was suffocating. She could bear it no longer. She wanted to disappear. Slowly, she made out her own form as well, small and lonely, huddled next to Alexandra's bed. That couldn't be right. She wasn't supposed to be there anymore. Marie had made her leave. She'd already left.

She jolted awake, warm and damp, covered in a thin sheen of sweat, blankets crumpled underneath her. The gentle rolling motion of the ferry registered and then the details of the modest cabin: the pitcher of water on the nightstand near her bed and the bare electric bulb hanging precariously from the ceiling.

She turned at once to check on the grand duchess in the little bassinet beside her bed. The baby slept soundly. Lena sighed in relief, yet her heart still raced. She needed fresh air. She reached for one of the periodicals in the basket near her bed and used it to prop the cabin door ajar, so she could hear the baby when she awoke.

Lena approached the railing outside of her cabin. A crisp breeze ruffled her hair and a seagull cried as it flew off from its perch on the deck above her. She focused on the distant shoreline. Through the gauze of coastal fog, she made out the fuzzy figures of grazing sheep and cows and the golden spires of Saint Petersburg cathedrals, tips twinkling in the distant sunlight. From here, it all looked so grand and peaceful.

A sharp wind gusted and Lena bundled deeper into her coat. When she was a little girl in Archangel and the first frost hit, she'd draw her warmest bear fur close around her body, determined to accompany her mother to another birth even if the howling wind frightened her. Now she'd never see her parents, never hear Anton's merry laugh, or play again with the lopsided chess pieces he carved from wood. But hadn't she fulfilled Anton's wish? She'd escaped Archangel. As she pulled farther and farther away, the easier it became to remember without bitterness. Her life lay free before her.

"I thought you were taking a nap, seamstress. You had a long night."

The familiar tone of his velvety voice made her skin tingle. She felt the color in her face, already flushed red from the cold, deepen as Pavel approached.

"You still move without making a sound," she commented. "It could get you in trouble someday. Now that you're no longer in the dowager's employ, you may want to change your habit."

"Many things could get me in trouble, so I may as well do as I please." When Pavel smiled, dimples appeared in the hollows of his cheeks.

She tried to return his smile, but away from their established roles, she felt awkward. She hadn't yet reconciled herself to the sight of Pavel in civilian clothes, a dark greatcoat and plain trousers, rather than his elaborate palace uniform. He didn't wear his fez or turban either. His hair was shorn close to his head. He still cut an impressive figure, but seemed more accessible somehow.

"What did Marie name the child?" Pavel asked.

"Charlotte. After her grandmother and her husband's grandmother." Lena glanced back at her cabin. It would be difficult to pass the girl to the couple in Copenhagen, to let her go and never find out what was to become of her. But what else could she do? Lena didn't want to dwell on the thought. "So Marie made you a member of the Preobrazhensky Guard. Congratulations."

"The title means nothing outside of Russia, but I appreciate the gesture. She gave me an honorary last name as well. Rubalov. Do you like it?"

"Pavel Rubalov," she said, testing the sound. "Paul Rubalov."

He leaned forward on the railing, smiling slyly. "You remember my given name from America."

Lena looked down at the waves lapping against the side of the boat. "Rubalov has a nice ring to it, but what will your family think?"

His smile collapsed. "We have no attachment to the other name. It was the name of the man who kept my parents as slaves."

"Oh." Lena felt her cheeks warm with embarrassment.

He looked past her, at the forests lining the retreating coastline. "Rubalov is as good a name as any. I'll use it from now on."

"What will you do after we leave the grand duchess with Marie's people?"

"The dowager empress gave me money. I'll start over again." He dipped his head. Even though he was much taller than Lena, he seemed to look up at her. "What about you? Nothing holds you back? What about your family?"

"I'm not leaving much behind."

He continued to stare at her.

"Once I started to work for the Romanovs, I hardly saw my family anyway," she added.

"What about your roommate?" he teased. "Did you even tell her good-bye? Surely you could have invented a story for her, some good gossip."

Lena tapped her foot against the deck. Masha wouldn't intercept any more of her letters or ask Lena when she would take a Cossack lover. She wasn't sure if she'd miss Masha or not.

Pavel laughed softly. "I see it in your face. You're ready for a change. I understand. I'm ready for a change as well. But I don't know that I'll get one."

He nodded toward the other side of the ferry's walkway. A well-dressed young couple strolled toward them on the deck, openly staring. The man's expression betrayed no more than mild curiosity. But as the cold ocean wind blew her hair from her face, Lena saw the woman crumple her nose and purse her lips.

Her look bored into Lena's soul. It reminded her of what she saw on Masha's face when Lena spoke to Pavel, only much worse. She wondered how Pavel could bear it. She didn't think she could manage. Lena turned to the woman. She smiled sweetly, but arched her eyebrows, the way Marie might. "If you have something to say," Lena told the woman, her voice ice, "come right on out and say it. Otherwise, allow us our privacy."

The woman scowled and began to walk at a decidedly swifter pace, passing Lena and Pavel without a word.

Pavel smiled again. "You developed a lady's wit at the palace. Now you have the heart of a lioness as well."

"My time with the dowager empress granted me courage," Lena said.

"She has that effect. Marie is a stubborn woman, but a great lady."

"Will it be better for you elsewhere? Will people always stare?"

Pavel leaned forward on the railing. His hands were so near hers. "I understand some places are better than others," he told her. "Have you traveled in Europe before?"

"I've never traveled anywhere," she said.

"So this is your opportunity to see the world. As for me, I don't intend to wander forever."

"You'll return home?" she asked. "To Virginia. You never did tell me about it. Your family is there?"

"A brother and some nephews I've only met once." Pavel squeezed his large hands together. They were finely groomed, as well kept as every other part of him, but she saw now the whitish scars and calluses, where his skin had torn, healed over, and been re-torn. Lena knew those scars. They came from hard, blistering work tilling fields. The scars on the hands of the men and women in Archangel were much the same.

"My parents have passed," he continued. "They had difficult lives. They both died young. They were born into slavery. But it wasn't much better afterward. They wanted me to leave. They encouraged it. They wanted me as far away as possible."

So much lay beneath Pavel's smooth exterior. "That's what my brother Anton wanted for me as well. My parents were born serfs. It's not the same, but—"

"It's not the same."

"No," she said. "But they had difficult lives. My brother wanted something better for me."

Pavel lowered his voice. "I ran as far as I could. Halfway around the world. I wanted something better. But now I want to return home. Does that make sense?"

He brushed her hand with his fingers. Her skin flamed. Her heart jumped. The wind lashed her cheeks, but now she scarcely noticed the cold. With as much subtlety as she could muster, she moved her hands away. She shoved them in her pockets, and felt the cool metal of the necklace Marie had given her before they left.

"You can go inside the cabin if you like," Lena said quickly. "It's cold. I don't want to trouble you." She tapped her foot on the wooden plank of the deck nervously.

Pavel removed a pack of cigarettes from his coat pocket and offered her one. She shook her head.

"I don't mind the cold if you don't." He lit a match. His long, elegant fingers moved to shield the light from the wind.

"I'm from up north," Lena said. "I'm used to the cold. I'll stay out here until the baby cries."

Pavel dipped his head again. "Then I haven't scared you."

"You scared me," she admitted, heart racing.

Pavel took a deep drag on the cigarette. It smelled like cloves, like the tsar's cigarettes. Wisps of smoke dissipated in the air around them. "What are your plans?"

Lena tried to stall. "I'll take the grand duchess to Marie's servants in Copenhagen. They'll take care of her."

"Marie told me. I meant afterward."

Lena sensed where this was headed. "I don't know."

"Perhaps we could decide together."

Lena could no longer see the land, only shimmering waves of gold and green on the horizon. She remembered Olga chasing her puppy, Alexandra's kind encouragements when Lena spoke English, even Masha's playful teasing. *What kind of man pleases you, Lenichka, a fair Ukrainian or a swarthy Tatar?*

Pavel leaned forward, his voice low. He met her gaze. "Would you like to see Virginia with me?"

For a moment, she wanted it all back, wanted everything as it had been, the security of knowing her place in the world and the shape of her days. She ached for the familiar. But she knew she couldn't have remained content in that world, not when this other, greater world beckoned. Her service with the Romanovs would fade over time into beautiful memories. Now she had a chance to create new memories.

She slipped her hand into Pavel's and their fingers intertwined.

SAINTE-FOY-LE-GRANDE
OCTOBER 1941

Charlotte stood at the window in her old room, brushing her hair and staring at the broad country sky and low hills to the south. The familiar view brought her back over twenty years. She was watching her mother lean against the kitchen sink. In the bright July sunlight, tears glistened on her mother's cheeks. Dull black newsprint stained her thumbs and forefingers. The newspaper report about the Romanov murder was spread open and before them on the table.

After she read it, her mother couldn't stop crying.

Charlotte remembered feeling puzzled. She had been sixteen at the time, more concerned with her boyfriend who planned to enlist in the army and her own nascent plans to leave for Paris once the fighting ceased. They knew families whose sons had died in battle, or been maimed by gas, or wilted to nothing struggling with the influenza that followed in the war's wake. Yet it was the regicide in distant Siberia that finally broke her mother.

"So you knew everything," Charlotte told Kshesinskaya.

"I watched over you the best I could, as Dowager Empress Marie and your parents asked." Kshesinskaya sat on Charlotte's bed, on the same bedspread and blankets Charlotte used to snuggle in with her mother on cold nights. Kshesinskaya's hair hung loose around her shoulders, jet-black at the ends but graying at the roots, her true self.

"I watched over you for so long, but then the Germans took my son. The Nazis had him in one of their camps. I had to give them something. You know what they would have done to him? I thought about it all the time, all the horrors I'd heard."

Kshesinskaya shrugged her frail shoulders, tried to erect her strong Russian front. She wore a thick wool sweater, but Charlotte could make out the arch of her delicate bones as she trembled. Unwillingly, Charlotte softened. How many times had she imagined what the Germans would do to Laurent? She understood too well now how such a threat played tricks on the mind.

"I came here to warn your parents that the German officer

knew," Kshesinskaya said. "Your adoptive parents . . . your parents.
I'm sorry. I'm trying to get this right."

The day she found her mother crying over the Romanovs,
Charlotte realized she'd grown taller. That was when she first knew
the time had come for them to switch roles. She'd hugged her
from behind to comfort her. Her mother had turned and drawn
her close, damp hands smelling of flour and yeast. She'd nestled
her head in Charlotte's shoulders. "At least we kept you safe," she
said between muffled sobs.

She might never hold her mother again. No one stood between her and the world.

"They're safe?" Charlotte asked.

"They left a few hours ago. They're headed for Spain. It's where
you should go. If I were younger, I'd go with you."

Charlotte stared at her mentor, trying to imagine her as a
younger woman. Kshesinskaya looked frail and malnourished,
but then she'd always been so thin. Before the occupation, she ate
what she pleased and her waist remained tiny. Charlotte had
watched other dancers eye her with envy. Now she remembered
the photographs of Kshesinskaya in her heyday when she danced
in Russia, when she was the tsar's mistress.

"You knew Nicholas II well," Charlotte said. And then, just
to experience how it felt rolling off her tongue, she added, "my
father."

Kshesinskaya gave a sad smile. "Our affair ended amicably. He
married your mother, who was lovely. Some people didn't care for
Empress Alexandra, but I found her a fine woman, simply out of
place in that world. She would have loved you."

"If she'd kept me?"

"The doctors told her it was a stillbirth. They had to tell her something."

"Did Marie Romanov tell them to say that?" Charlotte snapped.

Kshesinskaya bowed her head and nodded.

"She told Alexandra I was dead," Charlotte said, voice rising.

"The dowager empress believed she was doing the right thing. She cared for you. If she hadn't spirited you away, you would have died in that terrible house in Siberia."

"She couldn't see the future. She didn't know."

"Everything happens for a reason." Kshesinskaya reached past Charlotte and picked up a framed photograph from the night-stand, Charlotte in a romantic-style long tutu, a flower tucked behind her ear. Her mother had taken the picture after a performance of *Giselle*. Charlotte had been part of the corps de ballet.

Kshesinskaya tapped the photo with a slender finger. "How old were you here?"

Charlotte hesitated. "Seventeen."

"If you had stayed with your family, you would have been dead before this picture was taken."

Charlotte stared at the photograph. She was bent at the knee, arms curved into a circle before her, each finger delicately pointing up or forward. She felt jealous of the girl in the picture, so guile-less and perfect and effortlessly happy. She wanted to be that person again. Her gaze traveled to the photograph she'd taken from her parents' safe. The four grand duchesses. Her sisters. Tatiana, the second-oldest daughter of the tsar, looked about seventeen when the photo was taken. Tatiana even had the same expression Charlotte bore at that age, sure nothing could ever hurt her.

"When did you find out?" she asked Kshesinskaya.

"In 1927. Marie was still alive and living in Denmark. She had received a visitor, a German. This conversation scared her. All those years she had been so careful and then at the very end of her life she let it slip. Of course she always thought it would be the Bolsheviks after you, not the Germans. This man, Herr Krause, took her by surprise. She contacted your parents. You'd moved to Paris by then."

"She didn't even know where I lived?" Charlotte said.

"Marie was so out of touch in her final years. But as I said, everything happens for a reason. When your parents told Marie you'd moved to Paris, she contacted me and asked me to look out for you."

"And you believed Marie's story without any proof."

Kshesinskaya leaned forward and touched Charlotte's hand gently. Charlotte didn't squeeze her hand in return, but didn't pull away either. "I took one look at you and knew. You looked just like Grand Duchess Tatiana. And your eyes." Kshesinskaya lowered her gaze again. "You have the tsar's eyes. I know them well."

A tentative knock on the bedroom door interrupted their discussion. Kshesinskaya patted Charlotte's hand, looking relieved. "That would be your husband. You and Laurent need to go to Spain. One of the armies will win. They're the same. Cruel. You know what the Bolsheviks did to your family. You know what the Nazis are trying to do. You can't let either of them find you. Promise me that at least." Kshesinskaya stood and moved to the door. "If you ever need help, you can always contact me."

"You won't be around forever." Charlotte clamped her mouth shut, regretting the harsh words. "I'm sorry."

Kshesinskaya shrugged again. "You only state the obvious. I won't be around forever. I understand. But there are others. I'll make sure you always know how to find them and they always know how to find you. For now, let your husband help. He still cares for you." She slipped out of the room.

Luc brushed past Kshesinskaya on his way inside, hobbling, favoring his good leg. He reminded Charlotte of the retreating French soldiers making their way through the city before the German tanks rolled down the boulevards. The soldiers cried for water and dropped to their knees on the streets.

Still, despite the bruising on Luc's face and his swollen lip, he looked better. He'd managed to shower and change into some of her father's old clothes. Now he wore a simple shirt that hung loose on his shoulders and black trousers so long he'd pinned them at the ankles. He leaned against the wall to support himself. "I thought you'd fallen asleep," he told her. "Then I heard Kshesinskaya."

"I can't sleep."

The bed creaked as Luc took the weight off his leg and sat down. Without asking, Charlotte folded the trousers to expose the bindings around the wound. It looked purplish and splotchy, but not jagged and black as she'd feared. She placed her hand gently on his calf muscle. "Does it hurt?"

"No, Your Highness."

Charlotte withdrew her hand. "Don't call me that." She couldn't break down. Not now. Not in front of Luc. But she heard her voice shake as she added, "How could my parents keep something like this from me?"

"I'm sure they thought it best. Based on what we experienced a few hours ago, I'd say they were right. Besides, you'll have a chance to ask them."

She wanted to believe Luc. Once they had made it to Spain, she'd find her parents. She'd hold her mother again and feel warm and safe.

Luc's hand closed over hers, warm and strong as he stroked the inside of her wrists. A pang of desire stirred deep within her. It had been so long since anyone touched her this way.

And then she saw the bottle of black hair dye in his other hand.

"I don't know if I'll like you with darker hair," she said.

"It's not for me." He set the bottle down on the bed. He ran his fingertips through her hair and lightly caressed the back of her neck, but the moment had passed. She felt only a hollow echo of desire.

"I don't understand," she said.

"The Germans will send out pictures and descriptions. You need to look different. I'll help. It won't take long. Kshesinskaya brought a car for you and Laurent. She'll take the train back to Paris. Kshesinskaya brought money too. She says she'll buy your flat, if you won't take the money any other way."

"What about you?" Charlotte's hands started to shake. "You're not well. We'll wait a few days until you're better."

Luc gave one of his half smiles. She remembered the man she'd fallen in love with, that lazy smile she'd found so damn irresistible. "Try to get a few hours' rest," he said. "You need to leave before daylight."

"What will you do?"

Luc leaned forward, his elbows on his knees, careful not to press too hard on his bad leg. He put his head in his hands, massaging his forehead.

"I'm sorry, Charlotte," he said quietly. "Laurent deserves a father. You should have someone at your side to help. But that person can't be me."

She pulled back. He'd always been good at disguising his emotions. Right now he may as well have been made of stone. She should have known. For all she thought he'd changed, he never wanted a child. And he resented her for it.

"I wouldn't want you to stay with us out of obligation or pity," she said coldly. "I manage well enough on my own."

"It's not that," he said.

"Then what?" A wave of panic disoriented her. She was remembering something the German had said in that terrible cellar. He'd told her they could all be hanged for what they'd found in the car, or words to this effect. "What drop were you going to make for the courier?"

The stony mask crumbled. Luc put his hands down and looked up at her. It took Charlotte a moment to comprehend, but then she realized Luc was smiling. He reached for his pocket and withdrew a thick and ragged sheet of white paper that looked like it had been torn from a butcher's block. The map was rough and obviously made in haste. Marks were made around the perimeter of the city.

"The locations of all the German checkpoints," Luc said.

"You have to come with us," she whispered, pulse racing. "You must get this to your contact."

"I intend to go on to Spain," he said. "But not with you. Charlotte, I killed the German officer. How do you think we escaped? How do you think I got this back?"

Deep down she'd known. She couldn't think of anything to say.

"If they find all three of us together, God knows what they'll do to you and Laurent. How could I live with myself?"

"They might not do anything," she began, "if I went to them instead."

"You know you can't do that either," Luc said.

"They'll kill you," Charlotte said, her desperation mounting and threatening to collapse in on itself. "If I'm with you, we have something to offer."

"There's a train station in Bergerac," he said quietly. "That's where I'm heading. They're looking for three people. Perhaps they won't notice one."

Charlotte drew in a deep breath. She had already looked into the abyss, trapped in that cellar, fearing for Laurent's life. She could do this. She reminded herself this might be the last time she saw him. She had been robbed of closure the first time Luc left her. She wouldn't let that happen again.

She bent forward, brushing her lips against his. He returned the kiss, but felt strange and unfamiliar. Perhaps it was the swelling. She brushed his hair away from his eyes.

"I'll send someone to help you. Once we're in a safe house in Spain. I'll tell them what happened. We'll find you."

He put his hands flat on her cheeks and tipped his forehead to hers. He pulled her toward him once more and she kissed him again, not caring now that it felt different this time. It was meant to feel different now. They were different people.

L.A. THIS WEEK
News and Events for Hollywood, the Hills, and Beyond
BATTLE ROYALE!

Self-declared Romanov heir apparent Grand Duke Alexei has been hobnobbing with royalty for years, all the time keeping his eyes on the prize: restoration of the monarchy in Russia. When Romanov faced a challenge from local attorney Michael Karstadt, he thought he might have to turn in his orb and scepter. According to Mr. Romanov, Karstadt planned to "perpetuate the greatest hoax on the Russian people since they were led to believe bullets magically flew off of the Grand Duchess Anastasia in 1918." And all with the help of Alameda University Professor Veronica Herrera.

Mr. Karstadt's family claimed a fifth daughter had been born to Nicholas and Alexandra Romanov in 1902 and smuggled out of the country long before the Russian Revolution. "Utter nonsense," Romanov huffs, "a fiction without a shred of evidence."

Evidence is what ultimately brought the "False Mikhail," as Mr. Romanov calls him, back down to live among the serfs. DNA tests proved Michael Karstadt was a fake. "When he secured the assistance of an academic, we were concerned. But now we know that Mikhail is only the latest in a long string of imposters." Mr. Romanov further assures, "The actual Romanov heir will claim the throne. We will seize sublime destiny."

In recent years, rumblings inside of Russia indicate restoration isn't far-fetched. But in modern politics, is a tsar really acceptable, even as a figurehead? If so, will more "False Mikhails" make plays for the Russian throne?

Nineteen

Veronica stared at the endless rows of red brake lights shining in the darkness before her. She'd started the first leg of her annual night-before-Thanksgiving journey home to Bakersfield, the slow drive north through the San Fernando Valley. Apparently, every human being on the face of the planet had decided to embark on the exact same route at the exact same time. The traffic would thin out when she ascended the Grapevine, the low mountain range separating the Los Angeles basin from the rest of California. Then she would travel down and over to Highway 99, into the blanket of agribusiness pollution that constantly hovered over the once great Central Valley.

That leg of the journey always made the back of her neck prickle with anxiety. That's when it truly hit her. She would soon be back in her hometown, where she'd always be known as Ginger Herrera's strange granddaughter, the professor.

Except the next time Veronica made the drive to Bakersfield

she'd be behind the wheel of a U-Haul and no longer a professor. Veronica guessed that just made her strange.

The car ahead of her crept forward an inch or two. She gritted her teeth and tried to ward off the first pangs of a headache, to make herself numb.

The day after Veronica returned from her disastrous trip to New York, Regina Brack called her into her office, formed a steeple underneath her chin, and tapped her index fingers together. She may as well have brandished the grim reaper's ax. While Dr. Brack delivered her canned speech, Veronica stared at a new row of dead butterflies pinned to the boards on the wall behind Dr. Brack's desk. Most of the professors on Veronica's review committee had "grave concerns" regarding the "disturbingly slim and inconsistent" nature of Veronica's research. Furthermore, Veronica's student reviews, while "adequate overall," had not been sufficiently glowing to overcome her thin publishing record.

As Dr. Brack droned on, Veronica noticed a well-worn copy of *L.A. This Week* on the dean's desk. Veronica had already read the short article inside. A local professor of Russian history had been duped by an accomplished con man.

Knowing what was to come, Dr. Brack advised Veronica to submit a resignation, effective at the end of the semester, rather than endure the humiliation of a failed review. Veronica knew it was over. She'd been placed in Dr. Brack's kill jar and there was no escape. Her career was dead.

Once again, the brake lights on the car before her dimmed. Veronica pulled forward, another few inches closer to home. In two short weeks, she would join the ranks of the unemployed. She couldn't afford her rent without a paycheck. All of her savings had long since been drained to pay back her student loans. She planned to stay in her old bedroom in her grandmother's house while she looked for work. Veronica gripped the steering wheel tighter and practiced the smile she planned to use with her aunts. It might not be so bad. Maybe something would come up at a community college in Bakersfield. And it wasn't so far to drive back down to Los Angeles for an interview.

Still, Jess said Abuela had already been grumbling: Veronica was always welcome, but where was she supposed to find room for all of her sewing projects now?

Veronica's cousin Inez pushed her glasses up on her nose and made another elaborate gesture in the air. They sat together at a folding card table in the living room of her cousin's house in Bakersfield, right in the center of the action: high-definition TV and football. The commotion of the game was punctuated every so often by stomping feet. Some of her cousins had retreated upstairs to blast *Rock Band* on one of the spare televisions.

How different Inez seemed now from the giggling girl at the *quinceañera*. According to Abuela, Inez had recently been awarded a medal in the statewide academic decathlon, special emphasis in world history. Veronica could just make out Inez's words over the blare of football across the room and the drums at the beginning of Metallica's "Enter Sandman."

"The Romans were fantastic engineers," Inez told her. "That's what I wrote about. Did you know the Roman aqueducts provided water for more people than live in New York City? And engineers predicted the eruption of Mount Vesuvius. Some of the engineers on Pompeii tested the water for sulfur levels because the fish were dying . . . I got a fifty-dollar iTunes gift card along with the medal!"

"Fifty big ones," Veronica said. "Wow."

That came out more sarcastically than she'd intended. Actually, Veronica felt a twinge of jealousy over the gift card. These are the glory years, kid. That's what she wanted to tell Inez. Enjoy them while you can. In a few years, Inez would start applying for universities. And then she'd discover the acclaim she received as a prodigy in Bakersfield was replicated in every backwater town in the country, among all sorts of kids, and every one of those smartasses wanted the same spots in the same schools. Later on they'd want the same jobs.

If Inez wasn't careful, she'd end up like Veronica, scraping together money for rent, endlessly paying off student loans. And to what end? To move back home?

Veronica squeezed her eyes shut. She'd vowed not to wallow, at least not in the presence of others. The solitary crying jags were awful enough, but at least then she only hurt herself.

"You made it!" Jess's booming voice jolted Veronica from her brooding. Jess hovered above her, black hair spilling over her shoulders. She bounced Carlos on her hip and bent to kiss Veronica's cheek, smelling of baby powder and daisies. "We should have carpooled." She turned to Carlos. "See what a lucky boy you are? See that big bear?"

The enormous teddy bear had elicited the appropriate "oohs" and "aahs." Veronica even spotted a sidelong glance of amazement from a great-aunt who once told her she'd never get married because she was too smart for her own good.

Veronica didn't bother to mention that she'd re-gifted the bear. It had arrived in her office right before Thanksgiving break, along with flowers and a notecard that read "I'm sorry" in familiar, elegant handwriting. She'd given the flowers to the student who answered phones at the front desk. She tried to trash the note, but somehow couldn't bring herself to do so. Instead, she'd tossed it into the desk drawer full of junk she never used. Perhaps when they moved her replacement into the office, that person would find the note and wonder what happened.

"Why don't you hold Carlos?" Jess said.

Little brown spots danced before Veronica's eyes. "I don't think . . ."

Veronica hesitated. She expected to hear the hissing voices in her head, but they failed to materialize. Instead, she heard her cousin's voice faintly, like something in a dream. "What's wrong?"

"Nothing." Nothing. That was it. The hissing voices weren't there. Veronica realized she hadn't heard them since she submitted her resignation. She felt emboldened. "I'd love to hold Carlos."

Once Veronica's words registered, Jess broke into a huge smile. "Grab some hand sanitizer. It's in my purse."

Veronica rubbed vanilla-scented germ fighter into her hands and then Jess placed Carlos in her arms. The sprawl of his limbs cuddled up against her chest.

"See!" Jess said triumphantly. "He likes you. And he doesn't like just anybody. Speaking of, where's that handsome boyfriend of yours? The Russian prince?"

The chasm swelled in Veronica's chest, gaping, demanding attention and pity. She glanced at the empty chair next to her, mocking her. She stuffed her feelings back down her throat. Veronica bounced Carlos gently in her lap and was rewarded with a smile. "It didn't work out," she said.

"Oh." Jess may have lacked tact, but she blushed a little. "I'm sorry. You guys were cute together. Well, it's his loss."

Veronica nodded. A prickling sensation grazed the back of her neck. She twisted her head. Abuela was watching, eyebrows lifted. Veronica had arrived too late the night before to really talk with her grandmother. She'd fallen into her old bed almost as soon as she got home. Veronica imagined the conversations about Michael that would transpire later when they were back in the cocoon of Abuela's house. *I knew right away he was trouble. Too slick. Too charming. Too good to be true.*

"Veronica?" Inez tapped the table impatiently. "My mom told me you've been to Italy. Did you visit Pompeii? Did you see the ruins?"

Carlos shifted in Veronica's arms. Sensing a crying jag, she passed him back to Jess. "We hit a bunch of cities. In Italy, I only went to Rome." Veronica remembered ordering coffee at a tourist trap of a café across from the Colosseum, watching the sky turn to violet as the sun set over the ancient arches, giggling with her friends. Nearly fifteen years had passed since. She could hardly wrap her head around the passage of time. "I didn't have much money, but I had a great time."

Inez's expression brightened. "Maybe one day we can go to Pompeii together. I can show you everything from my report. You like that stuff, right?"

"Sounds great." It did sound great. Veronica found herself warming to the idea. "Let's plan a trip. You'll turn eighteen in three years, right? We'll go then."

"I babysit," Inez said cautiously. "How much would a trip like that cost?"

"We'll find the money. I'll save each month. We can go after you graduate." She extended her hand. "Deal?"

"Deal," Inez agreed. They shook on it.

Veronica caught a glimpse of her grandmother watching them. Abuela nodded toward the door. Veronica supposed she'd have to get this over with sooner or later. "I'll call your mom next week," she told Inez, withdrawing from the shake. "But I need to talk to my abuela now. Will you excuse me?"

Inez gave her a quick hug. "Thanks. I'm going to tell my mom."

Veronica watched Inez scamper off. For once, she'd done something right for her family. That had been easy. Facing Abuela, on the other hand . . .

The sun was so bright the frosty air caught Veronica by surprise. She'd grown accustomed to L.A. warmth and forgotten about Valley chill. She used her hand to shield her eyes. After nightfall, thick Tule fog would rise from the ground and wreak havoc on the freeway. But right now the bright light reflected off the cars lining the street.

Veronica heard the screen door slam behind her and then caught the scent of Abuela's facial powder and perfume. Natalya Rubalov's face flashed in Veronica's mind.

"Your eyes look puffy," her grandmother said. "Have you been crying?"

"I'm fine." Veronica pulled her thin sweater tighter and braced for the onslaught. Men were this. Men were that. Veronica's white father, etc. The same lines she'd heard since the first time her grandmother caught her writing "Veronica loves so and so" in her fifth-grade notebook.

Abuela took a seat next to her on the steps. She wore a new pink dress she'd made herself. Veronica actually liked the color. "How are you?" Abuela asked.

"This isn't exactly a great time to look for a job." Veronica wrapped her arms around her chest and began rocking to stay warm. "But I'll find something."

"Oh." Her grandmother tilted her head. How different she looked from Natalya. Both of them were neatly kept older women, but there was more artifice in her grandmother's appearance. Still, the familiarity felt reassuring. Veronica wouldn't have traded Abuela's presence right now for anything in the world.

"I'm glad to hear it," Abuela said at last.

"I thought you'd be more upset."

"I am upset," Abuela admitted. "But the most important thing is for you to be happy. Maybe you'll find a job or a career that makes you happier than academia."

Veronica raised her eyebrows in surprise. "Thank you."

"I want you to be happy. I want you to be secure. I want you to be safe."

"Even if you have to give up your sewing room for a little while?"

"Even if." Abuela paused. "I know you won't be there forever. Then I'll get my projects back out. I need to make a dress for your aunt Ana's wedding next summer. Of course it's her third marriage, so I won't make anything too fancy."

Veronica ran her hands through her hair. Abuela was still Abuela. But that was just as it should have been. Veronica was tired of defining herself against her family. She only wanted to enjoy them. She knew she could have done worse.

"That's not what I meant, though," Abuela said. "I'm sorry about what happened with your friend, Michael Karstadt. He seemed like a nice man."

"You're joking," was all Veronica could manage.

"I liked him." Abuela tugged sunglasses off the top of her head. Several strands of hair fell from her neat upsweep. "Even if he was an attorney."

"Then why were you so mean to him at the *quinceañera*?"

"I was only teasing." Veronica heard the tension in her grandmother's voice. "Do you blame me for driving him away?"

"No." Veronica looked down at her hands. She'd taken the time to buff her nails this morning and now she admired their smoothness. "I thought Michael was different. I can't explain."

"I know." Her grandmother scooted closer, caressing her shoulder, as she used to when Veronica came home from school with less than a perfect score on a spelling test. "I wish you'd known your mother better. She wanted to teach Spanish literature. That's why she went to study in Madrid."

"But she got knocked up with me," Veronica finished for her.

"Not that she regretted it for a second. It wasn't your fault, *mija*. I am so sorry if I ever made you think anything was your fault. Your mother would have gone back to school. I would have helped her. She only wanted to spend the first few years with you. Then she got sick." Abuela reached into her purse and took out a small pack of tissues. She removed her sunglasses and dabbed at her eyes. "I tried to raise you the way your mother would have wanted, as a strong, independent woman. I didn't mean you should never fall in love."

Veronica tried to picture her mother rocking her or feeding her. But these were false images. She had to rely on Abuela's memories. Veronica put her arm around her grandmother's thick waist and hugged her. "It's not your fault. And don't worry. I'm not Anna Karenina."

Abuela frowned. "The adulteress?"

Veronica grinned. "I mean I'm not going to throw myself in front of a train over Michael. Maybe I'm just meant to be alone."

"Maybe," Abuela said. "But haven't you noticed that car circling the block?"

"I don't hear anything."

"Of course not. It's a Prius. Didn't you tell me Michael Karstadt drove a Prius?"

Veronica's head shot up. Sure enough, a white Prius came to a soundless halt at the end of the street, backed up slowly, and then made a U-turn, still in silence. Her heart skipped a beat. "You invited him here?"

"You can't blame me for wanting to make things right."

"He's a liar. You don't want me to be with a liar, do you?"

Abuela pinched her eyebrows. "Just hear him out. Your mother would have . . ."

A chill passed through Veronica's chest. "My mother would have what?"

"I think your mother had a fascinating experience in Europe," Abuela said carefully. "When she came back she was different somehow."

Veronica opened her mouth, but Abuela stopped her. "Not just because she was pregnant. She suddenly had a new interest. Russian history. It seemed strange. She'd come back from Spain, not Eastern Europe. I always wondered what sparked her interest, but then we were so distracted when you were a baby and she passed away before I had a chance to ask her."

Veronica's lip twitched. "That is strange," she said at last. "Why didn't you tell me this until now?"

"I told you some, *mija*. I didn't talk about it too much because I didn't want to make you sad. But that copy of *Nicholas and Alexandra* you read? It was hers. She grew fascinated with the Romanovs around the same time you were born. I wasn't surprised you loved the book so much." Abuela rose to her feet and gave a little smile. "Anyway, just talk to this Michael Karstadt."

"Why me?" Veronica stood to meet her grandmother's gaze. "He's your guest. You entertain him."

"It's cold. I think I'll go in now."

Veronica's heart dropped to her stomach. "Wait."

Behind her, she heard a car door slam. Her grandmother went inside the house, shutting the door quietly in Veronica's face. Veronica spun around. Michael was already heading up the driveway.

Twenty

By now Lena had guided countless babies into the world. Still, she trembled with anticipation at the prospect of holding a newborn in her arms. Her hands weren't as steady as they'd once been, and so the excitement was tempered somewhat. Lena took particular care with the boy in her arms now.

Her daughter, Natalya, had been trying to get pregnant for years. She finally broke down and asked Lena for advice, even if all Lena offered were dubious tales from the Russian countryside. Lena had shrugged and told her youngest daughter to relax and let go of wanting a child so much. Three months later, Natalya was pregnant.

Mikhail yawned and fidgeted, but remained asleep. Lena cuddled him closer. As he napped, Lena watched her son-in-law, Anatoly Karstadt, play the role of proud papa. Anatoly was a large man, not fat, but tall and substantial. Strutting around the room with a cigar clenched between his teeth, he reminded Lena of a

Russian land baron lording over his serfs. He passed out cigars with little blue-and-gold bands and accepted each new stream of congratulations with manly pats on the shoulder, as though he, rather than poor exhausted Natalya, had endured hours of labor.

Lena regarded the cigars critically. She worried about the smoke damaging the baby's lungs, and the cost of the extravagance.

Before Mikhail's birth, Natalya had tearfully confided she and her husband were near financial ruin. He had invested heavily in a chain of failing restaurants and his temper grew shorter each day. Lena had nodded slowly while Natalya spoke, and tried not to say anything nasty about her son-in-law, knowing her daughter would only defend her husband. Instead, she patted Natalya's hand and promised to help.

Still, as Lena watched from across the room, she saw a side of her son-in-law she liked. Anatoly moved easily between the groups of relatives and friends gathered in the crowded brownstone, chattering in Russian and English. For all his bluster and bad temper and money problems, he had charm. Whenever he stopped to talk to someone, he focused his attention completely on them.

Her darling Natalya worked the room as well, charming despite her exhaustion. No one would possibly guess their financial problems. Lena supposed that was the point. Her daughter's laughter rang across the room in tinkling peals. With her dark golden skin, Natalya looked like her father, but her laugh was that of Lena's brother, Anton. Lena remembered Anton sitting by the roaring fire, showing her English books he'd brought home from school, patiently sounding out the letters in the strange alphabet.

Her daughter moved to another guest, lips parting in one of

her quirky smiles. Lena's heart fluttered a little before it sank; her daughter's smile was a feminine replica of Pavel's smile. The years sometimes jumbled in Lena's mind, but she realized over sixty-five years had passed since she'd agreed to accompany Pavel Rubalov to Virginia. It remained the best decision she'd ever made. And for all she hated the cigars her son-in-law passed to the guests, she liked their scent. It reminded her of Pavel's clove cigarettes.

After they left Grand Duchess Charlotte in Copenhagen, they spent several months in Virginia, near Pavel's brother and nephews. Opportunities for work were scarce and Lena saw the way people looked at them when they ventured out together. It made even Russian racism seem the picture of tolerance. Lena ended up spending most of her time in the house, safely out of sight and bored out of her mind.

Through one of his old connections, Pavel found a job in Brooklyn, working as an instructor at a boxing center for disadvantaged youths. Lena decided then she was meant to be a midwife, like her mother. Many European immigrants had amassed in New York City, all in need of her help. And then a flood of immigrants came from Russia after the Revolution.

"Looks like you're fading out there, *matushka*. Stay with us."

Her son-in-law hovered over her, a broad smile on his face. Since Pavel died the year before, Lena was prone to falling headfirst into memories and forgetting the world. But she was well into her eighties and had earned the right to fade from the world every now and again. She only needed to make sure she could still be summoned back.

Someone had turned on the television. Images of the moonwalk replayed on the news for the hundredth time. Lena had a difficult time believing the event had not been staged, no matter how many times Natalya assured her it really happened. Natalya didn't understand the duplicity of the powerful.

"Handsome fellow, isn't he?" Her son-in-law patted little Mikhail's head, a tad too roughly for Lena's comfort. Then he took a few satisfied puffs of his cigar.

"Very much so," she replied. "Now put out the cigar."

"Oh, you're not turning into some hippie health nut, are you?"

The words were spoken lightly enough, but with just a hint of menace, of the bully she knew he could be when provoked. Did her son-in-law really think he would intimidate her? Lena hadn't been scared in a long time. She couldn't even summon the sensation. "Put it out."

He smiled gamely, flattering her with the full force of his attentiveness. Then he stamped the cigar out on a nearby ashtray. "Five bucks down the drain."

Lena bit her tongue to hold back a sharp comment. "Well worth it, I'm sure."

"So you've been keeping up with the news?"

"I know." She rocked Mikhail gently. "We landed on the moon. It's really happened. Natalya explained."

Anatoly laughed softly and scratched the back of his neck. "I'm glad you're finally convinced. I heard on the news last night the commie bastards in the old country are seething. They can't believe we made it there first."

Lena gazed down at Mikhail. He'd stuffed his fingers in his mouth as he gurgled, content to look around the room. "I avoid thinking about the old country."

"Why? You left before the Revolution. You weren't forced out." He winked at her and inclined his head. "How come you never told us more? Natalya says you and Pavel worked for the royal family, but you won't say much else."

Lena's lips moved, but she couldn't manage to form the words. If it weren't for Marie and little Charlotte, she would have stayed. She would have remained close to Alexandra, followed the royal family into exile. Everyone knew the rest of that story. The servants were killed, alongside the family, in that dungeon in Siberia. The descriptions were so vivid: the horrific blast of gunfire, smoke rising in the still air, and then the tips of bayonets piercing tender skin as the grand duchesses collapsed.

She imagined feathers flying when it happened. Bullets must have riddled the down pillows the girls brought with them as they were marched downstairs. They'd wanted to make the chairs more comfortable for their parents and their sickly little brother. Lena pictured feathers floating to the floor over the family's lifeless bodies. And, if she had been there, her own eyes staring vacantly at the blood-spattered wall.

Only Marie's insistence that five girls meant one too many had saved her. An unwanted baby saved her life.

After news of the family's murder broke, Lena ached to reveal her secret. The Bolsheviks murdered children. One had escaped their notice. But Lena worried. She may have been safe in America, but she assumed Grand Duchess Charlotte still lived in Europe, close to the Soviet Union. If the Bolsheviks knew, they would find her and kill her, just as they'd murdered her parents and siblings.

"Matushka?"

Lena looked at her son-in-law, his face creased with worry. Her hand started to shake once more and she held Mikhail even tighter. The way she'd held Charlotte when they ran through the halls of Peterhof with Marie.

She wouldn't be around forever. That became more apparent every day, as her body throbbed with pain and her movements slowed. Marie was long gone. What if Charlotte needed her help?

"What's the matter?" Anatoly took her arm. It felt even frailer in his large, muscular hand. "You look as though you saw a spirit."

Lena cupped Mikhail's head in her hands as she moved him farther up her arm, feeling the weight of her years keenly. She never found out what became of Anton. She trusted Marie to keep him safe, but what happened after the Revolution, when the Romanovs lost power? What had become of him? Of her parents? Of people like Masha? They'd all been spirits for a long time. Lena squeezed her eyes shut.

"I served as an attendant for Empress Alexandra," she began. "I met the tsar. I played with the grand duchesses. Pavel was made a member of the Preobrazhensky Guard, the most loyal of the tsarist regiments. He took the name Rubalov. He didn't want the name of slave owners."

"I know. You've told us before." Anatoly sounded disappointed. "But I think you should write it down. Preserve your memories for this guy." Lena opened her eyes as he mimed a playful chucking of Mikhail's chin.

"We promised to keep their secrets." Lena knew she could keep the secret of the grand duchess forever, as she'd promised Marie. But should she? "We promised to watch over them."

She grabbed Anatoly's wrist. He didn't resist, but his expression registered shock. This felt right, the same way it had felt right to say yes when Pavel asked her if she wanted to come to America. She'd sworn to keep the secret, but she'd also sworn to keep the fifth grand duchess safe.

"I will tell you in the strictest confidence. I will tell Natalya as well, and when he's old enough I want you to tell your son. But it stays in our family. I will make it worthwhile for you to keep this secret. I can help you with money."

Anatoly grimaced, but nodded. Lena felt a sudden burst of strength. She recognized the sensation. It felt the same as when she realized she needed to return to Marie and rescue the baby grand duchess, all those years before.

"In 1901, Empress Alexandra was desperate for a son. She had four daughters, but the country had no heir." Lena remembered the furrows on Alexandra's forehead as she'd reached out and clutched Lena's wrist.

It's all right. Lena wished she could have whispered in the empress's ear, right before they shot her dead in that basement in Siberia, right before her head slumped lifeless over her chest. *Your children didn't all die. We saved one of them.*

"Alexandra asked for my advice on how to conceive a boy," Lena continued. "This is what I told her . . ."

PARIS

JULY 1974

"You won't marry this girl?" Charlotte sat across from her son at the table. Sunlight streamed into the freshly painted kitchen. "This is what you came to tell me?"

Usually, the morning light in the flat buoyed her mood. Charlotte lived alone, save for a stray tabby who showed up at her back door in the evening for bits of stewed chicken and a chin scratch. But she was safe and healthy and mobile, if slower these days. She lived in the city she loved and made her way to Kshesinskaya's old ballet studio once or twice a week. She took care of the finances, leaving the teaching to younger women now. But she liked to come in and sit opposite the long wooden barre, tapping her silver cane in time to the music and shouting out instructions to erring students. Not a terrible life for a woman over seventy.

This morning, however, the light only accentuated the harshness of Laurent's features as he sat with his hands clasped, pouting at her table. His expression set a spark off in her memory. Luc's face when she first told him she was pregnant. Same shock and disappointment. He'd wanted out. He wanted away from her.

Charlotte's hands curled into fists. All that rejection, all that trouble, and yet she still missed Luc every day. "You must make the honorable choice," she insisted.

Laurent sighed and gazed out the window, still tall and dark blond and handsome as Apollo, his face tanned from all the time in the Madrid sun. But the telltale signs of aging had started to crease the edges of his eyes and mouth. "It's not only me. She doesn't want to get married. She's an American. From California, no less. She doesn't want to move to Spain. I can't force her."

Suddenly, Charlotte felt very tired. How could he just leave this girl, hardly out of childhood herself from the sound of it, to raise a child in another country? At least Luc had remained in the same city and spent time with Laurent.

Charlotte folded her hands in front of her on the table. She hated looking at them now, the age spots, the withering skin, and chipped nails. She wanted to cover her hands with gloves, but this would date her as well. She didn't want to settle gracefully into old age, she wanted to fight it every step of the way.

Here was yet another issue with aging. Her once-focused mind now meandered when she needed it most. "This girl can't understand how difficult it is to raise a child alone," she said. "Have her come to see me. I'll tell her all about it. She sounds so young."

"She is young. That's why she went home. She has family. They'll help her." The corners of Laurent's lips curled, almost into a smile, and this reminded her of Luc as well. "Although her mother sounds like a real piece of work."

"Are they wealthy?" Charlotte asked. "Do they need money?"

Laurent closed his eyes and rubbed his temples. He'd suffered from frequent nosebleeds as a child. More recently, migraines had started to plague him.

Charlotte hesitated. "You feel a headache coming?"

He nodded. "Stress."

Watching Laurent in pain made her anger evaporate. Charlotte wished she could take him in her arms and rock him to sleep. If only parenting could stay so simple. Over the past thirty years, Charlotte had read everything she could find on the Romanov family, and so Laurent's physical troubles now made sense. Empress Alexandra had suffered from migraines as well. The nosebleeds were a symptom of his hemophilia, which had thankfully taken a mild form. The doctors said it couldn't be transmitted to children through fathers. This girl's child might become a carrier, but she was not in immediate danger.

At least not from that. "Tell me about her family." Charlotte tried a gentle tone, sure if she handled this correctly, she could make Laurent see sense. "Tell me where they live. We need to watch over them."

Laurent gave a raspy laugh, but his face scrunched again in pain. "Oh come on, Mother. Not this again."

Charlotte would never have spoken in that tone to her own

mother, not even when she was an adult, not even when she'd confronted her mother and asked why she hadn't told her who she really was. Charlotte had spoiled Laurent. It was coming back to haunt her now. "Don't you remember anything I told you about the war?" she said. "Who we are? The unique problems of our family?"

"You expected me to stay celibate?" Laurent said.

"Of course not. But how will you protect a child who lives so far away?"

"You're paranoid." Laurent's voice took on the condescending note he affected whenever she brought up this subject. He sounded like his father.

"Matilda Kshesinskaya told me about the Bolshevik spies in France between the wars," Charlotte said. "They kidnapped Romanovs and took them back to the Soviet Union. They tortured them, killed them. And these were distant relatives. If the Soviets find me they will kill me. If they find you, they will kill you. If they find this girl and her baby, they will kill them as well."

"We are in a détente," Laurent said.

"So they'll take more care to make it look like an accident."

"Damn it, Mother, no one is looking for extra Romanovs. No one cares about any of that anymore."

Charlotte slammed her fist on the table. Startled, Laurent dropped his hands to his sides. She'd tried to reason with him. That hadn't worked. Charlotte felt strong now, despite her age. Her son still needed her, even if he didn't realize it yet. She would force him to see sense. She would force him to treat this problem with the respect it warranted. "The Nazis wanted us too. Do you have any idea what we went through? They took us to an abandoned casino. I saw blood on the roulette wheels."

"I know. You hid my face. You didn't want me to look."

Charlotte stopped abruptly. She'd thought Laurent too young to remember, that's why she kept repeating the story.

"I know what you sacrificed for me." His voice started to break. "And I know what Papa did."

Charlotte went rigid. Over the years, the memory of Luc's face faded, and then came back to her with such startling clarity it scared her, as though she would wake up and find him smiling next to her, still young but no longer angry. She remembered him that last night, sitting next to her on her childhood bed, eyes closed, holding his palm open on her cheek, trying to keep his lower lip from trembling. He hadn't wanted to leave. Who would? Who wants to be brave? Who wouldn't rather be safe instead? But he couldn't live with himself if he'd stayed and put them in even greater danger. He made the sacrifice and left separately, hoping the Nazis would follow him and not her.

After the war, she tried to find Luc. But he'd vanished, like so many others.

"I remember everything," Laurent said, breaking her concentration. "But you can't expect me to marry this girl. Neither one of us wants that."

"What about me?" she asked desperately. "I can't have a relationship with my own grandchild?"

"I'm sorry," Laurent said softly. "I don't know what else to do. She's like Danae in the story, taking Perseus over the ocean to save him. It's too late."

Charlotte closed her eyes. She remembered taking Laurent in her arms during the last days of the war, to show him the constellations in the broad Spanish sky. He'd liked Perseus and Andromeda and the Kraken the best. He'd pointed to the stars that formed the throne of Andromeda's vain mother, Cassiopeia, and recited the story from heart.

He'd disappointed her. Just as Luc had when she told him she was pregnant. But Luc had redeemed himself. Perhaps Laurent would as well.

In the meantime, she would take matters into her own hands. She straightened her back, rolled her shoulders. "I know someone who can help us. A woman who lives in America. She'll be nearer to the girl than we will be."

Laurent looked at her with his sleepy eyes. Luc's eyes, the slight hooding of the lids. "She won't accept help."

"Not financial help. Protection. You don't even need to tell her. It's probably better if you don't." Charlotte touched the cross around her neck. "I know someone who will make sure the girl and her baby are safe. Matilda Kshesinskaya told me about her long ago."

BRIGHTON BEACH, BROOKLYN

JULY 1981

A priest in a black robe held a heavy iron chain with a secure round ball at the end. He swung the device languidly over the casket, releasing incense in little puffs. The strong scent in the hot and heavy air almost overpowered Charlotte. Her legs ached, she had been standing for so long. The choir lifted their voice in song and she clutched her long candle tighter, wishing she could release it and fan herself with her hands. She felt as though she'd entered another world. She supposed that was the point.

Charlotte watched the other mourners file past the open casket, engulfed in flowers and wreaths. She shuffled slowly to the end of the line. Perspiration speckled her forehead and the backs of her knees. She hated feeling her body give out. Laurent had hinted perhaps Charlotte was too old for this trip. A part of her wished she had listened. After all, she was only seventeen years younger than the woman in the coffin, and she had lived longer than most. Laurent finally relented, but insisted he would go with her.

She owed Lena her life. The least she could do was pay her final respects.

Charlotte had contacted Lena seven years ago, after she spoke to Laurent: Lena Rubalov, Brooklyn Heights, New York. Husband named Pavel. Daughter named Natalya.

Charlotte had trouble pressing the buttons on the phone, but when she said her name the woman on the other end of the line had drawn in a deep breath.

"Yes," she'd said softly. "I know who you are. I've been waiting to hear from you. I hoped you were still alive."

Charlotte had poured out her story, everything about her life. And then she told Lena about Laurent, how much she loved him but she was afraid she had spoiled him.

"That is your Russian blood," Lena murmured sympathetically. "We ruin boys."

She'd confided that Laurent fathered a child who was living in California, with her mother's family. Charlotte understood times were different now, as Laurent frequently reminded her. Soviet agents weren't lurking around every corner, ready to snatch anyone with a drop of Romanov blood. Still, it seemed wrong on so many levels. She should be near her granddaughter.

"No." Lena sprang to life. Even over the static of the transatlantic connection, Charlotte knew the old woman had bolted out of her chair. "She can't know. It's not safe."

"If I had known, I could have protected Laurent better." The bitterness rose quickly to Charlotte's throat, even after so many years. "My parents made a mistake not to tell me sooner. Matilda Kshesinskaya made a mistake not to tell me." She hesitated and left the last sentence unsaid. *You made a mistake not to tell me.*

She didn't need to say the words aloud. Lena had understood well enough. "We were all sworn not to tell," Lena said.

"My husband died because of the secret. If I had known—"

"What could you have done? He sacrificed himself for you. Honor his memory. Protect his granddaughter. My family will find her."

One of the other mourners brushed her shoulder, a large man who walked with a swagger. Charlotte shook her head, forced herself back into the present. She watched the man approach Laurent, who now stood at the end of the line of mourners. She beamed proudly at her handsome boy, stately and gentle. Her son had made a mistake, but now he was going to help make it right.

Laurent moved out of the line and followed the man outside, stooping slightly to pass under the low arch of the church doors. He was built so differently from Luc. He'd inherited his height from Charlotte, and perhaps his grandmother, Alexandra.

The large man snapped his fingers at a stocky boy of about twelve, who looked solemn for his age in a gray suit and a dark tie. The boy had an olive complexion and light brown eyes, almost hazel, like those of his handsome grandfather, Pavel, in the picture next to Lena's casket. He obeyed his father instantly.

After receiving the news of Lena's death, Charlotte wanted to speak directly to Lena's daughter. But Natalya had been in deep mourning, too distraught to speak with anyone, or so Charlotte was told. Instead, with the help of an interpreter, she'd been in contact with Lena's son-in-law, Anatoly Karstadt.

The mourner in front of her stepped forward. Charlotte realized it was her turn now. She turned away from Anatoly and Laurent and stood before the casket, but she couldn't look down. Slowly, with sharp jolts of pain shooting up her calves, she slid her feet into fifth position. Then she peered down over her lit candle.

Lena's gray hair hung in soft waves just to her shoulders. Her hands had been folded softly on her chest, serenely clutching an orthodox cross. It looked like Charlotte's cross. Instinctively, Charlotte put her hand to her throat, expecting the reassuring cool feel of the metal, the little stinging sensation in her hand where the ends of the cross poked her skin. But her memory had failed once more. The cross was no longer around her neck, but in a box in her handbag.

Charlotte wondered what more she would have said to Lena, had they met in person before Lena's passing. What did they have in common? What jokes or stories could they share? Probably nothing. But then what did any of that matter? Charlotte crossed herself with her thumb and two fingers, as she'd learned was the Russian custom. It had been worth it, hadn't it? Lena's sacrifices to protect her. She'd had her parents, the joy of performing, the hard thrill she felt dancing, the good years with Luc before things fell apart. Laurent. The great love of her life. Now there was a girl out there somewhere, with Laurent and Luc and Charlotte in her.

If Lena hadn't helped her, she would have been a grand duchess of Russia for sixteen years. And then nothing.

"Thank you for my life," she whispered. She bent down to kiss Lena's cold cheek.

Charlotte released her feet from fifth position and shuffled forward again, away from the casket. Then she turned to the church doors, looking past the ancient wooden icons with their long faces and mournful eyes. She ignored John the Baptist, hands raised to heaven, and the Virgin Mary gazing adoringly at her child. She stared instead at Laurent and Anatoly Karstadt as they spoke outside.

Charlotte moved closer, adjusting the small knob attached to the back of her right ear. The artificial amplification of her hated hearing aid would prove useful now. She could only pick up a few of the English words, which Laurent spoke with a heavy accent: Los Angeles, her family, what should be done. Anatoly Karstadt's eyes started to wander. This all meant little to him. She could read it in his bored expression. Charlotte's heart fell. His son—Mikhail, wasn't it?—said something Charlotte couldn't make out. Anatoly's face turned grim. He turned and slapped his son hard across the cheek.

Charlotte gasped. Laurent paled underneath his Spanish tan.

"This is all right," she heard Laurent say, a slight tremor betraying his anxiety. "The boy is only telling the truth. Her mother was my student. I shouldn't have been involved with her at all. Now she's gone and I feel terrible. But I want to help."

Anatoly shrugged. Charlotte felt too warm, and not just from the oppressive heat in the church. She didn't trust Anatoly Karstadt. They should have approached Lena's daughter, no matter what anyone said. Charlotte resolved to find Natalya and speak with her after the service. She had to make this right.

Then Charlotte's gaze fixed on Anatoly's son, Mikhail, cheeks still flushed red from the slap. He nodded and looked squarely at Laurent. He'd asked Laurent a good question. He wasn't like his father. She could tell. She saw Lena in this boy. He put the needs of others before his own needs. He would protect Laurent's daughter.

Mikhail must have sensed she was staring because he looked over his shoulder and right at Charlotte. The boy's hazel eyes met hers.

"Hello there," she said cautiously. She knew a little English, but felt nervous using it in front of these Americans.

The boy grinned shyly. Charlotte curled her fingers around the velvet jewelry box in her handbag and approached the boy.

Twenty-one

Veronica heard Michael's footsteps thud as he approached her cousin's house. He may have been quick, but he wasn't exactly light on his feet. Veronica focused her attention on the tall stems of the irises growing on either side of the porch, and tried to ignore the fluttering in the pit of her stomach. She hadn't counted on seeing him again so soon. Putting her head in her hands, she cradled her chin and tried to breathe.

The footsteps came to a halt before her, but she couldn't look at him.

"Veronica? Please. Hear me out."

He spoke in the same lilting, gentle voice she remembered, the one she'd found so at odds with his larger-than-life presence when they first met in her office. It washed over her, not exactly breaking her emotional defenses but exposing their delicate edges.

She opened her eyes. Michael's shoes, clean black dress shoes, just as she would have expected, entered her field of vision.

Slowly, she raised her head. Everything about him looked vital and strong, from the high color in his cheeks to the immaculately pressed suit and those gorgeous hazel eyes. She remembered the tattoo encircling his bicep and had a sudden urge to touch it. All of the sensations she'd been fighting, the desire to be enfolded into his arms, came rushing back. The impulse almost overpowered her, but she remained strong.

"May I sit down?" he asked.

He'd lied to her, let her think he was something he was not. Yet somehow she couldn't find it in her to order him away.

"You were very clear back in New York," she said slowly. "You said 'I failed you.' I would have given anything to hear an explanation then. You gave me nothing. Now I'm beginning to feel better, you show up again, and I'm right back to feeling awful."

"I couldn't give you an explanation in New York, not in front of Alexei Romanov. I'm sorry. But I needed to make sure the time was right."

"You needed time to fabricate more lies?"

"It's not like that. Please give me a few minutes. That's all I ask. If you don't like what I have to say, tell me to leave and I'll go."

Out of the corner of her eye, Veronica saw Abuela take a quick peek out from behind the curtains of her cousin's kitchen window. Then in a flash she was gone. Before the curtain fell back into place, she saw another figure behind Abuela, Jess.

As far as Veronica was concerned, the day had already been ruined. She just hoped Abuela and Jess didn't get their hopes up too high. She turned around one more time, to make sure no one was watching at the window, and then nodded. Michael took a seat beside her on the porch step, where Abuela had sat a few minutes before.

Questions played along the tip of Veronica's tongue. "I hear you and my grandmother have become friends. She invited you here?"

"Yes. It was nice of her. I usually go out to see my mom at Christmas, but Thanksgivings have been lonely since my divorce." He scratched the back of his neck, staring at the ground. The armor around Veronica's heart chipped away a little more.

Michael dipped his head so he was looking up at her. "I think we've reached an impasse. You can't think of anything worse a man can do than lie. I can't think of anything worse than endangering someone you love. That's what I would have done if I had been up front with you."

Someone you love. Her heart did a little flip, but she still didn't have the answers she wanted. "What happened in New York put me in danger. Now you're here. I have to ask. Are you putting my family in danger as well?"

He flinched. She wanted to retract her words, but before she could speak, he said, "No. I waited long enough to make sure of that. But what happened makes me sick inside."

She hunched farther into her sweater, still fighting the November chill in the air.

"I was scared," she said, "but I don't think anything would have happened to me. I think Alexei Romanov had something else in mind. Look what happened when we got back here." She heard her voice rising. "Didn't you see that blurb in *L.A. This Week*? He made us both sound like fools."

"I'm sorry," Michael said.

"Not that I need much help on that front," Veronica added. "I'm not making tenure. I had to resign. My career is over. I'm moving back here next month."

He raised his brows, looking startled. "To Bakersfield?"

"My grandmother didn't tell you that part."

"She just told me . . . God, Veronica. I'm sorry."

She eyed him, still wary.

"None of that part's on you," she said. "But it's disappointing, you know? I used to imagine how my life would look after I had my Ph.D. I was almost there. I was engaged, pregnant, had a good job. And then it all vanished, one by one—my baby, my fiancé, and now finally my career." She took a deep breath. Why did she always reveal so much to him? "Maybe it was never meant to be. I just wish I had something more to show for it all." Veronica gestured toward the house and then around the yard, not even sure what she meant.

"You have your family," he said.

"I guess so. I was always so focused on school. I'll try to make up for lost time with them."

"You have a wonderful family. Maybe you have more than you know."

"I get it," she said. "You don't need to ram the sentimentality down my throat."

Michael laughed softly and raised his hands in apology. "Never. I didn't mean it like that. Let me try a different angle. My mother's story about her mother and the fifth grand duchess. What did you think? Take me out of the equation. Did you believe it?"

"Did I believe it?" Veronica sighed and shook her head. "I want to believe it, but I'm an academic, at least for another week or so. I still think like an academic. I want proof. Your mother can't produce anything more than a letter. Alexei Romanov was right. Without an heir, there's no evidence."

Michael withdrew a small velvet jewelry box from his pocket and slipped it into her hand. For a second, Veronica thought he might bend down on one knee and propose to her. She knew it was crazy, but she couldn't stop her heart from thumping wildly in her chest. "What is this?"

"Open the box and see."

Curiosity compelled her. When she flipped the box open, it made a click. Inside, she found a thin silver chain and a tiny Russian Orthodox cross with the distinctive third bar angled down. She held it up to the sunlight. "You're plying me with gifts now?"

He laughed a little as she examined the tarnished edges of the crucifix, pressing one of its pointy edges. "All right. I give up," she said. "What is this?"

"Originally, this necklace belonged to Dowager Empress Marie," he told her. "She gave it to my grandmother to present to the fifth grand duchess."

Veronica snapped the box shut. "Nice try. I feel like I've been through all of this before, though."

"My grandmother, Lena, saved the baby, but couldn't return to Russia. That was the agreement. She'd fallen in love with the man assigned to protect her on the journey, my grandfather. He was from America. They eventually settled in New York."

Michael reached into the inside pocket of his jacket. She thought he was going to present her with another box, but this time he withdrew his phone. "Okay. I'm new at using this, but I have to admit it's convenient." He fiddled with the phone, pressing some buttons. "I want you to see them."

She shielded her eyes from the sunlight, the slender silver chain still between her fingers, cross dangling. The photograph on the screen was black and white. Based on the stains and fraying evident in the digital image, the original photograph must have been taken decades earlier. A tall, dark, attractive man in what looked like a regimental uniform stood next to a short, pale, smiling young woman. It took Veronica a few minutes to absorb the details. Then she recognized Lena, Michael's grandmother, from Natalya's photograph. She softened a bit more.

"You know about Lena," he said. "My grandfather, Paul, was originally from the south. He was born about ten years after the Civil War ended. You can imagine what his life was like. He'd won money as a boxer when he was a teenager and was able to travel. Eventually, he found work as a footman for Marie. They called him Pavel in Russia. And Marie gave him the last name Rubalov."

Excitement and the old thrill of discovery began to build inside of her once more. She had read about Paul/Pavel, the African-American boxer who worked for the royal family at the turn of the century. No one knew what happened to him.

"Before he left, Marie made Pavel a member of the Preo-brazhensky Guard. Lena and Pavel were loyal servants to the end. They turned the fifth grand duchess over to a Danish couple Marie trusted. The girl was named Charlotte and the family eventually settled in the southern region of France. Charlotte moved to Paris and had a son named Laurent. They were forced to relocate to Spain during the Nazi occupation. I understand Laurent grew infatuated with Spain. Later, he taught at the University of Madrid."

The University of Madrid—where her mother had studied and her father had taught literature. Her father. The specter rising up after all these years. Trembling, Veronica grabbed Michael's hand. "Why are you telling me this?"

Michael placed his phone back inside his jacket. "As you know, he was an academic. I guess it runs in the family. At any rate, I can't say the claim is likely to be honored at this point. Still, a direct descendant seemed to please Grigori's crowd."

Veronica's head was spinning and the voices had returned at last, although now they only shouted *What is he saying?*

Michael squeezed her hand. "Grand Duchess Charlotte's son, Laurent, had an affair with your mother. Laurent Marchand is your father."

He still held her hand in his, yet now he seemed distant. "My family has kept track of you for years." His voice rolled over her in low waves. "Charlotte and Laurent asked us to do this. My grandmother would have wanted it. She was an incredible woman, Veronica. I wish you could have known her. My grandmother, Lena, found out about you before she died. She did everything in her power to keep you safe. You're Alexandra's great-granddaughter. You're the Romanov heir."

Little sounds emitted from Veronica's throat, not really words, more like gurgling, and she couldn't make them stop.

"Take it easy," he told her. "It's not every day you hear you're heir to one-sixth the earth's surface."

"You think?" Veronica whispered. "I never even knew my father and now you're telling me he was some lost Romanov?"

Michael looked at her steadily and gave one firm nod.

Veronica could manage no more than a shake of her head. "If that's true, and I'm not saying I believe you, why did you wait so long to tell me? Why let me think you were the one?"

"Remember I told you I'd been to a family reunion in Russia, last Christmas?" Veronica nodded. "While we were there, my mother and I learned Alexei Romanov had become involved with a dangerous group of people. He's older now. Maybe he's grown more desperate. Originally, I used a fake family tree to approach

Alexei Romanov on behalf of myself and my family. I kept the lie to protect you, Veronica. I wanted his attention on me, not on you. We were afraid if he discovered the truth, you could be in danger. And we were sworn to protect you."

"Why tell me now?"

"Alexei Romanov thinks he's won. He's proven I'm an imposter, so he can finally leave me alone. And telling you here, away from Los Angeles, felt right. My grandmother Lena was the one who insisted your identity needed to be kept a secret. But now is the time. She'd understand."

Veronica's mind raced, her thoughts nothing more than a cluttered mess. "You really thought I needed protecting?"

"Grand Duchess Charlotte was persecuted during the war. We think Luc—her husband, your grandfather—died because of it. Lena swore to Marie she would protect the grand duchess and keep the secret safe."

"And you?" Veronica said. "You felt you had to keep it from me?"

Michael looked away, took a deep breath, and exhaled slowly. Then he turned back to her. "It's important to believe in something bigger than yourself."

Veronica's lip twitched. "Why should I believe any of this?"

He held her gaze. "If you take a DNA test, you'll see. I don't want anything from you, Veronica. There's no reason for me to make this up. If you don't want to know, don't take the DNA test. Do whatever you want. But I wasn't going to walk away without letting you know, no matter what you decide. No matter what you decide about me."

A strange, tingling sensation sailed down her back. "Oh my God," she breathed out. "But I don't look anything like the Romanovs."

"That's not true. The resemblance is there, especially considering the removal by several generations. I saw it from the beginning, but then I was looking."

"Why didn't Alexei Romanov see it?"

"He was focused on me, just as you were. That was the plan all along."

Veronica couldn't form a coherent thought. Michael wound his fingers around hers. They felt warm and comforting.

"So when you met Jessica and she talked about me?"

"Meeting Jess was a happy accident. I knew you lived in Los Angeles. I'd always wanted to meet you. My mother found a couple of your articles on the Romanov family. I wondered how you'd grown interested in Russian history. I assumed Laurent told your mother and that sparked your interest. My mother and I thought you knew more. I thought maybe you knew about your father and his family history. Anyway, it seemed logical to meet you and see."

"Logical?" The word came choking out. "Even if all of this is true, how can I trust you? Maybe you just want to get close to the heir. Or you just came to me out of some archaic sense of duty."

"I care about you. I want to help you, regardless of what you decide to do with this news."

Veronica thought about this for a moment, gnawing on her lip. "The article in *L.A. This Week* . . . it embarrassed you?"

He scratched his neck again and looked away. "Most of my clients are Russian. Some of them follow that stuff."

"So yes."

"Some of them found it strange," he said carefully.

"Have you lost clients?" When he didn't answer, she added,

"Maybe I should go public. I could explain why you did this. Maybe it would help."

"Veronica, my family has gone through so much to protect you. All I ask is that you give this decision some thought before you act. If you go public, you'll have to deal with Alexei Romanov and Grigori and all his thugs."

"Remember what I told you before. I expect the truth. I expect it from myself more than anyone else. Your family protected me, but if all of this is true, I need to start taking care of myself." She hesitated. "Charlotte isn't still alive, is she?"

He shook his head sadly. "She passed away shortly after Lena did."

"And Laurent?" She couldn't bring herself to call him Father.

"You can meet him if you want," Michael said. "I think he would like that. I think you will like him, actually."

Veronica put her head in her hands.

"You don't have to decide right now," Michael added softly.

Veronica nodded, too overwhelmed to speak further. It was all starting to hit her now. She actually understood what he was saying.

"It is true," he added. "I understand you need more than my word. But it is true."

She felt the tears coming, and let them slip. "Then will you help me?"

He smiled. "Help crown you Tsarina Veronica? Or do you prefer Empress?"

She shrugged. "It's not like I have anything else going on right now. Once my final set of exams are graded, my schedule is wide open."

"You can still work on your biography of Alexandra," Michael said. "So what if it doesn't go to an academic press. Think of all the material you'll have to work with now."

Veronica turned back toward her cousin's house. No one was spying from the kitchen window, but she would have to go back inside eventually. "Should I tell them? It's not every day you find out your weird cousin is the heiress to the Russian throne."

"Maybe hold off on that." He glanced at her seriously. "I think you should figure out where things stand before you make anything public, even within your own family."

Veronica felt her spirits rising. "Okay. Will you help me with this at least? I'll keep the cross hidden." She held out the necklace. Michael took it and lifted the soft strands of hair that grazed her neck. She shivered pleasantly. He shut the clasp on the chain and she tucked the orthodox cross under her shirt.

"Perfect," he said.

Veronica remembered Abuela's comments about her mother, how she'd suddenly been interested in Russian history when she returned from her semester abroad. "Did you tell my grandmother?" she asked.

"I felt I should. I think she knows how to keep a secret." He shook his head. "I know she didn't think much of me at first, but I like your grandmother."

"You could help me then," Veronica said. "A man who gets along with Abuela can get along with anyone. And I'll need good advice if I'm going to navigate all this. Your family has a tradition of loyal servitude, after all."

"Loyal servitude," he said. "You make it sound so grand."

"Come on, counselor. This could be fun."

"That's all you want? An advisor?"

Veronica stood up and offered Michael her hand. "You shouldn't keep Abuela waiting. You're her guest. She'll want to fuss over you all night. And my cousin fries a mean turkey if you're into that kind of thing. Significant cardiac event in a pan, I call it. I stick to the mashed potatoes and cranberries, but there's plenty of that as well."

She saw the start of another smile play on his lips. "So you're not going to answer my question."

Veronica helped him up from the porch. "We'll see. For now, let's just try to enjoy my family."

"If you're really going to pursue this . . ." His fingers curled around hers. ". . . when do we discuss taking over the world?"

"Not the whole world. Just Russia. That's only one-sixth of the earth's surface, you know." Veronica opened the front door. "We'll talk about it tomorrow. But not until after I drive Abuela to all the Black Friday sales."

"Your priorities are clearly in order," he said. "You'll make a fine tsarina."

Veronica put her finger on her lips and led him inside.

ACKNOWLEDGMENTS

I am fascinated by the fate of the last Russian royal family and the subsequent string of claimants to the throne. In *Anastasia: The Lost Princess*, James B. Lovell discussed the case of Suzanna DeGraaff, a woman who once claimed to be a fifth daughter of Nicholas and Alexandra. Though Charlotte Marchand is fictional, Ms. De-Graaff's story first inspired me to create a Romanov survival story that focused on a secret grand duchess.

Numerous books and Web sites helped give me a sense of late imperial Russia, Paris during the Nazi Occupation, and family feuding between modern-day Romanov factions. Robert K. Massie's *The Romanovs: The Final Chapter* and Carolly Erickson's *Alexandra: The Last Tsarina* were particularly helpful during the early stages of this project. I got to know Jim Hercules, the real-life inspiration for Pavel/Paul, in Greg King's *The Court of the Last Tsar*.

I am indebted to my amazing agent, Erin Harris of Folio Literary Management, and my magnificent editor, Vicki Lame at St. Martin's Press. I also want to thank my insightful and patient early readers: Melissa Jackson, Mary Pessaran, Lou Ann Barnett, Alan Klima, Kate Campbell, Deborah Grinnell, Caren Halvorsen, and Mary Anne Cox. Finally, thank you to my family—Karen, Jon, Brett, and Liz—for your love and support.

SELECTED BIBLIOGRAPHY

Erickson, Carolly. *Alexandra: The Last Tsarina*. New York: St. Martin's Press, 2001.

King, Greg. *The Court of the Last Tsar: Pomp, Power, and Pageantry in the Reign of Nicholas II*. Hoboken, NJ: Wiley, 2006.

King, Greg and Penny Wilson. *The Fate of the Romanovs*. Hoboken, NJ: Wiley, 2003.

Lovell, James B. *Anastasia: The Lost Princess*. New York: St. Martin's Press, 1991.

Massie, Robert. *The Romanovs: The Final Chapter*. New York: Ballantine, 1995.

Ousby, Ian. *Occupation: The Ordeal of France 1940–1944*. New York: Random House, 1999.

Perry, John Curtis and Constantine Pleshakov. *The Flight of the Romanovs: A Family Saga*. New York: Basic Books, 2001.

Radzinsky, Edvard. *The Last Tsar: The Life and Death of Nicholas II*. New York: Doubleday, 1992.

1. At several points in the story, Veronica feels drawn to Alexandra Romanov in an almost supernatural sense. Have you ever experienced a similar connection with a historical figure? A distant relative? What connects us to someone in the past?

2. After her failed engagement, Veronica erects self-protective emotional walls. What qualities does Michael possess that break down these walls? What is his main appeal? To what extent is Veronica attracted to the world Michael represents?

3. Veronica's grandmother encourages her to prioritize professional success over romance. Why? Is Abuela's opinion shaped more by Veronica's intellectual talents or by her own experiences?

4. Ultimately, is Michael justified in keeping his secrets from Veronica? Did he truly protect Veronica? Was this an act of self-protection on his part?

5. At the end of the story, Veronica is presented with a potentially life-changing revelation. What do you think she will do next? What would you do in her place?

6. Lena's loyalty to Alexandra implicitly defies the political views of her brother. What did the Romanovs and the monarchy in general represent to someone in Lena's position—security or tyranny? Both?

7. Lena and Alexandra develop a bond that transcends class. Lena and Pavel's attraction transcends the racial order of the time. Are the personal and the political intertwined? Do these relationships suggest Lena has a rebellious side?

8. Lena has a strained and distant relationship with her mother, yet ultimately chooses to follow in her footsteps professionally. Why? Does she admire her mother on some level?

9. After they leave Russia, what would life have been like for Lena and Pavel? What difficulties would they have encountered? How might they have dealt with these difficulties?

10. Charlotte endures the Nazi occupation of Paris seemingly without protest, until there is a clear and present threat to her son. Is it natural for most people to keep a low profile during military occupation? Without the threat to Laurent, do you think Charlotte would have found ways to rebel against the occupation?

11. Despite their estrangement, Charlotte remains attracted to her husband, Luc. Would she have felt the same way about Luc if they didn't share a common interest in Laurent?

12. Charlotte seems to feel her best days and her happiness lie entirely in the past. Was there more she could have done to embrace the present? Is it possible to find happiness in the present, even if you continue to dwell on the happiness of the past?

13. When Charlotte learns her true identity, she remains more interested in protecting Laurent, and later her granddaughter, than in pursuing her claim. Why? What experiences shape her reaction?

14. The narrative hinges on an alternate historical timeline. Outside of fiction, is there any reason to consider "what might have happened" historical questions?

15. The last Romanovs remain a popular subject of fiction. Why do you think this is? Are we more attracted to their lives, or to the sordid way they died? Is there beauty in tragedy?

16. To some extent, Veronica, Lena, and Charlotte all feel awkward and like outsiders in their respective worlds. In what ways? How do they deal with these feelings? Do their feelings about their relative places in the world evolve over time?